White Doves
at Morning

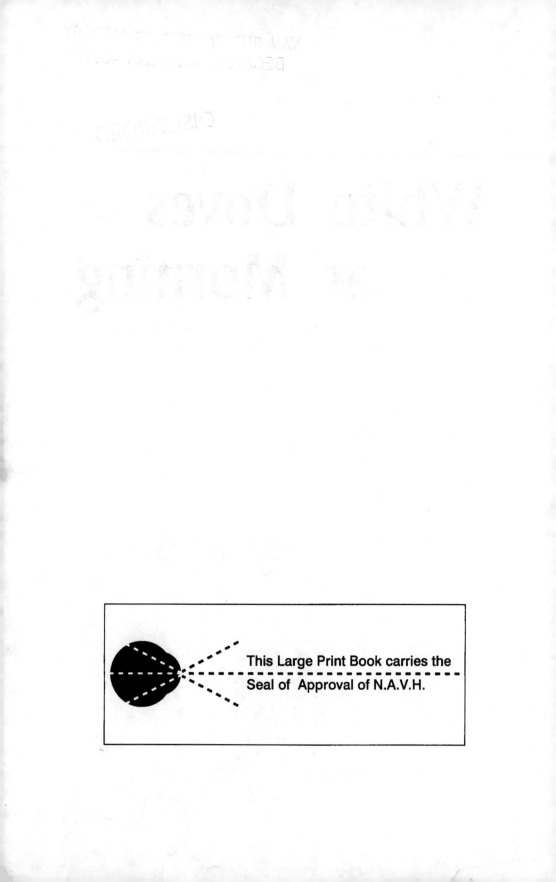

White Doves at Morning

at Morning

James Lee Burke

Waterville, Maine

Copyright © 2002 by James Lee Burke

Published in 2004 by arrangement with Simon & Schuster, Inc.

The text of this Large Print edition is unabridged.
Other aspects of the book may vary from the original edition.

Set in 16 pt. Plantin by Elena Picard.

Printed in the United States on permanent paper.

Library of Congress Cataloging-in-Publication Data

Burke, James Lee, 1936–
    White doves at morning : a novel / James Lee Burke.
      p. cm.
    ISBN 1-4104-0173-1 (lg. print : sc : alk. paper)
    1. United States — History — Civil War, 1861–1865 —
Fiction.   2. Louisiana — History — Civil War, 1861–1865 —
Fiction.   3. Large type books.   I. Title.
PS3552.U723W48 2004
813′.54—dc22   2003060587

for Dracos and Carrie Burke

I would like to thank Pamela Arceneaux at the Williams Research Center of New Orleans and C. J. LaBauve of New Iberia for their help with historical detail in the writing of this book.

Chapter One

1837

The black woman's name was Sarie, and when she crashed out the door of the cabin at the end of the slave quarters into the fading winter light, her lower belly bursting with the child that had already broken her water, the aftermath of the ice storm and the sheer desolate sweep of leaf-bare timber and frozen cotton acreage and frost-limned cane stalks seemed to combine and strike her face like a braided whip.

She trudged into the grayness of the woods, the male shoes on her feet pocking the snow, her breath streaming out of the blanket she wore on her head like a monk's cowl. Ten minutes later, deep inside the gum and persimmon and oak trees, her clothes strung with air vines that were silver with frost, the frozen leaves cracking under her feet, she heard the barking of the dogs and the yelps of their handlers who had just released them.

She splashed into a slough, one that bled out of the woods into the dark swirl of the river where it made a bend through the plantation. The ice sawed at her ankles; the cold was like a hammer on her shins. But nonetheless she worked her way upstream, between cypress roots that made her think of a man's knuckles protruding from the shallows. Across the river the sun was a vaporous smudge above the bluffs, and she realized night would soon come upon her and that a level of coldness she had never thought possible would invade her bones and womb and teats and perhaps turn them to stone.

She clutched the bottom of her stomach with both hands, as though holding a watermelon under her dress, and slogged up the embankment and collapsed under a lean-to where, in the summer months, an overseer napped in the afternoon while his charges bladed down the cypress trees for the soft wood Marse Jamison used to make cabinets in the big house on a bluff overlooking the river.

Even if she had known the river was called the Mississippi, the name would have held no significance for her. But the water boundary called the Ohio was another matter. It was somewhere to the north, somehow associated in her mind with the Jordan, and a black person only needed to wade across it to be as free as the children of Israel.

Except no black person on the plantation could tell her exactly how far to the north this river was, and she had learned long ago never to ask a white person where the river called Ohio was located.

The light in the west died and through the breaks in the lean-to she saw the moon rising and the ground fog disappearing in the cold, exposing the hardness of the earth, the glazed and speckled symmetry of the tree trunks. Then a pain like an ax blade seemed to split her in half and she put a stick in her mouth to keep from crying out. As the time between the contractions shrank and she felt blood issue from her womb between her fingers, she was convinced the juju woman had been right, that this baby, her first, was a man-child, a warrior and a king.

She stared upward at the constellations bursting in the sky, and when she shut her eyes she saw her child inside the redness behind her eyelids, a powerful little brown boy with liquid eyes and a mouth that would seek both milk and power from his mother's breast.

She caught the baby in her palms and sawed the cord in half with a stone and tied it in a knot, then pressed the closed eyes and hungry mouth to her teat, just before passing out.

The dawn broke hard and cold, a yellow

light that burst inside the woods and exposed her hiding place and brought no warmth or release from the misery in her bones. There was a dirty stench in the air, like smoke from a drowned campfire. She heard the dogs again, and when she rose to her feet the pain inside her told her she would never outrun them.

Learn from critters, her mother had always said. They know God's way. Don't never ax Master or his family or the mens he hire to tell you the troot. Whatever they teach us is wrong, girl. Never forget that lesson, her mother had said.

The doe always leads the hunter away from the fawn, Sarie thought. That's what God taught the doe, her mother had said.

She wrapped the baby in the blanket that had been her only protection from the cold, then rose to her feet and covered the opening to the lean-to with a broken pine bough and walked slowly through the woods to the slough. She stepped into the water, felt it rush inside her shoes and over her ankles, then worked her way downstream toward the river. In the distance she heard axes knocking into wood and smelled smoke from a stump fire, and the fact that the work of the plantation went on rhythmically, not missing a beat, in spite of her child's birth and possible death reminded her once again of her own insignificance and the words Master had used to her yesterday afternoon.

"You should have taken care of yourself, Sarie," he had said, his pantaloons tucked inside his riding boots, his youthful face undisturbed and serene and without blemish except for the tiny lump of tobacco in his jaw. "I'll see to it the baby doesn't lack for raiment or provender, but I'll have to send you to the auction house. You're not an ordinary nigger, Sarie. You won't be anything but trouble. I'm sorry it worked out this way."

When she came out of the water and labored toward the edge of the woods, she glanced behind her and in the thin patina of snow frozen on the ground she saw her own blood spore and knew it was almost her time, the last day in a lifetime of days that had been marked by neither hope nor despair but only unanswered questions: Where was the green place they had all come from? What group of men had made them chattel to be treated as though they had no souls, whipped, worked from cain't-see to cain't-see, sometimes branded and hamstrung?

The barking of the dogs was louder now but she no longer cared about either the dogs or the men who rode behind them. Her spore ended at the slough; her story would end here, too. The child was another matter. She touched the juju bag tied around her neck and prayed she and the child would be together by nightfall, in the warm, green place where lions lay on the beaches by a great sea.

But now she was too tired to think about any of it. She stood on the edge of the trees, the sunlight breaking on her face, then sat down heavily in the grass, the tops of her shoes dark with her blood. Through a red haze she saw a man in a stovepipe hat and dirty white breeches ride over a hillock behind his dogs, two other mounted men behind him, their horses steaming in the sunshine.

The dogs surrounded her, circling, snuffing in the grass, their bodies bumping against one another, but they made no move against her person. The man in the stovepipe hat reined his horse and got down and looked with exasperation at his two companions. "Get these dogs out of here. If I hear that barking anymore, I'll need a new pair of ears," he said. Then he looked down at Sarie, almost respectfully. "You gave us quite a run."

She did not reply. His name was Rufus Atkins, a slight, hard-bodied man whose skin, even in winter, had the color and texture of a blacksmith's leather apron. His hair was a blackish-tan, long, combed straight back, and there were hollows in his cheeks that gave his face a certain fragility. But the cartilage around the jawbones was unnaturally dark, as though rubbed with blackened brick dust, knotted with a tension his manner hid from others.

Rufus Atkins' eyes were flat, hazel, and rarely did they contain or reveal any definable emotion, as though he lived behind glass and the external world never registered in a personal way on his senses.

A second man dismounted, this one blond, his nose wind-burned, wearing a leather cap and canvas coat and a red-and-white-checkered scarf tied around his throat. On his hip he carried a small flintlock pistol that had three hand-smoothed indentations notched in the wood grips. In his right hand he gripped a horse quirt that was weighted with a lead ball sewn inside the bottom of the deerhide handle.

"She done dropped it, huh?" he said.

"That's keenly observant of you, Clay, seeing as how the woman's belly is flat as a busted pig's bladder," Rufus Atkins replied.

"Marse Jamison says find both of them, he means find both of them, Rufus," the man named Clay said, looking back into the trees at the blood spots in the snow.

Rufus Atkins squatted down and ignored his companion's observation, his eyes wandering over Sarie's face.

"They say you filed your teeth into points 'cause there's an African king back there in your bloodline somewhere," he said to her. "Bet you gave birth to a man-child, didn't you, Sarie?"

"My child and me gonna be free. Ain't your bidness no more, Marse Rufus," she replied.

"Might as well face it, Sarie. That baby is not going to grow up around here, not with Marse Jamison's face on it. He'll ship it off somewhere he doesn't have to study on the trouble that big dick of his gets him into. Tell us where the baby is and maybe you and it will get sold off together."

When she didn't reply to his lie, he lifted her chin with his knuckle. "I've been good to you, Sarie. Never made you lift your dress, never whipped you, always let you go to the corn-breaks and the dances. Isn't it time for a little gratitude?" he said.

She looked into the distance at the bluffs on the far side of the river, the steam rising off the water in the shadows below, the live oaks blowing stiffly against the sky. Rufus Atkins fitted his hand under her arm and began to lift her to her feet.

She seized his wrist and sunk her teeth into his hand, biting down with her incisors into sinew and vein and bone, seeing his head pitch back, hearing the squeal rise from his throat. Then she flung his hand away from her and spat his blood out of her mouth.

He staggered to his feet, gripping the back of his wounded hand.

"You nigger bitch," he said.

He ripped the quirt from his friend's grasp and struck her across the face with it. Then, as though his anger were insatiable and fed upon itself, he inverted the quirt in his hand and whipped the leaded end down on her head and neck and shoulders, again and again.

He threw the quirt to the ground, squeezing his wounded hand again, and made a grinding sound with his teeth.

"Damn, I think she went to the bone," he said.

"Rufus?" the blond man named Clay said.

"What?" he answered irritably.

"I think you just beat her brains out."

"She deserved it."

"No, I mean you beat her brains out. Look. She's probably spreading her legs for the devil now," the blond man said.

Rufus Atkins stared down at Sarie's slumped posture, the hanging jaw, the sightless eyes.

"You just cost Marse Jamison six hundred dollars. You flat put us in it, Roof," Clay said.

Rufus cupped his mouth in hand and thought for a minute. He turned and looked at the third member of their party, a rodent-faced man in a buttoned green wool coat and slouch hat strung with a turkey feather. He had sores on his face that never healed, breath that stunk of decaying teeth, and no work history other than riding with the paddy rollers, a ubiquitous crew of drunkards and white trash who worked as police for plantation interests and terrorized Negroes on the roads at night.

"What you aim to do?" Clay asked.

"I'm studying on it," Rufus replied. He then turned toward the third man. "Come on up here, Jackson, and give us your opinion on something," he said.

The third man approached them, the wind twirling the turkey feather on his hat brim. He glanced down at Sarie, then back at Rufus, a growing knowledge in his face.

"You done it. You dig the hole," he said.

"You got it all wrong," Rufus said.

He slipped the flintlock pistol from Clay's side holster, cocked it, and fired a chunk of lead the size of a walnut into the side of Jackson's head. The report echoed across the water against the bluffs on the far side.

"Good God, you done lost your mind?" Clay said.

"Sarie killed Jackson, Clay. That's the story you take to the grave. Nigger who kills a white man isn't worth six hundred dollars. Nigger who kills a white man buys the scaffold. That's Lou'sana law," he said.

The blond man, whose full name was Clay Hatcher, stood stupefied, his nose red in the cold, his breath loud inside his checkered scarf.

"Whoever made the world sure didn't care much about the likes of us, did He?" Rufus said to no one in particular. "Bring up Jackson's horse and get him across the saddle, would you? Best be careful. I think he messed himself."

After she was told of her daughter's death and the baby who had been abandoned somewhere deep in the woods, Sarie's mother left her job in the washhouse without permission and went to the site where her daughter had died. She followed the blood trail back to the slough, then stood on the thawing mudflat and watched the water coursing southward toward the river and knew which direction Sarie had been going when she had finally been forced to stop and give birth to her child. It had been north, toward the river called the Ohio.

Sarie's mother and a wet nurse with breasts that hung inside her shirt like swollen eggplants walked along the banks of the slough until late afternoon. The sun was warm now, the trees filled with a smoky yellow light, as though the ice storm had never passed through Ira Jamison's plantation. Sarie's mother and the wet nurse rounded a bend in the woods, then saw footprints leading up to a leafy bower and a lean-to whose opening was covered with a bright green branch from a slash pine.

The child lay wrapped in a blanket like a caterpillar inside a cocoon, the eyes shut, the mouth puckered. The ground was soft now, scattered with pine needles, and among the pine needles were wildflowers that had been buried under snow. Sarie's mother unwrapped the child from the blanket and wiped it clean with a cloth, then handed it to the wet nurse, who held the baby's mouth to her breast and covered it with her coat.

"Sarie wanted a man-child. But this li'l girl beautiful," the wet nurse said.

"She gonna be my darlin' thing, too. Sarie gonna live inside her. Her name gonna be Spring. No, that ain't right. Her name gonna be Flower," Sarie's mother said.

Chapter Two

In the spring of 1861 Willie Burke's dreams took him to a place he had never been and to an event he had not experienced. He saw himself on a dusty Texas road south of Goliad, where the wind was blowing in the trees and there was a hint of salt water or distant rain in the air. The soldiers around him were glad of heart, their backs strung with blanket rolls and haversacks, some of them singing in celebration of their impending freedom and passage aboard a parole ship to New Orleans.

Then their Mexican warders began forming up into squads, positioning themselves on one side of the road only, the hammers to their heavy muskets collectively cocking into place.

"Them sonsofbitches are gonna shoot us. Run for hit, boys," a Texas soldier shouted.

"*¡Fuego!*" a Mexican officer shouted.

The musket fire was almost point-blank.

19

The grass and tree trunks alongside the road were striped with blood splatter. Then the Mexicans bayoneted the wounded and fallen, smashing skulls with their musket butts, firing with their pistols at the backs of those still trying to flee. In the dream Willie smelled the bodies of the men piled on top of him, the dried sweat in their clothes, the blood that seeped from their wounds. His heart thundered in his chest; his nose and throat were clotted with dust. He knew he had just begun his last day on Earth, here, in the year 1836, in a revolution in which no Irishman should have had a vested interest.

Then he heard a woman, a prostitute, running from one officer to the next, begging mercy for the wounded. The musket fire dissipated, and Willie got to his feet and ran for the treeline, not a survivor, but instead cursed with an abiding sense of shame and guilt that he had lived, fleeing through woods while the screams of his comrades filled his ears.

When Willie woke from the dream in a backroom of his mother's boardinghouse on Bayou Teche, he knew the fear that beat in his heart had nothing to do with his dead father's tale of his own survival at the Goliad Massacre during the Texas Revolution. The war he feared was now only the stuff of rumors, political posturing, and young men talking loudly of it in a saloon, but he had no doubt it was coming, like a crack in a dike that would eventually flood and destroy an entire region, beginning in Virginia or Maryland, perhaps, at a nameless crossroads or creek bed or sunken lane or stone wall meandering through a farmer's field, and as surely as he had wakened to birdsong in his mother's house that morning he would be in it, shells bursting above his head while he soiled his pants and killed others or was killed himself over an issue that had nothing to do with his life.

He washed his face in a bowl on the dresser and threw the water out the window onto the grassy yard that sloped down to the bayou. By the drawbridge a gleaming white paddle-wheeler, its twin stacks leaking smoke into the mist, was being loaded with barrels of molasses by a dozen Negro men, all of whom had begun work before dawn, their bodies glowing with sweat and humidity in the light from the fires they had built on the bank.

They were called wage slaves, rented out by their owner, in this case, Ira Jamison, on an hourly basis. The taskmaster, a man named Rufus Atkins, rented a room at the boardinghouse and worked the Negroes in his charge unmercifully. Willie walked out into the misty softness of the morning, into the residual smell of night-blooming flowers and bream spawning in the bayou and trees

21

dripping with dew, and tried to occupy his mind with better things than the likes of Rufus Atkins. But when he sat on a hole in the privy and heard Rufus Atkins driving and berating his charges, he wondered if there might be an exemption in heaven for the Negro who raked a cane knife across Atkins' throat.

When Willie walked back up the slope and encountered Atkins on his way into breakfast, he touched his straw hat, fabricated a smile and said, "Top of the morning to you, sir."

"And to you, Mr. Willie," Rufus Atkins replied.

Then Willie's nemesis, his inability to keep his own counsel, caught up with him.

"If words could flay, I'd bet you could take the hide off a fellow, Mr. Atkins," he said.

"That's right clever of you, Mr. Willie. I'm sure you must entertain your mother at great length while tidying the house and carrying out slop jars for her."

"Tell me, sir, since you're in a mood for profaning a fine morning, would you be liking your nose broken as well?" Willie inquired.

After the boarders had been fed, including Rufus Atkins, Willie helped his mother clean the table and scrape the dishes into a barrel of scraps that later they would take out to their farm by Spanish Lake and feed to their hogs. His mother, Ellen Lee, had thick, round, pink arms and brown hair that was turning gray, and a small Irish mouth and a cleft in her chin.

"Did I hear you have words with Mr. Atkins?" she asked.

Willie seemed to study the question. "I don't rightly recall. It may have been a distortion on the wind, perhaps," he replied.

"You're a poor excuse for a liar," she said.

He began washing dishes in the sink. But unfortunately she was not finished.

"The times might be good for others but not always for us. Our livery is doing poorly, Willie. We need every boarder we can get," she said.

"Would you like me to apologize?" he asked.

"That's up to your conscience. Remember he's a Protestant and given to their ways. We have to forgive those whom chance and accident have denied access to the Faith."

"You're right, Mother. There he goes now. I'll see if I can straighten things out," Willie replied, looking through the back window.

He hurried out the door and touched Rufus Atkins on the sleeve.

"Oh, excuse me, I didn't mean to startle you, Mr. Atkins," he said. "I just wanted to tell you I'm sorry for the sharpness of my tongue. I pray one day you find the Holy Roman Church and then die screaming for a priest."

★ ★ ★

When he came back into the house his mother said nothing to him, even though she had heard his remarks to Rufus Atkins through the window. But just before noon she found him in his reading place under a live oak by the bayou and pulled up a cane chair next to him and sat down with her palms propped on her knees.

"What ails you, Willie?" she asked.

"I was just a little out of sorts," he replied.

"You've decided, haven't you?" she said.

"What might that be?"

"Oh, Willie, you're signing up for the army. This isn't our war," she said.

"What should I do, stay home while others die?"

She looked emptily at the bayou and a covey of ducklings fluttering on the water around their mother.

"You'll get in trouble," she said.

"Over what?"

"You're cursed with the gift of Cassandra. For that reason you'll always be out of place and condemned by others."

"Those are the myths that our Celtic ancestors used to console themselves for their poverty," he replied.

She shook her head, knowing her exhortations were of little value. "I need you to fix the roof. What are your plans for today?" she asked.

"To take my clothes to Ira Jamison's laundry."

"And get in trouble with that black girl? Willie, tell me I haven't raised a lunatic for a son," she said.

He put a notebook with lined pages, a pencil, and a small collection of William Blake's poems in his pants pockets and rode his horse down Main Street. The town had been laid out along the serpentine contours of Bayou Teche, which took its name from an Atakapa Indian word that meant snake. The business district stretched from a brick warehouse on the bend, with huge iron doors and iron shutters over the windows, down to the Shadows, a two-story, pillared plantation home surrounded by live oaks whose shade was so deep the night-blooming flowers in the gardens often opened in the late afternoon.

An Episcopalian church marked one religious end of the town, a Catholic church the other. On the street between the two churches shopkeepers swept the plank walks under their colonnades, a constable spaded up horse dung and tossed it into the back of a wagon, and a dozen or so soldiers from Camp Pratt, out by Spanish Lake, sat in the shade between two brick buildings, still drunk from the night before, flinging a pocketknife into the side of a packing case.

Actually the word "soldier" didn't quite describe them, Willie thought. They had been mustered in as state militia, most of them outfitted in mismatched uniforms paid for by three or four Secessionist fanatics who owned cotton interests in the Red River parishes.

The most ardent of these was Ira Jamison. His original farm, named Angola Plantation because of the geographical origins of its slaves, had expanded itself in ancillary fashion from the hilly brush country on a bend of the Mississippi River north of Baton Rouge to almost every agrarian enterprise in Louisiana, reaching as far away as a slave market in Memphis run by a man named Nathan Bedford Forrest.

Willie rode his horse between the two buildings where the boys in militia uniforms lounged. Some were barefoot, some with their shirts off and pimples on their shoulders and skin as white as a frog's belly. One, who was perhaps six and a half feet tall, his fly partially buttoned, slept with a straw hat over his face.

"You going to sign up today, Willie?" a boy said.

"Actually Jefferson Davis was at our home only this morning, asking me the same thing," he replied. "Say, you boys wouldn't be wanting more whiskey or beer, would you?"

One of them almost vomited. Another

threw a dried horse turd at his back. But Willie took no offense. Most of them were poor, unlettered, brave and innocent at the same time, imbued with whatever vision of the world others created for them. When he glanced back over his shoulder they were playing mumblety-peg with their pocket-knives.

He was on a dirt road now, one that led southward into the sugarcane fields that stretched all the way to the Gulf of Mexico. He passed a hog lot and slaughterhouse buzzing with bottle flies and a brick saloon with a railed bar inside, then a paint-skinned, two-story frame house with a sagging gallery that served as New Iberia's only bordello. The owner, Carrie LaRose, who some said had been in prison in the West Indies or France, had added a tent in the side yard, with cots inside, to handle the increase in business from Camp Pratt.

A dark-haired chub of a girl in front of the tent scooped up her dress and lifted it high above her bloomers. "How about a ride, Willie? Only a dollar," she said.

Willie raised himself in the saddle and removed his hat.

"It's a terrible temptation, May, but I'd be stricken blind by your beauty and would never find my home or dear mother again," he said.

The girl grinned broadly and was about to

shout back a rejoinder, when she was startled by a young barefoot man, six and a half feet tall, running hard after Willie Burke.

The tall youth vaulted onto the rump of Willie's horse, grabbing Willie around the sides for purchase while Willie's horse spooked sideways and almost caved with the additional weight.

Willie could smell an odor like milk and freshly mowed hay in the tall youth's clothes.

"You pass by without saying hello to your pal?" the young man said.

"Hello, Jim!"

"Hello there, Willie!"

"You get enough grog in you last night?" Willie asked.

"Hardly," Jim replied. "Are you going to see that nigger girl again?"

"It's a possibility. Care to come along?" Willie said.

The young man named Jim had hair the color of straw and an angular, self-confident face that reflected neither judgment of himself nor others. He pulled slightly at the book that protruded from Willie's pocket and flipped his thumb along the edges of the pages.

"What you're about to do is against the law, Willie," Jim said.

Willie looked at the dust blowing out of the new sugarcane, a solitary drop of rain that made a star in the dust. "Smell the salt?

It's a fine day, Jim. I think you should stay out of saloons for a spell," he said.

"That girl is owned by Ira Jamison. He's not a man to fool with," Jim said.

"Really, now?"

"Join the Home Guards with me. You should see the Enfield rifles we uncrated yesterday. The Yankees come down here, by God we'll lighten their load."

"I'm sure they're properly frightened at the prospect. You'd better drop off now, Jim. I don't want to get you in trouble with Marse Jamison," Willie said.

Jim's silence made Willie truly wish for the first time that day he'd kept his own counsel. He felt Jim's hands let go of his sides, then heard his weight hit the dirt road. Willie turned to wave good-bye to his friend, sorry for his condescending attitude, even sorrier for the fear in his breast that he could barely conceal. But his friend did not look back.

The last house on the road was a ramshackle laundry owned by Ira Jamison, set between two spreading oaks, behind which Flower sat in an open-air wash shed, scrubbing stains out of a man's nightshirt, her face beaded with perspiration from the iron pots steaming around her. Her hair was black and straight, like an Indian's, her cheekbones pronounced, her skin the color of coffee with milk poured in it.

She looked at the sun's place in the sky and set the shirt down in the boiling water again and went into the cypress cabin where she lived by the coulee and wiped her face and neck and underarms with a rag she dipped into a cypress bucket.

From under her bed she removed the lined tablet and dictionary Willie had given her and sat in a chair by the window and read the lines she had written in the tablet:

A owl flown acrost the moon late last night.

A cricket sleeped on the pillow by my head.

The gator down in the coulee look like dark stone when the sunlite turn red and spill out on the land.

There is talk of a war. A free man of color who have a big house on the bayou say for the rest of us not to listen to no such talk. He own slaves hisself and makes bricks in a big oven.

I learned to spell 3 new words this morning. Mr. Willie say not to write down hard words lessen I look them up first.

A band played on the big lawn on the bayou yesterday. A man in a silk hat and purple suit tole the young soldiers they do not haf to worry about the Yankees cause the Yankees is cowards. The brass horns were gold in the sunshine. So was the sword the man in the silk hat and purple suit carry on his side.

Mr. Willie say not to say aint. Not to say he dont or she dont either.

This is all my thoughts for the day.

Signed,
Flower Jamison

She heard Willie's horse in the yard and glanced around her cabin at the wildflowers she had cut and placed in a water jar that morning, her clean Sunday dress, which hung on a wood peg, the bedspread given to her by a white woman on Main, now tucked around the moss-stuffed mattress pad on her bed. When she stepped out the door Willie was swinging down from his horse, slipping a bag of dirty clothes loose from the pommel of his saddle.

He smiled at her, then squinted up at the sunlight through the trees and glanced back casually at the house, as though he were simply taking in the morning and his surroundings with no particular thought in mind.

"You by yourself today?" he asked.

"Some other girls are ironing inside the big house. We iron inside so the dust don't get on the clothes," she said.

"Could you give a fellow a drink of water?" he said.

"I done made some lemonade," she replied,

and waited for him to enter the cabin first.

He removed his hat as though he were entering a white person's home, then sat in the chair at the table by the window and gazed wistfully out onto the young sugarcane bending in the breeze off the Gulf. His hair was combed but uncut and grew in black locks on his neck.

"What did you write for us today, Flower?" he asked, his gaze still focused outside the cabin.

She handed him her tablet, then stood motionlessly, her hands behind her.

He put the tablet flat on the table and read what she had written, his elbows on the table, his fingers propped on his temples. His cheeks were shaved and pooled with color that never seemed to change in hue.

"You look at the world only as a poet can," he said.

He saw her lips say the word "poet" silently.

"That's a person who sees radiance when others only see objects. That's you, Flower," he said.

But she disregarded the compliment and felt the most important line she had written in the notebook was one he had not understood. In fact, she was not quite sure what she had meant when she made the entry. But the martial speech of the man in the silk hat still rang in her ears, and the hard gold light beating on his sword and the brass instruments of the band hovered before her eyes like the angry reflection off a heliograph.

"Is there gonna be a war, Mr. Willie?" she asked.

"Why don't you sit down? I'm getting a crick in my neck looking up at you," he said. "Look, y'all are going to be free one day. Peace or war, it's just a matter of time."

"You gonna join the army, ain't you, suh?"

In spite of his invitation she had made no movement to sit down at the table with him, which would have caused her to violate a protocol that was on a level with looking a white person directly in the face. But after having shown her obedience to a plantation code that systematically degraded her as well as others, she realized she was now, of her own volition, invading the privacy and perhaps exposing the weakness of a man she genuinely admired and was fond of.

For just a moment she wondered if it was true, as white people always said, that slaves behaved morally only when they were afraid.

"I try not to study on it," Willie replied. Then, as though to distract himself from his own thoughts, he told her of his father's participation in the Texas Revolution, the massacre of prisoners at Goliad, the intercession of a camp follower who probably saved his father's life.

"A prostitute saved all them men from being killed?" she said.

"She surely did. No one ever learned her name or what became of her. The Texans called her the Angel of Goliad. But think of the difference one poor woman made," he said.

She sat down on her bed, her knees close together, her hands folded in her lap.

"I ain't meant to be prying or rude. You're always kind to the niggers, Mr. Willie. You don't belong with them others," she said.

"Don't call your people niggers," he said.

"It's the only name we got," she said, with a sharpness in her voice that surprised her. "You gonna let the Yankees kill you so men like Marse Jamison can make more money off their cotton? You gonna let them do that to you, suh?"

"I think I should go now. Here, I brought you a book of poems. They're by an English poet named William Blake." He rose from his chair and offered her the book.

But she wasn't listening now. Her gaze was fixed outside the door. Through the criss-cross of wash lines and steam drifting off the wash pots scattered throughout the yard, she saw Rufus Atkins rein his carriage, one with a surrey on top, and dismount and tether his horse to an iron weight attached to a leather strap he let slide through his fingers.

"You best go, Mr. Willie," she said.

"Has Mr. Rufus been bothering you, Flower?"

34

"I ain't said that."

"Mr. Rufus is a coward. His kind always are. If he hurts you, you tell me about it, you hear?"

"What you gonna do, suh? What you gonna do?" she said.

He started to speak, then crimped his lips together and was silent.

After he was gone she sat by herself in the cabin, her heart beating, her breasts rising and falling in the silence. Out of the corner of her eye she saw Rufus Atkins' silhouette break across the light.

He stepped inside the cabin, his wide-brimmed hat on his head, his gaze sweeping over the room, the taut bedspread on her mattress, the jug of lemonade on her table, the cut flowers in the water jar.

He removed a twenty-dollar gold piece from his watch pocket and flipped it in the air with his thumb, catching it in his palm. He rolled it across the tops of his knuckles and made it disappear from his hand. Then he reached behind her ear and held the coin in her face.

"Deception's an art, Flower. We all practice it. But white people are a whole sight better at it than y'all are," he said.

When she didn't reply, he smiled wanly. "Young Willie bring you his wash?" he asked.

"Yes, suh," she replied.

"I hope he wasn't here to get anything else washed," he said.

She lowered her eyes to the floor. Atkins sat down at the table and removed his hat and wiped his face with a handkerchief.

"Flower, you are the best-looking black woman I've ever seen. Honest to God truth," he said. He picked up the jug of lemonade and drank out of it.

But when he set the jug down his gaze lighted on an object that was wedged under her mattress pad. He rose from the chair and walked to her bed.

"I declare, a dictionary and a poetry book and what looks like a tablet somebody's been writing in. Willie Burke give you these?" he said.

"A preacher traveling through. He ax me to hold them for him," she said.

"That was mighty thoughtful of you." He folded back a page of her tablet and read from it. " 'A cricket slept on the pillow by my head.' This preacher doesn't sound like he's got good sense. Well, let's just take these troublesome presences off your hands."

He walked outside and knelt by a fire burning under a black pot filled with boiling clothes. He began ripping the pages out of her writing tablet and feeding them individually into the flames. He rested one haunch on the heel of his boot and watched each page blacken in the center, then curl around the edges, his long hair and clipped beard flecked with gray, like pieces of ash, his skin as dark and grained as scorched brick.

Then he opened the book of poems and wet an index finger and methodically turned the pages, puckering his lips as he glanced over each poem, an amused light in his face.

"Come back inside, Marse Rufus," she said from the doorway.

"I thought you might say that," he replied, rising to his feet, his stomach as flat and hard as a board under his tucked shirt and tightly buttoned pants.

At four-thirty the next morning, April 12, 1861, a Confederate general whose hair was brushed into a greased curlicue on his pate gave the order to a coastal battery to fire on a fort that was barely visible out in the harbor. The shell arced across the sky under a blanket of stars, its fuse sparking like a lighted cigar tossed carelessly into a pile of oily rags.

Chapter Three

By afternoon of the same day the telegraph had carried the news of the bombardment of Fort Sumter to New Iberia, and Camp Pratt, out on Spanish Lake, was suddenly filled with young men who stood in long lines before the enlistment tables, most of them Acadian boys who spoke no English and had never been farther from Bayou Teche than the next parish. The sky was blue through the canopy of oak trees that covered the camp, the lake beaten with sunlight, the four-o'clocks blooming in the shade, the plank tables in front of the freshly carpentered barracks groaning with platters of sausage, roast chickens, boudin, smoked ducks, crab gumbo, dirty rice, and fruit pies that had been brought in carriages by ladies who lived in the most elegant plantation homes along the bayou.

Willie's tall friend, Jim Stubbefield, sat barefoot in his militia uniform, his back against a cypress tree by the water's edge, and drank from a cup of buttermilk and looked with puzzlement at the festive atmosphere in the camp. He turned to a young man in civilian clothes sitting next to him and said, "Robert, I think the fates are not working properly here. I enlisted two months ago and no one seemed to notice."

His friend was named Robert Perry. His hair grew over his collar and was the color of mahogany, his face handsome, his blue eyes never troubled by fear or self-doubt or conflict with the world around him.

"I'm sure it was just an oversight on the community's part," he said.

Jim continued to stare in a bemused way at the enlistment lines, then his gaze locked on one individual in particular and he chewed on a piece of skin on his thumb and spit it off his tongue.

"I think I've made a mistake," he said.

"A man with your clarity of vision? Seems unlikely," Robert said.

"Look there. Willie's joining up. Maybe at my urging."

"Good for Willie," Robert said.

"I doubt Willie has it in him to shoot anyone," Jim said.

"Do you?"

"If they come down here, I figure they've asked for it."

"I doubt if it was easy for Willie to come

here. Don't rob him of his self-respect," Robert said, rising to his feet, pressing a palm down on Jim's shoulder.

"Your father owns over a hundred and eighty niggers, Robert. You ought not to be lecturing to the rest of us."

"You're entirely right, Jim," Robert said. He winked at Jim and walked toward the recruitment table, where Willie Burke had just used quill and ink to enter his name among a long list of French and Spanish and Anglo-Saxon ones, many of them printed by an enlistment officer and validated by an X.

But Robert soon realized Jim's premonitions about their friend were probably correct, that the juncture of Willie Burke and the Confederate army would be akin to a meeting of a wrecking ball and a crystal shop.

Captain Rufus Atkins stepped out of a tent, in a gray uniform and wide-brimmed ash-colored hat with a gold cord and a pair of tiny gold acorns tied around the crown. A blond man, his hair as greasy as tallow, wearing a butternut uniform with corporal's chevrons freshly sewn on the sleeves, stood behind him. The corporal's name was Clay Hatcher.

"Where do you think you're going, young Willie?" Atkins asked.

"Back home," Willie answered.

"I think not," Atkins replied. He looked

out at the lake and the moss blowing in the trees, the four-o'clocks riffling in the shade. "One of the privies needs dipping out. After you finish that, spread a little lye around and that will be it until this evening. By the way, are you familiar with the poetry of William Blake?"

"Never heard of him," Willie replied.

"I see. Better get started, young Willie. Did you bring a change of clothes?" Atkins said.

"Excuse me, sir, but I didn't join the army to ladle out your shitholes. On that subject, can you clear up a question that has bedeviled many in the community? Is it true your mother was stricken with the bloody flux when you were born and perhaps threw the infant away by mistake and raised the afterbirth instead?"

The corporal to the side of Rufus Atkins pressed his wrist to his mouth to stop from snickering, then glanced at Atkins' face and sucked in his cheeks.

"Let me gag and buck him, Cap'n," he said.

Before Atkins could answer, Robert Perry walked up behind Willie.

"Hello, Captain!" Robert Perry said.

"How do you do, Master Robert?" Atkins said, bowing slightly and touching his hat. "I saw you signing up earlier. I know your father is proud."

"My friend Willie isn't getting off to a bad

start in the army, is he?" Robert said.

"A little garrison duty, that's all," Atkins said.

"I'm sure if you put him in my charge, there will be no trouble," Robert said.

"Of course, Master Robert. My best to your father," Atkins said.

"And to your family as well, sir," Robert said, slipping his hand under Willie's arm.

The two of them walked back toward the lake to join Jim Stubbefield at the cypress tree. Willie felt Robert's hand tighten on his arm.

"Atkins is an evil and dangerous man. You stay away from him," Robert said.

"Let him stay away from me," Willie replied.

"What was that stuff about William Blake?"

"I have a feeling he found a book I gave to a Negro girl."

"You did what?" Robert said.

"Oh, go on with you, Robert. You don't seem bothered by the abolitionist tendencies of Abigail Dowling," Willie said.

"I love you dearly, Willie, but you're absolutely hopeless, unteachable, beyond the pale, with the thinking processes of a stump, and I suspect an extra thorn in Our Savior's crown," Robert said.

"Thank you," Willie said.

"By the way, Abigail is not an abolitionist. She's simply of a kind disposition," Robert said.

"That's why she circulated a petition begging commutation for John Brown?" Willie said. He heard his friend make a grinding noise in his throat.

That evening Willie bathed in the clawfoot tub inside the bathhouse on the bayou, then dried off and combed his hair in a yellowed mirror and dressed in fresh clothes and walked outside into the sunset and the breeze off the Gulf. The oaks overhead were draped with moss, their limbs ridged with lichen, and the gardenias and azaleas were blooming in his mother's yard.

Next door, in a last patch of yellow sunshine, a neighbor was boiling crabs in an iron pot on a woodfire. The coolness of the evening and the fecund heaviness of the bayou and a cheerful wave from his neighbor somehow made Willie conclude that in spite of the historical events taking place around him all was right with the world and that it should not be the lot of a young man to carry its weight upon his shoulders.

He strolled down East Main, past the Shadows and the wide-galleried, gabled overseer's house across the street, past other homes with cupolas and fluted columns that loomed as big as ships out of the floral gardens that surrounded them.

He paused in front of a shotgun cottage with ventilated green shutters set back in live oak and pine trees, its windows lighted in the gloom, a gazebo in the side yard threaded with bougainvillea. He heard a wind chime tinkle in the breeze.

The woman who lived inside the cottage was named Abigail Dowling. She had come to New Iberia from Massachusetts as a nurse during a yellow fever epidemic and had stayed, working both in the clinic and teaching in a private school down the street. Her hair was thick, chestnut-colored, her skin without blemish, her bosom and features such that few men, including ones in the company of their wives, could prevent themselves from casting furtive glances at.

But for many her ways were suspect, her loyalties questionable, her candor intimidating. On one occasion Willie had asked her outright about rumors he'd heard.

"Which rumors might that be?" she said.

"A couple of Negroes who disappeared from plantations out by Spanish Lake," he replied.

"Yes?" she said, waiting.

"They got through the paddy rollers. In fact, it looks like they got clean out of the state. Some say you might be involved with the Underground Railroad, Miss Abigail."

"Would you think less of me?" she replied.

"A lady who hand-feeds those with yellow jack and puts their lives ahead of her own?" he said.

But she was not reassured.

Now, in the gloaming of the day, he stood on her gallery and tapped on her door, his straw hat in hand, a discomfort in his chest he could not quite define.

"Oh, good evening, Miss Abigail, pardon me for dropping by unexpectedly, but I thought you might like to take a walk or allow me to treat you to a dessert down at the café," he said.

"That's very nice of you," she said, stepping outside. She wore a plain blue cotton dress, buttoned not quite to the throat, the sleeves pushed up on her arms. "But someone is due to drop by. Can we just sit on the steps for a bit?"

"Sure," he said, hoping his disappointment did not show. He waited for her to take a seat on the top step, then sat on the step below her.

"Is something bothering you, Willie?" she asked.

"I enlisted today. Out at Camp Pratt. I'm just in the Home Guards now, but I suspect we'll be formed into regular infantry directly."

The darkening sky was full of birds now, sweeping above the chimneys, the oaks loud with cicadas and the throbbing of tree frogs.

After a long silence, she said, "I'm sure in your own mind you did the right thing."

"My own mind?" he said, and felt his face

color, both for his rudeness in mimicking her statement and because he was angry at himself for seeking absolution from her, as though he were not possessed of either humanity or a conscience himself.

"I don't judge you, Willie. Robert Perry is enlisting, too. I think the world of you both," she said.

"Robert believes in slavery. I don't. He comes from a wealthy family and has a vested interest in seeing the Negro race kept subservient. That's the difference between us," he said, then bit his lip at the self-righteousness in his voice.

"Robert is reading for the law. He doesn't plan to be a plantation or slave owner." She paused when she saw the injury in Willie's eyes. "Why are you enlisting?"

Because I'm afraid to be thought a coward, a voice inside him said.

"What?" she said.

"Nothing. I said nothing," he replied. He looked out at a carriage passing in the street. Don't say anymore, for God's sakes, he told himself. But his old enemy, his impetuosity, held sway with him once again.

"I think all this is going to be destroyed. By cannon shot and fire and disease, all of it wiped out," he said, and waved his hand vaguely at the palm trees in the yards, the massive houses hidden inside the live oaks, a paddle-wheeler churning on the Teche, its lighted windows softly muted inside the mist.

"And you make your own life forfeit for a cause you don't respect? My God, Willie," Abigail said.

He felt the back of his neck burning. Then, when he believed matters could get no worse, he looked up and saw Robert Perry rein his horse in the dusk and dismount and enter the yard, removing his hat.

"Good evening, Miss Abigail. You too, Willie. Did I break in on something?" Robert said.

Robert waited for a reply, his face glowing with goodwill.

Two hours later Willie Burke was on his fourth glass of whiskey in the brick saloon next to Carrie LaRose's brothel. The plank floor was scattered with sawdust and burned by cigars and stained with tobacco juice around the cuspidors. Hand towels hung from brass rings along the bar, and above the bar mirror was a painting of a reclining nude, her bottom an ax-handle wide, her stomach like a soft pink pillow, her smile and pubic hair and relaxed arms an invitation to enter the picture frame with her.

Willie wanted to concentrate on the lovely lines of the woman in the painting and forget the events of the day, particularly the fact he had been so foolish as to enlist in the Home Guards. But the man standing next to him, one Jean-Jacques LaRose, also known as Scavenger Jack, was giving a drunken lecture to anyone within earshot, pounding his fists on the bar, denouncing Secessionists, Copperheads in the North who encouraged them, and people stupid enough to join the army and serve their cause.

Unlike his sister, Carrie LaRose, who owned the bordello next door, Scavenger Jack operated on the edges of legitimate society, hauling away Chitimacha burial mounds that he mixed with manure and sold for high-grade fertilizer, exporting weevil-infested rice to plantation operators in the West Indies whose food costs for their workers were running too high, and, rumor had it, luring ships onto a reef with a false beacon off Key West in order to salvage the cargo.

He was a huge man, his black hair and beard streaked with red, a scar across his nose like a flattened worm. His bull neck was corded with veins, his teeth like tombstones, his shoulders so broad they split the seams of his coat.

"Let me ax you gentlemen somet'ing. When them Yankees blockade our ports, 'cause that's what they gonna do, how you gonna get your sugar and salt and cotton out of Lou'sana, you? Round up the crawfish and pile it on their backs?" he said to his audience.

"Now, Jean-Jacques, there's more involved

here than money," said a member of the town council and part owner of the bank, an older man with an egg-shaped, pleasant face. "The Negroes have already heard about the firing on Fort Sumter. A lady in St. Martinville caught her cook with cyanide this morning. But I worry more about the Negro male population being turned loose on our women. That's the kind of thing these abolitionists have encouraged."

"Them rich people couldn't convince y'all to fight for their cotton, no. So they got all them newspapers to start y'all t'inking about what's gonna happen to your jelly roll. That done it when nothing else did," Jean-Jacques said.

"That's not called for, Jean-Jacques. We're all serious men here and we speak respectfully of one another," the older man said.

"What y'all fixing to do is ruin my bidness. You t'ink a black man who work all day in the field got nothing on his mind except sticking his pole up your wife's dress?" Jean-Jacques said.

"You should give some thought to your words, sir," the older man said, lowering his eyes, his throat coloring. Then he collected himself and said to the bartender, "Give my friend Jean-Jacques another drink."

Jean-Jacques belched so loudly the men at the billiard table turned around, startled.

"Better enjoy your own drink, suh. The liquor in here come off my boats. What y'all gonna drink after them Yankees shut me down?" Jean-Jacques said.

But Willie had long ago given up listening to the self-serving arguments about the moral validity of Secession. Rarely did logic and humanity have any influence over the discussion. Instead, the most naked form of self-interest always seemed to drive the debate, as though venality and avarice had somehow evolved into virtues. He thought about the slave girl Flower and the fact that her literacy had to be concealed as though it were an object of shame.

He wondered if Rufus Atkins had found Flower's notebook as well as the collection of William Blake's poems. What had he done? Why had he not listened to his mother or his friend Jim Stubbefield?

He drank the rest of the whiskey in his glass, then sipped from a pitcher of warm beer that he was using as a chaser. He looked at the mouth and breasts of the woman in the painting and through the open window heard someone playing a piano in the brothel next door. His head reeled and the room seemed to tip sideways, and his ears buzzed with sound that had no meaning. The oil lamps in the saloon were like whorls of yellow color inside the cigar smoke that layered the ceiling. The whiskey had brought him no relief and instead had only created a hunger in his loins that made him bite his lip when he looked at the woman above the bar mirror.

Oh Lord, quiet my desires, he thought. And immediately focused his gaze on the woman's form again. He swallowed the rest of his whiskey in one gulp and thought he was going to fall backward.

"Gag and buck," he said to no one.

"What did you say, Willie?" Jean-Jacques asked.

"What does 'gag and buck' mean?"

"You don't want to find out. You ain't gone and signed up for the army, you?"

"I did."

"Po' Willie, why ain't you come to see me first?" Jean-Jacques said, and cupped his hand on the back of Willie's neck.

"You're a criminal," Willie said.

"But I got my good points too, ain't I?"

"Undoubtedly. Oh, Jean-Jacques, I've made a mess of things," Willie said.

Jean-Jacques put his mouth close to Willie's ear. "I can put you on a boat for Mexico when it's the right time. Let's go next door to my sister's and get your ashes hauled," he said.

"That's a grand suggestion, and please don't hold it against me for not acting on it. But I have to puke," Willie said.

He reeled out the back door into an overgrown coulee and bent over behind a tree just as an enormous volume of whiskey and beer and pickled food surged out of his stomach. He gasped for breath, then rinsed his face in a rain barrel and dried it on his shirt. The night air was soft with mist, the moon buried in the clouds above the cane fields. Next door the piano player was playing a minstrel song titled "Dixie's Land." Willie shouldered a mop propped against a cistern and began a parody of close-order drill in the yard behind the brothel, then flung aside the flap on the tent in the side yard and marched through the row of cots inside, counting cadence for himself, "Reep . . . reep . . . reep," saluting two naked people caught at the worst possible moment in their coupling.

He continued out the far end of the tent and on down the road, passing a horseman whose face was shadowed by a wide hat. The wind changed, and he saw dust blowing out of the fields and a tree of lightning splinter across the sky. He left the road and crossed the dirt yard of the laundry where Flower worked and walked through the iron pots in the backyard and the wash that was flapping on the clotheslines and stopped by the back window of her cabin.

"Flower?" he said.

He heard her rise from her bed, then push open the wood flap on the window with a stick.

"What you doing, Mr. Willie?" she asked.

"Did Rufus Atkins come upon the poetry book I gave you?"

"Yes, suh, he did."

"Did he report you?"

"No, suh, he ain't done that. I mean, he didn't do that."

"Come close, so I can see your face."

"You don't sound right, Mr. Willie," she said.

"Did Rufus Atkins make you do something you didn't want to?"

"I ain't got no control over them things. It don't do no good to talk about them, either."

"I've done you a great harm, Flower."

"No, you ain't. I mean, no, you hasn't. You better go back home now, Mr. Willie."

He was about to reply when he heard horses out on the road.

"Who's that?" he said.

"The paddy rollers. Oh, suh, please don't let them catch you here," she said.

He walked back through the yard and the darkness of the oaks that grew on each side of the laundry. He was sweating now, the wind suddenly cold on his face. He heard thunder crack in the south and rumble across the sky, like apples tumbling down a wooden chute. He stepped out on the road and walked toward the lights in the saloon and the tinny music in Carrie LaRose's brothel, his pulse beating in his wrists, his palms

53

damp, a tightness in his throat he could not quite explain.

There were six riders spread across the road in front of him, led by a seventh man in a rain slicker and flop hat, like cavalry advancing on an enemy position, their saddles hung with pistols and coils of rope and braided whips, their faces bladed with purpose.

"Hold your hands out by your sides, friend," the leader said.

"I think not. Unless you have governance over a white man talking a walk," Willie said.

The leader rode his horse forward. Lightning rippled through the clouds overhead and the wind flattened the tops of the young cane in the fields. The leader of the horsemen leaned down on his pommel, the saddle creaking with the shift in his weight.

"We've got five niggers unaccounted for tonight. It isn't a time for cleverness, Mr. Willie," he said.

"Oh, it's Captain Atkins, is it? This is a coincidence. I'm on a mission of recovery myself. I took my laundry to the black girl, what's her name, Flower, the one owned by Mr. Jamison? I think I dropped one or two of my books out of my saddlebags. You didn't find them, did you?"

"Maybe you and I will have a talk about that later," Atkins said.

"Mr. Jamison often visits at the Shadows.

I'll mention it to him. Is there anything I should report about amorous relationships on your part with his niggers?" Willie said.

Atkins' ringed finger clicked up and down on the stitched top of his pommel.

"A word of caution to you, Mr. Willie. You were at the home of the abolitionist woman this evening. Now I see you in a neighborhood where five slaves didn't report for bell count. Be aware there are others besides I who feel you bear watching," Atkins said.

"Say again?"

"Robert Perry saved his little tit-sucking momma's boy of a friend from being gagged and bucked today. Don't expect that kind of good fortune again," Atkins said.

"Thank you, sir. It's a great honor to be excoriated by a miserable fuck and white trash such as yourself," Willie said.

He brushed past Atkins' horse and walked through the other riders, the cane in the fields whipping in the wind, dust and rain now blowing across the lighted front of the saloon.

He heard Atkins' boot heels thud against his horse's sides and barely had time enough to turn before Atkins rode him down, whipping the lead ball on the butt of his quirt handle across Willie's head.

He felt the earth rush up at him and explode against his face. Then the booted legs of the paddy rollers surrounded him and through a misting rain he thought he heard the song "Dixie's Land" again.

"Since he likes the abolitionist woman so much, dump him in the nigger jail," Atkins said.

Then Willie was being lifted over a saddle, his wrists and feet roped together under the horse's belly. As the horse moved forward blood dripped out of Willie's hair onto his shirtsleeves and the dust from the horse's hooves rose into his nostrils.

But a huge man stepped into the middle of the road and grasped the horse's bridle.

"You're a constable and I cain't stop you from taking him in, Mr. Atkins. But if there's another mark on him in the morning, I'm gonna strip the clothes off your body on Main Street and lay a whip to your back, me," Jean-Jacques LaRose said.

Atkins was dismounted, his stature diminutive in contrast to Jean-Jacques LaRose. He pressed his quirt against Jean-Jacques' chest, bowing the braided leather back on itself.

"Would you care to see your sister's business establishment shut down? . . . You don't? . . . I knew you were a man of reason after all, Jack," he said. He tapped his quirt softly on Jean-Jacques' chest.

A half hour later Willie lay on a wood bunk inside a log jail, an iron manacle around his ankle. Two Negroes sat on the dirt floor against the far wall, barefoot, their knees drawn up before them. Their clothes were torn, their hair bloody. They smelled of funk and horse barns and night damp and fish that had soured on their stomachs. He could hear them breathing in the dark.

"You men ran from your owners?" Willie asked.

But they would not answer him. In the glow of the moon through the barred window their faces were running with sweat, their eyes red, their nostrils cavernous. He could see the pulse jumping in one man's throat.

He had never seen fear as great in either man or beast.

Chapter Four

Later that same night Flower left her cabin and crossed the cane field through layers of ground fog that felt like damp cotton on her skin. She entered a woods that was strung with air vines and cobwebs and dotted with palmettos and followed the edge of a coulee to a bayou where a flatboat loaded with Spanish moss was moored in a cluster of cypress trees.

The tide was going out along the coast. In minutes the current in the bayou would reverse itself, and the flatboat, which looked like any other that was used to harvest moss for mattress stuffing, would be poled downstream into a saltwater bay where a larger boat waited for the five black people who sat huddled in the midst of the moss, the women in bonnets, the men wearing flop hats that obscured their faces.

Two white boatmen, both of them gaunt, with full beards, wearing leather wrist guards and suspenders that hitched their trousers almost to their chests, stood by the tiller. One of them held a shaved pole that was anchored in the bayou, his callused palms tightening audibly against the wood.

A white woman with chestnut hair in a gray dress that touched the tops of her shoes had just walked up a plank onto the boat, a heavy bundle clasped in both arms. One of the white men took the bundle from her and untied it and began placing loaves of bread, smoked hams, sides of bacon and jars of preserves and cracklings inside the pilothouse.

Flower stepped out of the heated enclosure of the trees and felt the coolness of the wind on her skin.

"Miss Abigail?" she said.

The two white men and the white woman turned and looked at her, their bodies motionless.

"It's Flower, Miss Abigail. I work at the laundry. I brung something for their trip," she said.

"You shouldn't be here," Abigail said.

"The lady yonder is my auntie. I known for a long time y'all was using this place. I ain't tole nobody," Flower said.

Abigail turned to the two white men. "Does one more make a difference?" she asked.

"The captain out on the bay is mercenary, but we'll slip her in," one of them said.

"Would you like to come with your auntie?" Abigail asked her.

"There's old folks at Angola I got to care for. Here, I got this twenty-dollar gold piece. I brung a juju bag, too." Flower walked up the plank and felt the wood bend under her weight. The water under her was as yellow as paint in the moonlight. She saw the black head and back and S-shaped motion of a water moccasin swimming across the current.

She placed the coin in Abigail's hand, then removed a small bag fashioned out of red flannel that was tied around her neck with a leather cord and placed it on top of the coin.

"How'd you come by this money, Flower?" Abigail asked.

"Found it."

"Where?"

Flower watched the moss moving in the trees, a sprinkle of stars in the sky.

"I best go now," she said.

She walked back across the plank to the woods, then heard Abigail Dowling behind her.

"Tell me where you got the gold piece," Abigail said.

"I stole it out of Rufus Atkins' britches."

Abigail studied her face, then touched her hair and cheek.

"Has he molested you, Flower?" she said.

"You a good lady, Miss Abigail, but I ain't

a child and I ain't axed for nobody's pity," Flower said.

Abigail's hand ran down Flower's shoulder and arm until she could clasp Flower's hand in her own.

"No, you're neither a child nor an object of pity, and I would never treat you as such," Abigail said.

"Them two men yonder? What do you call them?" Flower asked.

"Their names?"

"No, the religion they got. What do you call that?"

"They're called Quakers."

Flower nodded her head. "Good night, Miss Abigail," she said.

"Good night, Flower," Abigail said.

A few minutes later Flower looked back over her shoulder and saw the flatboat slip through the cypress trees into a layer of moonlit fog that reminded her of the phosphorous glow given off by a grave.

Three days later Willie Burke was walked in manacles from the Negro jail to the court, a water-stained loft above a saloon, and charged with drunkenness and attacking an officer of the law. The judge was not an unkindly man, simply hard of hearing from a shell burst at the battle of Buena Vista in 1847, and sometimes more concerned with the pigeons whose droppings splattered on his desk than the legal matter at hand.

Through the yellow film of dirt on the window Willie could see the top of a palm tree and a white woman driving hogs down the dirt street below. His mother and Abigail Dowling and his friend Jim Stubbefield sat on a wood bench in the back of the room, not far from Rufus Atkins and the paddy rollers.

"How do you plead to the charges, Mr. Burke?" the judge asked.

"Guilty of drunkenness, Your Honor. But innocent of the rest, which is a bunch of lies," Willie replied.

"These men all say you attacked Captain Atkins," the judge said, gesturing at the paddy rollers.

Willie said something the judge couldn't understand.

"Speak louder!" the judge said.

"I'd consider the source!" Willie replied.

"We have two sides of the same story, Mr. Burke. But unfortunately for you the preponderance of testimony comes from your adversaries. Can you pay a fifty-dollar fine?" the judge said.

"I cannot!"

The judge cupped his ear and leaned forward. His face was as white as goat's cheese, his hair like a tangle of yellowish-gray flaxen.

"Speak louder!" he yelled.

"I have no money, sir! I'll have to serve a

penal sentence!" Willie said.

"Can you pay twenty-five dollars?" the judge said.

"No, I cannot!"

"I'll pay his fine, me," a voice at the back of the room said.

The judge leaned forward and squinted into the gloom until he made out the massive shape of Jean-Jacques LaRose.

"The only fine you'll pay will be your own, you damn pirate. Get out of my court and don't return unless you're under arrest," the judge said.

"May I speak, Your Honor?" Abigail Dowling said.

The judge stared at her, his glasses low on his nose, his head hanging forward from his black coat and the split collar that extended up into his jowls like pieces of white cardboard.

"You're the nurse from Massachusetts?" he asked.

"Yes, sir, that's correct!" she yelled.

"Everybody in this proceeding is red-faced and shouting. What's the matter with you people?" the judge said. "Never mind, go ahead, whatever your name is."

Abigail walked out of the gloom into a patch of sunlight, her hands folded in front of her. She wore an open-necked purple dress with lace on the collar and a silver comb in the bun on top of her head.

"I know Mr. Burke well and do not believe him capable of harming anyone. He's of a gentle spirit and has devoted himself both to his studies and works of charity. His accusers —"

She paused, her right hand floating in the direction of Rufus Atkins and the paddy rollers. "His accusers are filled with anger at their own lack of self-worth and visit their anger with regularity on the meek and defenseless. It's my view their testimony is not motivated by a desire for either truth or justice. In fact, their very presence here demeans the integrity of the court and is an offense to people of goodwill," she said.

The judge looked at her a long moment. "I hope the Yankees don't have many more like you on their side," he said.

"I'm sure their ranks include much better people than I, sir," Abigail said.

It was quiet in the room. One of the paddy rollers hawked softly and leaned over and spit in his handkerchief. The judge pinched his temples.

"You want to say anything, Captain Atkins?" he asked.

"I haven't the gift of elocution that Miss Dowling has, since I wasn't educated in a Northern state where Africans are taught to disrespect white people," he said. "But that man yonder, Willie Burke, attacked an officer of the law. You have my word on that."

The judge removed his glasses and pulled on his nose.

"You're a member of the militia?" he said to Willie.

"Yes, sir, I am!"

"Will you stop shouting? It's the sentence of this court that you return to your unit at Camp Pratt and be a good soldier. You might stay out of saloons for a while, too," the judge said, and smacked down his gavel.

After the judge had left the room, Willie walked with his mother and Abigail and Jim toward the door that gave onto the outside stairway.

"Where's Robert today?" Willie asked, hoping his disappointment didn't show.

"Mustered into the 8th Lou'sana Vols and sent to Camp Moore. The word is they're going to Virginia," Jim said.

"What about us?" Willie asked.

"We're stuck here, Willie."

"With Atkins?"

Jim laid his arm across Willie's shoulders and didn't answer. Outside, Rufus Atkins and the paddy rollers were gathered under a live oak. The corporal named Clay Hatcher turned and looked at Willie, his smile like a slit in a baked apple.

It rained late that afternoon, drumming on Bayou Teche and the live oaks around Abigail Dowling's cottage. Then the rain stopped as suddenly as it had begun and a strange green light filled the trees. Out in the mist rising off the bayou Abigail could hear the whistle on a paddle-wheeler and the sound of the boat's wake slapping in the cypress trunks at the foot of her property.

She lighted the lamp on her desk and dipped her pen in a bottle of ink and began the letter she had been formulating in her mind all day.

She wrote *Dearest Robert* on a piece of stationery, then crumpled up the page and began again.

Dear Robert,
Even though I know you believe deeply in your cause, candor and conscience compel me to confess my great concern for your safety and my fear that this war will bring great sorrow and injury into your life. Please forgive me for expressing my feelings so strongly, but it is brave young men such as yourself who ennoble the human race and I do not feel it is God's will that you sacrifice your life or take life in turn to further an enterprise as base and meretricious as that of slavery.

She heard the clopping of a horse in the street and glanced up through the window and saw Rufus Atkins dismount from a huge buckskin mare and open her gate. He wore polished boots and a new gray uniform with a gold collar and a double row of brass buttons on the coat and scrolled gold braid on the sleeves.

She put down her pen, blotted her letter, and met him at the front door. He removed his hat and bowed slightly.

"Excuse my intrusion, Miss Abigail. I wanted to apologize for any offense I may have given you in the court," he said.

"I'm hardly cognizant of anything you might say, Mr. Atkins, hence, I can take no offense at it," she replied.

"May I come in?"

"No, you may not," she replied.

He let the insult slide off his face. He watched a child kicking a stuffed football down the street.

"I have a twenty-dollar gold piece here," he said. He flipped it off his thumb and caught it in his palm. "Years ago a card sharp fired a derringer at me from under a card table. The ball would have gone through my vest pocket into my vitals, except this coin was in its way. See, it's bent right in the center."

She held his stare, her face expressionless, but her palms felt cold and stiff, her throat filled with needles.

"I lost this coin at the laundry and had pretty much marked off ever finding it," he said. "Then two days ago the sheriff found a drowned nigger in Vermilion Bay. She had this coin inside a juju bag. She was one of the escaped slaves we'd been looking for. I wonder how she came by my gold piece."

"I'm sure with time you'll find out, Mr. Atkins. In the meanwhile, there's no need for you to share the nature of your activities with me. Good evening, sir."

"You see much of Mr. Jamison's wash girl, the one called Flower? The drowned nigger was her aunt."

"In fact I do know Flower. I'm also under the impression your interest in her is more than a professional one."

"Northern ladies can have quite a mouth on them, I understand."

"Please leave my property, Mr. Atkins," she said.

He bowed again and fitted on his hat, his face suffused with humor he seemed to derive from a private joke.

She returned to her writing table and tried to finish her letter to Robert Perry. The sky was a darker green now, the oaks dripping loudly in the yard, the shadows filled with the throbbing of tree frogs.

Oh, Robert, who am I to lecture you on doing injury in the world, she thought.

She ripped the letter in half and leaned her head down in her hands, her palms pressed tightly against her ears.

Her journey by carriage to Angola Plantation took two days. It rained almost the entire time, pattering against the canvas flaps that hung from the top of the surrey, glistening on the hands of the black driver who sat hunched on the seat in front of her, a slouch hat on his head, a gum coat pulled over his neck.

When she and the driver reached the entrance of the plantation late in the afternoon, the western sky was marbled with purple and yellow clouds, the pastures on each side of the road an emerald green. Roses bloomed as brightly as blood along the fences that bordered the road.

In the distance she saw an enormous white mansion high up on a bluff above the Mississippi River, its geometrical exactness softened by the mist off the river and columns of sunlight that had broken through the clouds.

The driver took them down a pea-gravel road and stopped the carriage in front of the porch. She had thought a liveried slave would be sent out to meet her, but instead the front door opened and Ira Jamison walked outside. He looked younger than she had expected, his face almost unnaturally devoid of lines, the mouth soft, his brown hair thick and full of lights.

He wore a short maroon jacket and white shirt with pearl buttons and gray pants, the belt on the outside of the loops.

"Miss Dowling?" he said.

"I apologize for contacting you by telegraph rather than by post. But I consider the situation to be of some urgency," she said.

"It's very nice to have you here. Please come in," he said.

"My driver hasn't eaten. Would you be so kind as to give him some food?"

Jamison waved at a black man emerging from a barn. "Take Miss Dowling's servant to the cookhouse and see he gets his supper," he called.

"I have no servants. My driver is a free man of color whom I've hired from the livery stable," she said.

Jamison nodded amiably, his expression seemingly impervious to her remark. "You've had a long journey," he said, stepping aside and extending his hand toward the open door.

The floors of the house were made of heart pine that had been sanded and buffed until the planks glowed like honey. The windows extended all the way to the ceiling and looked out on low green hills and hardwood forests and the wide, churning breadth of the Mississippi. The drapes on the windows were red velvet, the walls and ceiling a creamy white, the molding put together from ornately carved, dark-stained mahogany.

But for some reason it was a detail in the brick fireplace that caught her eye, a fissure in the elevated hearth as well as the chimney that rose from it.

"A little settling in the foundation," Ira Jamison said. "What can I help you with, Miss Dowling?"

"Is your wife here, sir?"

"I'm a widower. Why do you ask?"

She was sitting on a divan now, her hands folded in her lap, her back not touching the fabric. He continued to stand. She paused for a long moment before she spoke, then let her eyes rest on his until he blinked.

"I'm disturbed by the conduct of your employee Captain Atkins. I believe he's molesting one of your slaves, a young woman who has done nothing to warrant being treated in such a frankly disgusting fashion," she said.

Ira Jamison was framed in the light through the window, his expression obscured by his own silhouette. She heard him clear an obstruction from his throat.

"I see. Well, I'll have a talk with Mr. Atkins. I should see him in the next week or so," he said.

"Let me be more forthcoming. The young woman's name is Flower. Do you know her, sir?" she said, the anger and accusation starting to rise in her voice.

He sat down in a chair not far from her. He pressed one knuckle against his lips and seemed to think for a moment.

"I have the feeling you want to say something to me of a personal nature. If that's the case, I'd rather you simply get to it, madam," he said.

"I've been told she's your daughter. It's not my intention to offend you, but the resemblance is obvious. You allow an employee to sexually harm your own child? My God, sir, have you no decency?"

The skin seemed to shrink on his face. A black woman in a gray dress with a white apron appeared at the doorway to the dining room.

"Supper for you and your guest is on the table, Mr. Jamison," she said.

"Thank you, Ruby," he said, rising, his face still disconcerted.

"I don't think I'll be staying. Thank you very much for your hospitality," Abigail said.

"I insist you have supper with me."

"You insist?"

"You cast aspersions on my decency in my own home? Then you seem to glow with vituperative rage, even though I've only known you five minutes. Couldn't you at some point be a little more lenient and less judgmental and allow me to make redress of some kind?"

"You're the largest slave owner in this state, sir. Will you make 'redress' by setting your slaves free?"

"I just realized who you are. You're the abolitionist."

"I think there are more than one of us."

"You're right. And when they have their

72

way, I'll be destitute and we'll have bedlam in our society."

"Good," she said, and walked toward the door.

"You haven't eaten, madam. Stay and rest just a little while."

"When will you be talking to Captain Atkins?" she asked.

"I'll send a telegraph message to him this evening."

"In that case, it's very nice of you to invite me to your table," Abigail said.

As he held a dining room chair for Abigail to sit down, he smelled the perfume rising off her neck and felt a quickening in his loins, then realized the black woman named Ruby was watching him from the kitchen. He shot her a look that made her face twitch out of shape.

Chapter Five

After Willie reported to Camp Pratt and began his first real day of the tedium that constituted life in the army, he knew it was only a matter of time before he would empower Rufus Atkins to do him serious harm. One week later, after an afternoon of scrubbing a barracks floor and draining mosquito-breeding ponds back in the woods, he and Jim Stubbefield were seated in the shade on a bench behind the mess hall, cleaning fish over a tub of water, when Corporal Clay Hatcher approached them. It was cool in the shade, the sunlight dancing on the lake, the Spanish moss waving overhead, and Willie tried to pretend the corporal's mission had nothing to do with him.

"You threw fish guts under Captain Atkins' window?" Hatcher said.

"Not us," Willie said.

"Then how'd they get there?" Hatcher asked.

"Be fucked if I know," Jim said.

"I was talking to Burke. How'd they get there?" Hatcher said.

"I haven't the faintest idea, Corporal. Have you inquired of the fish?" Willie said.

"Come with me," Hatcher said.

Willie placed his knife on the bench, washed his hands in a bucket of clean water, and began putting on his shirt, smiling at the corporal as he buttoned it.

"You think this is funny?" Hatcher said.

"Not in the least. Misplaced fish guts are what this army's about. Lead the way and let's straighten this out," Willie said.

He heard Jim laugh behind him.

"I can have those stripes, Stubbefield," Hatcher said.

"You can have a session with me behind the saloon, too. You're not a bleeder, are you?" Jim said.

Hatcher pointed a finger at Jim without replying, then fitted one hand under Willie's arm and marched him to the one-room building that Rufus Atkins was now using as his office.

"I got Private Burke here, sir," Hatcher said through the door.

Atkins stepped out into the softness of the late spring afternoon, without a coat or hat, wearing gray pants and a blue shirt with braces notched into his shoulders. He had shaved that morning, using a tin basin and mirror nailed to the back side of the building, flicking the soap off his razor into the shallows, but his jaws already looked grained, dark, an audible rasping sound rising from the back of his hand when he rubbed it against his throat.

"He says he didn't do it, sir. I think he's lying," Hatcher said.

Atkins cut a piece off a plug of tobacco and fed it off the back of his pocketknife into his mouth.

"Tell me, Private, do you see anyone else around here cleaning fish besides yourself and Corporal Stubbefield?" he said.

"Absolutely not, sir," Willie replied.

"Did Corporal Stubbefield throw fish guts under my window?"

"Not while I was around," Willie said.

"Then that leaves only you, doesn't it?" Atkins said.

"There could be another explanation, sir," Willie said.

"What might that be?" Atkins asked.

"Perhaps there are no fish guts under your window," Willie said.

"Excuse me?" Atkins said.

"Could it be you still have a bit of Carrie LaRose's hot pillow house in your mustache, sir?" Willie said.

Atkins' eyes blazed.

"Buck and gag him. The rag and the stick. Five hours' worth of it," he said to the corporal.

"We're s'pposed to keep it at three, Cap," Hatcher said.

"Do you have wax in your ears?" Atkins said.

"Five sounds right as rain," Hatcher replied.

Willie remained in an upright ball by the lake's edge for three hours, his wrists tied to his ankles, a stick inserted between his forearms and the backs of his knees, a rag stuffed in his mouth. A stick protruded from each side of his mouth, the ends looped with leather thongs that were tied tightly behind his head.

Water ran from his tear ducts and he choked on his own saliva. The small of his back felt like a hot iron had been pressed against his spine. He watched the sun descend on the lake and tried to think of the fish swimming under the water, the wind blowing through the trees, the way the four-o'clocks rippled like a spray of purple and gold confetti in the grass.

Out of the corner of his eye he saw Rufus Atkins mount his horse and ride out of the camp. The pain spread through Willie's shoulders and wrapped around his thighs, like the tentacles of a jellyfish.

Jim Stubbefield could not watch it any longer. He pulled aside the flap on the corporal's tent and went inside, closing the flap behind him. Hanging from Jim's belt was a bowie knife with a ten-inch blade that could divide a sheet of paper in half as cleanly as a barber's razor.

Hatcher was combing his hair in a mirror attached to the tent pole when Jim locked his arm under Hatcher's neck and simultaneously stuck the knife between his buttocks and wedged the blade upward into his genitals.

"You cut Willie loose and keep your mouth shut about it. If that's not acceptable, I'll be happy to slice off your package and hang it on your tent," Jim said.

Two minutes later Corporal Hatcher cut the ropes on Willie's wrists and ankles and the thong that held the stick in his mouth. Willie stumbled back to the tent he and Jim shared and fell on his cot. Jim sat down next to him and gazed into his face.

"What's on your mind, you ole beanpole?" Willie said.

"You have to stop sassing them, Willie," Jim said.

"They cut bait, didn't they?" Willie said.

"What do you mean?" Jim asked.

"I outlasted them. They're blowhards and yellow-backs, Jim."

"I put a bowie to Hatcher and told him I'd make a regimental flag out of his manhood," Jim said.

"Go on with you?" Willie said, rising up on his elbows. "Hey, come back here. Tell me you didn't do that, Jim."

But Jim had already gone out the tent flap to relieve himself in the privy.

Willie got up from his cot and walked unsteadily behind the mess hall and picked up the severed pieces of rope that had bound his wrists and ankles and the salvia-soaked gun rag that had been stuffed in his mouth and the sticks that had been threaded under his knees and pushed back in his teeth. He crossed the parade ground to Corporal Clay Hatcher's tent and went inside.

A small oil lamp burned on the floor, a coil of black smoke twisting from the glass up through an opening in the canvas. Hatcher slept on his side, in a pair of long underwear, his head on a dirty pillow, his mouth open. The inside of the tent smelled like re-breathed whiskey fumes, unwashed hair, and shoes someone had worn for long hours in a dirt field.

Willie kicked the cot. Hatcher lifted his head uncertainly from the pillow, his pale blue eyes bleary with sleep.

Willie threw the sticks and pieces of rope and thong into his chest.

"God love Jim for his loyalty to a friend. But you finish your work, you malignant cretin, or one morning find glass in your mush," Willie said.

Hatcher sat up, his lips caked with mucus. "Finish my work?" he said stupidly.

"Did your mother not clean your ears when she dug you out of her shite? You and Atkins do your worst. I'll live to piss in your coffin, you pitiful fuck."

Hatcher continued to stare at Willie, unable to comprehend the words being spoken to him, the bad whiskey he had drunk throbbing in his head.

Willie started for him.

"I'm coming. I got to relieve myself first," Hatcher said, jerking backward, clutching his groin under the coarse cotton sheet. His throat swallowed in shame at the fear his voice couldn't hide.

Except for the house servants, Ira Jamison's slaves were free to do as they wished on Sunday. Until sunset they could visit on other plantations, sit upstairs at a white church, play a card game called pitty-pat, roll dice, or dance to fiddle music. Even though Jamison's slaves were forbidden to possess "julep," a fermented mixture of water, yeast, and fruit or cane pulp, Jamison's overseers looked the other way on Sunday, as long as no slave became outrageously drunk or was sick when he or she reported for bell count on Monday.

On Sunday mornings Flower usually put on her gingham dress and bonnet and walked one and a half miles to a slat church house, where a white Baptist minister conducted a service for slaves and free people of color after he had completed services at the white church in town. He was considered a liberal minister and tolerant man because he often allowed one of the congregation to give the homily.

This morning the homilist was a free man of color by the name of Jubal Labiche, who actually never attended services in the church unless he was asked to give the sermon. He owned slaves and, upstream from town, a brick kiln on Bayou Teche. Behind a long tunnel of oak trees on the St. Martinville Road he had built a house that sought to imitate the classical design of his neighbors' houses, except the columns and porch were wood, not marble, the workmanship utilitarian, the paint an off-white that seemed to darken each year from the smoke of stubble fires.

He was a plump, short man, his eyes turquoise, his skin golden, his hair flattened with grease against his scalp. Even though it was warm inside the building, he wore a checkered silk vest with his suit, a gold watch as fat as a biscuit tucked in the pocket.

"We're living in troublesome times, sisters and brothers," he said. "We hear rumors of wars and our hearts are made uneasy and we know not who to believe. That's why we have to turn to the Scripture and listen to the words of Jesus and his followers.

"No one loved God more than St. Paul. He was bound and jailed and whipped, but no matter how great his suffering, he never listened to false prophets. When the Ephesians were of a rebellious mind, this is what he told them . . ."

Jubal Labiche fitted on his spectacles and looked down at the Bible that rested on the podium in front of him.

" 'Servants, be obedient to them that are your masters according to the flesh, with fear and trembling, in singleness of your heart, as unto Christ,' " he read.

The people seated on the plank benches knotted their hands in their laps uncomfortably or looked at their shoes, or glanced furtively at the white minister, a sheep-shorn rail of a man with a long nose and pointed chin. Some of the people in the congregation nodded assent, before anyone perceived a glimmer of dissent in their eyes.

Flower looked directly into Jubal Labiche's face. He stared back at her, then raised his eyes, as though he were caught in a sudden spiritual moment. He began a long prayer of thanks to God during which the congregation would say in unison "Amen" or "Yes, Lord" whenever he paused.

After the service Jubal Labiche was climbing into his carriage when Flower walked past him. He stepped back down in the road and automatically started to touch his hat, then lowered his hand.

"You seemed to have great interest in the homily," he said.

"St. Paul wrote down that slaves is s'pposed to do what the master say?" she asked.

"He's telling us to put our faith in the Lord. Sometime the Lord's voice comes to us through those who know more about the world than a simple servant such as myself," he replied, bowing slightly.

"How come we cain't learn from the Bible ourself? How come it got to be read to us?"

"I guess I'm not really qualified to talk about that," he said.

"I guess you ain't," she said.

She turned and walked down the dirt road through the cane fields, her bonnet in her hand, her hair blowing. She could almost feel his eyes burrowing into her back.

But all the way home she found no release from the words Jubal Labiche had read to the congregation. Was it the will of God that people should own one another? If that was true, then God was not just. Or was the Scripture itself a white man's fraud?

She warmed a tin cup of coffee and fixed a plate of corn bread and molasses, peas, and a piece of fried ham and sat down to eat by her back window. But her food was like dry paper in her mouth. She felt a sense of abandonment and loneliness she could not describe. Outside, the wind was hot blowing across the cane fields, and the blue sky had filled with plumes of dust.

God wanted her to be a slave and Jesus, His son, was a teacher of submission?

She looked through her front door at the empty yard and laundry house. The widow who ran the laundry for Ira Jamison was away for the day, gone with a suitor who owned a hunting cabin on stilts back in the swamp.

Flower walked across the backyard, through the wash pots and clotheslines, and entered the back door of the laundry. The widow's bedroom door was open, and on the dresser was a leather-bound edition of the King James Bible.

It took her less than five minutes to find the lines Jubal Labiche had read aloud from Paul's letter to the Ephesians. Labiche had carefully avoided reading the passages that followed his selective excerpt, namely, that Christians should live and perform "not with eye-service, as men-pleasers; but as the servants of Christ, doing the will of God from the heart; with goodwill doing service, as to the Lord, and not to men."

And a bit farther on: "For we wrestle not against flesh and blood, but against principalities, against powers, against the rulers of the darkness of this world, against spiritual wickedness in high places."

She closed the cover on the book and went back to her cabin and finished her lunch, a strange sense of both confidence and tranquility in her heart, which she did not as yet quite understand.

Before sunset she walked downtown and bought a peppermint stick from the drugstore for a penny. She ate it on the bank of the bayou, not far from the boardinghouse operated by Willie Burke's mother. She watched the dusk gather in the trees along the bayou and the water darken and the sunfish and gars rolling in the shallows. The western sky was red and black now and she could smell the rain falling on the fields somewhere out on the rim of the earth.

She stood up from the bank and brushed off her dress and started to walk back to the quarters behind the laundry, before the paddy rollers came out on the roads. But now, for some unexplained reason, the thought of encountering them did not fill her with apprehension.

Then she realized the origin of the feelings that had flooded through her after she had gone into the widow's bedroom and hunted through the New Testament for the excerpt from St. Paul. She could read. No one could ever take that gift from her, and no one could hide knowledge or the truth about the world from her again.

At sunrise the next morning she heard Rufus Atkins' horse in the yard, then heard him swing down from the saddle and approach her door. She was undressed, and she gathered up her clothes and sat on her bed and held them in her lap and over her breasts. He stepped inside the door, smelling of tobacco and cooked bacon, steam rising from his uniform in the morning coolness.

He removed the bent twenty-dollar gold piece from the watch pocket of his trousers and began working it over the tops of his knuckles.

"I got to go to bell count," she said.

"No, you don't."

"All the niggers got to be there, suh. The widow don't abide lateness."

"Not you, Flower. You can do almost any goddamn thing you want. You're a juicy bitch and you know it."

"Ain't right you talk to me like that, suh."

"I'm not here for what you think," he said. He walked to the back window and looked out on the cane field. The sun had just broken the edge of the horizon, like a soft red lump of molten metal.

"Marse Jamison is establishing a slaves council on all his plantations," Atkins said. "That means the slaves will lay out the punishment for anybody who breaks the rules. Marse Jamison reserves only one right — to overturn a punishment if he thinks it's too severe . . . Are you listening?"

"I'm not dressed, suh."

Atkins took a deep breath and went outside the door. She heard him light a cigar and lean against the railing on her small gallery. She put on her work dress and lit the kindling in her stove and washed her face in the water bucket, then pushed her coffeepot over the flames that leaked around one of the iron pothole lids. She heard Atkins clear his throat and spit and then felt his weight bend the floorboards in the cabin.

"You're going to be on the slaves council for the laundry and two of the plantations up the road," he said.

"This don't sound like Marse Jamison," she said.

"What do you care? It gives you a little power you didn't have before."

"What if I say I don't want it?"

"I'd say you were a mighty stupid black girl."

"Tell him the stupid black girl don't want it."

He removed the cigar from his mouth and tossed it through the back window.

"You're a handful, Flower. In lots of ways," he said, biting down on his lip.

"You been in my bed, Marse Rufus. But it ain't gonna happen again."

"Say that again?"

"You heard me. I ain't afraid of you no more."

It was silent inside the cabin. Outside, the wind off the Gulf rustled the cane and flapped the clothes drying in the yard.

"I wouldn't be talking out of school, Flower. There are houses in Congo Square for girls who do that," he said.

"I ain't afraid."

He took a step toward her, his eyes roving over her face and the tops of her breasts. Her hand touched the oyster knife she kept on the table next to the stove.

Atkins rubbed his mouth and laughed.

"Damned if being white makes any man less of a fool. If I ever get rich I'll buy you and carry you off on my saddle and keep you as my personal strumpet. You believe that? It's a fact. Wouldn't lie to you, girl," he said.

His eyes seemed to be laughing at her now, as though he were reliving each moment he had probed inside her, put her nipples in his mouth, lifted her up spread-eagled across his loins. She turned away and picked up the coffeepot and burned her hand. Behind her, she heard him walk out the door, his boots knocking with a hollow sound on her gallery.

I hope the Yankees kill you, she said under her breath.

But the vehemence in her thoughts brought her little solace.

★ ★ ★

When she was a child, Abigail Dowling's father, who was a physician and a Quaker, taught her that a lie was an act of theft as well as one of deceit. A lie stole people's faith in their fellow man, he said, and the loss was often irreparable, whereas a monetary one was not.

In early August of 1861 the first casualty lists from Manassas Junction made their way back to New Iberia. The postmaster sat down behind the counter where he daily sorted the mail into pigeonholes, an eyeshade fastened on his forehead, and went down the alphabetized row of names from the 8th Louisiana Volunteers with his finger. Then he removed his glasses and placed them on his desk and with some very tiny nails he tacked all the lists to the post office wall.

He put on his coat and went out the front door and walked toward the end of Main, where he lived in a tree-shaded house behind the Episcopalian church. Without apparent cause he began to sway from side to side, as though he were drunk or possessed of epilepsy. When he collapsed against a hitching rail, a black deliveryman picked him up and sat him down in a chair against the front wall of the grocery. Then two white men took him inside and peeled off his coat and fanned his face and tried to get him to drink a glass of water.

Abigail stared through the grocery window at the scene taking place inside.

"What happened?" she asked the black man.

"Mr. LeBlanc's son got kilt in Virginia," the black man said.

"How did he learn?" she asked.

"I reckon it come t'rew the wire or the mail, Miss Abigail. That po' man."

Abigail hurried inside the post office. The wind through the open door and windows was lightly rattling the casualty lists against the wall. Her heart beating, she read the names of the soldiers under the captions "Wounded" and "Killed" and saw none there she could put a face with. She let out her breath and pressed her hand against her heart, then felt shame that her joy was at the expense of the families who would never see their soldier boys again.

When she turned to leave the post office she glanced at the floor and saw a sheet of paper the wind had blown loose from the nails. She picked it up, her hand beginning to tremble. At the top of the page was the caption "Missing in Action." The third name in the column was that of Lieutenant Robert S. Perry.

She walked stone-faced down the street to her house, her ears ringing, unaware of the words spoken to her by others on the street or the peculiar looks they gave her when she didn't respond to their greetings.

Later, she did not remember drawing the curtains inside her house, filling it with summer heat that was almost unbearable, nor did she remember pacing from one room to the other, her mind drumming with her father's words about his experience as a surgeon with Zachary Taylor's troops in Mexico.

"I saw a lad, not more than a tyke really, struck by an exploding cannonball. It blew him into small pieces. We buried parts of his fingers and feet. I had to pick them up with forceps and put them in a sack," her father had said.

Why had she lectured Robert on slavery, trying to inculcate guilt in him for deeds that were his family's and not his? Were her piety, the sense of righteousness with which she bore her cause like a personal flag, even her sexual modesty, were all these virtues in which she prided herself simply a vanity, a self-deception that concealed the secret pleasure she took in the superiority of her education and New England background?

Could she deny she was not guilty of pride, the most pernicious of the seven deadly sins? Or of carnal thoughts that took hold of her sleep and caused her to wake hot and wet in the middle of the night?

She saw Robert's face before her, the shine like polished mahogany in the thickness of his hair, his eyes that were the bluest and most beautiful she had ever seen in a man.

She saw him on a meandering, pebble-bottomed creek, surrounded by green hills, saw him rise from behind earthworks and walk with an extended sword toward a line of dark-clad soldiers, perhaps boys from Massachusetts, who in unison fired their muskets in a roar of dirty black smoke and covered Robert's face and chest and legs with wounds that looked like the red lesions of the pox.

What about her participation in the Underground Railroad? she asked herself. She had told slaves of the land across the Ohio, filling them with hope, in some cases only to see them delivered into the hands of bounty hunters. Worse, she had personally put Flower's aunt on a boat that overturned and drowned her.

She wanted to cut the word "traitor" into her breast.

She fell asleep in her clothes, the late afternoon heat glowing through the curtains in her bedroom. She became wrapped in the sheet, her body bathed in sweat, and she dreamed she was inside a tunnel, deep underground, the wet clay pressing against her chest, pinning her arms at her sides, her cries lost inside the heated blackness.

She awoke in a stupor, unsure of where she was, and for just a moment she thought she heard Robert's voice in the room. She pulled her dress over her head and flung it on the floor and, dressed only in her underthings, went into the backyard and opened the valve on the elevated cistern that fed trapped rainwater into the bathhouse.

She closed the bathhouse door behind her, stripped off her undergarments, and sat in the tub while the wood sluice that protruded through the wall poured water over her head and shoulders and breasts. It was late afternoon now, almost evening, and the light breaking through the trees was green and gold and spinning with motes of dust. Somewhere a bird was singing.

You don't know that he's dead, she told herself.

But when she closed her eyes she saw shells bursting in a field, geysering dirt into the air, while men crouched in the bottom of a trench and prayed and begged and pressed their palms against their ears.

Poseur, she thought. *Self-anointed bride of Christ, walking among the afflicted. Hypocrite. Angel of Death.*

She put her head down and wept.

Later, she opened all the windows of her house to let in the evening's coolness and tried to sort out her thoughts but could not. Her skin felt dead to the touch, her heart sick, as though it had been invaded by invisible worms. She thought she understood why primitive people, during mourning rituals, tore their hair and gouged their bodies with stone knives. She lit an oil lamp on her living room table and began a letter to a Quaker church in Bradford, Massachusetts, resigning her title of deacon.

Then she saw a man walk into her yard, wearing a gray officer's uniform and a soft white hat. He removed his hat when he stepped onto the gallery, and knocked on her door.

"Mr. Jamison?" she said.

"Yes. I was visiting in town and heard of your distress. Your neighbors and friends were concerned but didn't want to show a disrespect for your privacy. So I thought I should call upon you," he said.

"Please come in," she said.

He stood in the middle of the living room, his face rosy in the light from the oil lamp, his thick hair touching his collar.

"I understand you've been longtime friends with Robert Perry," he said.

"Yes, that's correct," she replied.

"Are you and Lieutenant Perry engaged, Miss Abigail?"

"No, we're not," she said, clearing her throat. "Could I offer you some tea?"

"No, thank you." He smiled self-effacingly. "I arrived at your door in a peculiar fashion. By steamboat. Would you take a ride with me?"

She turned and saw out the back window the lighted compartments and decks of a huge boat, with paddle wheels on both its starboard and port sides; a roped gangway extended from the deck to the bank.

"The cook has prepared some dinner for us. It's a beautiful evening. As I told you, I'm a widower. It took me some time to learn it's not good to lock ourselves up with our losses," he said.

The dining room on the steamboat was aft, and through the back windows, in the failing summer light, she could see the boat's wake swelling through the cypress trees and live oaks and elephant ears along the bayou's banks. Ira Jamison poured a glass of burgundy for her.

"I wasn't aware you were in the army," she said.

"I've taken a commission in the Orleans Guards. Actually I attended the United States Military Academy with the intention of becoming an engineer. But after my mother's death I had to take over the family's business affairs," he replied.

"Is it true you're instituting some reforms on your plantations?" she said.

"It hurts nothing to make life a little better for others when you have means and opportunity. I wish I'd done so earlier. No one has to convince me slavery is evil, Miss Abigail. But I don't have an easy solution for it, either," he said.

When he turned toward the galley, looking for the waiter, she studied his profile, the lack of any guile in his eyes, the smooth texture of his complexion, which did not seem consistent with his age.

He looked back at her, his eyes curious, resting momentarily on her mouth.

"You don't like the wine?" he asked.

"No, it's fine. I don't drink often. I'm afraid I have no appetite, either," she replied.

He moved her glass aside and folded his hands on top of the tablecloth. They were slender, unfreckled by the sun, each nail pink and trimmed and rounded and scraped clean of any dirt. For a moment she thought he was going to place one hand over hers, which would have both embarrassed and disappointed her, but he did not.

"Perhaps Lieutenant Perry is a prisoner or simply separated from his regiment. I haven't been to war, but I understand it happens often," he said.

She rose from her chair and walked to the open French doors that gave onto the fantail of the boat.

"Did I upset you?" he asked behind her.

"No, no, not at all, sir. You've been very kind. Thank you also for ensuring that your employee did not harm Flower again," she said.

There was a brief silence. For a moment she thought he had not heard her above the throb of the boat's engines.

"Oh yes, certainly. Well, let's get our pilot to turn around and we'll dine another evening. It's been a trying day for you," he said.

She felt his hand touch her lightly between the shoulder blades.

The next morning she went to the small brick building on Main that served as stage station and telegraph and post office. Mr. LeBlanc sat behind the counter, his eyeshade fastened on his forehead, garters on his white sleeves, sorting newspapers from Baton Rouge, New Orleans, and Atlanta that he would later place in the pigeonholes for the addressees.

He had married a much younger woman and their son had been born when Mr. LeBlanc was fifty-two. He was a religious man and had opposed Seccession and had dearly loved his son. Abigail imagined that his struggle with bitterness and anger must have been almost intolerable. But he held himself erect and his clothes were freshly pressed, his steel-gray hair combed, his grief buried like a dead coal in his face.

"I'm sorry for your loss, Mr. LeBlanc," Abigail said.

"Thank you. May I get your mail for you?" he said, rising from his chair without waiting for an answer.

"Have you heard anything else about casualties among the 8th Louisiana Volunteers?" she said.

"There's been no other news. The Yankees were chased into Washington. That brings joy to some." Then he seemed to lose his train of thought. "Are you a subscriber to one of the papers? I can't remember."

He hunted through the pile of newspapers on his desk, his concentration gone.

"It's all right, Mr. LeBlanc. I'll come back later. Sir? Please, it's all right," she said.

She went back outside and walked up the street toward her house, staying in the shade under the colonnade. Men tipped their hats to her and women stepped aside to let her pass, more deferentially and graciously than ordinary courtesy would have required of them. Her face burned and sweat rolled down her sides. Again she felt a sense of odium and duplicity about herself she had never experienced before and heard the word *traitor* inside her head, just as if someone had whispered the word close to her ear.

That evening Ira Jamison was at her door again, this time with a carriage parked in front. He was out of uniform, dressed in white pants and black boots and a green coat.

"I thought you might like to take a ride into the country," he said.

"Not this evening," she replied.

"I see." He looked wistfully down the street, his face melancholy in the twilight. A mule-drawn wagon, mounted with a perforated water tank, was sprinkling the dust in the street. "I worry about you, Miss Abigail. I've read a bit about what some physicians are now terming 'depression.' It's a bad business."

He looked at her in a concerned way.

"Come in, Mr. Jamison," she said.

After he was inside, she did not notice the glance he gave to his driver, who snapped the reins on the backs of his team and turned the carriage in the street and drove it back toward the business district.

He sat by her on the couch. The wind rustled the oak trees outside and blew the curtains on the windows. She saw heat lightning flicker in the yard, then heard raindrops begin ticking in the leaves and on the roof.

"I'll do whatever I can to help find the whereabouts of Robert Perry," he said.

"I'd appreciate it very much, Mr. Jamison."

"This may be an inappropriate time to say this, but I think you're a lady of virtue and principle, and also one who's incredibly beautiful. Whatever resources I have, they'll be made immediately available to you whenever you're in need, for whatever reason, regardless of the situation."

She was sitting on the edge of the couch, her shoulders slightly bent, her hands in her lap. She could feel the emotional fatigue of the last two days wash through her, almost like a drug. Her eyes started to film.

"It's all right," he said, his arm slipping around her.

He leaned across her and pulled her against him and spread his fingers on her back, pressing his cheek slightly to hers. Then she felt his lips touch her hair and his hand stroking her back, and she placed her hands on the firmness of his arms and let her forehead rest on his chest.

He tilted her face up and kissed her lightly on the mouth, then on the eyes and cheeks and the mouth again, and she put her arms around his neck and held him tighter than she should, letting go, surrendering to it, the heat and wetness in her own body now a balm to her soul rather than a threat, the wind blowing the curtains and filling the room with the smell of rain and flowers.

He extinguished the oil lamp and laid her back on the couch. He bent down over her and she felt his tongue enter her mouth, his hand cup one breast, then the other, and slide down her stomach toward her thighs. His breath was hoarse in his throat. He pressed her leg against the swelling hardness in his pants.

She twisted her face away from him and sat up, her hands clenched in her lap.

"Please go, Mr. Jamison," she said.

"I'm sorry if I've done something wrong, Miss Abigail."

"The fault isn't yours," she replied.

He hesitated a moment, then stood up and pushed his hair out of his eyes.

"If I can make this up —" he began.

"You need to fetch your driver, sir. Thank you for your kind offer of assistance," she said.

For the first time she realized one of his eyes was smaller than the other. She did not know why that detail stuck in her mind.

That night she woke feverish and sweaty and tangled in her sheets, her head filled with images from a dream about a sow eating her farrow. She did not fall asleep again until dawn.

Two days later she was walking home from the grocery, stepping around mud puddles in the street, an overly loaded wicker basket in each of her hands. Rufus Atkins stopped his buggy and got down and tried to take one of the baskets from her.

"Don't do that," she said.

"Marse Jamison says to look after you," Atkins said.

"Take your hand off my basket."

"Sorry, Miss Abigail. I got my orders." He winked at her, then pulled the basket from her hand and swung it up behind the buggy seat. He reached for the other basket.

"He has also ordered you to stop molesting women in this community," she said.

"What are you talking about?" Atkins asked.

"The telegraph message he sent you."

"He didn't send me a telegraph message. He told me something about not letting the overseers impregnate any of the nigger wenches. But he didn't send me a telegraph message."

She stared at him blankly.

Atkins laughed to himself. "Look, Miss Dowling, I don't know what kind of confusion you're under, but Marse Jamison is giving the niggers a little self-government so's he can get himself installed in Jefferson Davis' cabinet. Davis is famous for the nigger councils on his plantations. Is this what you're talking about?"

"Give me back my basket," she said.

"By all means. Excuse me for stopping. But your nose was so high up in the air I thought you might walk into a post and knock yourself unconscious," he said.

He dropped her grocery basket in the mud and drove off, popping his buggy whip above the back of his horse.

Two weeks later the Confederate War Department notified the parents of Robert Perry their son had been separated from his regiment during the Battle of Manassas Junction

102

and that he was alive and well and back among his comrades.

That same night, while the moon was down, Abigail Dowling rowed a runaway slave woman and her two small children to a waiting boat, just north of Vermilion Bay. All three of them were owned by Ira Jamison.

Chapter Six

In the spring of the following year, 1862, Willie and Jim marched northward, at the rear of the column, along a meandering road through miles of cotton acreage, paintless shacks, barns, corn cribs, smokehouses, privies, tobacco sheds cobbled together from split logs, and hog pens whose stench made their eyes water.

The people were not simply poor. Their front porches buzzed with horseflies and mosquitoes. The hides of their draft animals were lesioned with sores. The beards of the men grew to their navels and their clothes hung in rags on their bodies. The children were rheumy-eyed and had bowed legs from rickets, their faces flecked with gnats. The women were hard-bitten, dirt-grained creatures from the fields, surly and joyless and resentful of their childbearing and apt to take an ax to the desperate man who tried to put a fond hand on their persons.

Willie looked around him and nodded. So this is why we came to Tennessee, he thought.

Two months earlier he and Jim had been on leave from the 18th Louisiana at Camp Moore and had stood in front of a saloon on upper St. Charles Avenue in New Orleans, dipping beer out of a bucket, watching other soldiers march under the canopy of live oaks, past columned homes with ceiling-high windows and ventilated green shutters, regimental bands playing, the Stars and Bars and Bonnie Blue flags flying, barefoot Negro children running under the colonnades, pretending they were shooting one another with broomsticks and wood pistols.

It was a false spring and the air was balmy and filled with the smells of boiled crawfish and crabs and pralines. The sky was ribbed with pink clouds, and palm fronds and banana trees rattled in the breeze off Lake Pontchartrain. Out on the Mississippi giant paddle-wheelers blew their whistles in tribute to the thousands of soldiers turning out of St. Charles into Canal, the silver and gold instruments of the bands flashing in full sunlight now, the mounted Zouaves dressed like Bedouins in white turbans and baggy scarlet pants.

Women threw flowers off the balconies into the columns of marching men. Prostitutes from Congo Square winked at them from under their parasols and sometimes hoisted their skirts up to their thighs and beyond.

"Maybe there's something glorious about war after all," Jim said.

"We might have to rethink that statement later on, Jim," Willie replied.

"I hear a trip to Congo Square is two dollars," Jim said.

"The fee for the doctor to stick an eight-inch hot needle up your pole is an additional three," Willie said.

"If I had a lady like Abigail Dowling on my mind, I'd have the same elevated sentiments." Jim looked at the prostitutes hiking their skirts across the boulevard and sucked his teeth philosophically. "But I'm afraid my virginity is going to die a beautiful and natural death in old New Orleans tonight."

Now New Orleans was surrounded by Federal gunboats and the city's surrender was expected any day.

Where were Louisiana's troops? Willie asked himself.

In Tennessee, protecting hog farmers and their wives, one glance at whom would make any man seriously consider a life of celibacy, Willie said to himself.

As the column crested a rise he could see the great serpentine length of the army he was marching in, the mismatched gray and butternut uniforms, some regiments, like his own, actually wearing blue jackets, all of them heading toward a distant woods on the west bank of the Tennessee River.

But his deprecating thoughts about his surroundings and the governance of the Confederate military were not the true cause of his discontent. Nor did he think any longer about the heaviness of the Enfield rifle on his shoulder or the blisters on his feet or the dust that drifted back from the wheels of the ambulance wagons.

In the pit of his stomach was an emptiness he could not fill or rid himself of. When the sun broke through the clouds that had sealed the sky for days, lighting the hardwood forest in the distance, a bilious liquid surged out of his stomach into the back of his mouth and his bowels slid in and out of his rectum. A vinegary reek rose from his armpits into his nostrils, not the smell of ordinary sweat that comes from work or even tramping miles along a hard-packed dirt road, but the undisguised glandular stench of fear.

"What day is it?" Willie said.

"Saturday, April 5," Jim replied. "Why's that?"

"I don't know. I don't know why I asked. What's that place up yonder called?"

"To my knowledge, it doesn't have a name. It's a woods."

"That's foolishness, Jim. Every place has a name."

"There's nothing there except a Methodist

church house. It's called Shiloh. That's it. Shiloh Church," Jim said.

They camped late that afternoon in a clearing among trees on the edge of a ravine. The floor of the forest and the sides of the ravine were layered with leaves that had turned gray under the winter snow and were now dry and powdery under their feet. The sun was an ember in the west, the trees bathed in a red light like the radiance from a smithy's forge.

Willie sat on a log and pulled off his shoes and massaged his feet. The odor from his socks made him avert his face and hold his breath. All around him men were stacking their weapons, breaking rations out of their haversacks, kicking together cook fires. The wind was blowing off the river, and the canopy of hickory and chestnut and oak trees flickered against the pinkness of the sky. In the knock of axes, the plunking of a banjo being tuned, the smell of corn mush and fatback frying, it was not hard to pretend they were all young fellows and good friends assembling for a camp meeting or coon hunt.

Maybe that's all it would be, Willie thought. Just another long stroll across the countryside, a collective exercise that would be unmemorable once the grand illusion became obvious to them all.

Jim poured water from his canteen into a

big tin cup, then carefully measured out two spoonfuls of real coffee into the water, not chicory and ground corn, and set it to boiling on a flat stone in the center of his cook fire. His face looked composed and thoughtful as he squatted by the fire, his skin sun-browned, his sideburns shaggy, the road dust on his face streaked where his sweat had dried.

Willie went to the field kitchen and got a pan of corn mush, his unlaced shoes flopping on his feet, then squatted next to Jim and greased the bottom of a small frying pan with a piece of salt bacon and poured the mush on top of it and stuck the pan in the coals.

"What's the first thing you're going to do when we get back home?" he asked Jim.

"Start my own shipwright business. Build the first clipper ship to come out of New Iberia, Lou'sana," Jim said.

"Steam is making museum pieces of the clippers, Jim."

"That's good. I won't have competitors," Jim said.

Willie lowered his head so his voice wouldn't travel.

"Are you scared?" he asked.

"If you was as scared as I am, you'd run for home. I'm just too scared to get my legs moving," Jim said.

"You put on a good act, you ole beanpole.

But I don't think you're scared of anything," Willie replied.

Jim stood up with his tin cup of boiling coffee and poured half of it into Willie's cup. He rubbed Willie on the top of the head.

"No blue-bellies can do in the likes of us," he said.

"That's right, by God. Here, our mush is ready," Willie said.

"I can't eat. I think I got a stomach cold. Can't hold anything down," Jim said, walking into the shadows so Willie could not see his face.

The sun dipped below the hills and suddenly the woods were cooler, the sky the color of coal dust, without moon or stars, the tree branches knocking together overhead. To the north there were fires on the bluffs above the river and Willie thought he could feel the vibrations of gun carriages and caissons through the ground.

Five men and a drummer boy from the 6th Mississippi, in butternut pants and homespun shirts, were sitting around a fire, six feet away, smoking cob pipes, laughing at a joke.

"Who's out there?" Willie asked them, nodding toward the north.

" 'Who's out there?' Where the hell you been, boy?" a tall man with a concave face said.

"Corinth."

"Them bluffs and ravines is crawling with

Yankees. They been out there for weeks," the man said.

"Why not leave them be?" Willie asked.

"We done turned that into a highly skilled craft, son. But the word is we're going at them tomorrow," the man said.

Willie felt his stomach constrict and sweat break on his forehead. He went out of the firelight, into the trees, and vomited.

Fifteen minutes later Jim came back to the fire and sat down on the log beside Willie, his sheathed bowie knife twisting against the log's bark. Willie sniffed the air.

"What have you been up to?" he asked.

Jim opened his coat to reveal a half-pint, corked bottle stuck down in his belt. The clear liquid it contained danced in the fire-light.

"This stuff will blow the shoes off a mule," he said.

Three soldiers with a banjo, fiddle, and Jew's harp were playing a dirge by the edge of the ravine. The men from the 6th Mississippi were lying on their blankets or in their tents, and the drummer boy sat by himself, staring into the fire, his drum with crossed sticks on top resting by his foot. He wore an oversized kepi, and his scalp was gray where his hair had been bowl-cut above his ears. His dour face, with downturned mouth and impassive eyes, was like a miniature painting of the Southern mountain man to whom sorrow and adversity are mankind's natural lot.

"You get enough to eat?" Jim said to him.

"Pert' near as much as I want," the boy replied.

"Then I guess we'd better throw away this mush and bacon here," Jim said.

"Hit don't matter to me," the little boy said, his face as smooth and expressionless as clay in the light from the fire.

"Come over here and bring your pan," Jim said.

The boy dusted off the seat of his pants and sat on a stump by Willie. He watched while Willie filled his pan, then he ate the mush with a spoon, his thumb and index finger all the way up the handle, scraping the food directly into his mouth.

"What's your name?" Willie asked.

"Tige McGuffy," the boy said.

"How old might you be, Tige?" Willie asked.

"Eleven, pert' near twelve," the boy said.

"Well, we're mighty pleased to meet you, Tige McGuffy," Willie said.

"This mush with bacon is a treat. I ain't never quite had it prepared like that," Tige said. "How come you was puking out in the trees?"

"Don't rightly know, Tige," Willie said, and for the first time that day he laughed.

Out on the edge of the firelight the musicians sang,

"White doves come at morning
Where my soldier sleeps in the ground.
I placed my ring in his coffin,
The trees o'er his grave have all
    turned brown."

Jim stood up and flung a pinecone at them.

"Put a stop to that kind of song!" he yelled.

As the campfires died in the clearing, Jim and Willie took their blankets out in the trees and drank the half-pint of whiskey Jim had bought off a Tennessee rifleman.

Jim made a pillow by wrapping his shoes in his haversack, then lay back in his blankets, gazing up at the sky.

"A touch of the giant-killer sure makes a fellow's prospects seem brighter, doesn't it?" he said.

Willie drew his blanket up to his shoulders and propped his head on his arm.

"Wonder how a little fellow like Tige ends up here," he said.

"He'll get through it. We'll all be fine. Those Yankees better be afraid of us, that's all I can say," Jim said.

"Think so?" Willie said.

Jim drank the last ounce in the whiskey bottle. "Absolutely," he replied. "Good night, Willie."

"Good night, Jim."

They went to sleep, their bodies warm with alcohol, with dogwood and redbud trees in bloom at their heads and feet, the black sky now dotted with stars.

Chapter Seven

They woke the next morning to sunlight that was like glass needles through the trees and the sounds of men and horses running, wagons banging over the ruts out on the Corinth Road, tin pots spilling out of the back of a mobile field kitchen.

They heard a single rifle shot in the distance, then a spatter of small-arms fire that was like strings of Chinese firecrackers exploding. They jumped from their blankets and ran back to the clearing where they had cooked their food and stacked their Enfields the previous night. The air was cinnamon-colored with dust and leaves that had been powdered by running feet. Their Enfields and haversacks lay abandoned on the ground.

The men from the 6th Mississippi were already moving northward through the trees, their bayonets fixed. Tige McGuffy was strapping his drum around his neck, his hands shaking.

"What happened to the 18th Lou'sana?" Jim said.

"Them Frenchies you come in with?" Tige said.

"Yes, where did they go?" Willie asked, his heart tripping.

"West, toward Owl Creek. A kunnel on horseback come in before dawn and moved them out. Where'd y'all go to?" Tige replied.

Willie and Jim looked at each other.

"I think we're seriously in the shitter," Jim said.

"How far is this Owl Creek?" Willie said.

Before Tige could answer a cannon shell arced out of the sky and exploded over the canopy. Pieces of hot metal whistled through the leaves and lay smoking on the ground. Tige hitched up his drum, a drumstick in each hand, and ran to join his comrades.

"Let's go, Jim. They're going to put us down as deserters for sure," Willie said.

Jim went back into the trees and retrieved their blankets while Willie repacked their haversacks. They started through the hardwoods in a westerly direction and ran right into a platoon of Tennessee infantry, jogging by twos, their rifle barrels canted at an upward angle, a redheaded, barrel-chested sergeant, with sweat rings under his arms, wheezing for breath at their side.

"Where might you two fuckers think you're going?" he said.

"You sound like you're from Erin, sir," Willie said.

"Shut your 'ole and fall in behind me," the sergeant said.

"We're with the 18th Lou'sana," Jim said.

"You're with me or you'll shortly join the heavenly choir. Which would you prefer, lad?" the sergeant said, raising the barrel of his carbine.

Within minutes men in gray and butternut were streaming from every direction toward a focal point where other soldiers were furiously digging rifle pits and wheeling cannon into position. Through the hardwoods Willie thought he saw the pink bloom of a peach orchard and the movements of blue-clad men inside it.

The small-arms fire was louder now, denser, the rifle reports no longer muted by distance, and he could see puffs of rifle smoke exploding out of the trees. A toppling minié ball went past his ear with a whirring sound, like a clock spring winding down, smacking against a sycamore behind his head.

Up ahead, a Confederate colonel, the Bonnie Blue flag tied to the blade of his sword, stood on the edge of the trees, his body auraed with sunlight and smoke, shouting, "Form it up, boys! Form it up! Stay on my back! Stay on my back! Forward, harch!"

There seemed to be no plan to what they were doing, Willie thought. A skirmish line had moved out into the sunlight, into the drifting smoke, then the line broke apart and became little more than a mob running at the peach orchard, yelling in unison, "Woo, woo, woo," their bayonets pointed like spears.

Willie could not believe he was following them. He wasn't supposed to be here, he told himself. His commanding officer was the chivalric Colonel Alfred Mouton, not some madman with a South Carolinian flag tied to his sword. Willie fumbled his bayonet out of its scabbard and paused behind a tree to twist it into place on the barrel of his Enfield.

The redheaded sergeant hit him in the back with his fist.

"Move your ass!" the sergeant said.

Out in the sunlight Willie saw a cannonball skip along the ground like a jackrabbit, take off a man's leg at the thigh, bounce once, and cut another man in half.

The sergeant hit him again, then knotted his shirt behind the neck and shoved him forward. Suddenly Willie was in the sunlight, the sweat on his face like ice water, the peach orchard blooming with puffs of smoke.

Where was Jim?

The initial skirmish line wilted and crumpled in a withering volley from the orchard. A second line of men advanced behind the first, and, from a standing position, aimed and fired into the pink flowers drifting down from the peach trees. Willie heard the Irish sergeant wheezing, gasping for breath behind him. He waited for another fist in the middle of his back.

But when he turned he saw the sergeant standing motionless in the smoke, his mouth puckered like a fish's, a bright hole in his throat leaking down his shirt, his carbine slipping from his hand.

"Get down, Willie!" he heard Jim shout behind him.

Jim knocked him flat just as a wheeled Yankee cannon, in the middle of a sunken road, roared back on its carriage and blew a bucket of grapeshot into the Confederate line.

Men in butternut and gray fell like cornstalks cut with a scythe. The colonel who had carried the Bonnie Blue flag lay dead in the grass, his sword stuck at a silly angle in the soft earth. Some tried to kneel and reload, but a battery none of them could see rained exploding shells in their midst, blowing fountains of dirt and parts of men in the air. Many of those fleeing over the bodies of their comrades for the protection of the woods were vectored in a cross fire by sharpshooters rising from rifle pits on the far side of the sunken road.

Then there was silence, and in the silence

Willie thought he heard someone beating a broken cadence on a drumhead, like a fool who does not know a Mardi Gras parade has come to an end.

Through the morning and afternoon thousands of men moved in and out of the trees, stepping through the dead who flanged the edge of the woods or lay scattered across the breadth of the clearing. Columns of sunlight tunneled through the smoke inside the woods, and the air smelled of cordite, horse manure, trees set on fire from fused shells, and humus cratered out of the forest floor. Willie had lost his haversack, cartridge box, the scabbard for his bayonet, and his canteen, but he didn't know where or remember how. He had pulled a cartridge pouch off the belt of a dead man who had already been stripped of his shirt and shoes. Then he had found another dead man in a ravine, with his canteen still hung from his neck, and had pulled the cloth strap loose from the man's head and uncorked the canteen only to discover it was filled with corn whiskey.

He had never been so thirsty in his life. His lips and tongue were black from biting off the ends of cartridge papers, his nostrils clotted with dust and bits of desiccated leaves. He watched a sergeant use his canteen to wash the blood from a wounded man's face and he wanted to tear the canteen from the sergeant's hands and pour every ounce of its contents down his own throat.

Jim's canteen had been split in half by a minié ball early in the morning, and neither of them had eaten or drunk a teaspoon of water since the previous night. They had collapsed behind a thick-trunked white oak, exhausted, light-headed, their ears ringing, waiting for the group of Tennessee infantry, to which they now belonged through no volition of their own, to re-form and once again move on the sunken road that the Southerners were now calling the Hornets' Nest.

The leaves on the floor of the forest were streaked with the blood of the wounded who had been dragged back to the ambulance wagons in the rear. Some men had talked about a surgeon's tent, back near the Corinth Road, that buzzed with green flies and contained cries that would live in a man's dreams the rest of his life.

Looking to the south, Willie could see horses pulling more cannons through the trees, twenty-four-pounders as high as a man, the spoked wheels knocking across rocks and logs. He pointed and told Jim to look at the cannons that were lumbering on their carriages through the hardwoods, then realized he could not hear.

He pressed his thumbs under his ears and swallowed and tried to force air through his ear passages, but it was to no avail. The rest of the world was going about its business, and he was viewing it as though he were trapped under a glass bell.

The cannons went past him, silently, through the leaves and scarred tree trunks, lumbering toward the peach orchard and the sunken road, as silently as if their wheels had been wrapped with flannel. He lay back against the trunk of the white oak and shut his eyes, more tired than he had ever been, convinced he could sleep through the Apocalypse. He could feel a puff of breeze on his cheek, smell water in a creek, hear his mother making breakfast in the boarding-house kitchen at dawn's first light.

Then he heard a sound, like a series of doors slamming. He jerked his head up. Jim was standing above him, his lips moving, his consternation showing.

"What?" Willie said.

Jim's lips were moving silently, then audible words came from his mouth in mid-sentence.

"— got us some water. That fellow from the 6th Mis'sippi we were talking to last night, the one who looked like he got hit across the face with a frying pan, he toted a whole barrel up here strapped to his back," Jim said.

He squatted down with a tin cup and handed it to Willie.

"Where's yours?" Willie asked.

"I had plenty. Drink up," Jim said, his eyes

sliding off Willie's face.

There was a black smear of gunpowder on the cup's rim where Jim had drunk, but the water level in the cup was down only an inch. Willie drank two swallows, a little more than half the remaining water, and returned the cup to Jim.

"Finish it up, you ole beanpole, and don't be lying to your pal again," Willie said.

Jim sat down against the tree bark.

"You hit any of them today?" he asked.

"I couldn't see through the smoke most of the time. You?" Willie replied.

"Maybe. I saw a fellow behind a rick fence go down. A ball hit him in the face," Jim said. He looked into space, his jaw flexing. "I was glad."

Willie turned and looked at Jim's profile, a gunpowder burn on his right cheek, the bitter cast in his eye.

"They're no different from us, Jim," he said.

"Yes, they are. They're down here. We didn't go up there."

A young lieutenant strolled through the enlisted men sitting on the ground. He wore a goatee that looked like corn silk, and a wide-brimmed cavalry officer's hat, with a gold cord strung around the crown, a bared sword carried casually on his shoulder. Blood had drained from inside his coat onto the leather flap of his pistol holster.

"Our cannoneers are about to start banging doors again, gentlemen. Then we're going to have another run at it," he said.

"We been out there eleven times, suh," a private on the ground said.

"Twelve's a charm. Stuff your fingers in your ears," the lieutenant said, just as over twenty cannons fired in sequence, almost point-blank, into the sunken road and the woods beyond.

Then the cannon crews began to fire at will, the barrels and gun carriages lurching off the ground, the crews turning in a half-crouch from the explosion, their hands clamped over their ears. They swabbed out the barrels, then reloaded with more case shot, canister, and grape. They snipped the fuses on explosive shells so they detonated as airbursts immediately on the other side of the sunken road. When they ran short of conventional ordnance, they loaded with lengths of chain, chopped-up horseshoes, chunks of angle iron and buckets of railroad spikes.

Through the smoke Willie and Jim could see bits of trees flying in the air, the staff of an American flag lopped in half, blue-clad men climbing out of their rifle pits, running for the rear, sometimes with a wounded comrade supported between them.

The barrage went on for thirty minutes. When it lifted, the sun looked like a broken egg yolk inside the smoke, the acrid smell of gunpowder so dense they could hardly breathe.

Willie and Jim advanced across the clearing with the others, once again the cry of the fox hunt rising hoarsely from their throats. They crossed the sunken road and stepped over the Federal dead who lay there and entered a woods where trees were split in two, as though divided by lightning, the bark on the southern side of the trunks hanging in white strips.

The ground was littered with Springfield rifle muskets, boxes of percussion caps, ramrods, haversacks, canteens, torn cartridge papers, entrenching shovels, kepis, bloody bandages, bayonets, cloth that had been scissored away from wounds, boots and shoes, newspaper and magazine pages that men had used to clean themselves.

Inside the smoke and broken trees and the fallen leaves that were matted together with blood was the pervasive buzzing of bottle flies. In the distance, over the heads of the Confederates who were out in front of him, Willie saw a white flag being waved by a Union officer in front of a silenced battery.

The firing ended as it had started, but in inverse fashion, like a string of Chinese firecrackers that pops with murderous intensity, then simply exhausts itself.

Willie and Jim slumped against a stone

fence that was speckled with lichen and damp and cool-smelling in the shade. Even the sunlight seemed filtered through green water. Jim's eyes were bloodshot, his face like that of a coal miner who has just emerged from a mine shaft, his teeth startling white when he grinned.

The tall man, with the concave face, from the 6th Mississippi, walked past them, his body bent forward. A huge barrel was mounted on his back with leather straps that were looped around his shoulders. The barrel had been hit in four places across the middle with either grapeshot or minié balls, and four jets of water were spraying from the holes, crisscrossing one another as the man labored with his burden back toward the sunken road.

"How about a drink, pard?" Jim said.

"What's that you say?" the man asked. His jaws were slack, unshaved, his peculiar, smoke-blackened, indented face like that of a simian creature from an earlier time.

"You're leaking. Give us a cup before it's all gone," Willie said.

"Take the whole shithouse," the man said.

He slipped the leather straps off his back and slung the barrel on a rock, where the staves burst apart and the water patterned on the leaves, then became only a dark shadow in the dirt.

Willie and Jim stared at him in disbelief.

"Want to make something of hit?" he asked.

"No, sir, not us," Willie said.

The man rubbed his hand on his mouth and looked about him as though he didn't know where he was. A rivulet of dried blood ran from his ear canal into his whiskers.

"Where's the little fellow, what's-his-name, Tige?" Willie asked.

"Gone. Him and his drum, both gone," the man said.

"Gone where?" Willie asked.

"Into their cannon. Right into their goddamn cannon," the man said.

His eyes were wet, the whites filled with veins that looked like crimson thread, his teeth like slats in his mouth.

When Willie and Jim found their outfit later in the afternoon, it was as though they had journeyed to a different war. Five hundred men of the 18th Louisiana were spread along the tree-dotted edge of a ravine, their blue jackets now turned inside out in order to show the white linings. In front of them, up a long green incline, was a hardwood forest unscarred by rifle or cannon fire, and inside the forest were three regiments of Federal infantry and batteries of wheeled artillery whose jack screws had been twisted to their maximum extension in order to point the cannon barrels straight down the slope.

Willie and Jim walked through the bottom of the ravine, the leaves almost ankle-deep, their clothes rent, their saliva still black when they spat. Their friends stared at them quizzically, as though they were visitors from a foreign world. Willie and Jim knelt behind a tree on the northern rim and stared out at the scene in front of them.

The slope was partially in shadow now, the air cool with the hint of evening. When the wind blew down the slope Willie could see wildflowers inside the grass. The depressed muzzle of a cannon stared down the slope at him like a blunt-edged iron instrument poised to enter the throat of a surgical patient.

Off to the left Rufus Atkins stood among the trees, with two other officers, his head nodding, his gloves pulled tautly through his belt, while Colonel Alfred Mouton moved his index finger on a map that was spread across his wrist and forearm. Then Corporal Clay Hatcher walked past Willie, interdicting his line of vision.

"Where y'all been? Cap'n Atkins wrote y'all up as deserters," Hatcher said, stopping, his eyes, which reminded Willie of a rodent's, squinting in the gloom. He carried a Springfield rifle with a narrow brass tube mounted on top of the barrel.

"In the rear, catching up on our sleep. I see you've taken up the role of sniper. I think you've found yourself, Clay," Jim said.

Hatcher tried to stare them down, as he had tried on many other occasions, but the memory of his humiliation at their hands back at Camp Pratt was always in their eyes, their contempt and rejection of his authority like a salty cut on his soul.

"What's going on, Hatcher?" Willie asked.

"We're taking that battery up there," Hatcher said, his chin out.

"They're quit. We punched through them at the sunken road," Willie said.

"Tell that to them blue-bellies up in the trees," Hatcher said. "Where are your coats?"

"We lost them," Willie said.

"You might as well. We had to turn ours inside out. The Orleans Guards started firing on us."

For a moment Hatcher felt like a brother-in-arms, a noncommissioned officer looking out for his men, Willie and Jim, but he looked at the black stains around their mouths, the sweat lines that had dried in the dust on their faces, and he knew they were different from him, better than him, and he knew also they had already passed a test inside the crucible that now waited for him up the slope.

He turned his head and pretended to spit in order to show his lack of fear, even rubbing his shoe at a dry place in the leaves, then walked off, the weight of his scoped rifle balanced horizontally inside his cupped palm, rehearsing a scowling look of disdain for the next enlisted man who should wander into his ken.

Willie crunched through the leaves toward the place where Colonel Mouton and his staff were talking. Mouton wore a thick beard and a wide hat with a plum-colored plume in it and a long coat and knee-length calvary boots outside his pants. His coat was stiff on one side with dried mud splatter, one eye watery where a shaft of sunlight cut across his face. He stopped in mid-sentence.

"What is it you want, Private?" he asked.

"We were at the Hornets' Nest, sir. The sunken road, over to the east. They surrendered," Willie said.

"We're aware of that. But thank you for coming forward," Mouton said.

"Sir?" Willie said.

"Yes?" Mouton said, distracted now, his eyes lifting for a second time from the map.

"They're whipped. We went at them twelve times and whipped them," Willie said.

"You need to go rejoin your comrades, Private," Mouton said.

Willie turned and walked away without saluting, glancing up the slope at the artillery pieces that waited for them inside the shadows and the cooling of the day, twenty-four-pounders loaded with the same ordnance Willie had seen used at the sunken road. He stopped behind a tree and leaned over, then slid down his rifle onto his knees, shutting his eyes, clasping the holy medal that hung from his neck.

The sun was low on the western horizon now, the sky freckled with birds. Colonel Mouton rode his horse out onto the green slope in front of the ravine and waited for his regiment to move out of the trees and join him in the failing light. A hawk glided over the glade, its shadow racing behind it, and seemed to disappear into the redness of the sun.

Mouton spoke first in French, then in English, repeating the same statements three times in three different positions so all would hear his words.

"The 16th Louisiana and the Orleans Guards were supposed to be on our flanks, gentlemen. Unfortunately they have not arrived. That means we have to kick the Yankees off that hill by ourselves. You are brave and fine men and it is my great honor to serve with you. Our cause is just and God will not desert us. In that spirit I ask you to come with me up that hill and show the invaders of our homeland what true courage is.

"God bless and love every one of you."

Then he raised his saber in the air, turned his horse northward, and began the long walk up the slope into an enfiladed box where they would be outnumbered three to one and fired upon from the front and both flanks simultaneously.

As Willie marched up the slope with Jim, his heart thudding in his chest, he kept waiting for the crack of the first rifle shot, the one that would ignite the firestorm for which no soldier could ever adequately prepare himself. His own stink rose from his shirt, and there was a creaking sound inside his head, as though he were deep underwater, beyond all the physical laws of tolerance, and the pressure was about to rupture his eardrums.

The standard bearer was in front of him, the white stars and crossed blue bars on a red field rippling and popping in the wind, the standard bearer tripping over a rock, righting himself, his kepi falling to the ground, stepped on by the man behind him.

But it was not a rifle shot that began the battle. A cannon lurched and burst with flame against the darkness of the trees, and suddenly there was sound and light in the midst of the 18th Louisiana that was like the earth-rending force inside a hurricane, like a wind that could tear arms and legs out of sockets, rip heads from torsos, disembowel the viscera, blow the body lifelessly across the ground, all of it with such a grinding inevitability that one simply surrendered to it, as he might to a libidinous and heavy-handed lover.

Colonel Mouton's horse twisted its head sideways, walleyed, whinnying, then went down, its rib cage pocked with grapeshot. Mouton separated himself from the saddle and rose to his feet, shot in the face, and tried to pull a revolver from his holster. He fell to one knee, his left hand searching in the air for support, then toppled forward into the grass.

A piece of case shot spun through the air and embedded four inches into the upper thigh of the standard bearer. He sagged on the flagstaff, like an elderly man grown weary of an arduous climb, then pivoted and looked imploringly into Jim's face.

"They sight on the guidon! Don't take it!" Willie said.

But Jim shifted his rifle to his left hand and slipped the staff from the grasp of the wounded man. With almost superhuman strength he held the colors aloft in the sunset with one hand, his Enfield gripped in the other, stepping over the fallen, while minié balls made whirring sounds past his ears.

Willie heard the mortal wound before he saw it, a plopping sound, a minié fired from the woods that struck Jim's brow and blew out the back of his head.

He saw the battle flag tilt, then the cloth fall across his own face, blinding him. When he ripped it aside and flung it from his hand, Jim lay on his side, in the grass, an unbruised buttercup an inch from his sight-less eyes.

Suddenly he could no longer hear the roar of the guns or the airbursts over his head. But inside his own mind he heard himself speak Jim's name.

Jim? Hey, you ole beanpole, get up. We've got fish to catch, dances to go to. This is all a lark, not worth our dying for.

The sound of the war came back, like a locomotive engine blowing apart. The ends of his fingers were wet with Jim's blood, his shirt splattered with Jim's brain matter.

In fifteen minutes two hundred and forty members of the 18th Louisiana, just short of half, were casualties. They retreated back down the slope, dragging their wounded with them, many of their weapons left on the field.

But Willie did not go with them. He picked up his Enfield and slipped Jim's bowie knife and scabbard from his belt, and ran in a crouch toward the sunset and the trees that bordered Owl Creek. A cannon shell screamed past his head, its breath like a hot scorch on his neck.

He splashed across the stream and went deep into the hardwoods, where round boulders protruded from the humus like the tops of toadstools. He paused long enough to thread the scabbard of the bowie knife onto his own belt, then he cut northward, running through the undergrowth and spiderwebs draped between the tree trunks, gaining elevation now, the sun only a burnt cinder between two hills.

He smelled tobacco smoke and saw two blue-clad pickets, puffing on cob pipes, perhaps sharing a joke, their kepis at a jaunty angle, their guns stacked against the trunk of a walnut tree. They turned when they heard his feet running, the smiles still on their faces. He shot one just below the heart, then inverted the Enfield, never breaking stride, and swung the barrel like a rounders bat, breaking the stock across the other man's face.

He pulled a .36 caliber navy revolver from the belt of the man he had shot and kept running, across the pebbled bottom of a creek and a stretch of damp, cinnamon-colored soil that was printed with the tracks of grouse and wild turkeys, past a dried-out oxbow where a grinding mill and waterwheel had rotted and started to cave into the streambed, through box elder and elm trees, right into the back of a huge, black-bearded Union private, who was urinating with his phallus held in both hands.

On the ground by his foot lay a dirty handkerchief spread with vest watches, marriage and Masonic rings, coins, a gold toothpick, cigars, tightly folded and compressed currency, a clay pipe, a condom made from an animal's bladder, even false teeth carved from whalebone.

The Union soldier almost lost his footing, then righted himself, as though on the deck of a ship, and pushed his phallus back inside his fly. His sleeves were rolled, and the hair on the backs of his arms was peppered with grains of dirt. He reached out casually for a Sharp's carbine that was hung by its strap from a branch just behind him.

"Lose your way home, Johnny?" he asked.

Willie cocked the pistol and fired a ball into the middle of his forehead, saw the man disappear momentarily inside the smoke, then heard the man's great deadweight strike the ground.

It was almost dark and lightning flickered inside the clouds that once again had sealed the sky. He wandered for what seemed hours and saw feral hogs snuffing and grunting among the dead, their snouts strung with lights. He heard the heavy, iron-rimmed wheels of caissons and gun carriages and ammunition and hospital wagons rumbling on the old Hamburg–Savannah Road. The wind changed, and he smelled water in a stagnant pond somewhere, and another odor with it that made him clear his mouth and spit.

After all the balls were gone from his revolver, he used the knife at least twice in the woods, clenching his hand on one man's throat while he drove the blade repeatedly into the heart cavity. Another he hit from behind, a whiskered signal corpsman with a terrible odor whom he ran upon and seized around the neck and stabbed and left either wounded or dying at the bottom of a rocky den overlooking the Tennessee River.

The clouds overhead were marbled with lightning that rippled across the entirety of the sky. Below the bluffs he could see dozens of paddle-wheelers on the river, their cabins and pilothouses dark, their decks packed with men. He heard gangplanks being lowered with ropes onto the bank, saw lanterns moving about in the trees and serpentine columns of men wending their way into a staging area where a hydrogen balloon rocked inside a net that moored it to the ground.

He headed west, away from the river, and recrossed the Hamburg–Savannah Road and again smelled the thick, heavy odor of ponded water and sour mud, threaded with another odor, one that was salty and gray, like fish roe drying on stone or a hint of copulation trapped in bedsheets.

Veins of lightning pulsed in the clouds, and through the trees he saw a water pond, of a kind boys would bobber-fish in for bluegill and sun perch. Except now the water was red, as dark as a dye vat, and bodies floated in it, the clothes puffed with air.

He saw a figure, one with white ankles and feet, run from the pond through the woods, some thirsty and abandoned soul, he thought, who had probably tried to scoop clear water out of the reeds and had fouled his throat and was now running through the peach orchard they had raked with grapeshot earlier in the day. Willie kept going west, toward the Corinth Road, and found a bloodstained stub of bread that had been dropped in a glade scattered with mushrooms. He ate it as he walked, then heard someone moving in the trees and saw a miniature Confederate soldier in butternut and an oversized kepi, looking at him, his feet and face cut by thorns and branches, his pants hitched tightly under his ribs, a pair of drumsticks shoved through his belt.

"Is that you, Tige?" Willie asked.

The boy continued to stare at him, shifting from one foot to another, as though trying to take the weight off a stone bruise.

"You're one of the fellows who give me the mush and bacon. Where'd everybody go?" the boy said.

"Not sure. I ran everywhere there is and then ran out of space. Ran myself silly in the head while I was at it. So I turned around. Hop aboard," Willie said, turning his back for the boy to climb on.

But the boy remained motionless, breathing through his mouth, his eyes blinking inside the dust and sweat on his face.

"You got blood all over you. You're plumb

painted with it," he said.

"Really?" Willie said. He wiped his cheek with the flat of his hand and looked at it.

"How far is Vicksburg if you float there on the river?" the boy asked.

"This river doesn't go there, Tige."

The boy crimped his toes in the dirt, the pain in his feet climbing into his face now, his strength and resolve draining from his cheeks.

"I gone all the way to the peach orchard," he said.

"I bet you did. My pal Jim was killed today. He was a lot like you. Too brave to know he was supposed to be afraid. He didn't know when to ask for help, either," Willie said.

"It don't seem fair."

"What's that?" Willie asked.

"We whupped them. But most all the fellows I was with is dead," the boy said.

"Let's find the road to Corinth. I'll tell you a story about the ancient Greeks while we walk," Willie said.

The boy climbed onto Willie's back and locked his arms around Willie's neck. His bones were so light they felt filled with air, like a bird's, rather than marrow. Then the two of them walked through a forest that was unmarked by war and that pattered with raindrops and smelled of wet leaves and spring and freshly plowed fields.

They rested on the wooded slope of a creek bed, then rose and continued on through trees until they could see cultivated acreage in the distance and lightning striking on the crest of a ridge. Willie set Tige down on a boulder that looked like the top of a man's bald head and arched a crick out of his back while the rain ticked on the canopy over their heads.

"So this Oedipus fellow was a king but he married his mother and blinded hisself and become a beggar, even though he could figure out riddles and was the brightest fellow around?" Tige said.

"That pretty well sums it up," Willie said.

"Them ancient Greeks didn't have real high standards when it come to smarts, did they?" Tige replied.

Willie was sitting on a log, his legs spread, grinning at Tige, when he heard the jingle of bridle chains, the creak of saddle leather, the thud of shoed hooves on damp earth. He looked at Tige's face and saw the alarm in it as Tige focused on a presence behind Willie's head.

Willie stood up from the log, drawing the bowie from its scabbard, letting it hang by his thigh. He looked up at a bareheaded specter of a man in a brass-buttoned gray coat that was pushed back over the scrolled hilt of a cavalry saber.

"Light it up, Sergeant," the mounted man in the gray coat said.

The sergeant who walked beside him scratched a lucifer match on a candle lamp and touched the flame to three wicks inside it and lifted the bail above his head. The shadows leapt back into the trees and Willie saw the gold stars of a colonel sewn on the horseman's collar, the hair deeply receded at the temples, the severity of a hawk in his face.

Other mounted officers appeared out of the undergrowth and overhang, and farther back in the trees lean, dismounted men in slouch hats and kepis were leading their horses by the bridles, pulling them up the slope of a coulee that snaked along the edge of a cornfield.

Willie stared, intrigued, at the man with the hawklike face. On his last leave in New Orleans he had seen his picture in the window of a photographer's studio on Canal Street. There was no mistaking who he was, nor misinterpreting the inflexible posture, the martial light in the eyes, the adversarial expression that seemed untempered by problems of conscience.

"You don't seem aware of military protocol," the colonel said.

"Private Willie Burke at your orders, sir," Willie said, removing his kepi, bowing in a thespian fashion. "That young gentleman yonder is my pal Tige McGuffy, of the 6th Mississippi."

"I'm very happy to make your acquaintance," the colonel said. There was a lump of chewing tobacco in his jaw, and his mouth looked like a ragged hole inside his triangular, untrimmed beard. He leaned in the saddle and spat a long brown stream into the leaves. "You look to be wounded."

"Not me, sir. They killed my pal Jim Stubbefield, though. You didn't happen to know him, did you?" Willie replied.

The colonel wiped his lips with his wrist. "No, I didn't. Where's your regiment?" he asked.

"I haven't seen them in a while. But I'm glad you raised the subject. Perhaps you could tell me the names of the thumb-sucking incompetent sods who got Colonel Mouton shot in the face and the 18th Louisiana destroyed," Willie said.

The sergeant turned with the candle lamp, staring incredulously at Willie, waiting for the colonel's command.

But the colonel waved a finger in disapproval.

"You been out yonder?" he asked Willie, nodding toward the north, his horse resting one hoof.

"That I have. They've been reinforced up to their eyes and I suspect at daybreak they may kick a telegraph pole up your ass," Willie replied.

"I see," the colonel said, dismounting, the

tiny rowel on his spur tinkling when his boot touched the ground. He opened a saddlebag and removed a folded map, then studied Willie's face, which in the candlelight and rain looked like yellow and red tallow that had started to melt. "Can you point out where these Yankees are staging up?"

"I think I'm either bent for the firing squad or being on my way with Tige here, Colonel."

"Matters not to me. But it will to the men we may lose tomorrow," the colonel said.

Willie thought about it. He yawned to clear the popping sound from his ears. He felt as though he were sliding to the bottom of a black well, the invective he had delivered a senior officer echoing in his head like words spoken in a dream. When he closed his eyes the ground seemed to move under his feet. He took the map from the colonel's hand, then returned it to him without opening it.

"Colonel Forrest, is it?" Willie said, blowing out his breath.

"That's correct."

"This light is mighty poor. Will one of your fellows take care of Tige, perhaps carry him to the Corinth Road?" he said.

"It will be our pleasure," the colonel said.

"They're going to rip us apart, sir. I saw them offload maybe a hundred mortars," Willie said, then realized he had just used the word "us."

The colonel bit off a chew of plug tobacco and handed the plug to Willie.

"I don't doubt you're a brave man and killed the enemy behind his own lines today. Wars get won by such as yourself. But don't ever address me profanely or disrespectfully again. I won't have you shot. I'll do it myself," he said.

Then the colonel directed an aide to build a fire under a canvas tarp and to bring up dry clothes and bread and a preserve jar of strawberry jam for Willie and Tige, and bandages and salve for Tige's feet, and that quickly Willie found himself back in the mainstream of the Confederate army, about to begin the second day of the battle of Shiloh.

Chapter Eight

The first day Abigail Dowling reported to work as a volunteer nurse at the Catholic hospital on St. Charles Avenue, she realized her experience with the treatment of yellow fever had not adequately prepared her for contrasts.

At first it was heartening to see the Union ironclads anchored on the river, plated and slope-sided, their turreted cannons an affirmation of the North's destructive potential, the American flag popping from the masts. But somehow the victory of her own people over the city of New Orleans rang hollow. She had anticipated seeing anger in the faces of the citizenry, perhaps feelings of loss and sorrow, but instead she saw only fear and she didn't know why.

The hospital was two stories, constructed of brick that was webbed with ivy, set far back under live oak trees, with a scrolled-iron veranda on the second story. Two wings extended out toward the street, creating a garden-like area in the center that was planted with pink and gray caladium, banks of philodendrons and elephant ears, climbing roses, banana trees, bamboo, crepe myrtle and azaleas, whose blooms puffed in the wind and tumbled on the grass.

She walked with a white-clad nun down a long wood hallway that glowed from hours of polishing done by women who prayed inside sweltering habits while they scrubbed floors on their hands and knees. The intermittent statues of the saints, daily dusted from the crowns of their heads to the soles of their feet, could have been the votive patrons of cleanliness and order. Then Abigail passed a Union sentry and entered the ward for Confederate prisoners who had survived surgery in field hospitals and had been shipped south from Shiloh on commandeered riverboats.

Abigail fought to keep her face empty of expression when she looked upon the men in the rows of beds, the covered ceramic slop jars set neatly in front of each bed. Field surgeons had often sawed the limb right at the trunk, offering no chance for a prosthesis. Some men had only sockets for eyes, a scooped-out hole for a nose, a mouth without a jaw, a tube of useless flesh for an arm or leg after the bone had been removed.

The lucky ones had stumps that ended in puckered scar tissue that was still pink with circulation. But some had been condemned to die the death of the damned twice, their limbs cut without benefit of ether or laudanum by a field surgeon using a saw he cleaned on an old shirt soaked in whiskey. Then, when they thought their ordeal was over, they discovered that gangrene had taken hold under their bandages and their swollen flesh had turned the color of an eggplant.

"Some of the nuns put rosewater on a handkerchief and pretend they have a cold," the sentry at the door told her. His accent was a distorted echo of her own, Boston or New York or Rhode Island, a man who had probably operated a dray or worked in a fish market or at the firehouse.

"I'm not bothered by it," she replied.

"Come back at night. When we have to close the windows because of the mosquitoes and they start pitching around in their sleep, knocking over slop jars and yelling out and such," he said.

The sentry was thin and nice-looking, with startling blue eyes, a fresh haircut and a trimmed mustache. A bayonet was fixed on the rifle that was popped butt-down between his feet.

"Yesterday, when I got off the boat, I heard a great commotion by the Mint," she said.

"The Rebs tore down our flag and ripped it up in the street. They're not gracious losers."

"I see," she said.

"One of them is about to get a taste of General Butler today. You know what the general said? 'They don't respect our stars, they'll feel our stripes.' Pretty clever, if you ask me," the sentry said.

"I don't quite follow you," she said.

"Go down to the Mint this evening and get an eyeful."

She started to walk away.

"Don't feel sorry for these Rebs, ma'am. They've lorded it over the darkies all their lives and never had to work like the rest of us. Now, they're going to get their comeuppance. If you want to see an example of His Southern Highness, check behind the screens at the end of the room," the sentry said.

Later, as she was carrying out slop jars to the lime pit in back, she glanced through an opening between two mobile partitions fashioned from mosquito netting. Propped up on pillows by the window was a bare-chested and handsome man wrapped with bandages across his rib cage and lower back and shoulder. The bandages on the rib cage were spotted with two dark red circles the size of quarters.

The shutters on the window were open, and the dappled light that filtered through the philodendron shifted across his face like gold leaves floating on water. His eyelids looked as thin as paper, traced with tiny blue veins. His breath was so shallow he seemed barely alive.

"Colonel Jamison?" she said.

He turned his head on the pillow and opened his eyes, his brow furrowed, like a man waking from an angry dream. His lips were dry and gray, and he seemed to rethink a troubling idea in his head, then correct the expression in his face, as though by choice he could manifest the personae he wanted to present to the world.

"Miss Abigail? You have a way of showing up in the most unexpected fashion," he said.

"You were taken prisoner at Shiloh?" she said.

"Truth be known, I don't remember it very well. For sure, they planted three balls in me. Would you mind putting a teaspoon of lemon water in my mouth?"

When she picked up the bowl from the nightstand his mouth opened and waited like a communicant's. She placed the teaspoon of crushed ice and mint leaves and lemon on his tongue. His throat made a dry, clicking sound when he swallowed and for just a moment color seemed to bloom in his cheeks. On the nightstand were a gilded leather-bound Bible and a saucer with three conically shaped .36 caliber pistol rounds on it.

She tried to remember the name of his regiment. Was it the Orleans Guards?

"Do you have news of a soldier named Willie Burke? He was with the 18th," she said.

149

A shadow seemed to slide across Jamison's brow.

"On the first day we were supposed to be on their flank. There was a great deal of confusion. They went up the slope on their own."

"Do you know of Willie?" she asked again.

"No, I know no one by that name. I was wounded the following day. If I live through this war, I'll always be associated with the destruction of the 18th Louisiana. I hope the balls they dug out of my flesh somehow atone for my failure."

She studied his face and could not decide if what she saw there was remorse or self-pity. His fingers touched hers.

"I apologize for my behavior in your home, Miss Abigail. I'm an aging widower and sometimes give in to romantic inclinations that are the product of my years," he said.

His eyes tried to hold hers, but she turned from him and picked up a partially covered wooden bucket filled with encrusted bandages. An odor rose into her nostrils that made the skin of her face stretch against the bone.

"The surgeon says my intestines were probably damaged. There's a term for it," he said.

"Peritonitis?"

"Yes."

She pressed down the lid on the wooden bucket and let her face show no expression.

When she returned from the lime pit he was looking out the window at a sunshower falling on the live oaks and floral gardens between the hospital and the street.

"Flower is attending me. She'll be here this evening," he said.

"Pardon?" Abigail said.

"I had her brought from New Iberia. She's a good girl, isn't she?"

He turned his head on the pillow and smiled. For the first time she looked upon him with pity and wondered if indeed, as her religion taught, there were those who found genuine redemption in their last days.

Her thoughts were still on the colonel and his illegitimate daughter, the slave girl Flower, when she took a public carriage downtown that evening and walked to the room provided her by the Sanitary Commission. She stopped at the open-air market and bought a fried catfish sandwich and sat on a bench by the river, watching the paddle-wheelers in the sunset and the children playing in the street. The wind smelled of wet trees and rain falling on warm stone in a different part of the city, and when she closed her eyes she felt more alone than she had ever felt in her life.

She had dedicated herself to the plight of the infirm and the abandoned and the oppressed who had no voice, hadn't she? Why this unrelieved sense of loneliness, of always feeling that the comforting notion of safe harbor would never be hers?

Because there was no one solidly defined world she belonged to, no one family, no one person, she thought. She saw herself in an accurate way only twice during any given twenty-four-hour period, at twilight and at false dawn, when the world was neither night nor day, when shadows gave ambiguity a legitimacy that sunlight did not.

Amid the cries of children wheeling barrel hoops down the street and a band playing in front of a saloon, she heard another sound, a guttural shout, like a visceral cheer from a single individual who spoke for many. Then she heard collective laughter and yelling, a crowd moving up the street toward the U.S. Mint, a mixture of soldiers trying to maintain the appearance of discipline, loafers from the saloons, drunk prostitutes, a dancing barefoot Negro in green felt pants and a red-and-white-striped hat, a man with a peg leg stumping his way along the edge of things, a dwarf carrying a parasol over his head, grinning with a mouthful of tombstone teeth.

In the center of the crowd was a disheveled and terrified white man, his hands shackled behind him with a chain and heavy metal cuffs. He wore a thin mustache that looked grease-penciled on his upper lip, like an actor playing a villain in a cheap melodrama. He twisted his head back and forth, pleading to anyone who would listen. But his words were lost in their jeers.

"What did he do?" Abigail asked an elderly man with a goatee sitting next to her, his hands folded on the crook of a cane.

"He was wearing a piece of the ripped flag in his buttonhole," the man replied.

Then she remembered the account given her by the sentry, something about a man who had torn down the Stars and Stripes from the front of the U.S. Mint.

"The army knows it was he?" she asked.

"I don't think they care. He's a cardsharp by trade," the elderly man replied.

She set down her sandwich on the piece of newspaper it had come wrapped in and stood up from the bench.

"My God, what are they going to do?" she said. When the man on the bench didn't reply, she tried again. "Who's in charge of this?"

His eyes looked at her casually, as though he were considering the implications of her accent before he answered.

"General Butler. 'Spoons' Butler to some. He has a way of ending up with people's silverware. Where you from, anyway?" the man said.

She walked hurriedly toward the balloon of people who surrounded the man in manacles, her shoes splashing in water. She jerked on a soldier's arm.

"What are you going to do to this man?" she asked.

"Whatever it is, it's none of your business. Go back to the edge of the street," the soldier replied.

"You take me to your commanding officer," she said.

"Maybe you should kiss my smelly bum, too," he said.

"*What* did you say?" she said.

He shifted his rifle to his left hand and spun her in the opposite direction, then pushed her hard between the shoulder blades, snapping her head back. When she turned around again, the other soldiers had already worked their captive inside the building.

Someone on the second story pulled aside the curtains above the empty flag staff that protruded from the bricks. She could see the man in manacles fighting now, butting the soldiers with his head, spitting at their faces.

She tried to push her way inside the door and was shoved back by a sentry. She heard the crowd roar behind her and looked up, just as the manacled man was hoisted onto the windowsill, a narrow-gauge greased length of rope looped around his throat. He fell three feet into space before the rope came taut.

But his neck did not snap. Brick mortar

shaled from his shoes and fell on her head and shoulders as he twisted on the rope and his feet kicked against the wall.

She fought her way back through the crowd and suddenly found herself inside the collective odor of its members, the dried sweat under the perfume and caked body powder, the dirty hair, the wine breath and decayed meat impacted between their teeth, all of it washing over her in a fetid wave as they shouted out their ridicule of the man whose eyes bulged like walnuts above them, some twisting their own heads and sticking their tongues out the sides of their mouths in mockery.

She pushed her way to the edge of the crowd into the open. She dropped her purse in a mud puddle and almost fell down when she tried to pick it up. The whistle of a steamboat screamed on the river and one of the ironclads fired off a cannon in celebration of the hanging. Then a black woman took her around the waist and walked with her toward the open-air market and the empty bench where a cat was eating the sandwich Abigail had left behind.

"You gonna be all right, Miss Abigail. No, no, don't watch what them people are doing no more. You and me are just gonna keep putting one foot after the other and not worry about them folks back yonder," the black woman said.

"Is that you, Flower?" Abigail said.

"Sure it is, Miss Abigail. I ain't gonna let you down, either," Flower said.

"That poor man."

"No, no, do what I tell you and don't be looking over there," Flower said, touching Abigail's eyes with her fingers. "You a brave lady. I wish I was as brave as you. One day everybody gonna know how brave you been, how much you done for us. I'm gonna see to it."

When they sat down on the bench together they clenched hands like schoolchildren. The palm and banana trees along the levee clattered in the wind off the river, and the deepening color of the sky made her think of the purple cloak Jesus was supposedly made to wear at his crucifixion. The street was empty now. The manacled man hung like a long, narrow exclamation mark against the wall of the Mint.

"My own people did this. Those who claim to be the voice of justice," Abigail said.

"But we didn't. That's what counts, Miss Abigail. You and me didn't do it. Sometimes that's about all the relief the world give you," Flower said.

"It's not enough," Abigail said.

Chapter Nine

Flower Jamison walked through Jackson Square, past St. Louis Cathedral, and down cobbled streets under colonnades and scrolled-iron balconies that dripped with bougainvillea and passion vine. A man in a constable's uniform was lighting the gas lamps along the street, and the breeze smelled of freshly sprinkled flower beds on the opposite side of a gated wall, spearmint, old brick that was dark with mold, and ponded water in a courtyard where the etched shadows of palm fronds moved like lace across a bright window.

The moon rose above the rooftops and chimneys and cast her shadow in front of her, at first startling her, then making her laugh.

She walked past the brothels in Congo Square, two-story wood-frame buildings, their closed shutters slitted with an oily yellow light from inside. The only customers now were Yankee soldiers, boys, really, who entered the houses in groups, never singly, loud, boisterous, probably with little money, she thought, anxious to hide their fear and innocence and the paucity of their resources.

She passed a house that resonated with piano music and offered only mulatto women to its customers, what were always called quadroons, no matter what the racial mix of the woman actually was. A baby-faced soldier not older than seventeen sat on the front step, flicking pebbles with his thumb into the yard, a kepi cocked on his head. He watched her pass and then for some unaccountable reason tipped his kepi to her.

She nodded at him and smiled.

"Some other fellows went inside. I was just waiting on them," he said.

The overseer who had brought her from New Iberia had placed her with a husband and wife who were free people of color and lived in an elevated cottage overlooking Basin and the drainage ditch that sawed its way down the middle of the street to a sinkhole that was gray with insects. She ate supper with the husband and wife, then waited for the husband to drive her to the hospital on St. Charles.

He was a light-skinned man who ran a tannery and looked more Indian than African. He seemed irritable as he pulled a pair of gloves over his palms, vexed somehow by her presence or his need to transport her back and forth to her work.

"Is something wrong, suh?" she asked.

"The overseer tole me yesterday you're Ira Jamison's daughter," he said.

"He ain't said it to me. No white person ever has."

"I seen you walking past them houses down there tonight. Flirting wit' a Yankee soldier on the porch," he said. He wagged his finger back and forth. "You don't do that when you stay at my house."

"Colonel Jamison is a prisoner of war. He cain't hurt you, suh."

"I bought my freedom, girl. I ain't ever gonna lose it. If you come to New Orleans, scheming to get free, you better not drag me into it, no," he said, pulling down his shirt to expose a circular scar that looked like dried plaster, of a kind left by a branding iron poorly laid on.

Flower knew she should have been depressed by the hostility and fear of her host and the hanging she had witnessed that evening, but oddly she was not. In fact, since the day an overseer had arrived in New Iberia from Angola Plantation and had told her Colonel Jamison was in New Orleans, badly wounded, asking for her, she could hardly deal with the strange and conflicting emotions that assailed her heart.

She remembered when she had seen him for the first time as a little girl, dressed in skintight white breeches and a blue velvet jacket, his hair flowing behind him as he galloped his horse across a field of alfalfa and jumped a fence like a creature with invisible wings. A teenage boy picking cotton in the row next to hers had said, "He ride that hoss just like he rode yo' mama, Flower."

The boy's mother had slapped him on the ear.

Flower did not understand what the boy had meant or why his mother had been provoked to such a level of anger, which to Flower, even as a child, was always an indicator of fear.

She saw Marse Jamison again, on a Christmas Day, when her grandmother brought her to work with her in the big house. Flower had peeked out from the kitchen and had seen him talking with other men by the fireplace, the whiskey in his glass bright against the flames. When he saw her watching him, he winked and picked up a piece of hard candy from a crystal plate and gave it to her.

In that moment she believed she was in the presence of the most important man in the world.

She did not see him again for fifteen years.

Then, on what might become his deathbed, he had asked for her. She felt herself forgiving him for sins that he had neither acknowledged nor had asked forgiveness for, and she wondered if she were driven less by charity than by weakness and personal need. But people were what they did, she told herself, not what they said or didn't say, but what they did. And Colonel Ira Jamison had sent for his daughter.

Now she enclosed him in mosquito-netting at night and sponge-bathed him and changed his bandages and brought his food from the hospital kitchen on a cloth-covered tray. He was melancholy and remote, but always grateful for her attentions, and there were moments when his hand lingered on hers and his eyes seemed to turn inward and view a scene she could hardly imagine, a field churning with smoke and terrified horses or a surgeon's tent where human limbs were piled like spoiled pork.

He read until late at night and slept with the flame turned low in the lamp. On one occasion, when the oil had burned out, she found him sitting on the side of the bed, his bare feet in a pool of moonlight, his face disjointed with his own thoughts.

"The war won't let you sleep, Colonel Jamison?" she asked him.

"The laudanum makes you have strange dreams, that's all," he replied.

"It ain't good to take it if you don't need it no more," she said.

"I suspect your wisdom may be greater than mine, Flower," he said, and looked at her fondly.

But tonight when she reported to the hospital he was not reading either the Bible or one of the several novels he kept on his nightstand. Instead, he sat propped up on pillows with a big ledger book spread open on his knees. The pages were lined with the first names of people — Jim, Patsy, Spring, Cleo, Tuff, Clotile, Jeff, Batist — and beside each name was a birthdate.

As he turned the pages and read the lists of names, which must have numbered almost two hundred, he moved his lips silently and seemed to count with his fingers. He extinguished the lamp and went to sleep with the ledger book under his pillow.

In the morning a new sentry was on duty at the entrance to the ward. His cheeks were pink, his hair so blond it was almost white. He straightened as she walked by, clearing his throat, a hesitant grin at the corner of his mouth.

" 'Member me?" he said.

"No," she said.

"Sitting on the porch at that house on Congo Square? Place I probably didn't have no business?" he said.

"Oh yes, how do you do?" she said.

He shifted his hands on his rifle barrel and looked past her out the window, his eyes full of light, thinking about his response but finding no words that he felt would be very interesting to anyone else.

"I'm on our regimental rounders team. We're gonna play some Vermont boys soon as I get off duty," he said.

"Rounders?"

"It's a game you play with a ball and a bat. You run around bases. That's how come it's called 'rounders.'" He grinned at her.

"It's nice seeing you," she said.

"Ma'am, I didn't go in that place last night," he said hurriedly, before she could walk away.

"I know you didn't," she said.

He had just called her "ma'am," something no white person had ever done. She looked back over her shoulder at him. He was twirling his kepi on the point of his fixed bayonet, like a child intrigued with a top.

That night, when she returned to the hospital, Ira Jamison was in an ebullient mood, one she did not understand in a dying man. He had two visitors, men with coarse skin and uncut hair, with a lascivious look in their eyes and the smell of horses in their clothes. They pushed the screens around the bed and lowered their voices, but she heard one man laugh softly and say, "Ain't no problem, Kunnel. We'll move the whole bunch up into Arkansas, safe and sound, ready to fetch when the shooting is over."

After they were gone she brought Ira Jamison hot tea and a piece of toast with jam. The ledger book with the lists of names was on the nightstand. On top of it was a page of stationery that Jamison had been writing on. Her eyes slipped across the salutation and the words in the first paragraph as she propped up the tray on Jamison's lap.

"Who was them men, Colonel?" she said.

"Some fellows who do work for me from time to time."

"They got dirty eyes," she replied.

He looked at her curiously.

"I could have sworn you were reading the letter I was writing to a friend," he said.

"How could I do that, suh?"

"I don't know, but you're no ordinary —"

"Ordinary what?"

"No ordinary girl. Neither was your mother."

"I ain't a girl no more, Colonel."

She picked up his soiled bedclothes from the floor and carried them to the laundry.

During the night, out in the foyer where she kept a cot, she overheard a Union physician talking to one of the nurses.

"You say he's mighty cheerful? By God, he should be. I thought sure we'd be dropping him into a hole, but his specimen has been clear two days now. The colonel will probably be back abusing his darkies in no time. I guess if I ever wanted to see a nonsuccess in the treatment of a patient, my vote would be for this fellow."

Flower sat up on her cot, her body still warm from sleep. The ward was dimly lit by oil lamps at each end, the air heavy with the smell of medicine and bandages and the sounds of snoring and night dreams. She walked softly between the rows of beds to the screened enclosure where Jamison slept, unable to think through the words she had just heard. She stood over his bed and looked down at the mound of his hip under the sheet and the pale smoothness of his exposed shoulder.

His face was turned into the shadows, but even in sleep he was a handsome man, his body firm, without fat, his skin clear and unwrinkled, his mouth tender, almost like a girl's.

Had he known his life was out of danger and not bothered to tell her? Was he that indifferent about the affections and loyalties of others?

She had other questions, too. What about the visitors whose clothes smelled of horse sweat and whose eyes moved up and down her body? Why had the colonel been reading from a ledger book that contained the names of all his slaves?

He had completed the letter he had been

writing and had stuck it inside the cover of the ledger book and had slipped the book under his pillow. She eased the sheets of paper out of the book and unfolded them in the light that was breaking through the window. Each line of his flowing calligraphy was perfectly linear, each letter precise, without swirls or any attempt at grandiosity. She began reading, moving her lips silently, tilting the page into the grayness of the dawn.

Dear Colonel Forrest,
I have good news from the Union surgeon and am on my way to a fine recovery. However, I am still haunted by the destruction of the 18th Louisiana Regiment at Shiloh and the fact the Orleans Guards, partially under my command, were not there on their flank when they advanced so bravely into Yankee artillery.

But conscience and honor require me to state I also have a practical concern. I plan to enter politics once the war is over. Because my name will be associated in a causal fashion, fairly or unfairly, with the tragedy of the 18th Louisiana, I think accepting a parole will not contribute to my chances of gaining high office. Neither do I relish the prospect of eating dried peas in a Yankee prison camp. I'm also quite sick of being tended by unwashed niggers in a Yankee hospital that stinks of urine —

She heard a Catholic sister pass on the other side of the screen and she refolded the letter and replaced it inside the ledger book.

Jamison woke and stared straight up into her face. For the first time she noticed that one of his eyes was smaller than the other, liquid, with a bead in it, like a glimmering, narrow conduit into a part of his mind he shared with no one.

"What are you doing?" he asked.

"What you brung me here for. To tend you. To carry out your slop jar, to fetch your food, to wash the sweat off your skin, to listen to your grief. That's why you brung me, ain't you, suh?"

He propped himself up on one elbow and looked at her with a new and cautionary awareness.

On her way out the door to catch the public car back to Basin Street, she saw Abigail Dowling sitting on a stone bench under a live oak tree, next to a double-amputee who was sleeping in a wheelchair, his head on his chest, the bandaged stubs of his legs sticking out into space.

"Could I sit down, ma'am?" she said.

"You don't have to ask," Abigail replied.

"What do the word 'par-old' mean?"

"Say it again."

"Par-old. Like something somebody don't want."

"You mean 'parole'? P-a-r-o-l-e?"

"That's it."

"Prisoners of war are exchanged sometimes so they don't have to go to a jail or a prison camp. Or sometimes they sign an oath of allegiance and just go back home. But you say there's somebody who doesn't want a parole?"

Flower watched the ice wagon turn off St. Charles and enter the hospital driveway. The driver stopped and chatted with a Creole woman who was cutting flowers and laying them delicately in a straw basket. Vapor rose from the tarp covering the sawed blocks of ice that had been brought in ships all the way from New England, and were now melting and running off the tailgate of a dray on a dappled, pea-gravel driveway lined with pink and gray caladium. Blue-streaked, white-crusted blocks of ice carefully packed in sawdust that could refrigerate medicines and numb the pain in suffering men, now melting needlessly because a man and a lady wanted to exchange pleasantries in a floral garden in New Orleans, Louisiana.

She felt her breath catch in her throat.

"Are you all right, Flower?" Abigail asked.

"I can read. I can write some, too. Nobody know it, though, except Willie Burke, 'cause he taught me."

"What is it you're trying to tell me?"

Flower loosened the drawstring on the

168

cloth bag she carried and removed the dictionary given her by Willie Burke. She flipped the pages to the P's and ran her finger down a page until she located the word her mind had unclearly formed and associated with an idea and an image which now seemed inextricably linked.

" 'Possession,' " she said.

"Pardon?" Abigail said.

"Colonel Jamison got one eye smaller than the other. It got a wet blue gleam in it. I didn't know what that look meant. It's possession, Miss Abigail. It's the control he got over other people that keeps him alive. Not love for no family, no cause, no little nigger baby who was found almost froze to death in a woods."

Abigail put her arm around her shoulders and squeezed her.

"I'll always be your friend," she said.

But Flower rose from her grasp and walked quickly to the street, her face obscured in the shadows, her back shaking.

After she returned to the hospital that evening, the sky turned black and the wind began to blow hard out of the south. She could hear rain hitting on the window glass and the open shutters vibrating against the latches that moored them to the bricks. When she looked out the window she saw leaves whipping in circles and the highest limbs in the oak trees thrashing against the sky and spiderwebs of lightning bursting inside the clouds.

"Sounds like cannons popping out there, don't it?" the young sentry said. He sat in a chair by the end of the ward, near the foyer where she kept her cot. His rifle was propped between his legs.

"Have you been in the war?" she asked.

"The Rebs potshot at us out on the river. They floated burning rafts past us so they could see us on the far bank. But they didn't hit nobody."

When she made no reply, he added, "I hear we're going up to Baton Rouge and kick their behinds. I'm ready for it."

"You be careful," she said.

"I ain't afraid."

"I know you're not," she said.

He pulled a cigar box from under his chair and shook it.

"You want to play checkers?" he asked.

"You ain't s'pposed to be sitting down."

"The lieutenant's a good fellow. Bet you don't know how."

She went to the kitchen and began washing Colonel Jamison's supper dishes. His food and drink were never served on the same dishware or in the same glasses or cups used by the other patients. His own china, along with his reading matter, personal stationery, nightgown, underwear and socks, even a tailored gray Confederate uniform, had all been brought to him by an Angola Plantation overseer, with permission, through Union lines. Flower dried each dish and cup and fork and knife with a soft cloth and placed them inside a big tin breadbox painted with flowers and set the breadbox inside a cabinet. She glanced outside and saw a closed carriage roll by under the trees, a driver in a black slouch hat and slicker backlit against the flicker of lightning through the canopy.

She looked in on Colonel Jamison, who was sleeping with a pillow over his head, perhaps to muffle the boom of thunder outside. She wondered if he dreamed of the boys who had died under his command or if in his sleep he relived only his own fear and wounding on the battlefield. She glanced at the three pistol balls lying in a saucer on his nightstand and knew the answer to her own question.

When she walked back to the foyer the sentry was looking out the window at the leaves blowing against the glass and the white flicker of electricity through the tops of the trees. He had left his rifle at his post, the bayonet-tipped barrel propped tautly against the wall.

"I was kidding you about not knowing how to play checkers. I saw you reading a book back there in the foyer. That puts you one up on me," he said.

"You cain't read?"

"Folks in my family is still working on making their X." He grinned and looked at his feet.

"I can teach you how," she said.

He grinned again. His eyes went away from her, then came back. "You gonna play checkers with me?" he asked.

"I wouldn't mind," she replied.

He placed two chairs at a small table by the window and removed a folded cloth painted with checker squares from his cigar box and flattened the cloth on the table. The checker pieces were carved from wood and looked like big buttons, domed on the top and painted green or red. He lined them up on the cloth squares and glanced out the window just as lightning popped in a yard on the opposite side of the street.

"Wonder what that carriage is doing out there?" he said.

"It's the hearse. They take the bodies out the back door," she replied.

There was a disjointed expression in his face.

"A hearse?" he said.

"They don't want the other patients to see the bodies. There's a room behind the kitchen where they take the ones who are gonna die."

He looked emptily down the long rows of beds in the ward and at the rectangular shadows they cast.

"I bet most of the dead is probably Rebs who got gangrene 'cause their people didn't look out for them," he said.

"Probably," she said, avoiding his eyes.

He glanced out the window again, then shook a thought out of his face and pushed a checker piece forward with his index finger.

"Your move. I ain't showing no mercy, either," he said.

Later, after she had looked in on the colonel for the final time that evening, she pulled the blanket across the length of clothesline she had strung by her cot and lay down and closed her eyes. In her sleep she heard the rain hitting hard on the window glass and she dreamed of birds flying from their cages, flapping their wings loudly in their newfound freedom.

Sometime after midnight she heard a door open and felt a draft course through the corridors and swell against the walls and ceiling. Then in the coldness of the moment she heard the heavy sound of men's boots on the floor and smelled rainwater and horses and an odor like old clothes moldy with damp.

She pulled the sheet over her head and drew her knees up toward her chest and fell deeper into the dream of birds thropping through the sky, high above the hunters whose guns fired impotently into the air.

But the dream would not hold. A scorched odor, like dry oak pitched on a flame, made her open her eyes. The thunder had stopped and in its vacuum she heard wind and leaves scraping on stone and a door fluttering on its hinges, then the wet, crunching sound of horses' hooves and iron-rimmed carriage wheels sinking in pea gravel.

She rose from her cot and drew aside the blanket that hung from the clothesline stretched across her nook. It was still dark outside and clouds of ground fog rolled and puffed between the palms and live oak trunks. She stepped into the hallway that fed into the ward and saw her friend, the sentry, still seated in his chair, his back to her, his chin on his chest. His rifle was propped against the table they had played checkers on. A brass lamp was knocked askew on the wall above his head, oil oozing from the slit through which the wick extended, igniting in the flame, dripping to the floor like a string of melted gold coins.

The sentry's kepi lay crown-down on the table.

Oh, Lordy, they gonna shoot you for sleeping on guard duty, she said to herself.

But even as she heard the words inside her, she knew they were a deception. She stepped into what should have been the periphery of his vision and saw the paleness in his cheeks and the dark area, like a child's bib, under his chin. A barber's razor with a pearl handle lay in a circle of blood at his feet.

At the end of the ward the screens had been moved aside from the colonel's bed. The sheet he had slept under trailed on the floor like a handkerchief half-pulled from a man's pocket. She ran toward the kitchen to find the night nurse, the Confederate amputees propping themselves up at the sound of feet. The brass lamp still burned on the colonel's nightstand. She glanced at the saucer where he had kept the three .36 caliber pistol balls that had been removed from his body, hoping that perhaps in some way what she had always known about him and denied, namely, that first and last and foremost he thought of no one except himself and his own possessions, was not true.

The saucer was bare, his overturned slop jar running on the floor.

Chapter Ten

Lieutenant Robert Perry had always slept
without dreaming, or at least without
dreaming of events or places or people he remembered in daylight. The world was a fine
place, filled with birdsong and the smell of
horses and wood smoke at dawn and fish
spawning in swamps where the sunlight
glowed like a green lantern inside the cypress. In fact, in the quietness of the dawn
and the faint pinkness spreading across the
cane fields and the cabins of the slaves and
the horses blowing in the pasture, Robert
sometimes believed he was witness to the
quiet hush of God's breath upon the world.

Now sleep came to him fitfully and took
him to places to which he did not want to
return. The geographical designations —
Manassas Junction, Winchester, Front Royal,
Cross Keys — were names that never appeared in the dreams. His nocturnal recollec-
tion of these places came to him only in

images and sounds: a night picket cocking back the hammer on a rifle, a man calling for water, another caught inside a burning woods, a stretcher bearer sitting on the lip of a crater in the middle of a railroad track, holding his ears, screaming, kicking his feet.

When Robert would finally fall into a deep slumber before dawn, he would awake suddenly to the whistling sound of a shell arcing out of its trajectory, then discover the world outside his tent was silent, except perhaps for a cook rattling pans in the back of a wagon. He would lie with his arm across his eyes, his palm resting on the coolness of his revolver, breathing slowly, reciting his morning prayers, waiting for his mind to empty of dreams he told himself had no application in the waking day.

The previous evening he had received a letter from Abigail Dowling, one that perplexed him and also saddened his heart, because even though he had already learned of Jim Stubbefield's death, he had not accepted it, each morning waking with the notion Jim was still alive, in the Western campaign with the 18th Louisiana, the youthful confidence on his face undisturbed by either war or mortality. In Robert's haversack was a *carte de visite*, taken by a photographer at Camp Pratt, showing Willie, Robert and Jim together for the last time, Jim standing while they sat, a hand on each of their shoulders, a gentle scarecrow posed between two smiling friends.

God fashions the pranksters to keep the rest of us honest, Jim. Wasn't right of you to die on us, old pal, he thought, almost resentfully.

But the other portions of Abigail's letter disturbed him as well, although with certainty he could not say why. He sat on a Quaker gun, in front of a cook fire, in the cool, smoky dawn above the Shenandoah Valley, and unfolded her letter and read it again.

Dear Robert,
I saw your father and he said you know of Jim's death at Shiloh. I just wanted to tell you how sorry I am at the loss of your friend. Also I need to confide some thoughts of my own to you about the war and what I perceive as a great evil that has fallen upon the land. Please forgive me in advance if my words are hurtful in any way.

I helped prepare the body of a young Union soldier who had been guarding Confederate amputees in the hospital where I have been working in New Orleans. His throat had been cut by men in the employ of Colonel Ira Jamison. Colonel Jamison was offered a parole, but evidently for reasons of political gain he refused it and had a boy of seventeen murdered in order to establish himself as an escaped prisoner of war. I believe this man to be the most despicable human being I have ever met.

I witnessed the hanging of a gambler whose only crime was to possess a piece of a ripped Union flag. The execution was ordered by none other than General Butler himself, supposedly with the approval of President Lincoln. I would like to believe the deaths of the gambler and the young soldier were simply part of war's tragedy. But I would be entertaining a deception. Colonel Jamison and General Butler are emblematic of the arrogance of power. Their cruelty speaks for itself. The young sentry, the gambler, and Jim Stubbefield are their victims. I think there will be others.

Please write and tell me of your health and situation. Day and night you are in my thoughts and my prayers.

Affectionately,
Your friend,
Abigail

The Quaker gun he sat on was a huge log lopped free of branches that had been dragged into the earthworks and positioned to look like a cannon. Robert looked into the cook fire, then across an open field at timbered hills, where, if he listened carefully, he would hear axes chopping into wood, trees crashing among themselves, blue-clad men wheeling light artillery through the under-brush. The wind blew inside the earthworks and the pages of Abigail's letter fluttered in his hands.

"You think we're going across?" he asked a lieutenant sitting next to him.

The man was named Alcibiades DeBlanc. He was heavily bearded and was smoking a long-stem pipe, one leg crossed on his knee. When he removed the pipe from his mouth his cheeks were hollow and his mouth made a puckered button.

"Perhaps," he said.

Robert stood and looked across the field again. There were two round green hills next to each other in the distance, a stream that fed between them and woods on each side of a dammed pond at the bottom of the stream. A Union officer rode out of the trees and cantered his horse up and down the edge of the field. Robert thought he saw sunlight glint on brass or steel inside the trees.

"What troubles you? Not the Yanks, huh?" Alcibiades asked.

Robert handed him Abigail's letter to read. The earthworks were stark, constructed from huge baskets that had been braided together out of sticks and packed solidly with dirt and mud and rocks. Logs supported by field stones were laid out horizontally against the walls of the rifle pits so sharpshooters could stand on them and fire across the field. Alcibiades finished reading the letter and re-folded it and handed it back to Robert.

"She wants to marry you," he said.

"It's that simple?" Robert said.

Across the field a shell exploded in a black puff of torn cotton high above the mounted officer's head. But the officer was unper-turbed and wheeled his horse about and can-tered it along the rim of the woods, where men in blue were forming a skirmish line be-hind the tree trunks.

"I don't know how many times we have to whip them to make them understand they're whipped," Alcibiades said.

"You didn't answer my question," Robert said.

"She loves you dearly, no doubt about it, and she'll marry you the day you turn your slaves loose and denounce all this out here," his friend said, waving his hand at the churned field, the horses that lay bloated and stiff in the irrigation ditches, the dead sol-diers who'd had their pockets pulled inside out and their shoes stripped from their feet.

Robert put away Abigail's letter and stared at the shells bursting over the hills in the dis-tance. Ten minutes later he advanced with the others in a long gray and butternut line through the whine of minié balls and the tra-jectory scream of a Yankee mortar Southerners called Whistling Dick. On either side of him he could hear bullets and canister and case shot thudding into the bodies of friends with whom he had eaten breakfast only a short time ago.

The hills in the distance reminded him of a woman's breasts. That fact made him clench his hands on the stock of his carbine with a degree of visceral anger he did not understand.

Jean-Jacques LaRose loved clipper ships, playing the piano, fistfighting in saloons, and the world of commerce. He thought politics was a confidence game, created to fool those gullible enough to trust their money and well-being to others. The notion of an egalitarian society and seeking justice in the courts was another fool's venture. The real equalizer in the world was money.

Early on he knew he had a knack for business and how to recognize cupidity in others and how to use it to drive them against the wall. In business Scavenger Jack took no prisoners. Money gave him power, and with power he could flaunt his illiteracy and whorehouse manners and stick his bastard birth status in the faces of all those who had sent him around to their back doors when he was a child.

According to the gospel of Jean-Jacques LaRose, anyone who said money was not important was probably working on a plan to take it from you.

He was childish, slovenly, sentimental, a slobbering drunk, a ferocious barroom brawler who could leave a saloon in splinters, true to his word, honest about his debts, at least when he could remember them, and absolutely fearless when it came to running the Union blockade out on the salt.

He also loved the ship he had bought five years before the war from a famous French shipbuilder in the West Indies. It was long and sleek, and was constructed both with boilers and masts and could outdistance most of the Union gunboats that patrolled the mouth of the Mississippi or the entrances to the waterways along the wetlands of Louisiana.

In no time Jean-Jacques discovered that the Secession he had opposed was probably the best stroke of historical luck he could have fallen into. He took cotton out and brought coffee and rum in, with such a regular degree of success two men from the state government and one from the army came to him with a proposal about slipping through the blockade with a cargo of Enfield rifles.

Seems like the patriotic thing to do, Jean-Jacques told himself.

He picked up the rifles in the Berry Islands, west of Nassau. Cockneys who carried knives on their belts worked all night loading the hold, and the ship's captain Jean-Jacques paid in gold coin was an evil-smelling man who had a rouged West Indian boy in his cabin. But at false dawn Jean-Jacques' visitors were gone. The sails popped with a fresh breeze, and as the tide lifted him over the sandbar at the entrance to the cove where he had anchored, the waves were green and the coconuts floating inside them thudded against the solidness of the hull and the gulls hung on the breeze above his wake like a testament to his good fortune. It was going to be a splendid day, he told himself.

At noon he passed over reefs of fire coral, through small islands that swarmed with land crabs, and saw the steel-gray backs of porpoises arcing out of the water and stingrays and jellyfish toppling from the waves that slid against his bow. The air was hot and close and smelled like brass, like hurricane weather, but the sky was clear, the water lime-green with hot blue patches in it like floating clouds of India ink. He saw a ship briefly on the southern horizon, one with stacks and black smoke trailing off its stern, but the ship disappeared and he gave it no more thought.

Not until he was south of Dry Tortugas, in no more than fifteen feet of water, when the wind dropped, his sails went slack, and a Parrott gun at Fort Jefferson lobbed a round forty yards off his bow.

His boilers were cold. Jean-Jacques ran up a Spanish flag. Another round arced out of its trajectory, this one a fused shell that exploded in a dirty scorch overhead and showered his deck with strips of hot metal.

Then he felt the wind at his back, like the collective breath of angels. The sails on his masts filled and soon Fort Jefferson and the Straits of Florida were just a bad memory.

He sailed on a westerly course far south of New Orleans to avoid the noose the Yankee navy had placed around the city, then turned north, toward Cote Blanche Bay, leaving the murky green pitch and roll of the Gulf, entering the alluvial fan of the Mississippi that flowed westward like a river of silt.

He waited for nightfall to go in. But even though the moon was down, the sky flickered with heat lightning, and at three in the morning two Yankee ships opened up on him, at least one of them using cast-iron cannonballs, hooked together with chain, that spun like a windmill and could cut a deckhand in half.

The twin paddle-wheels on his port and starboard were churning full-out, the boilers red-hot, one mast down on the deck, the sails ripped into shreds. Lightning rippled across the sky and in the distance he saw the low, black-green silhouette of the Louisiana coastline. But he knew he would not reach it. Grapeshot that was still glowing rained across the entirety of the ship, fizzing when it hit the bilge down below, blowing the windows out of his cabin, setting fires all over the deck. Then a Confederate shore battery boomed in the darkness and he saw a shell spark across the sky and light up a Yankee gunboat as though a flare had burst inside its rigging.

As if obeying a prearranged understanding, all the firing ceased and Marsh Island slid by on his port side and he sailed into the quiet waters of Cote Blanche Bay at low tide, scraping across a sandbar, drifting into the smell of schooled-up shrimp and flooded saw grass and sour mud and huge garfish that had died in hoop nets and floated swollen and ratchet-jawed to the surface.

He believed it was the most lovely nocturnal scene he had ever set his eyes on. He breathed the night air into his lungs, uncorked a wine bottle and, with the bottle upended, drank most of it in one long, chugging swallow, until he lost his balance and fell backward over a shattered spar. One by one, his four crew members found him, all of them still scared to death, none of them seriously hurt. They threw roped buckets overboard and drenched the fires on deck, then drank a case of wine and went to sleep on the piles of canvas that had fallen from the masts.

The next day Jean-Jacques discovered his

real problems had just begun.

Two dozen mule-drawn wagons and twice that many blacks and Confederate enlisted men arrived in a forest of persimmon, pecan, and live oak trees to take possession of the Enfield rifles. The floor of the forest was dotted with palmettos, the air hazy and golden with dust. The officer in charge of the transfer was Captain Rufus Atkins.

"I thought you was off fighting Yankees," Jean-Jacques said.

"Currently on leave from the 18th Lou'sana," Atkins said.

It was warm inside the trees. The wind had died and the bay looked like a sheet of tin. Atkins wiped his face with a handkerchief.

"We need to settle up," Jean-Jacques said.

"This is Mr. Guilbeau. Assistant to the gov'nor. He'll make everything right for you, Jack," Atkins said.

"I don't use that name. My name is Jean-Jacques, me."

"Sorry, I thought your friends called you otherwise," Atkins said.

The man named Guilbeau was tall and had a long face, like a horse's, and a narrow frame and a stomach that protruded in a lop-sided fashion, like a person whose liver has calcified. He dropped the tailgate on a wagon and set a crimson carpetbag on it that was woven with a floral design. He unsnapped the wood latches on the bag, then lifted a gold

187

watch from his vest pocket and clicked it open and looked at the time.

Jean-Jacques stuck his hand inside the bag and picked up a sheaf of bills that was tied with string.

"Script?" he said.

"It's the currency of your country, sir," Guilbeau said.

"Wipe your ass wit' it," Jean-Jacques said.

Guilbeau hooked his little finger in his ear, then examined the tip of it.

"Would you prefer a promissory note?" he asked.

"I paid gold for them guns."

"Sorry you feel so badly used. Maybe you can share your complaint with some of our boys who had to fight with flintlocks at Shiloh," Guilbeau said.

"I seen you befo'. Wit' Ira Jamison," Jean-Jacques said.

Guilbeau put a twist of chewing tobacco in his mouth and chewed it thoughtfully in one jaw. He spit in the leaves at his feet and lifted the carpetbag from the tailgate of the wagon and walked it down to the bank and dropped it in the rowboat in which Jean-Jacques had come ashore.

Jean-Jacques watched the black men load the cases of Enfields into the wagons. Most of them were barefoot, their clothes in tatters, sweat sliding down their faces in the heated enclosure of the trees. His own men were hung over and sick, sleeping under a shade tree on the bank. He no longer felt like a ship's captain but instead like an object of contempt who stands by impotently while thieves sack his house. He opened and closed his hands and bit down on his lip, but continued to do nothing while the black men crunched back and forth in the leaves and flung the British rifles heavily into the wagons, case upon case, latching up the tailgates now, the armed enlisted men in the wagon boxes lifting the reins off the mules' backs.

"Ain't right what y'all doing," Jean-Jacques said.

"We'll be mixing it up with the blue-bellies soon. You're welcome to join us. Be a lot of opportunities if this war comes out right," Atkins said.

"Ira Jamison got his thumb in this," Jean-Jacques said.

"That's about like saying there's crawfish in Lou'sana, Jack," Atkins said.

"Tell him the man who steals from me don't just walk away, no."

"My regards to your sister. She's an exceptional woman. Two thirds of the soldiers at Camp Pratt can't be wrong," Atkins said.

He mounted his horse and rode to the head of the wagon train. Jean-Jacques watched as the wagons creaked over the live oak roots, snapping pecan husks under the iron rims of the wheels, the sun-heated dust floating back into his face.

Saturday afternoon he rode his horse to the brick saloon next to his sister's brothel and stood at the bar and ordered a whiskey. The bartender served him without speaking, and others returned his greeting obliquely, an obstruction in their throats, their eyes not meeting his.

A bearded man with a pinned-up sleeve, his arm taken at Manassas Junction, looked him boldly in the face, then tossed his cigar hissing into a spittoon six inches from Jean-Jacques' shoe.

"I'm glad you got a good aim, you," Jean-Jacques said.

But the ex-soldier studied the brown spots on the back of his hand and took no pleasure in Jean-Jacques' sense of humor.

A cotton trader from up on the Red River, whom he had known for years, was sitting at a table behind him, one corner of the opened newspaper he was reading held down with a beer glass to stop it from fluttering in the breeze that blew through the door.

"Pretty damn hot today, huh?" Jean-Jacques said.

"Why, yes it is," the man said, leaning forward in his chair, his eyes focusing outside.

Jean-Jacques picked up his whiskey and approached the cotton trader, but the cotton trader rose from the table, gathering up his hat hurriedly, and went out the door. Jean-Jacques stared after him, then looked about for an explanation. Every back in the saloon was turned to him.

He looked down at the opened newspaper and tried to make sense out of the headlines. But the only words he recognized on the page were those of his own name, in the first paragraph of an article that might as well have been written in Chinese.

He ripped the page from the newspaper and stuffed it in his pocket, then walked out of the coolness of the building into the late afternoon heat and angrily swung up on his horse. Inside the bar the customers were talking among themselves again, buying drinks for one another, their cigars glowing inside the dim bourbon-scented darkness of the Saturday afternoon haunt he had always taken for granted.

He rode to the cabin he owned on the bayou south of town, among a grove of cypress trees that stood on high ground above the floodline. He kept a pirogue there and fishnets and cane poles, a worktable where he carved duck decoys for his hunting blind, a pantry full of preserves and smoked fish and beef and corked bottles of wine and rum. Red and yellow four-o'clocks bloomed in the shade and bamboo and elephant ears grew along the water's edge. It was a place that had always made him happy and secure in his feelings about the world and himself when no other place did, but today, in spite of the gold-green evening light and the wind blowing through the trees, a pall like a black film seemed to descend on his soul.

He snicked away at a mallard duck he was carving from a block of cypress wood, then felt the knife slip with his inattention and slice across the edge of his finger.

He crimped his finger in the cone of his right hand and went outside to fill a bucket with rainwater from the cistern. Next door the slave girl named Flower, who worked at the laundry not far from his sister's brothel, was buying carp off a flat-bottomed boat piled with blue-point crabs and yellow catfish that looked like mud-slick logs.

"You hurt yourself, Mr. Jean?" she asked, setting down her basket and taking his hand.

"I passed my hand under the knife and it cut me," he said, dumbly, looking down from his height at the top of her head.

"Here, I'm gonna wash it out, then put some cobweb on it. You got some clean cloth we can tie it up with?" she said.

"No, I ain't got nothing like that," he said.

She went to the buggy she had driven to the bayou and removed a clean napkin from a basket of bread rolls and came back, shaking it out.

"Here, we're gonna get you fixed up. You

gonna see," she said.

She went inside the cabin with him and washed and dressed his hand. It felt strange having a black woman care for him, touching and examining his skin, turning his wrist over in her fingers, when he had not asked help of her and when she was not obligated to offer any.

"Why you came back from New Orleans, you?" he said.

"This is where I live," she replied.

"You could have been free."

"My family ain't . . . it isn't free. They're still up at Angola."

She held his hand tightly and when she pulled the bandage knot tight with her teeth he felt a reaction in his loins that made him glance away from her face. She put his hand down and made ready to go.

"Why you look so sad, Mr. Jean?" she asked.

"I was in the saloon. People treated me like I done somet'ing wrong. Maybe I was drunk in there and I done somet'ing I don't remember."

"Sometime people are just that way, Mr. Jean. It don't mean . . . it doesn't mean you done anything wrong."

He was seated in a chair by the window. He looked out on the bayou at a white man in a pirogue raking moss from the tree limbs that the man would later sell for stuffing in mattresses. Jean-Jacques remembered the crumpled newspaper page from his pants pocket and smoothed it on the tabletop. His finger moved down a column of print and stopped.

"My name's right there. See? But I don't know why, me. Maybe they're writing in there about my ship getting shot up, huh?" he said.

She walked around behind him and peered over his shoulder. He could smell the red hibiscus she wore in her hair and a clean, crisp odor in her clothes. Her breastline rose and fell on the corner of his vision.

"You a good man, Mr. Jean. You always been good to people of color. You ain't got to . . . I mean, you don't have to pay attention to what somebody write in a paper about you," she said.

"You can read that?" he said, turning in his chair, his finger still spear-pointed in the middle of the article.

"I reckon," she said.

He stared at her stupidly. Then his eyes blinked.

"What it say?" he asked.

" 'Unlike Colonel Jamison, who risked his life to escape from a prison hospital, a local gentleman by the name of Jean-Jacques LaRose tried to extract gold from our treasury in payment for rifles that should have been donated to our soldiers. This man's greed should sicken every patriot.' "

Jean-Jacques looked at the man harvesting moss from the tree limbs that extended over the bayou. The man was white-haired and old, his clothes mended in many places, and he was struggling to free his rake from where it had become entangled in the branches over his head. If the man was lucky, he would make perhaps a half-dollar's wage for his day's work.

"Men who work for Ira Jamison cheated me. They give me script for guns I bought with gold. Then they made me out a traitor," Jean-Jacques said.

It was quiet a long time inside the cabin. Flower's weight shifted on the floor boards.

"Mr. Jean, Colonel Jamison is moving all his slaves up into Arkansas. A whole bunch is already gone. Maybe they never gonna be free," Flower said.

"What you saying?"

"Miss Abigail is looking to hire a boat."

He looked sharply into her face. "Boat for what?" he asked.

"I ain't . . . I haven't said."

"My ship was raked with grape out on the salt. I got one mast down and holes in the boiler." He looked thoughtfully out the window. The old man was gone and the bayou was empty, wrinkled now with wind and sunlight.

"I see," she said.

195

"But I got another one, me. Tied up in a backwater, just outside Baton Rouge," he said.

Sergeant Willie Burke stood on a promontory above the Mississippi River and looked down at the gathering dusk in the trees on the far shore. The late sun was molten and red in the west, and down below he could see dark shapes, like the backs of terrapins, floating in the water, oscillating slowly, sliding off logs that had snagged in jams on sandbars. Except they were not terrapins. They were men, and their blue blouses were puffed with air, their wooly hair bejeweled with drops of water, their wounds pecked clean and bloodless by carrion birds that perched on their heads or necks or the pockets of air in their uniforms.

They had been members of the Louisiana Native Guards, originally a regiment of free black men in the service of the Confederacy. After the fall of New Orleans, they had been reorganized by the Federals into the 1st Louisiana Infantry and assigned to guard the railway leading into New Orleans.

There were stories about captured Negro soldiers who were being sold into slavery, and also rumors about Negro soldiers who had not been allowed to surrender. Willie wondered if those floating down had died under a black flag, one that meant no quarter.

Clay Hatcher and another man just like him, rodent-eyed, despised inside the womb, went out each night by themselves and did not tell others of what they did. But at dawn, when they returned to camp, there was a sated gleam in their eyes, a shared knowledge between them, like pride in an erotic conquest.

Hatcher had used a nail file to saw sixteen narrow indentations along the stock of the scoped Springfield that he kept cleaned and oiled in the way a watchmaker cleans and oils the delicate mechanisms inside a fine clock. Hatcher had also taken to wearing a woman's garter high up on his right shirtsleeve, the purpose of which, he claimed, was to keep his forearm and wrist unencumbered when crawling up on a target.

Each day or night a story passed on the river and Willie wondered why those who wrote about war concentrated on battles and seldom studied the edges of grand events and the detritus that wars created: livestock with their throats slit, the swollen carcasses of horses gutshot by grape or canister, a burning houseboat spinning around a bend at night, with no one aboard, the flames singeing the leaves in the gum trees along the bank, a naked lunatic drifting by on a raft, a cowbell hanging from his throat, a Bible open in his hand, yelling a sermon at the soldiers on the shore, a pimp from Baton Rouge trying to put in to shore with a boatload of whores.

But who was he to reflect upon the infinite manifestations of human insanity, he asked himself. The hardness of his body, his sun-browned skin, the sergeant's stripes that were already becoming sun-bleached on his sleeve, were all a new and strange way of looking at himself, but in truth he didn't know if he had grown into the person he had always been or if a cynical and insentient stranger lived inside him.

He no longer questioned the authority or wisdom of those who had power over his life, no more than he would question the legitimacy of the weather in the morning or the rising and setting of the sun. He also kept his own counsel and did not express his disapproval of others, even when they committed cruel or atrocious acts. The ebb and flow of armies was not his to judge anymore. Years from now the great issues of the war would be forgotten and the consequences of his actions would have importance only to himself. He was determined he would never be ashamed of them, and that simple goal seemed to be honor enough.

He could not believe that to some degree he had probably earned a footnote in history by having scouted for Nathan Forrest at the battle of Shiloh. But if someone were to ask him of his impressions about the colonel, he would reply he recalled little about him, other than the fact he was a coarse-skinned, profane man who bathed in horse tanks and put enough string tobacco in his mouth to clog a cannon, and if Willie saw him amid a gathering of grocery clerks, he would probably not recognize him nor wish to do so.

He watched the cooks butcher a flock of chickens they had taken from the farm of a widow downstream. She had refused the Confederate script a major had tried to give her and had pleaded in French for him not to take her poultry, that they were her only source of eggs for a sickly grandchild. When the major took his brass trainman's watch from his pocket and hung it across her palm, she swung it by the chain and smashed it on a stump.

Willie stared down from the promontory at the body of a dead Negro soldier caught on a snag, the current eddying around the crown of his head, the closed eyes and up-turned face like a carved deathmask superimposed on the water's surface. Downstream a flat-bottomed boat was headed north, its decks covered with canvas, a Southern flag flying from the stern, its windows filled with the sun's last red glow.

Willie smelled the chickens frying in skillets over a fire. He got his mess kit from his tent and sat on a log with his comrades and waited for the food to be done.

Chapter Eleven

It was sunset on the river now, and Abigail Dowling sat next to Flower Jamison on a rough-hewn bench in the pilothouse of Jean-Jacques LaRose's salvage boat as it moved northward against the current, past a wooded promontory dotted with campfires and the biscuit-colored tents of Confederate soldiers. The river was swollen and dark yellow from the summer rains, and back in the shadows under the overhang the water roiled with gars feeding on dead livestock.

Abigail thought about the work that lay ahead for her that night, and the prospect of it made her throat swallow. She had helped transport escaped slaves out of the wetlands, onto boats that waited for them in salt water, but this was not the same. This time she was going into the heart of enemy country, into a primitive and oftentimes cruel area not tempered by either the mercies of French Catholicism or its libertine and pagan form of

Renaissance humanism. And she was taking others with her.

The conflicts of her conscience seemed endless, like the thinking processes of a neurotic and self-concerned girl incapable of acquiring her own compass, she thought. In moments like these she longed for the presence of her dead father. What was it he had once said about the obligations and restraints of those who fight the good fight of St. Paul? "We will do many things in the service of justice. But shedding blood isn't one of them. The likes of us have a heavy burden, Abby."

In more ways than one, she thought.

The air smelled like sulfur and distant rain and smoke from cypress stumps that had been chain-pulled out of the dirt and set burning while still wet. Abigail looked out the back door of the pilothouse at the riverwater cascading in sheets off the paddlewheel. For a moment she thought she saw a blue-sleeved arm and shoulder roll out of the froth in the boat's wake, then be lapped over and disappear. She rose to her feet and stared at the water's surface, the waves from the boat now sliding into the shore.

"Something wrong, Miss Abigail?" Flower asked.

"No, the light's bad. I imagine things sometimes," she replied.

Jean-Jacques turned from the wheel and looked at her but said nothing. They followed the channel markers through a wide bend in the river and passed lighted plantation homes couched among cedar and oak trees, a half-sunken gunboat whose cannons and boilers had been removed, a slave cemetery whose banks were eroding into the river, cotton acreage that was still under cultivation in spite of the war, and a pine woods that had been sawed into a stump farm. Then the moon broke from behind the clouds and the river loomed up ahead of them, straight as far as the eye could see, immense, rain-dented, tree-lined, wrinkled with wind, blown with leaves and dust out of the fields.

Abigail looked over Jean-Jacques' shoulder at the raindrops striking against the glass.

"You're a problem of conscience for me," she said.

He turned around and squinted his eyes to show his incomprehension.

"I took advantage of your resentment toward Ira Jamison," she said.

"When this is all over, who you t'ink is gonna come out on top?"

"The Union," she replied.

"Remember who hepped you," he said.

But the rum on his breath belied his cavalier attitude. If they were caught, his fate and that of the two white men who fed the boiler belowdecks would not be an easy one. At best they would be sent to a prison where the convicts were literally worked to death.

But chances were they would never make trial and would die on a tree.

Nor would the fate of Flower Jamison be much better. Although Abigail had never witnessed an instance of branding or hamstringing herself, she had heard stories and had known slaves who turned to stone if they were questioned about the scars on their bodies.

But when she tried to imagine her own fate, she realized once again her risks were like those of a rear echelon officer in a war. Slavers might hate her; a bounty hunter could spit on her skirts; and a newspaper editorialist could refer to her as "Miss Lover-of-all-Darkies." But if they didn't respect *her*, they respected money, and they knew her family had been rich, at least at one time, and her father had been the friend of United States presidents from both the North and South and had served at the side of Jefferson Davis in the War of the Mexican Cession. It was doubtful she would ever die on a tree or experience the touch of a hot iron on her back.

Flower was sleeping with her head on her chest, the hat she had woven from palmetto leaves quivering from the vibration of the engines. Her face looked troubled, as though she had walked through a spiderweb in her dreams.

Abigail squeezed her hand.

"You're the bravest person I've ever known," she said.

Flower's eyes opened like the weighted eyelids on a doll.

"Brave about what?" she asked, unsure of where she was.

"We're almost there," Abigail said.

Flower smiled sleepily.

"My gran'mama never thought she could be free. I cain't believe this is happening, Miss Abigail," she said.

The river was blanketed with rain rings now, the moon buried deep in clouds, like a pool of scorched pewter. Jean-Jacques steered his boat past a lighted plantation home on a bluff, then rounded a bend where the land flattened and the river had risen into groves of willow and gum trees and out in a field a trash fire was burning inside the mist, the sparks fanning over the water.

Jean-Jacques blew out his breath and looked through the glass at the canvas that was stretched across the deck, swelling in the wind and tugging against the ropes that held it, canvas that in reality sheltered nothing except a few crates of tools and plowshares. He reached into his shirt and lifted a religious medal to his lips and kissed it.

"Lord, if you cain't forgive me all my sins, just don't remember them too good, no. Thank you. Amen," he said.

He steered the boat close to shore, until

the overhang scratched against the gunnel and the top of the pilothouse, then shut down the paddle-wheel while his boatmates slipped the anchors on the bow and stern. Curds of yellow smoke rose from the trash fire burning in the field. A black man walked through the trees toward the boat, the fire bright behind him. He stood motionless on the bank, squinting at the darkened windows in the pilothouse.

"That's my uncle!" Flower said, and ran out on the deck.

"Why don't she yell it at them people in that plantation house back yonder?" Jean-Jacques said.

"We'll be back in a few minutes. It's going to be fine," Abigail said.

Lightning rippled through the clouds over the river. Jean-Jacques' face looked dilated, his eyes like black marbles. He pulled the cork from a green bottle and drank from the neck.

"Miss Abigail, my heart done aged ten years tonight. Get back quick with them colored people. Don't make me grow no older, no," he said.

"Fifteen minutes. You'll see," she said, and winked at him.

She and Flower went down the plank the boatmates had propped against the bank and followed Flower's uncle up an eroded coulee through a stand of gum trees. The mist was gray and damp, like a cotton glove, the air tannic with the smell of dead leaves that had pooled inside stagnant water. The coulee led like a jagged wound through a sweet potato field, steep-sided, thick with ferns and air vines, the soft clay at the bottom laced with the stenciled tracks of deer and possums and raccoons.

Lightning jumped between the clouds, and Abigail saw perhaps two dozen adults and children sitting down on each side of the stream at the bottom of coulee, their faces frightened, their belongings tied inside blankets.

A tall, thick-necked black woman, with cheekbones as big as a hog's, wearing an ankle-length gray dress, rose to her feet, her eyes fastened on Abigail.

"This the one?" she asked Flower, nodding at Abigail.

"There ain't . . . there isn't a better white person on earth," Flower said.

"Some white mens from Baton Rouge has talked slaves into running and turned them in for the bounty," the older black woman said.

"You're Flower's grandmother?" Abigail said.

"That's right."

"I don't blame you for your suspicions. But we don't have much time, ma'am. You must trust me or otherwise return to your home.

You have to make that decision now," Abigail said.

Flower's grandmother picked up her bundle in one hand and took the hand of a little boy in another.

"The paddy rollers are scared of the Yankees. They was looking along the river with lanterns," she said.

"Then let's be gone," Abigail said.

They walked single file back down the coulee toward the river, the sparks from the fire in the field drifting over their heads. A thunderous clap of lightning struck in the trees, and behind her Abigail heard an infant begin to cry. She stepped out of the line and worked her way back to a teenage girl who was walking with an infant not over three or four months old in each arm.

"Cain't carry them both. I gots to go back," the girl said.

"No, you don't," Abigail said, and took one of the babies from her.

The line of people splashed ankle-deep down the coulee toward the sound of the river coursing through the willow trees in the shallows. Then they heard someone snap a dry branch off a tree and throw it angrily aside with a curse, as though an object of nature had deliberately targeted him for injury. A balloon of light burst out of the tree trunks and flooded the bottom of the coulee.

"Tell me y'all ain't the most bothersome

bunch of ungrateful pea brains I ever seen," a voice said from behind the lantern.

His name was Olin Mayfield. He had a jug head and a torso that looked as soft as mush. He wore a slicker and a slouch hat whose brim had gone shapeless in the rain and an army cap-and-ball .44 revolver on his hip. When the light of his lantern swung into his face his eyes were as green and empty of thought as stagnant water in a cattle tank.

"No, I ain't gonna hit you. Just get your worthless asses out of the ditch and follow me back to the quarters. Colonel Jamison is gonna flat shit his britches," he said and laughed. He crouched down to pull a woman up by her hand.

Then he stiffened, his nostrils swelling with air, as though the odor of a dangerous animal had suddenly wrapped itself around him. He rose from his crouch, turning, hoisting the lantern above his head, and stared straight into the face of Jean-Jacques LaRose.

Abigail watched the next events take place as though she were caught in a dream from which she could not wake. Olin Mayfield's expression shaped and reshaped itself, as though he could not decide whether to grin or to scowl. Then he gripped the heavy Colt revolver on his hip and pulled it halfway from his holster, his lip curling up from his teeth, perhaps, Abigail thought, in imitation of an illustration he had seen on the cover of a dime novel.

The knife Jean-Jacques carried in his right hand was made from a wagon spring, a quarter-inch thick, reheated and beveled down to an edge that was sharp enough to shave with, mounted inside an oak handle with a brass guard. He thrust the blade through Olin Mayfield's throat and extracted it just as fast.

Mayfield's mouth opened in dismay as the blood drained out of his head and face and spilled down his chest. Then he slumped to his knees, his head tilted on his shoulder, as though the trees and sweet potato fields and the empty wagons in the rows had become unfairly torn loose from their fastenings and set adrift in the sky.

His lantern bounced to the bottom of the coulee and hissed in the stream but continued to burn. Then the entire band of escaping slaves bolted for the shoreline and the gangplank that led onto Jean-Jacques' boat.

Abigail was at the end of the line as it moved past Olin Mayfield. He lay on his side, his mouth pursed open, at eye level with her, his hands on his throat. When she looked at the twitch in his cheek and the solitary tear in one eye and the froth on his bottom lip she knew he was still alive, unable to speak or to fully comprehend what had happened to him.

"I'm sorry," she whispered.

She gathered the infant she was carrying closer to her and dashed after the others.

An hour later the rain stopped and the sky cleared and Abigail stood in the darkness of the pilothouse and looked out on the vast moonlit emptiness of the river and the black-green border of trees on the banks and the stump fires that smelled like burning garbage. She wondered if any sort of moral victory was possible in human affairs or if addressing and confronting evil only empowered it and produced casualties of a different kind.

The slaves had at first been terrified at the slaying of the paddy roller, but once they were in a new and seemingly secure environment, hidden inside the cargo hold or under the canvas on deck, the fear went out of their faces and they began to laugh and joke among themselves. Abigail had found herself laughing with them; then one man in the hold found a splintered piece of wood from a packing crate and hacked at the air with it, pretending he was executing Olin Mayfield. Everyone clapped their hands.

What had her father said? "We will do many things in the service of justice. But shedding blood isn't one of them." She drew a ragged breath and shut her eyes and saw again the scene in the coulee. What a mockery she had made of her father's admonition.

"You still t'inking about that man back there?" Jean-Jacques said. A palpable aura of rum and dried sweat and tobacco smoke rose from his skin and clothes.

"Yes, I am," she replied.

"He made his choice. He got what he deserved. Look out yonder. We got a lot more serious t'ings to deal wit'," he said.

They had just made a bend in the river and should have been churning past the Confederate encampment, unchallenged, on their way to New Orleans, with nothing to fear until they approached the Union ironclads anchored in the river north of the city. Instead, a ship-of-war with twin stacks was anchored close to the shore, and soldiers with rifles moved in silhouette across the lighted windows. A pair of wheeled cannons had been moved into a firing position on a bluff above the river and all the undergrowth and willows chopped down in front of the barrels. Abigail heard an anchor chain on the Confederate boat clanking upward through an iron scupper.

Jean-Jacques wiped his mouth with his hand.

"Maybe I can run it. But we gonna take some balls t'rew the starboard side," he said.

"Turn in to shore," she said.

"That don't sound like a good idea."

"Get everyone down below," she said.

"There ain't room," he said.

"You have to make some."

She pulled up her dress and lifted the bottom of her petticoat in both hands and began to tear at it. The petticoat was pale yellow in color and sewn with lace on the edges. Jean-Jacques stared at her, his face contorted.

"I ain't having no parts in this," he said.

"Get Flower to help you. Please do what I say."

He frowned and rubbed the stubble on his jaw.

"Leave me your knife," she said.

"My knife?"

This time she didn't speak. She fixed her eyes on his and let her anger well into her face.

He called one of his boat mates to take the wheel and went out on the deck and opened a hatch in front of the pilothouse. One by one the black people who were hidden under the canvas crawled on their hands and knees to the ladder and dropped down into the heat of the boiler room.

Abigail ripped a large piece out of her petticoat, and knelt on the floor with Jean-Jacques' knife and cut the cloth in a square the size of a ship's flag. Then she tied two strips from the trimmings onto the corners and went to the stern. She pulled down the Confederate flag from its staff and replaced it with the piece from her petticoat.

Jean-Jacques came back into the pilothouse and steered his boat out of the channel, into dead water, cutting the engines just as the Confederates came alongside.

"What we doing, Miss Abigail?" he asked. He watched two soldiers latch a boat hook onto his gunnel and throw a boarding plank across it.

She patted her hand on top of his. He waited for her to answer his question.

"Miss Abigail?" he said.

But she only touched her finger to her lips.

Then he glanced at the tops of his shoes and his heart sank.

A major, a sergeant and three enlisted men dropped down onto the deck. Jean-Jacques went outside to meet them, his smile as natural as glazed ceramic.

"Had a bad storm up there. It's cleared up all right, though," he said.

The faces of the soldiers held no expression. Their eyes swept the decks, the pilothouse, the canvas stretched across the front of the boat. But one of them was not acting like the others, Jean-Jacques noted. The sergeant, who was unshaved and wore his kepi low on his brow, was looking directly into Jean-Jacques' face.

"You see any Yanks north of here?" the major asked.

"No, suh," Jean-Jacques said.

The major lit a lantern and held it up at

eye level. He was a stout, bewhiskered man, his jowls flecked with tiny red and blue veins. A gray cord, with two acorns on it, was tied around the crown of his hat.

"You'll find them for sure if you keep going south," he said.

"I give a damn, me," Jean-Jacques said.

"They can confiscate your vessel," the major said.

"What they gonna do, they gonna do."

"What's your cargo?" the major asked.

Before Jean-Jacques could answer Abigail stepped out in front of him.

"You didn't see our yellow warning?" she said.

"Pardon?" the officer said.

"We have yellow jack on board," she said.

"Yellow fever?" the major said.

"We're taking a group of infected Negroes to a quarantine and treatment station outside New Orleans. I have a pass from the Sanitary Commission if you'd like to see it."

The enlisted men involuntarily stepped back, craning their necks, looking about.

"Where are these infected Negroes from?" the major asked.

"Up the river. There's been an outbreak on two plantations," Abigail answered, busying herself inside her purse. She handed him a Sanitary Commission identification card. He cupped it in his palm but did not look at it.

"Where are they?" he asked.

"In the cargo hold."

"Something's not right here," the major said.

"Why is that?" she replied.

"Is that blood on your shoes?" the major asked Jean-Jacques.

Jean-Jacques studied his feet. "That's what it look like."

"Happen to know where it came from?" the major asked.

"People tole me I busted a bottle on a fellow's head last night. I ain't sure about that, though. I t'ink I would remember it if I done somet'ing that bad, me."

"Why are you transporting the Negroes in the hold?" the major asked.

"It's an airborne disease. Sir, why don't you inspect them and come to your own conclusions?" Abigail said.

The major's eyes broke. He brushed at one nostril and thought for a moment.

"I'll do it, sir," the sergeant interrupted.

"Very well," the major said.

Willie Burke hooked his hand through the bail of the lantern and walked aft. He hesitated a moment, then grasped the iron ring on the hatch and lifted it. His face darkened as he stared down into the hold.

"What is it?" the major asked.

"There appear to be a couple of families down here, sir," Willie replied.

"And?" the major said.

Willie wiped his nose on his sleeve. "I think their yellow flag is one we should heed, sir."

"Close it up," the major said. He handed Abigail her identification card. "You appear to be a brave woman."

"I'm not," she replied.

"Don't you people do this again," he said.

"Sir?"

"You know what I mean," the major said, and gestured for his men to follow him.

Willie passed within inches of her. He wore a mustache now and his faded gray shirt was tight on his body, his skin browned by the sun, his black hair ragged on his neck. His armpits were looped with sweat stains and he smelled of campfire smoke and leaves and testosterone.

His dark eyes met hers for only a moment, then he was gone.

A half hour later Abigail stood on the stern, the Confederate camp far behind her, and once again she looked at the great emptiness of the river and the coldness of the stars. She had never felt more desolate in her life. In her victory, the joy of danger and adrenaline had been stolen from her, and she was left to contemplate the lighted face of a dying man on the edge of a coulee, a red-veined bubble forming on his lips.

Chapter Twelve

The winter of 1862 and the following spring were not a good time for Ira Jamison. The weather turned wet and blustery, the temperature dipping below freezing at night, and the wounds in his side festered. From his bedroom window on the second story of his home he saw his fruit trees wither, his fields lie fallow, and many of the slave cabins remain empty. In order to sleep he placed a lump of opium in his cheek. The smell of the infection in his wounds filled his dreams.

Even before his wife had died in childbirth, his life had been one of solitude. But solitude should not mean loneliness, his father had always said. A real man planted his feet solidly in the world, chose his own friends, male and female, in his own time, and was never alone except when he wanted to be, his father had said.

But when Ira Jamison's possessions were in jeopardy, he experienced a form of soul sick-

217

ness that did not seem connected to the loss of the material items themselves. His fireplaces seemed to give no heat, a tryst with an octoroon girl no solace. He wandered his house in his bathrobe, voices out of his childhood echoing from the coldness in the walls. For some reason the fissure in the living room hearth and chimney would catch his eye and obsess him, and he would find himself feeling the rough edges of the mortar and separated brick with his thumb, rolling a marble across the hearth to determine if the foundation of the house was still settling. On Christmas Eve he piled oak logs on the andirons and stoked the fire until his face was sweating. An oil painting of his mother looked down at him from above the mantelpiece. Her cheeks were red, her lips mauve-colored, her black hair pulled tightly behind her head. When his eyes lingered on the painting, he could almost smell her breath, like dried flowers, like cloth that had moldered in a grave.

She had liked to stroke his hair when he was a child and sometimes she pulled him into her skirts, smothering him with her smell. His father had said nothing on these occasions, but his eyes smoldered and one hand clenched and unclenched at his side.

His father was a rough-hewn Scotsman, mercurial in his moods, keenly aware of his wife's education and his lack of one, generous and loving with his son, but always fearful that his wife's indulgent and sentimental ways would make the boy a victim of a predatory world. He was a curious mixture of humanity, severity and self-irony, and Ira loved him fiercely and sought his approval in everything he did.

"Spare the rod to feel good about yourself and create a lazy Negro," his father used to say. Then he would add, with a smile, "Spare the rod enough and create an impoverished plantation owner. Truth is, lad, in spite of everything we're told, there's no difference between the African and white races. The day the Negroes figure that one out is the day they'll take all this from us."

Ira's father was built like a stump, his chest streaked with fine black hair. He enjoyed stripping to the waist and working alongside his Negroes to demonstrate he was their equal if not superior at any physical task, heaving sacks of sweet potatoes into a wagon, prizing a cypress tree out of clay, splitting firewood that cracked like a rifle shot.

One winter Ira's mother contracted pneumonia. The fever and deliriums passed but the cough never left her lungs and the handkerchief she often kept balled in her fist was sometimes freckled with blood. When she leaned down to kiss her son's head, her breath made the skin of his face tighten against the bone.

His father moved out of the main bedroom and slept on a leather couch in the library. Unlike some of his male neighbors, he did not visit the slave quarters at night. He didn't have to. As Ira learned at age ten, his father had another life in Baton Rouge.

Ira's father left him to play in the yard of a friend while he rode a livery horse down into the bottoms, an area of Baton Rouge that was still undrained, the streets lined with saloons and tanneries. But Ira had always been allowed to go anywhere his father went, and he slipped out of the yard and followed his father to a cottage, the only one on the street that was painted white and had ventilated green shutters on the windows and a vegetable garden in the side yard.

The front door was closed, even though the weather was warm. Hanging baskets of flowers and ferns swayed from the eaves of the gallery, creaking in the wind, their colors riffling in the shade. Ira sat on the top step and watched the paddle-wheelers and scows on the river and the Irish boat hands from New Orleans unloading stacks of cowhides that they dumped into smoking vats behind the tanneries. He felt himself dozing off, then he heard his father's voice and the laughter of a woman inside the cottage.

He rose from the step and walked into the side yard where the shutters of a window were opened behind a stand of banana trees.

He pushed aside the banana leaves and propped a wood box against the side of the cottage and pulled himself up to eye level on the windowsill, expecting to play a joke on his father and see his father's face light with surprise and goodwill.

Instead, he looked upon the naked, clay-colored back of a woman whose knees were splayed across his father's loins. Her head reared back and her mouth opened silently, then a sound broke from her lips that he had never heard a woman make before. She blew out her breath, as though the room had grown cold, bending down toward his father now, her knees and thighs clenching him as if she was mounted on a horse. Her back shuddered again and her hands touched his father's face with a tenderness and intimacy that somehow seemed stolen from his mother and misused by another.

Ira's thoughts made no sense and were like shards of glass in his head.

Then the box broke under his feet and he was left hanging from the sill, the woman's eyes fastening on his now, his father's uplifted face popping with sweat like pinpoints of dew on a pumpkin.

Ira fell into the banana stalks and ran through the yard, dirty and hot and itching with ants, his head ringing as though someone had clapped him on both ears.

A moment later his father appeared on the

gallery, barefoot, his shirt hanging outside his pants.

"Sit down with me, son," his father said.

"No," Ira said.

His father walked down the steps, his silhouette blocking out the sun. He touched Ira under each eye with his thumb.

"There's nothing to cry about," he said.

"Who is she?" Ira said.

"A woman I see sometimes." He took his son's hand and led him back up to the gallery. They sat together on a swing that was suspended on chains from an overhead beam. It was spring and the willows and cypresses along the riverbanks were filled with wind and green with new leaf.

"Your mother has the consumption. That means we can't have the normal life of a husband and wife. I just hope God and you both forgive my weakness," his father said.

"She's a nigger. She was sitting on top of you," the boy said.

His father had been stroking his head. But now he took his hand away and looked at the river and a hawk that hung motionlessly in the wind above the trees.

"Will you be telling your mother about this?" he asked.

"I hate you," Ira said.

"You tear my heart out, son."

"I hate you. I hate you. I hate you," Ira said.

Then he was running out of the yard and down the street in his short pants, running through mud puddles, past the grinning faces of whores and teamsters and drunk Irishmen, his legs and face splattered with water that was black and oily and smelled like sewage and felt like leeches on his skin.

Back at Angola Plantation, Ira refused to eat, fought with his British schoolmaster, and attacked a mulatto dressmaker at the dirt crossroads in front of the plantation store.

She was a statuesque, coffee-colored woman who wore petticoats and carried a parasol. She had been waiting for a carriage, fanning herself, her chin pointed upward, when Ira had gathered up a handful of rocks, sharp ones, and begun pelting her in the back.

The store clerk had to pick him up like a sack of meal and carry him across the pommel of his saddle to Ira's house.

His mother sat with him in the kitchen, her eyes and cheeks bright with the fever that never left her body. The light was failing outside, the clouds like purple smoke above the bluffs on the river. Ira could hear the pendulum swinging on the clock in the dining room, the soft chimes echoing off the walls.

"What frightens you so?" his mother said, stroking his head.

"I'm not afraid of anything," he replied.

"Something happened in Baton Rouge, didn't it? Something you're trying to hide from your mother."

He clenched his hands in his lap and looked at the floor.

"Is that why you hit the sewing woman with rocks? A well-dressed mulatto woman?" she said.

He scraped a scab on his hand with his thumbnail. His mother lifted his chin with her finger. Her black hair was pulled back like wire against her scalp, her dark eyes burning.

"You have my looks and my skin. If you don't inherit my family's bad lungs, you'll always be young," she said.

"He let her sit on him. He put her —"

"*What?*" his mother said, her face contorting.

"He had her breast in his mouth. They were naked. On a bed in Nigger Town."

"Get control of yourself. Now, start over. You can trust me, Ira. But you have to tell me the truth."

She made him go through every detail, describing the woman, the positions on the bed, the words his father had spoken to him outside the cottage.

"What is her name?" she asked.

"I don't know," he said, shaking his head.

"You must know. He must have used her name."

But Ira couldn't speak now. His face was hot, his eyes swimming with tears, his voice hiccuping in his throat. His mother rose from her chair and looked for a long time out the window. Ira's father was in the garden, snipping roses, placing them in a bucket of water. He did not see his wife watching him. Then he glanced up at the window and waved.

She turned back toward her son.

"You must never tell anyone about this," she said.

"Is Papa going to know I told?"

"You didn't tell me anything, Ira. This didn't happen," she said.

She walked close to him and pulled his face into the folds of her dress and rubbed the top of his head with both hands. He could smell an odor like camphor and animal musk in her clothes. He put his arms around her thighs and buried his face against her stomach.

"When you were a baby I bathed you every morning and kissed you all over. I kissed your hands and your little feet and your bottom and your little private places. You'll always be my little man. You're my good little man, aren't you?" she said.

"Yes," he replied.

She released him and, with no expression on her face, walked out of the room. For reasons he could not understand he felt a sense of numbness, violation, shame and desertion, all at the same time. It was a feeling that would come aborning in his dreams the rest of his life.

For his birthday a week later, his father had the cook bake a strawberry cake and fry a dinner basket of chicken and convinced Ira's mother to join the two of them and an elderly black body servant named Uncle Royal for a picnic on the southern end of their property, three miles down the river.

His father chose this particular spot because it had been the site of a Spanish military garrison, supposedly overrun and massacred by Atakapa Indians in the eighteenth century, and as a boy Ira's father had played there and dug up the rusted shell of a Spanish helmet and a horseman's spur with an enormous spiked rowel on it.

They spread a blanket in a glade and set fishing lines in the river, and for a birthday present his father gave him a windup merry-go-round with hand-carved wooden horses on it that rotated in a circle while a musical cylinder played inside the base.

The river was yellow from the spring rains, thick and choked with mud, swirling with uprooted trees that floated southward toward New Orleans. The wind was drowsy and warm, the glade dotted with buttercups and bluebonnets and Indian paintbrush, and for a while Ira forgot his father's infidelity and the brooding anger in his mother's eyes and the blood-spotted handkerchief that stayed balled in the palm of her hand.

The body servant, Uncle Royal, wore a tattered black coat, a white shirt, a pair of purple pants and looked like he was made of sticks. He was fascinated by the windup merry-go-round that rested in the center of the blanket, next to the cake.

"Where something like that come from, Master Jamison?" he asked.

"All the way from England, across the big pond," Ira's father said.

"Lord, what my gran'child would give to play with something like that," Uncle Royal said.

"I tell you what, Royal, the storekeeper in Baton Rouge has another one just like it. On my next trip there, I'll buy it for you as an early Christmas present," Ira's father said.

"You'll do that, suh?" Uncle Royal said.

"You bet I will, old-timer," Ira's father said.

Ira never admired his father more.

He and his parents ate the chicken and strawberry cake on the blanket while Uncle Royal fished, then Ira's father decided he would entertain his wife and son by climbing on a pyramid of pine logs that were stacked and penned with stobs on a grassy shelf six feet above the shallows.

He walked up and down on the crest of

the logs, perhaps twenty feet above the glade, his arms outstretched for balance, grinning idiotically.

"Watch this!" he called. Then he flipped up on his hands and held his feet straight up in the air, his muscular body quivering with tension.

The ground was soft and moist from a week's rain. A stob on the far side of the logs bent backward against the additional weight on the pile, then one log bounced down from the top, followed by another. Ira's father flipped back on his feet and balanced himself, smiling, looking about, waiting for the rush of blood to leave his head. Suddenly the entire pile collapsed and rumbled downward into the river, taking Ira's father with it.

Ira and his mother and Uncle Royal rushed to the edge of the bluff and stared down at the mudflat. Ira's father lay pinioned under a half-dozen crisscrossed logs, his legs in the water, his face white, his powerful arms trying to push away the weight that was crushing the air from his lungs.

Ira and Uncle Royal climbed down from the embankment and pushed and lifted and tugged on the logs that held his father, but to no avail.

"Go to the house. Come back with a team and chains," Ira's father said.

"I got to get your head up out of the water, Master," Uncle Royal said.

"I think my back's broken. You have to get help," Ira's father said.

"You gonna be all right, suh?" Uncle Royal asked.

"Don't be long," Ira's father replied.

Ira watched Uncle Royal climb back up the embankment, the clay shaling over his bare ankles.

"Come on, son," his mother said, reaching her hand down to Ira. Her eyes seemed to avoid both him and his father.

"I'm staying," he replied.

"No, you can't be out here by yourself," she said.

"Then you or Uncle Royal stay," he said.

"We have to get axes and saws and chains. We have to bring a whole crew of men back. Now you do what I say."

He crawled up the embankment, then looked back down at his father.

"We'll hurry," he said.

His father winked at him and tried to hold his smile in place.

"I can stay in if you want, Miz Jamison," Uncle Royal said.

"Get in the carriage," she replied.

Uncle Royal turned the carriage around, then got down from the driver's seat to help Ira's mother up the step.

"Drive to the crossroads," she said.

"To the sto'?" Uncle Royal asked.

"Yes, to the store."

"That's eight miles, Miz Jamison," Uncle Royal said.

"All the workers are in the fields. Drive to the crossroads. We'll find help there," she said.

"Miz Jamison, the river's going up a couple of inches every hour. It's all that rainwater."

"Do I have to hit you with the whip?" she said.

Ira and his mother and Uncle Royal and the wagonload of men they put together did not get back to the river until after dark. When the manager of the plantation store held a lantern over the water, Ira saw the softly muted features of his father's face just below the surface, the eyes and mouth open, one hand frozen in a death grasp on a broken reed he had tried to breathe through.

As he matured Ira did not grow in understanding of his father and mother's jealousies and the lack of love that consumed their lives. Instead, he thought of his parents with resentment and anger, not only because they had destroyed his home but also because they had made him the double instrument of his father's death, first as an informer of his father's adultery, then as an accomplice in his mother's deception and treachery.

He spent one year at West Point and told others upon his resignation that he had to return home to run his family's business affairs. But the reality was he did not like the confines of military life. In fact, he thought anyone who willingly ate dry bread and unsweetened black coffee and shaved and bathed in cold water was probably possessed of a secret desire to be used as cannon wadding.

At age twenty he was the master of his estate, a dead shot with a dueling pistol, and a man who did not give quarter in business dealings or spare the rod with his workers. His parents rested in a plot on a grassy knoll above the river, but he never visited their graves nor shared his feelings about the unbearable sense of loss that defined his childhood memories.

He learned not to brood upon the past nor to think analytically about the events that had caused him to become the hard-edged man he had grown into. The whirrings in his blood, the heat that would balloon in his chest at a perceived insult, gave an élan to his manner that made his adversaries walk cautiously around him. A man he had cuckolded called him out on the street in New Iberia. The cuckold's hand shook and his ball went wide, striking Ira in the arm. But Ira's aim didn't waver and he drove a ball through the man's mouth and out the back of his head, then sipped coffee at a saloon bar while a physician dressed his wound.

His young wife was at first bemused and

intrigued by his insatiable sexual desires, then finally alienated and frightened by them. In a fit of remorse and guilt about her participation in what she called her husband's lust, she confided the intimate details of her marriage to her pastor, a nervous sycophant with smallpox scars on his cheeks and dandruff on his shoulders. After Ira learned of his wife's visit to the minister, he rode his horse to the parsonage and talked to the minister in his garden. The minister boarded a steamboat in Baton Rouge the next day and was never seen in Louisiana again.

"What did you say to him?" Ira's wife asked.

"I told him he was to denounce both of us every Sunday from his pulpit. If he didn't, I was going to shoot him."

But there were moments in Ira Jamison's life that made him wonder if, like his father, more than one person lived inside his skin.

He was cleaning out his attic on a late fall afternoon when he came across the windup merry-go-round his father had given him on his eleventh birthday. He inserted the key in the base and twisted the spring tight, then pushed a small lever and listened to the tune played by the spiked brass cylinder inside.

For no reason he could quite explain he walked into the quarters, in a tea-colored sunset, among tumbling leaves and the smell of gas in the trees, and knocked on Uncle Royal's door.

"Yes, suh?" Uncle Royal said, his frosted eyes blinking uncertainly.

"You still have any young grandchildren?" Ira asked.

"No, suh, they grown and in the fields now. But I got a young great-gran'child."

"Then give him this," Ira said.

The old man took the merry-go-round from Ira's hand and felt the carved smoothness of the horses with the ends of his fingers.

"Thank you, suh," he said.

Ira turned to go.

"How come you to think of this now, Master Ira?" Uncle Royal asked.

"My father made you a promise he couldn't keep. So I kept it for him. That's all it means. Nothing else," he replied.

"Yes, suh," Uncle Royal said.

On the way back to the house Ira wondered if his words to Uncle Royal had become his way of saying good-bye forever to the innocent and vulnerable child who had once lived inside him and caused him so much pain.

Now the spring of 1863 was upon him, and he knew enough of history to realize that the events taking place around him did not bode well for his future. Some of his slaves had been shipped to unoccupied areas of Arkansas, but it was only a matter of time until the South fell and emancipation became a fact of life.

In the meantime someone had hijacked two dozen slaves from his property, taking them downriver to New Orleans through a Confederate blockade, murdering one of his paddy rollers in the bargain. Ira could not get the image of the dead paddy roller out of his mind. Three of his overseers had carted the body up to the front porch, stuffed in a lidless packing case, the knife wound in his throat like a torn purple rose.

Ira did not believe in coincidences. One of his own men had now died in the same fashion as the young sentry in the New Orleans hospital the night Ira escaped from Yankee custody.

Nor was it coincidence that a woman with a Northern accent was on board the boat that transported a cargo of Negroes supposedly infected with yellow jack to a quarantine area north of New Orleans the same night two dozen of his slaves had disappeared from the plantation.

Abigail Dowling, he thought.

Every morning he woke with her name in his mind. She bothered him in ways he had difficulty defining. She had a kind of pious egalitarian manner that made him want to slap her face. At the same time she aroused feelings in him that left his loins aching. She was the most stunning woman he'd ever seen, with the classical proportions of a Renaissance sculpture, and she bore herself with a dignity and intellectual grace that few beautiful women ever possessed.

The spring rains came and the earth turned green and the fruit trees bloomed outside Ira's window. But the name of Abigail Dowling would not leave his thoughts, and sometimes he woke throbbing in the morning and had images of her moaning under his weight. Nor did it help for him to remember that she had rebuffed him and made him feel obscene and sexually perverse.

He looked out upon the sodden fields and at an oak tree that was stiff and hard-looking in the wind. What was it that bothered him most about her? But he already knew the answer to his own question. She was intelligent, educated, unafraid and seemed to want nothing he was aware of. He did not trust people who did not want something. But most of all she bothered him because she had looked into his soul and seen something there that repelled her.

What was her weakness? he asked himself. Everybody had one. Maybe he had been looking in the wrong place. She seemed to have male friends rather than suitors or lovers. A woman that beautiful? He gazed out the window at the white bloom on his peach trees and a slave girl pulling weeds inside the drip lines. His side ached miserably. He placed a small lump of opium under his lip and felt a sensation like warm water leaking through his nervous system.

He had thought of Abigail Dowling as a flesh-and-blood replication of Renaissance sculpture, an Aphrodite rising from a tidal pool on the Massachusetts coast. He watched the slave girl drop a handful of weeds into her basket and get to her feet, the tops of her breasts exposed to his view. Maybe he had been only partially correct about Abigail's classical origins.

Were her antecedents on the island of Lesbos rather than Melos?

He wondered.

Chapter Thirteen

After the retreat from Shiloh, Willie began to dream about a choleric-faced man, someone he did not know, advancing out of a mist with a bayonet fixed to the end of his rifle. The choleric-faced man would not fall down when Willie fired upon him. He also dreamed about the sound of a distant siege gun coughing in a woods, then a shell arcing in a dark blur out of a blue sky, exploding in a trench full of men with the force of a ship's boiler blowing apart. He began to take his dreams into the waking day, and his anxieties and fears would be so great with the passage of each hour that contact with the enemy became a welcomed release.

That's when a line sergeant gave him what the sergeant considered the key to survival for a common foot soldier: You never thought about it before you did it and you never thought about it when it was over.

Nor did thinking make life easier for a

commissioned officer, Willie told himself later.

Lieutenant Willie Burke peered through the spyglass at the steam engine and the line of freight cars parked on the railway track. The sun was white in the sky, the woods breathless, the leaves in the canopy coated with dust. His clothes stuck to his skin; his hair was drenched with sweat inside his hat. There was a humming sound in his head, like the drone of mosquitoes, except the woods were dry and there were no mosquitoes in them.

But their eggs were in his blood, and at night, and sometimes in daylight, he would see gray spots before his eyes and hear mosquitoes humming in his head, as was now the case, and he wished he was lying in a cold stream somewhere and not sighting through a spyglass, breathing dust inside a sweltering woods.

The train was deserted, the steam engine pocked with holes from case shot. Two of the boxcars that had been loaded with munitions had burned to the wheels. Another boxcar, a yellow one with sliding doors that had carried Negro troops, was embedded from stem to stern with iron railroad spikes, like rust-colored quills on a porcupine.

The black soldiers, almost all of them newly emancipated slaves, untrained, with no experience in the field, had melted away into thickly wooded river bottoms and had taken a mule-drawn field piece with them, whipping the mules across the flanks, powdering dust in the air as they crushed through the palmettos and underbrush.

Willie moved the spyglass over the river bottoms but could see no movement inside the trees. The train tracks shimmered in the heat and he could smell the hot odor of creosote in the ties. He focused the glass far down the line on an observation balloon captured from the Federals. It was silver, as bright as tin, tethered to the earth by a rope that must have been two hundred feet long. A bearded man in a wicker basket was looking back in Willie's direction with a spyglass similar to his own.

Willie got down on one knee and gestured for Sergeant Clay Hatcher to do the same. The sudden movement made his head swim and his eyes momentarily go out of focus. He spread a map on the ground and tapped on it with his finger.

"That woods yonder is probably a couple of miles deep. Their officers are dead, so my guess is they're bunched up," he said.

Hatcher nodded as though he understood. But in reality he didn't. He carried a Henry repeater he had taken off the body of a Federal soldier. He was unshaved and sweaty, his kepi crimped wetly into his hair.

"Take two men and get around behind

them. When you do, I want you to make life very uncomfortable for them," Willie said.

Hatcher smiled.

"I can do that," he said.

"I don't think you follow me, Hatch."

Hatcher looked at him, his eyes uncertain.

"I want them to unlimber that field piece. You'll be on the receiving end of it. You up for that?" Willie said.

"As good as the next," Hatcher said.

"Better get moving, then," Willie said.

Hatcher kept his gaze on the map without seeming to see it.

"You want prisoners?" he asked.

"If they surrender," Willie said.

"The rumor is there ain't a great need for them in the rear."

"Well, you hear this. If I catch you operating under a black flag, I'll take you before a provost and you'll be off to your heavenly reward before the sun sets."

Hatcher nodded, his eyes looking at nothing, a lump of cartilage flexing in his jaw. "One of these days all this will be over," he said.

"Yes?"

"That's all. It'll be over and my stripes and those acorns on your hat won't mean very much."

"I look forward to the day, Hatch."

Willie watched Hatcher crunch across the floor of the woods toward the train track, his spine slightly bent, his clothes stiff with salt and dirt, his Henry repeater cupped in a horizontal position, like a prehistoric creature carrying a spear. Two other men joined him, both of them dressed in tattered butternut, and the three of them crossed the railway embankment and disappeared into the trees on the far side.

Willie wondered when Hatcher would eventually muster up the nerve to frame Willie's back in his rifle sights.

Someone touched him on the shoulder.

"Major is asking for you, Lieutenant," a soldier said. He could not have been over sixteen. There were no buttons on his shirt and the cloth was held against his chest by the crossed straps of his haversack and a bullet pouch. He wore a domed, round-brimmed straw hat that sat on his head like a cake bowl.

"How is he?" Willie asked.

"He falls asleep and says funny things," the boy answered.

Willie walked back through the woods to a bayou that was spangled with sunlight and draped with air vines that hung from the trees. The major lay on a blanket in the leaves, his head propped on a haversack stuffed with his rubber coat.

Back in the shade, under a mulberry tree clattering with bluejays, the feet of four dead soldiers stuck out from the gum blankets that had been pulled over their bodies. Their shoes had been taken and the blankets that covered them were spotted with the white droppings of birds.

Both of the major's arms were broken and hung uselessly at his sides. A bandage with a scarlet circle the size of a half dollar in the center was tied just below his heart. His muttonchop sideburns looked as thick as hemp on his jowls.

"I had a dream about snow. Everything was white and a red dog was barking inside some trees," the major said.

"We have a boat coming up the bayou, sir. We'll have you back at battalion aid soon," Willie said.

"We shot the living hell out of them, didn't we?"

"You bet," Willie said.

"I need to ask you something."

"Yes, sir."

"When we stopped that steamboat on the Mis'sippi, the one carrying yellow jack?"

Willie let his eyes slip off the major's face.

"Yes, sir, I remember it," he said.

"I had a feeling you knew the woman on board, the one with the Yankee accent."

"Could be, sir."

"I don't think those darkies had yellow jack. I think they were escaped slaves."

"Lots of things are out of our control, Major," Willie said. He was propped on one knee, his gaze fixed on the air vines that fluttered in the wind.

"I worked my whole life as a trainman. I owned nary a slave. I always thought slavery was a mistake," the major said.

Willie nodded. "Yes, sir," he said.

"Those who got through us on the river? They might have joined up with the colored outfit we just shot up, the ones who put the ball under my heart. That'd be something, wouldn't it?"

Willie's eyes returned to the major's and he felt something drop inside him.

"It's nothing to worry about. The boat will be here soon," the major said, and tried to smile.

"Sir —" Willie began.

"Watch your back, Willie. Hatcher and Captain Atkins are no good. They hate a young fellow such as yourself."

Then the major widened his eyes briefly and turned his face away, into the shadows, as though the world of sunlight and the activity of the quick held little interest for him.

When Willie got back to his position inside the edge of the woods, he sat very still on a log and waited for his head to stop spinning. Then he poured water out of his canteen into his palm and wiped his face with it. The boxcars on the track went in and out of focus and a pang like a shard of glass sliced across the lining of his stomach. For a moment he thought he would lose control of his sphincter muscle.

In the distance he saw snow egrets and black geese rising from the canopy in the river bottoms, then he heard the spatter of small-arms fire that meant Hatcher's group had made contact with the black soldiers who had fled the train.

Both the men with Hatcher carried captured Spencer rifles and bags of brass cartridges, and they, along with Hatcher and his Henry repeater, were laying down a murderous field of fire. The shooting went on for five minutes, then a field piece roared deep in the river bottoms and the gum trees overhead trembled with the shock and a cloud of smoke and grayish-orange dust rose out of the leaves into the sunlight. A moment later the field piece roared again and a second cloud of dust and smoke caught the light and flattened in the wind.

Willie looked through his spyglass at the observation balloon tethered by the railway track far down the line. The bearded man in the wicker basket was using a pair of handheld flags to semaphore a battery down below, one consisting of three rifled twenty-pounder Parrotts that had been removed from a scuttled Union gunboat.

One of the cannons fired, and a shell arced over the spot in the river bottoms where the dust clouds had risen out of the canopy. The round went long by thirty yards, and the man in the basket leaned over the side and whipped his flags in the air. The next round was short and the man in the basket semaphored the ground again.

Then all three Confederate cannons fired for effect, again and again, the fused shells whistling shrilly only seconds before they struck.

Uprooted trees and columns of dirt fountained into the air, and through the spyglass Willie could see shoes and pieces of blue uniform mixed in with the dirt and palmetto leaves.

The barrage went on for almost a half hour. When Willie and his platoon marched across the railway embankment and entered the bottoms, he saw a black soldier huddled on the ground, trembling all over as though he had malaria, his forearms pressed tightly against his ears. Deeper in the bottoms the ground was pocked with craters, the dirt still smoking, and the trees were decorated in ways he had not seen since Shiloh.

Back in the underbrush he saw one of Hatcher's men cut the ear from a dead man's head, fold it in a handkerchief, and place it carefully in a leather pouch.

So that's the way it goes, he thought. You turn a blind eye to slaves escaping downriver, and later they join up with the blue-bellies and perhaps drive a ball under your friend's heart, and you trap the poor devils under a barrage that paints the trees with their blood and nappy hair. Ah, isn't it all a lovely business, he thought.

He wondered what Abigail would have to say about his work and hers.

An hour later he passed out. When he woke, he was in a tent and rain was ticking on the canvas. Through the flap he saw two enlisted men digging a grave by the bayou. The major lay next to the mound of dirt, his face covered with his gray coat.

Chapter Fourteen

The morning did not feel like spring, Abigail thought. The air was hot and smelled of dust and trash fires, the sky gray, the clouds crackling with electricity. Then her neighbor's dogs began barking and she heard a banging noise down the Teche, like a houseful of carpenters smacking nails down in green wood. She walked out on the gallery and saw birds lifting out of the trees all the way down the street as a long column of soldiers and wagons rounded a bend in the distance and advanced toward the center of town.

The soldiers were unshaved, gaunt as scarecrows, some of them without shoes, the armpits of their butternut and gray uniforms white with salt, their knees patched like the pants on beggars. Three wagons carrying wounded passed in front of her. The teamsters in the wagon boxes were leaning forward, away from their charges, with handkerchiefs tied across their faces. The wind shifted, and she smelled the unmistakable odor of gangrene and of men who had become incontinent and left to sit in their own excretions. She saw no one with a surgeon's insignia in the column.

She walked out into the yard just as a mounted officer rode his horse to the head of the column. He wore a slouch hat, a sweat-peppered gray shirt, no coat, and a pistol in a shoulder holster on his chest. His face was narrow, his skin as coarse and dark as if it had been rubbed with the dust from a foundry.

He picked his hat off his head by the crown and combed back his hair with his fingers.

"Still in our midst, are you?" he said.

"This is where I live," Abigail replied.

"Bring as many ladies as you can find up to the Episcopalian church," he said.

"You don't need to tell me my obligations, Captain Atkins," she replied.

"There's nothing like hearing a Yankee accent behind our own lines. But I'm sure you've been loyal to the cause, haven't you?"

"Where is Willie Burke?"

"Can't rightly say. Saw him puking his guts out last week. Don't think he was quite up to blowing railroad spikes into freed niggers."

"What?"

"You haven't heard? The Yanks give them uniforms and guns and permission to kill

248

their previous owners. We waylaid a whole trainload of them. Made good niggers out of a goodly number."

Dry lightning rippled through the clouds. Atkins replaced his hat on his head and looked up at the sky.

"By the way, that was some of General Banks' skirmishers shooting behind us," he said. "They say he was a bobbin boy in one of your Massachusetts textile mills. Does not like rich people. No, sir. So he's turned his men loose on the civilian population. I hear they're a horny bunch. You might fasten on a chastity belt."

She wouldn't let the level of his insult register in her face, but the fact that he had insulted her sexually, in public, indicated only one conclusion about her status in the community: She was utterly powerless. She wanted to turn and walk away, but instead she fixed her eyes on the exhaustion in the faces of the enlisted men marching past her, the sores on the horses and mules, a mobile field kitchen whose cabinet doors swung back and forth on empty shelves.

"Captain Atkins, I suspect you may be a gift from God," she said.

His head tilted sideways, an amused question mark in the middle of his face.

"Sometimes we're all tempted to think of our own race as being superior to others," she said. "Then we meet someone such as yourself and immediately we're beset with the terrible knowledge that there's something truly cretinous at work in the Caucasian gene pool. Thank you for stopping by."

He studied her for a moment and scratched his cheek, his gaze slightly out of focus. He touched his horse with one spur and rode slowly toward the front of the column, his head bent down as though he were lost in thought. Then he reined his horse in a circle and rode back to Abigail's gate. He leaned with both arms on the pommel, the leather creaking under his weight. His flat, hazel eyes looked like they had been cut out of another face and pasted on his own.

He pointed at her with a dirt-rimmed fingernail. "A pox on you, you snooty cunt. Be assured your comeuppance is in the making," he said.

When Abigail arrived at the brick church at the far end of Main Street, the pews had been upended against the walls and the injured placed in rows on the floor. She peeled bandages from wounds that were rife with infection, scissored the trousers and underwear off men who had fouled themselves, and bathed their bodies with sponges and soap and warm water. A local physician, untrained as a surgeon, created an operating table by propping a door across two pews, then sawed limbs off men as though he were pruning trees. After each patient was carried away, he threw a bucket of water on the table and began on the next. There was no laudanum, and Abigail had to hold the heel of her hand in one man's mouth to keep him from biting through his tongue.

Outside, she heard men and horses running in the street, their gear clanking, a wheeled cannon bouncing off a parked wagon, then the spatter of small-arms fire in the distance.

"Are you with the 18th?" she asked a private who lay on a litter, a mound of bloody rags on the floor beside him.

He nodded. His eyes were receded in his face, his cheeks hollow. The bones in his chest looked like sticks under his skin. One pants leg had been cut away, and a swollen red line ran from a bandage on his thigh into his groin.

"What happened out there?" she asked.

"We divided our numbers and tried to fight on both sides of the bayou. They chewed us up. They been running us for six days."

"Do you know where Willie Burke is?"

"Lieutenant Burke?"

"Yes."

"Captain Atkins put him on rear guard."

"You mean now?"

"Yes, ma'am," the soldier said.

"Captain Atkins recently saw Lieutenant Burke?" she said.

But the soldier's eyes had lost interest in her questions.

"Fix my arms and my feet," he said.

"Pardon?"

"You know what I mean. Fix me," he said.

She started to speak, then gave up the pretense, the lie, that was in reality an insult to the dying. She folded his arms across his chest and lifted his good leg and pressed it close to the other, then tied his ankles with a strip of rag. His tin identification disk, with a leather thong looped through a hole at the top, was clenched tightly in his palm.

"Do you want me to write a letter to someone?" she asked.

"No, no letter," he said. His eyes filled with a terrible intensity and roved the vaulted ceiling above him, where a bird was battering itself against the glass windows, trying to escape into the treetops outside. "I stole money from a poor man once. I had a wife and wasn't good to her. I did mean things to others when I was a boy."

"I bet you were forgiven of your sins a long time ago," she said.

"Lean close," he said.

She bent down over his face, turning her ear to his mouth. His breath touched her skin like a moist feather.

"When I'm dead, set my tag so it's up and down between my teeth and knock my jaws shut," he whispered.

She nodded.

"If you got your tag in your mouth, they got to put your name on a marker," he said.

"I'll make sure. I promise," she said.

"I'm scared, ma'am. Ain't nobody ever been as scared as I am right now."

She raised her head and gazed down at him, but whatever conclusion he had reached about the unchartered course of his life or the fear that had beset him in his last moments had already drifted out of his face like ash off a dead fire.

The bird he had been watching dipped under the arch of the front doorway and lifted into the sky, its wings throbbing.

The next day Flower Jamison rose before sunup and lit her woodstove and fixed coffee that was made from chicory and ground acorns. Then she lit the lamp on her table and in the misty coolness between false dawn and the moment when the sun would break above the horizon she removed from under her bed the box of books and writing materials given her by both Willie Burke and later by Abigail Dowling and opened the writing tablet in which she kept her daily journal.

She no longer hid her books or her ability to read them from white people. But her fear of her literacy being discovered did not leave her as a result of any decision or conscious act of her own. It had simply gone away as she looked about her and saw both privation and the cost of war on distant battlefields indelibly mark the faces of those who had always exercised complete power and control over her life. She could not say that she felt compassion or pity for them. Instead, she had simply come to realize that the worst in her life was probably behind her, and adversity and struggle and powerlessness were about to become the lot of the plantation owners who had seemed anointed at birth and placed beyond the reach of the laws of mortality and chance and accident.

At least that is what she thought.

Outside her window the new cane was green and wet inside the mist and she could hear it rustling when the wind blew from the south. She placed her dictionary next to her writing tablet and began writing, pausing on every fourth or fifth word to look up a spelling:

Last night there was either shooting or thunder down the bayou. The dead were took out of the back of the church and laid on the grass under a oak tree. There were flashes of light in the sky and a loud explosion in the bayou. A free man of color say a yankee gunboat was blowed up and fish rained down in the trees and some hungry people picked them up with their hands for food to eat.

Miss Abigail ask me why I come back from New Orleans when I could stay there and be free. I told her this is my home and inside myself I'm free wherever I go. I told her I want to stay and help other slaves escape up the Mississippi to the north. I have been telling myself this too.

I cannot be sure this is exactly truthful. This is my thoughts for this morning.

Respectfully,
Flower Jamison

She looked back down at her words in the lamplight, then gazed out the window at the blueness of the dawn and a calf wandering out of the cane field. The calf caught a scent on the breeze and ran toward a cow that stood on the lip of the coulee in a grove of swamp maples.

Flower picked up her pencil and wrote at the bottom of the folded-back page in her tablet:

Post Script — I know I should hate him. But it is not what I feel. Why would a man not love his own daughter? Or at least look at her the way a father is suppose to look at his child? All people are the same under their skin. Why is my father different? Why is he cruel when he does not have to be?

Late that afternoon Flower filled the caulked cypress tub behind the slave quarters with water she drew from the windmill, then bathed and put on a clean dress and began her pickup route, stopping first at the back door of Carrie LaRose's brothel.

Carrie LaRose could have been the twin of her brother, Scavenger Jack. She was beetle-browed, big-boned, with breasts the size of pumpkins and red-streaked black hair that grew on her head like snakes. She wore a holy medal and a gold cross around her neck, a juju bag tied above her knee and paid a *traiteur* to put a gris-gris on her enemies and business rivals. Some said she had escaped a death sentence in either Paris or the West Indies by seducing the executioner, who bound and gagged another woman in Carrie's prison cell and took her to the guillotine in Carrie's stead.

Flower paid little attention to white people's rumors, but she did know one thing absolutely about Carrie LaRose, that she either possessed the powers of prophecy and knew the future or she was so knowledgeable about human weakness and the perfidious and venal nature of the world that she could predict the behavior of people in any given situation with unerring precision.

Cotton speculators, arms dealers, munitions manufacturers, and slave traders came to her bordello and had their palms read and their lust slaked in her bedrooms and gladly paid her a commission on their profits.

Early in the war a Shreveport cotton trader asked her advice about risking his cotton on a blockade runner.

"How much them British gonna pay you?" she asked.

"Three times the old price," the cotton trader replied.

"What you t'ink them textile mills in Mass'chusetts gonna pay?" she asked.

"I don't understand. We're not trading with the North," he said.

"That's what you t'ink. The cotton don't care where it grow. Them Yankees don't, either. They rather have it come up to the Mis'sippi than go t'rew the blockade to the British. The blockade runners gonna bring guns back to the Confederates."

The cotton traders who listened to Carrie increased their profits six- and sevenfold.

But those who sought her advice and the service of her girls and sometimes the opium she bought from a Chinaman in Galveston little realized she often listened to their confessions and manifestations of desire and infantile need by putting her ear to a water glass she pressed against the walls of their rooms. On Saturday nights her brothel roared with piano music and good cheer. On Monday mornings a New Orleans export-importer might discover a profitable business deal had been stolen from under his feet.

Flower stripped the sheets from the mattresses in the bedrooms and piled them in the hallway. Outside, the western sky was streaked with gold and purple clouds and under an oak tree in the dirt yard three paddy rollers were drinking whiskey at a plank table. The wind puffed the curtains and blew through the hallway, and Flower could smell watermelons and rain in a distant field. She thought she was by herself, then she heard a board creak behind her and turned around and saw Carrie LaRose sitting in a chair, just inside the kitchen door, watching her, a contemplative expression on her face.

"Why you want to do this shit, you?" Carrie asked.

"Ma'am?"

"I could set you up in your own house, make you rich."

Flower wadded up the dirty linen she had thrown in the hallway and the dresses of Carrie LaRose's higher-priced girls and tied them inside a sheet.

"Don't know what you mean, Miss Carrie," she said.

"Don't tell me that, no. In a week or two this town's gonna be full of Yankees and all you niggers are gonna be free. A pretty li'l t'ing like you can make a lot of money. Maybe you t'inking about selling out of your drawers on your own."

"You don't have the right to talk to me like that, Miss Carrie."

Carrie LaRose looked at her nails. She wore a frilled beige dress, her hair piled on top of her head, a silver comb stuck in back.

"You could have stayed in New Orleans and been free. But you come back here, to a li'l town on the bayou, where you're a slave," she said.

"I don't mess in your bidness, Miss Carrie. Maybe you ought to keep out of mine."

It was silent except for the muffled conversation of the paddy rollers in the yard and the wind popping the curtains on the windows. Flower could feel Carrie LaRose's eyes on her back.

"You come back 'cause of Ira Jamison. You keep t'inking one day he's gonna come to your li'l house and tell you he's your daddy and then all that pain he give you for a lifetime is gonna go away," Carrie LaRose said.

Flower felt the skin draw tight on her face.

"I'll be getting on my way," she said.

"He ain't wort' it, girl. Learn it now, learn it later. Ain't none of them wort' it. They want your jellyroll wit' the least amount of trouble possible. The day you make them pay for it, the day you got their respect."

"Yes, ma'am."

"Don't play the dumb nigger wit' me."

"I'm fixing to be free, Miss Carrie. It doesn't matter what anybody say to me now.

I can read and write. Words I don't know I can look up in a dictionary. I can do sums and subtractions. Miss Abigail and Mr. Willie Burke say I'm as smart as any educated person. I'm fixing to be anything I want, go anywhere I want, do anything I want, and I mean in the whole wide world. How many people can say that about themselves?"

Carrie LaRose propped her chin on her fingers and studied Flower's face as though seeing it for the first time. Then she looked away with an age-old knowledge in her eyes that made something sink in Flower's chest.

The wind was picking up now as she loaded her laundry bags into the carriage behind the brothel. The three paddy rollers were still at the plank table under the oak tree, their heads bent toward one another in a private joke. After the war had begun they had postured as soldiers, carrying the mail from the post office out to Camp Pratt or guarding deserters and drunks, but in reality everyone knew they were mentally and physically unfit for service in the regular army. One man was consumptive, another harelipped, and the third was feebleminded and had worked as a janitor in the state home for the insane.

Flower was about to climb up into the carriage when Rufus Atkins rode into the yard and stopped under the oak tree. He did not acknowledge her or even look in her direction. The three paddy rollers grinned at him and one of them lifted their whiskey bottle in invitation. Atkins dismounted and pulled his shoulder holster and pistol down over his arm and hung them from the pommel of his saddle. His eyes lit on Flower momentarily, seeming to consider her or something about her for reasons she didn't understand. Then the object of his concern, whatever it was, went out of his face and he took a tin cup from his saddlebags and held it out for the harelipped man to pour into. But he remained standing while he drank and did not sit down with the three men at the table.

Flower continued to stare at him, surprised at her own boldness. He stopped his conversation with the paddy rollers in mid-sentence and looked back at her, then set his cup down on the table and walked toward her, the leaves from the oak tree puffing into the great vault of yellow-purple sky behind him.

He wore boots and tight, gray cavalry pants with gold stripes down the legs, a wash-faded checkered shirt, and a slouch hat sweat-stained around the crown. A canvas cartridge belt with loops designed for the new brass-cased ammunition was buckled at an angle on his narrow hips.

"You have something you want to say, Flower?" he asked.

"Not really."

"You bear me a grudge?" he said.

"Miss Carrie in there knows prophecy. Some people say Mr. Willie Burke got the same gift. But folks such as me don't have that gift," she said.

"You're not making a whole lot of sense."

"I cain't read the lines in somebody's palm. But I know you're gonna come to a bad end. It's because you're evil. And you're evil because you're cruel. And you're cruel because inside you're afraid."

He stared into the distance, his fists on his hips, his weight resting casually on one leg. Rain was blowing off the Gulf, like spun glass across the sun. He shook his head.

"I tell you the truth, Flower, you're the damnedest nigger I've ever known and the best piece of rough stock I ever took to bed. That said, would you please get the hell out of here?" he said.

As she rode away in the buggy, she looked back over her shoulder and saw Rufus Atkins counting out a short stack of coins into the palm of each of the paddy rollers. A shaft of sunlight fell on the broad grin of the feeble-minded man. His teeth were as yellow as corn, his eyes filled with a liquid glee.

Chapter Fifteen

Willie Burke no longer knew if the humming sound in his head was caused by the mosquito eggs in his blood or the dysentery in his bowels. The dirt road along the bayou was yellow and hard-packed and the dust from the retreating column drifted into his face. He wore no socks and the leather in his shoes had hardened and split and rubbed blisters across his toes and on his heels. He watched the retreating column disappear around a bend, then ordered his men to fall out and form a defensive line along a coulee that fed into the bayou.

He lay below the rim of the embankment and peered back down the road. Houses were burning in the distance, and when he pressed his ear against the ground he thought he could hear the rumble of wheeled vehicles in the south, but he could see no sign of Union soldiers.

Where were they? he asked himself. Perhaps sweeping south of New Iberia to capture the salt mines down by the Gulf, he thought. It was shady where he lay on the embankment, and he could smell wildflowers and water in the bottom of the coulee and for what seemed just a second he laid his head down in the coolness of the grass and closed his eyes.

An enlisted man shook him by his arm.

"You all right, Lieutenant?" he asked.

"Sure I am," Willie said, his head jerking up. The side of his face was peppered with grains of dirt. He raised himself on his arms and looked down the road at the row of oaks and cypress trees that lined the bayou. He felt light-headed, disconnected in a strange way from the scene around him, as though it belonged somehow inside the world of sleep and he belonged in another place.

He could see a curtain of black smoke rising from the fields in the south now, which told him he had been right in his speculation that the Yankees' main force would concentrate on capturing the salt mines and, at worst, he and his men would not have to deal with more than a diversionary probe.

He looked at the empty road and the cinders rising in the sky from the fields and the wind blowing across the tops of the oak trees and wondered if he would see his mother and Abigail Dowling that evening. Yes, he most certainly would, he told himself. He would bathe in an iron tub and have fresh clothes and he would eat soup and perhaps even bread his mother had baked for him.

He thought about all these things and did not see the Yankee gunboat that came around a bend in the bayou, emerging from behind trees into the gold-purple light of the late afternoon, its port side lined with a half dozen cannons.

He saw a sailor jerk a lanyard at the rear of a Parrott gun, then a shell sucked past his ear and exploded against a tree trunk behind him, showering the coulee with leaves and branches and bits of metal and the sudden glare of the sun. Then he was running down the coulee with the others, away from the bayou and the gunboat that was now abreast of them, close enough for him to see the faces of the gun crews and the sharpshooters on top of the pilothouse.

The row of cannons fired in sequence, turning the boat against its rudder, blowing smoke across the water. He felt himself lifted into the air, borne above the treetops into a sky that was the color of a yellow bruise, his concerns of a second ago no longer of consequence. He struck the earth with a shuddering, chest-emptying impact that was oddly painless, and in a dark place that seemed outside of time, he thought he heard the sound of dirt falling around him like dry rain clicking on a wood box.

★ ★ ★

Abigail drove her buggy along the bayou road and passed a house with twin brick chimneys whose roof had been pocked by a stray cannon shell that had exploded inside and blown the windows onto the lawn. She passed families of Negroes and poor whites who were walking into town with bundles on their heads, and a barefoot Confederate soldier who sat on a log, without gun, hat or haversack, his head hanging between his knees. His teeth were black with gunpowder and a rag was tied across the place where his ear had been.

"Can I change your dressing, sir?" she asked.

"I haven't give it any real thought," he replied.

"Do you know where Willie Burke is?"

"Cain't say as I recall him," the soldier replied.

"Lieutenant Burke. He was on the rear guard."

"This hasn't been a day to be on rear guard. Them sons . . ." The soldier did not finish his sentence. "You wouldn't have any food on you, would you, ma'am?"

She fed the soldier and cleaned the wound on the side of his head and wrapped it with a fresh bandage, then drove farther down the Teche. She expected to see ramparts, batteries of Napoleon or Parrott guns arcing shells into the sky, sharpshooters spread along the lip of a coulee, or mounted officers with drawn sabers cantering their horses behind advancing infantry. Instead, a ragged collection of butternut soldiers was firing behind trees into the distance at no enemy she could see, then retreating, reloading on the ground, and firing again. The air inside the trees was so thick with musket and shotgun smoke that the soldiers had to walk out into the road to see if their fusillade had found a mark.

She heard a metallic cough down the bayou, like a rusty clot breaking loose inside a sewer pipe, then there was silence followed by a chugging sound ripping across the sky. The mortar round exploded in the bayou behind her and bream and white perch rained down through the top of a cypress and flopped on the ground.

A shirtless boy with his pants tucked inside cavalry boots that fit him like galoshes paused by the wagon and stared at her. He carried a flintlock rifle and a powder horn on a leather string that cut across his chest. His skin was gray with dust, his arms thin and rubbery, without muscular tone.

"There's Yankees down there, ma'am," he said.

"I don't see any," she said.

"You ain't suppose to see them. When you can see them, you put a ball in one of them." He grinned at his own joke and looked at the birds in the sky.

"Do you know Lieutenant Willie Burke?" she asked.

He thought about it and pushed a thumb under his right ear, as though it were filled with water or a pocket of air.

"Yes, ma'am, I do," he said.

"Where is he?"

"I think a boat or Whistling Dick got him."

"What?"

The boy's head jerked at a sound behind him.

"Oh Lord Jesus, here it comes," he said, and ran for the trees at the side of the road.

The mortar round reached the apex of its trajectory and chugged out of the sky, exploding in the yard of a plantation across the bayou. Abigail saw Negroes running from a cabin toward the back of the main house, some of them clutching children.

She had to use her whip to force her horse farther down the road. The retreating Confederates were behind her now, around a bend, and the road ahead was empty, whirling with dust when the wind gusted, the sky yellow as sulfur, ripe with the smell of salt, creaking with gulls that had been blown inland by a storm. She rode on another mile, her heart racing, then saw blue-clad foot soldiers come around a curve and fall out on each side of the road, lounging under shade trees, completely indifferent to her presence.

She passed through them, her eyes straight ahead. On a cedar-lined knoll above a coulee two filthy white men in leg irons with wild beards and a group of black men in cast-off Union uniforms were digging a pit. Next to it was a tarpaulin-covered wagon. A cloud went across the sun and raindrops began clicking on the trees and the water in the coulee and the tarpaulin stretched across the wagon.

A young, dark-haired Union lieutenant, with a mustache and clean-shaved cheeks, wearing a patch over one eye and a kepi, approached her buggy.

"You look like you're lost," he said.

"I live in New Iberia, but I've served with the Sanitary Commission in New Orleans. I'm looking for a Southern officer who's been listed as missing in action."

"We're a burial detail. The two men in chains are convicts. I recommend you not get within arm's length of them," the officer said.

The wind gusted out of the south, flapping the tarp on the wagon. An odor like incinerated cowhides struck her nostrils. The lieutenant walked back to his horse and returned with a pair of saddlebags draped over his forearm. He untied the flap on one of the bags and shook fifteen or twenty wooden and tin identification tags onto the carriage seat.

"These are the Rebs we've buried in the last week. I haven't been through the effects of the people in the wagon," he said. His eyes lost their focus and he gazed down the bayou, his face turned into the breeze.

"You said 'people.'"

"A number of them may be civilians, but I can't be sure. Some Rebs were in a house we raked with grape. It caught fire."

She picked up each identification tag individually and examined the name and rank on it. Some of the tags were scratched with Christian crosses on the back. Some of them stuck to her fingers.

"His name isn't among these. I'd like to look in the wagon," she said.

"I don't think that's a good idea," the officer said.

"I don't care what you think."

The officer rotated his head on his neck as though his collar itched him, then brushed at a nostril with one knuckle.

"Suit yourself," he said, and extended his hand to help her down from the buggy.

The officer gestured at the two convicts, who lifted the tarp by its corners and peeled it back over its contents.

The dead were stacked in layers. The faces of some had already grown waxy, the features uniform and no longer individually defined. Others bore the expression they had worn at the exact moment of their deaths, their hands still clutching divots of green grass. The body of a sergeant had been tied with a shingle across the stomach to press his bowels back inside the abdominal cavity. Those who had died in a fire were burned all the way to the bone. A Negro child lay on top of the pile, as though he had curled up there and gone to sleep.

The convicts were watching her face with anticipation.

"Want to put your hand in there?" one of them said.

"Shut up," the officer said.

"Where are your own dead?" Abigail asked.

"In a field mortuary," the officer replied.

"Does the little boy's family know?" she asked.

"I didn't have time to ask," he replied.

"Didn't have time?" she said.

The officer turned back to the convicts and the black laborers.

"Get them in the ground," he said.

One of the convicts picked the Negro boy off the pile by the front of his pants and lifted him free of the wagon. The boy's head and feet arched downward, his stomach bowing outward. His eyes were sealed as tightly as a mummy's. The convict flung him heavily into the pit.

"You bastard," Abigail said.

"Show some care there," the officer said to the convict. "And, madam, you need to step

271

out of the way or take your sensibilities down the road."

She stood aside and watched the laborers and the convicts lay the bodies of the dead side by side in the bottom of the pit. The black men and the convicts had all tied kerchiefs across their faces, and some of the black men had wrapped rags around their hands before they began pulling the dead out of the wagon by their feet and arms. The rain dripped through the canopy overhead and began to pool in the bottom of the pit.

But none of the dead, as least those who were recognizable, resembled Willie Burke.

"I hope you find him," the officer said.

"Thank you," she said.

"Where was he fighting?" he asked.

"On the rear guard."

"Well, those who serve there are brave fellows. Good luck," he said.

Then a huge black man wearing a shapeless hat and a Yankee coat without a shirt walked back down the road and grabbed the ankles of a blood-slick butternut soldier in the underbrush and dragged him into the open.

The black man pulled the kerchief off his nose and mouth. "This 'un bounced off the pile," he said.

"Thank you for telling me that," the officer said.

"You ain't axed, boss. Better come take a

look," the black man said.

"What is it?" the officer asked.

"He just opened his eyes."

Willie lay in the road, the rain ticking in the leaves around him. He could hear men spading dirt out of a pile and flinging it off the ends of their shovels. Abigail was on her knees beside him, lifting his head, pressing the lip of a canteen to his mouth.

"Where are you hit?" she asked.

"Don't know," he said.

She opened his shirt and felt his legs and turned him on his side. She put her fingers in his hair and felt the contours of his skull. Then she rebuttoned his shirt and looked back over her shoulder at the Union officer.

"Were you knocked unconscious?" she asked.

"I dreamed I was underground. There was a little Negro boy next to me. Where am I hit?"

"You're not," she whispered. She touched his lips with two fingers.

"What happened to the Negro boy?" he said.

But she wasn't listening. Her head was turned in the direction of the Union officer and the grave diggers.

"It wasn't a dream, was it?" he said.

"Don't say anything else," she said.

She folded a clean rag into a square and

moistened it and laid it across his eyes, then rose to her feet and approached the Union officer.

"I can take him back with me," she said.

The officer shook his head. "He's a prisoner of war," he said.

She looked back at Willie, then touched the officer on the arm. "Would you step over here with me?" she said.

"Miss, I appreciate your problem but —"

"He's from New Iberia. Let him die at home," she said. She fixed her eyes on the officer's.

"I don't have that kind of authority."

"You send your own to a field mortuary and bury others with no dignity at all. Are you a Christian man, sir?"

"The Rebs made this damn war. We didn't."

She stepped closer to him, her face tilting up into his. Her eyes were so intense they seemed to jitter in the sockets. "Will you add to the sad cargo I've seen here today?" she said.

His stare broke. "Load him up and get him out of here," he said.

On the way into New Iberia, Willie passed out again.

He awoke behind Abigail's cottage, humped on the floor of the buggy. It was almost dark and he could hear horses and wagons and men shouting at one another in the street.

"What's going on?" he said.

"The Confederates are pulling out of town," Abigail replied.

His face was filmed with sweat, his hair in his eyes. During the ride back he had dreamed he was buried alive, his body pressed groove and buttock and phallus and face against the bodies of the dead, all of them sweltering inside their own putrescence. His breath caught in his throat.

"My father was at the Goliad Massacre," he said.

"The what?"

"In the Texas Revolution. He was spared because he hid under the bodies of his friends. He had nightmares until he died of the yellow jack in '39."

"You're not well, Willie. You were having a dream."

He got out of the buggy and almost fell. The trees were dark over his head and through the branches he could see light in the sky and smoke rolling across the moon. The tide was out on the bayou and a Confederate gunboat was stuck in the silt. A group of soldiers and black men on the bank were using ropes and mules to try to pull it free, their lanterns swarming with insects.

"Where's my mother?" Willie said.

"She went out to the farm. The Federals are confiscating people's livestock."

He started walking toward the front of Abigail's cottage and the ground came up and struck him in the face like a fist.

"Oh, Willie, you'll never grow out of being a stubborn Irish boy," she said.

She got him to his feet and walked him into the bathhouse and made him sit down on a wood bench. She opened the valve on the cistern to fill the iron tub with rainwater.

"Get undressed," she said.

"That doesn't sound good," he said, lifting his eyes, then lowering them.

"Do what I say."

She looked in the other direction while he peeled off his shirt and pants and underwear. His torso and legs were so white they seemed to shine, his ribs as pronounced as whalebone stays in a woman's corset. He sat down in the tub and watched the dirt on his body float to the surface.

"I'm going to get you some clean clothes from next door. I'll be right back," she said.

He closed his eyes and let himself slide under the water. Then he saw the face of the Negro child close to his own, as though it were floating inside a bubble, the eyes sealed shut. He jerked his head into the air, gasping for breath. In that moment he knew the kind of dreams that would visit him the rest of his life.

Abigail returned with a clean shirt and a pair of socks and undershorts and pants borrowed from the neighbor.

"Put them on. I'll wait for you in the house," she said.

"Where are the Federals?"

"Not far."

"Do you have a gun?"

"No."

"I need one."

"I think the war is over for you."

"No, it's not over. Wars are never over."

She looked at the manic cast in his eyes and the V-shaped patch of tan under his throat and the tanned skin and liver spots on the backs of his hands. He looked like two different people inside the same body, one denied exposure to light, the other burned by it.

"I'm going to fix you something to eat," she said.

He watched her go out the door and cross the lawn in the shadows and mount the back steps to her cottage. The wind blew through the oaks and he could smell rain and the moldy odor of blackened leaves and pecan husks in the yard. When he rose from the tub the building tilted under his feet, as though something were torn loose inside his head and would not right itself with the rest of the world.

He sat on the wood bench and dressed in the cotton shirt and brown pants Abigail had given him. Civilian clothes felt strange on his body, somehow less than what a man should wear, effete in some way he couldn't describe. He picked up his uniform from the floor and rolled it into a cylinder and went inside the cottage.

"I have to find the 18th," he said.

"You'll go a half block before you pass out again," she said.

"Colonel Mouton was shot in the face at Shiloh. But he was back at it the next day. You don't get to resign, Abby."

"Who needs you more, Willie, your mother or the damn army?"

He smiled at her and began walking toward the front door, knocking into the furniture, as rudderless as a sleepwalker. She caught him by the arm and walked him into her bedroom and pushed him into a sitting position on the mattress. The room was dark, the curtains puffing in the wind.

"Lie down and sleep, Willie. Don't fight with it anymore. It's like fighting against an electrical storm. No matter what we do or don't do, eventually calamity passes out of our lives," she said.

"Do you see Jim Stubbefield's father?"

"Sometimes."

"He carried the guidon straight uphill into their cannons. They blew his brains all over my shirt. I'll never get over Jim. I hate the sons of bitches who caused all this."

He felt her fingers stroking his hair, then

he put his arms around her hips and pulled her body against his face and held her more tightly than was reasonable or dignified, burying his face in her stomach, touching the backs of her thighs now, raising his head to her breasts, gathering her dress in both his hands.

She lay down with him, and he kissed her mouth and eyes and neck and felt the roundness of her breasts and put his hand between her thighs, without shame or even embarrassment at the nakedness of his own need and dependence.

It was raining on the trees and the bayou, and he could smell grass burning inside the rain and hear the cough of the mortar round called Whistling Dick. He climbed between Abigail Dowling's thighs and kissed the tops of her breasts and put her nipples in his mouth, then kissed the flat taper of her stomach and raised himself up on his arms while she cupped his sex with her palm and placed it inside her.

He came a moment later, early on beyond any attempt at self-control, his eyes tightly shut. Inside his mind he saw an endless field of dead soldiers under a night sky rimmed by hills that looked like women's breasts. But even as his heart twisted inside him and his seed filled her womb, he knew the safe harbor and succor she had given him were an act of mercy, and the tenderness in her eyes and the caress of her thighs and the kiss he now felt on his cheek were the gifts granted to a needy supplicant and not to a lover.

He lay next to her and looked at the shadows on her face.

"I'm sorry my performance is not the kind Sir Walter Scott would have probably been interested in writing about," he said.

"Oh, no, you were fine," she said, and touched the top of his hand.

He stared at the ceiling, wondering why ineptitude seemed to follow him like a curse.

He heard a plank creak on the front gallery and a knock on the door.

"Miss Abigail, the Yankees set fire to the laundry. They attacked some girls in the quarters. You in there, Miss Abby?" the voice of Flower Jamison said.

Chapter Sixteen

Flower had to wait outside almost five minutes before Abigail Dowling finally came to the door. Then she saw Willie Burke step out of the bedroom into the glow of the living room lamp and her face tightened with embarrassment.

"I'm sorry. I reckon I caught y'all at supper," she said.

"Come in, Flower," Abigail said, holding back the door.

"How you do, Mr. Willie?" Flower said.

"Hello, Flower. It's good to see you again. Miss Abby says you've been doing splendidly with your lessons." His voice was thick, his cheeks pooled with color, as though he had a fever. His eyes did not quite meet hers.

"Thank you, suh," she said.

"What was that about the laundry?" Abigail asked.

"Some Yankees came across the fields and started pushing people out of the cabins.

They drug a corn-shuck mattress behind the laundry and chased down some girls and drug them back there, too. When they were finished they lit a cannonball and threw it through the kitchen window."

"Where'd they go?" Willie asked.

"To the saloon. They were carrying all the rum out the door."

"Did you see other troops? Soldiers in large numbers?" Willie asked.

"No," she said.

"You stay here tonight," Abigail said. "I'm going to take Mr. Willie to his mother's."

"Mr. Willie, you suppose to be in reg'lar clothes like that?" Flower said.

"Not exactly," he replied.

"Suh, there's bad things going on. Don't let them hurt you," she said.

"They're not interested in people like me," he said.

"I hid in the coulee, but I could hear what they were doing on the other side of the laundry. You don't want them to catch you, suh."

"You be good, Flower. The next time I see you, I'm going to have a new book for you," he said.

Please don't talk down to me, she thought. "Yes, suh. Thank you," she said.

Abigail and Willie walked out into the yard. Flower followed them as far as the gallery.

"Mr. Willie, put your uniform on," she said.

He grinned at her, then climbed into the buggy beside Abigail. Flower stood on the gallery and watched them ride away toward the center of town.

Miss Abby, aren't you a surprise? she thought.

The sky was red in the south, and pieces of burnt cane, like black thread, drifted into the yard. A riderless white horse cinched with a military saddle wandered in the street, its hooves stepping on the reins. The shutters and doors of every house on the street were latched shut.

By habit she did not sit down in a white person's home until she was in the kitchen. She wished she had taken her books and writing tablets from her cabin, and she wondered if the soldiers who had attacked the girls had found the box she kept under her bed and thrown its contents into the flames that had climbed out of the laundry's windows.

The fact that their uniforms were blue didn't matter, she thought. Their kind hated books, just as the paddy rollers did and Clay Hatcher and Rufus Atkins did and all those who feared knowledge because of what it could reveal to others about themselves.

The cannon fire had stopped and there was no sound of either horses or wagons in the streets, but she believed the quietness outside and the easy sweep of wind in the trees were like the deceptions that had always characterized the world she had grown up in. Nothing was ever as it seemed. A child was born in a cabin to a mother and a father and believed it belonged to a family not totally unlike the one that lived in the columned house up on the hill. Then one day the mother or the father or perhaps the child was sold or traded, either for money or land or livestock, and no one was supposed to take particular notice of the fact that the space occupied by a human being, made of flesh and blood, a member of a family, had been emptied in the time it took to sign a bill of sale.

But Flower had come to believe that moral insanity was not confined to people who lived in columned houses.

That day Yankee soldiers had come hot and dirty across a burned field, and while a Union flag flapped from a staff above their wagon, they had lined up to rape two fifteen-year-old girls whose mother was beaten back from the scene with a barrel slat.

Abigail Dowling loved human beings and nursed the dying and risked her life for the living and was detested as a traitor.

Willie Burke taught her to read and write. Then served in an army that had no higher purpose than to keep African people in bondage to ignorance and the overseer's lash.

She thought she had freed herself of her anger by helping other slaves escape up the Mississippi to Ohio. But an English poet in one of her books had used a term she couldn't forget. The term was "mind-forged manacles." They didn't get left on the banks of the Ohio River, she thought. They were the kind people carried to the grave.

What if she set about teaching others to read and write, just as Mr. Willie Burke had taught her, she thought. Each person she taught would in turn teach another, and that person another. If the Yankee soldier who stood guard in the hospital in New Orleans had not been murdered by Ira Jamison's men, she would have been able to give him what Mr. Willie had given her. But now she could create an even larger goal for herself. She could do something that was truly grand, influential in ways she had never imagined. By teaching one person at a time, she had the potential to empower large numbers of people to forever change their lives.

The thought made the blood rush to her head and she wondered if she was not indeed vainglorious and self-deluded. She heard the wind chimes tinkling on the gazebo and through the back window saw the moonlight inside the oak branches and shadows moving on the grass when the wind blew through the limbs overhead. Then a darkened steamboat passed on the bayou, its stacks blowing sparks on a roof, its wake slapping hard against the cypress trunks.

For just a moment she thought she saw the silhouette of a man on the bank, a stick figure backlit briefly by the red glow off the steamboat's stacks. She got up from the kitchen table and walked out into the yard. But the boat was gone and the bayou was dark again, and all she could see along the bank were the heart-shaped tops of flooded elephant ears beaded with drops of water as fat as marbles.

She went back inside the kitchen and sat down at the table and put her head down on her arms. She wondered where Ira Jamison was. She wondered what he would do when Yankee soldiers swept across his lands and drove off or killed his livestock and fired his barns and cotton fields and freed his slaves and gutted the inside of his house and perhaps stacked his furniture in the front yard for burning. She wondered what he would have to say when he was powerless, sick, and alone.

Then she wondered why she even cared.

When would she ever free herself of the father who not only refused to recognize her but who in a letter to Nathan Forrest said he was "quite sick of being tended by unwashed niggers"?

Maybe one day some of them would tend him in hell, she thought.

But the clear, bright edges of her anger would not hold, and again she fell back into the self-hating thoughts that invaded her soul whenever she meditated long upon the name of Ira Jamison.

An image flicked past a side window, like a shard of light out of a dream. She raised her head off her arms and stared out in the darkness, wondering if she had fallen asleep. The air smelled like leaves burning on a fall day. A twig snapped in the yard and she heard feet moving fast across the ground, then a shadow went across the kitchen window.

She locked down the bolt on the back door and walked to the front of the cottage and stepped out on the gallery. She looked up and down the street, but no one was there and the only lamp burning on the block was in the house of a mad woman. Then the riderless white horse thundered across the lawn and crashed through banana trees into the street, its eyes bulging in a ripple of heat lightning across the sky.

She went into the kitchen and fired the woodstove, then uncovered the water barrel by the pantry and dipped an iron pot with a long handle into the water and set it on top of the stove lid.

She locked the door in the living room and sat down in a chair by the front window. She wished she had a pistol or a rifle or a shotgun, it didn't matter what kind. She had never held one in her hands, but for a life-time she had watched white men handle them, take them apart, clean and oil them, load and cock and fire them, and she never doubted the degree of affection the owner of a gun had for his weapon nor the sense of control it gave him.

But Abigail Dowling owned no firearms and would allow none in her home. So Flower sat with her hands clenched in her lap, her heart beating, and wondered when Abigail would return home.

She heard a plank bend under someone's weight on the gallery. She waited for a knock, but there was only silence. The doorknob twisted and the door began to ease forward in the jamb before it caught against the deadbolt. Her heart hammered in her ears.

She rose from her chair. She could see no one in the yard and the angle of her vision prevented her from seeing who was on the gallery. She walked to the door and stood only inches from it, looking at the threadlike, cracked lines in the paint on the cypress boards, the exposed, square nailheads that were darkened with rust, a thimbleful of cobweb stuck behind a hinge.

"Who is it?" she asked.

"Got a message from the aid station for Miss Abigail Dowling."

"She cain't come to the door right now."

"The surgeon don't have a nurse. He says

288

for her to get down there."

"I'll tell her."

"She in the privy?"

"Who are you?"

But this time he didn't answer and she heard feet moving past the side window. She screwed down the wick in the living room oil lamp until the flame died, then hurried to the kitchen and took a butcher knife from a drawer. The fire glowed under the stove lids and the air was hot and close with the steam that curled off the pot she had set to boil. She stood motionless in the darkness, her clenched palm sweating on the wood handle of the knife.

The first man through the back door splintered it loose from the bolt with one full-bodied kick. Then he plunged into the kitchen with two other men behind him, all three of them wearing white cotton cloths with eye holes tied tightly across their faces. They went from room to room in the cottage as though she were not there, as though the knife in her hand were of no more significance than the fact she was a witness to a home invasion.

Then all three of them returned to the kitchen and stared at her through the holes in their masks. She could hear them breathing and smell the raw odor of corn liquor on their breaths.

"Where's she at?" one man said. He

wheezed deep down in his chest.

"Not here."

"That's helpful," he said, and looked at the broken door. He pushed it back in place with his foot. He grabbed her wrist and swung her hand against the stove and knocked the butcher knife to the floor. "When will she be back?"

"When she feel like it."

The man looked at the steam rising off the pot on the stove. He coughed into his hand, then breathed hard, as though fighting for air, the cloth of his mask sucking into his mouth. "You making tea?" he asked.

She looked at the wall, her arms folded across her chest, her pulse jumping in her throat.

"Let's get out of here," a second man said.

"We got paid for a night's work. We ought to earn at least part of it," the first man said.

The three men looked at one another silently, as though considering a profound thought.

"Sounds good to me," the third man said.

They walked Flower into the bedroom, releasing her arms when they reached the bed, waiting, the night air outside filled with the singing of tree frogs.

"You want to undress or should we do it for you?" the first man said. He turned his head, lifted his mask briefly, and spit out the window. "Enjoy it, gal. We ain't bad men.

Just doin' a piece of work."

For the next half hour she tried to find a place in her mind that was totally black, without light or sound or sensation of any kind, safe from the incessant coughing of a consumptive man an inch from her ear and the smell of chewing tobacco and testosterone that now seemed ironed on her skin. When the last man lifted his weight from her, the cloth across his face swung out from his mouth and his teeth made her think of kernels of yellow corn.

Chapter Seventeen

Abigail and Willie rode in her buggy to his mother's small farm by Spanish Lake, five miles outside of town. The house was dark inside the overhang of the oak trees, and the animals were gone from the pens and the barn. The front door of the house gaped open, the broken latch hanging by a solitary nail. A dead chicken lay humped on the gallery, its feathers fluttering in the wind. Willie stepped inside the doorway and lit a candle on the kitchen table. The rows of dishes and cups and jars of preserves on the shelves were undisturbed, but the hearthstones had been prized out of the fireplace and several blackened bricks chipped loose with a sharp tool from inside the chimney.

"I've heard tell about jayhawkers in the area," Abigail said.

"This bunch wore blue uniforms. Jayhawkers would have taken the food," he replied.

His words lingered in the air, the syllables touched with an angry stain she couldn't associate with the boy she used to know.

The entire rural landscape seemed empty of people as well as livestock. The ground was powdered with white ash, the pecan orchards sculpted in the moonlight, the sky full of birds that never seemed to touch the earth. They passed Camp Pratt and looked at the deserted barracks and the wind wrinkling the surface of the lake. Across the water there was a red glow in the bottom of the sky. Briefly they heard the popping of small-arms fire, then it was quiet again and there was no sound except the wind and the creaking of the trees.

"I'm sure your mother's all right," Abigail said.

He didn't speak for a long time. She looked at the profile of his face, the darkness in his eyes, the way his civilian clothes seemed inappropriate on his body.

"Do you regret this evening?" he asked.

"Pardon?" she said, looking straight ahead.

"You hear right well when you choose to."

"I don't do anything I don't wish to," she said. She could feel the intensity of his eyes on the side of her face.

"You're a damn poor liar, Abby."

"I know of no greater arrogance than for a man to tell a woman what she feels."

"Perhaps my experience is inadequate," he replied.

The buggy rumbled across a wood bridge that spanned a coulee. A large, emaciated dog with a bad hind leg climbed out from under the bridge and ran crookedly into a cane field, a red bone in its mouth.

"Hold up," Willie said.

He got down in the road and walked to the crest of the coulee. At the bottom of the slope, among the palmettos, were the bodies of three Union soldiers. Two lay facedown in the water, an entry wound in the back of each of their heads, the hair blown back against the scalp by the closeness of the muzzle blast. The third man lay on his side on the far bank, one eye staring back at Willie, the other covered by a black leather patch. The wrists of all three men had been tied behind them. Their weapons were gone and their pockets had been pulled inside out.

Abigail stood next to Willie.

"It's the officer from the burial detail," she said.

"Yes, it is. Poor fellow," Willie said. He looked off into the pecan orchards by the lake and up and down the road and out into the field.

"Who did this?" she asked.

"They call themselves guerrillas or irregulars. Most of them are criminals," he said.

"How do you know Confederates didn't do it, Willie?"

He paused before he replied, a vein working in his neck. "Because these men still have their shoes on, and secondly we don't murder prisoners of war," he said.

"The stories about Negro prisoners aren't true?" she said.

"I have to find my unit. Tell my mother I'm sorry I couldn't find her."

"Me? You take care of your own family. You stop this insanity," she said.

"The Yankees rape slave women and burn people's farms. I've seen them do it, Abby. It doesn't matter who starts a war. The only thing that matters is who finishes it."

His words came out with such ferocity that his head throbbed and he became short of breath. He thought he saw men moving through the trees but realized he was only looking at shadows.

"I think the war is poisoning your heart," she said.

The skin of his face felt as though she had slapped it.

They rode back toward New Iberia in silence, sullen, angry at each other, the most tender moment in their day now only a decaying memory, each wondering if the other was not either a stranger or an enemy.

Willie left her outside the town limits and

crossed through a cane field that was cut by the deep tracks of wheeled cannons, then stole a pirogue from a dock and paddled it across Bayou Teche to the far bank and walked through the yard of a deserted plantation house to a pecan grove by the St. Martinville Road.

The whole countryside seemed alive with movement, all of it the wrong kind. He saw Union soldiers sacking the home of Jubal Labiche, a slave-owning free man of color who operated a brick factory down the Teche and who had spent a lifetime courting the favor of plantation whites. Jubal had sent his daughters North to be educated, hoping they would marry there and rinse the family veins of the African blood that had always denied him full membership in white society. Now Union soldiers were stacking his imported furniture for a bonfire, smashing his crockery, and tearing his piano apart in the yard with an ax.

Freed slaves crisscrossed the road, running from one house to the next, like children trick-or-treating on Halloween, filling blankets and sheets with silverware, candelabras, tailored men's suits and ballroom dresses. A solitary artillery shell arced out of nowhere and exploded in a puff of pink smoke high above the bayou, and no one gave it notice, as though it were part of the celebration taking place below.

Willie backed away from the road and followed the bayou upstream, crossing through backyards and wash lines, keeping the trees and outbuildings between himself and the road. He crossed a coulee that smelled of rainwater and night-blooming flowers, then in a leaf-banked spot between a corn crib and a woodpile he tripped across the body of a dead Confederate soldier.

The soldier, who had been shot through the lungs, had probably been hit somewhere else and had crawled there to die. His skin was gray, his mouth gaping at the moon, the coughing of his blood still bright on the stones he had crawled across before his death. A pair of brass binoculars hung from his neck on a leather cord.

Willie removed the binoculars and found a long, horn-handled folding knife in the dead soldier's back pocket. He followed the blood trail backward to the edge of a cane field, looking for a gun, then entered the cane and hunted through the rows, but could find no weapons of any kind. He went back to the bayou, into the shadows of the cypresses and live oaks, and continued walking upstream toward St. Martinville, where he believed he would eventually encounter the rear guard of his own army. He carried his tightly rolled, blood-streaked, butternut uniform under his right arm.

Abigail had wanted him to surrender, to join the increasing number of deserters who offered every justification possible for leaving their brothers-in-arms to go it on their own. Their arguments were hard to contend with. Hunger, malaria, foot rot, leeches on a man's ankles and the eggs of crab lice in the seams of his clothes were a poor form of pay for marching uphill into canister or grape or repeater rifles the Yankees loaded on Sunday and fired all week.

If men deserted under those circumstances, it was only human and no one who had not paid the same dues had any right to condemn them, Willie thought. But by the same token few of them would probably ever make peace with themselves. They would always feel less about who they had become, robbed by their own hand of the deeds they had performed honorably, and excluded from the comradeship of the best and bravest men they would ever know.

Why was it so difficult for Abby to understand that?

Because she doesn't love you, his mind answered.

He had come to her like a beggar. He was not only a recipient of sexual charity, he was an object of pity and, in her own words, a man who had let the war poison his heart.

He sat down on top of an overturned pirogue and put his face in his hands. He could smell the odor of the dead Confederate soldier on his palms.

Five miles farther up the bayou he knelt among a cluster of palmettos behind a rick fence and used the dead soldier's binoculars to watch a scene that seemed created by the inhabitants of an outdoor mental asylum. A stack of furniture, oil paintings, and mattresses was burning in the backyard of a plantation home and black women dressed in brocaded evening gowns and Sunday hats with ostrich plumes on them danced in the firelight to a tune played by a bare-chested fiddler with braided hair, who wore a necklace strung with human fingers around his throat.

Between twenty and thirty white men in civilian clothes were passing rum bottles in wicker baskets from hand to hand and cooking a pig spitted on a trace chain over a bed of coals. Down by the bayou, a man was copulating with a black woman against the back wall of a stable, his white buttocks glowing with moonlight, her legs wrapped around him.

Willie focused his binoculars on the faces of the white men but recognized none of them. Some were armed with muskets, others with shotguns and hatchets, at least two with bows and feathered arrows. He had heard of both jayhawkers and guerrillas operating in Louisiana, the guerrillas under the command of a man named Jarrette, a Missourian who had ridden with Quantrill and Bloody Bill Anderson. The man apparently in charge of the group in the plantation yard wore a long sword in a metal scabbard and a butternut shirt and sky blue skintight pants, with a gold stripe down each leg. His hair was copper-colored, tangled on his shoulders, his face oily and poached in the firelight, the front of his hat pinned up on the crown so that he looked like he was facing into a gale.

They must be jayhawkers, Willie thought, deserters, conscription evaders, criminals of every stripe who hid in the swamps and preyed upon all comers. Certainly these seemed to be getting along well enough with freed slaves.

But guerrilla or jayhawker, it didn't matter. They both fought under a black flag and extended no mercy and took no prisoners.

The white man copulating with the Negro woman finished with her and reached down to pull up his trousers. When he did, the firelight caught his face and Willie recognized one of the manacled convicts who had almost buried him alive.

He was stuck. He couldn't cross the yard of the plantation without being seen, nor could he retrace his steps without risk of running into Federals who were undoubtedly advancing up the Teche toward St. Martinville. He climbed into a coulee and lay back against the incline and rested his arm across his eyes for what he thought would be no more than a few minutes. He could hear the black women dancing around the fire and ducks wimpling the water in the shallows and a bell clanging on a cow somewhere in a field. In seconds the war seemed to disappear like light draining out of his bedroom at the back of his mother's house.

An hour later he woke to the sound of running feet. The bonfire in the yard had collapsed into a pile of blackened wood, and the wind was kicking up cinders from it into the sky. The men in the yard were running into a pecan orchard, spreading along the same rick fence that rimmed the coulee where he had slept, some sprinting across the road into more trees. A drunken black woman tried to hold onto the arm of a man with a blue rag tied around his head. He shoved her in the face, knocking her back across a log. In less than two minutes the men from the yard had become motionless, their bodies and weapons absorbed by the shadows, their hats slanted down on their faces so their skin would not reflect light.

Down the road walked sixteen blue-clad soldiers in single file, their equipment clanking in the darkness, some of them with their rifles carried horizontally across their shoulders like broom handles. An arrow zipped through the darkness from behind a tree trunk, and the lead soldier stumbled and fell to the ground as though he had stepped in a hole and lost his balance. The other soldiers stopped and stared stupidly into the shadows, just before a volley of shotgun and musket fire from both sides of the road tore into their file.

The men from the plantation yard swarmed out of the shadows with bayonets, knives and hatchets, warbling the Rebel yell as they ran.

I guess you're not jayhawkers after all, Willie thought.

He leapt from the coulee and bolted across the backyard of the plantation toward St. Martinville. He looked back over his shoulder and saw the guerrillas at work in the road, chopping with their steel instruments like sugar harvesters cutting cane in the fall.

Two hours later, as the stars went out of the sky and the horizon turned gray in the east, his breath and his legs gave out simultaneously as though all his blood had suddenly been drained from his veins. He fell to his knees and crawled underneath an overturned rowboat inside a leaf-strewn stand of persimmon trees. With his uniform rolled under his cheek, he slept the sleep of the dead.

When he awoke the sun was a white flame in his eyes and the Yankee enlisted men who pointed their rifles in his face asked if he would mind accompanying them to a prisoner of war compound just up the road.

★ ★ ★

Three days later he sat under a shade tree and waited his turn to enter a wide galleried, notched and pegged house outside of St. Martinville. Inside the living room, behind a flat oak desk, sat General Nathaniel Banks. His dark hair looked like wire, coated in grease, stacked in layers, his upper lip like the bill on a duck. Outside the house, spread across two acres of pasture, upward of three hundred captured men milled about, most in patchwork butternut and gray uniforms. The prisoner compound was marked off with laths and string to which strips of rag were tied. Brass field pieces loaded with grape were positioned on the four corners of the square, and pickets armed with rifle-muskets or Spencer repeaters were posted at twenty-yard intervals along the string, or what came to be known as the "Deadline." Threaded in among the deserters and captured soldiers were members of the group Willie had seen ambush the squad of Federals on the St. Martinville Road, including the apparent leader, the man in a pinned-up cavalry hat and skintight pants with a gold stripe down each leg.

A Union sergeant tapped the sole of Willie's shoe with his own.

"Your turn inside," he said.

"Really, now? After three days I get to meet the Massachusetts bobbin boy?" Willie said.

The sergeant's kepi made a damp line across the back of his dark red hair. He wore a goatee and a poor excuse for a mustache and a silver ring with a tiny cross affixed to it on his marriage finger. He started to speak, then touched at a place on his lip and gazed off into space as though a thought had escaped his mind.

Willie got to his feet and started toward the house. Beyond the Deadline he saw a weathered red barn and seven or eight soldiers with rifle-muskets in the shade along the side wall, their weapons propped butt-down in the dirt.

The sergeant pulled Willie's sleeve.

"Listen, the general is handling these interviews because he lost some good men to a gang of cutthroats. You look to be a decent man. Use your head in there, Reb," he said.

"You have problems of conscience?" Willie said.

"A good man don't have to prove it," the sergeant said.

"You've lost me, Yank. Say again?"

"I think you're one on whom words are easily wasted," the sergeant said. He escorted Willie inside the house, where Willie stood in front of General Banks.

The general's boots and dark blue uniform were splattered with dried mud. He had tangled eyebrows and deep-set eyes that seemed filled with either conflicting or angry thoughts, and the skin at the top of his forehead was a sickly white. The odor of horse liniment and wood smoke and unrinsed soap emanated from his clothes. He peered down his nose at a list of names on a sheet of paper. By his left hand was Willie's crumpled uniform.

"Who are you? Or rather what are you?" he asked.

"First Lieutenant William Burke, 18th Louisiana Volunteers, at your service, sir."

"And these rags here are your uniform?"

"That appears to be the case, sir."

The general lifted up the uniform, revealing a pair of brass binoculars and a folding, horn-handled knife under it.

"These are your knife and your field glasses?" he asked.

"No, I took them off a dead man, probably a forward artillery observer. One of ours."

The general's eyes lingered on a neutral spot in space, then looked at Willie again, the cast in them somehow different now.

"Can you tell me why you're out of uniform?" he asked.

"I was prematurely stuffed into one of your burial wagons. The dead have a way of leaking their shite and other fluids all over their companions, sir."

The general drummed his fingers on the table, gazed out the window, brushed at his nose with his knuckle.

"You look like a civilian to me, Mr. Burke, a good fellow at the wrong place at the wrong time, one probably willing to sign an oath of allegiance and go about his way," he said.

"It's First Lieutenant Willie Burke, sir. I was at Shiloh and Corinth and a half-dozen places since. I'll not be signing a loyalty oath."

"Damn it, man, you were out of uniform!"

"I gave you a reasonable explanation, too!" Willie replied.

It was quiet inside the room. The wind ruffled the papers on the general's desk. Through the window Willie could see the weathered red barn in the distance and a sergeant who was ordering the line of seven or eight enlisted men around to the back side. One of them was arguing, and the sergeant grabbed him by his blouse and shoved him against the wall.

"Take a seat outside in the hall, Lieutenant. I'll continue our talk in a few minutes," he said.

The sergeant who had escorted Willie inside the house walked him into the breezeway and pointed at a chair for him to sit in. Then he shook his finger reprovingly in Willie's face.

"I come from a religious family, but I had to learn the only real pacifist is a dead Quaker. I decided to make an adjustment. Do you get my meaning?" he said.

"It escapes me," Willie said.

The sergeant went outside and returned with a frightened man who had a pie-plate face, arms like bread dough, and rows of tiny yellow teeth.

Willie had seen him around New Iberia. What was his name? He was simpleminded and did janitorial work. Pinky? Yes, that was it. Pinky Strunk. What was he doing here?

Through the open door Willie could hear the general questioning him.

"You were in possession of five Spanish reals. That's a lot of money for a working-man to have clanking in his pocket," the general said.

"Ain't no law against it. Not that I know of," Pinky answered.

"Sixteen of my men were ambushed and butchered on the St. Martinville Road. I think you're one of the men who looted the bodies," the general said.

"Not me. No, suh."

From behind the red barn there was a volley of rifle fire, then a cloud of smoke drifted out into the sunlight.

"Jesus God!" Pinky said.

"How did you come by five Spanish pieces-of-eight?" the general asked.

"Is that a firing squad out there, suh?"

"How did you come by the reals?"

"It's kind of private."

"Not anymore."

"Done a chore for a man. Me and two others."

"What might that be?" the general asked.

The man named Pinky blew his nose in a handkerchief.

"We was s'pposed to —" he began. But his voice faltered.

"Supposed to do what?"

"Fix an uppity nurse who don't know her place. I never stole in my life. Man who says so is a liar."

"Start over again."

"There's a Captain Atkins paid us to put the spurs to a troublesome white woman. She wasn't home so we give it to a darky instead. Three of us topped her. That's the long and the short of it. I ain't looted no dead Yankees."

"Sergeant, take this man to the provost-marshal. The paperwork will follow," the general said.

"Y'all sending me back home?" Pinky said. His eyes blinked as he waited for the general's response.

A half hour later Willie was standing once again in front of the general. Through the window he saw two Yankee soldiers escorting Pinky Strunk behind the barn, gripping him by each arm. He was arguing with them, twisting his face from one to the other.

"Sixteen of my men were butchered, their throats slit, their ring fingers cut off their hands. Don't be clever with me," the general said.

"The killers of your men are out yonder in the compound, General. Pinky Strunk isn't one of them," Willie said.

"Then you'd damn well better point them out."

A ragged volley of rifle fire exploded from behind the barn.

"Would you have a chew of tobacco on you, sir?" Willie asked.

That evening he stood at the barred window of a brick storehouse on the bank of Bayou Teche and watched the sun descend in a cloud of purple smoke in the west. It was cool and damp-smelling inside the storehouse, and the oaks along the bayou were a dark green in the waning light, swelling with wind, the air heavy with the fecund odor of schooled-up bream popping the surface of the water among the lily pads.

Other men sat on the dirt floor, some with their heads hanging between their knees. They were looters, rapists, guerrillas, jayhawkers, grave robbers, accused spies, or people who just had very bad luck. In fact, Willie believed at that moment that the nature of the crimes they had committed was less important than the fact that anarchy had spread across the land and the deaths of these men would restore some semblance of order to it.

At dawn, the general had said.

How big a price should anyone have to pay to retain his integrity? Willie asked himself. How did he come to this juncture in his life?

Arrogance and pride, his mind answered.

He could hear his heart pounding in his ears.

Chapter Eighteen

Flower Jamison did not sleep the night she was raped. She bathed in the iron tub behind Abigail Dowling's cottage, then put back on the same clothes she had worn before the attack and sat alone in the darkness, looking out on the street until Abigail returned home.

"What happened?" Abigail asked, staring at the splintered door in the kitchen.

"Three men broke in and raped me," Flower replied.

"Federals broke in here? You were ra—"

"They were civilians. They were looking for you. They took me instead."

"Oh, Flower."

"What one man more than any other wants to hurt you? A man who hates you, who's cruel through and through?"

"I don't know."

"Yes, you do," Flower said.

"Rufus Atkins threatened me. Out there, in

the street. Yesterday," Abigail said.

Flower nodded her head.

"I saw him give money to three men be-hind Carrie LaRose's house earlier today."

"That doesn't prove anything."

"Yes, it does. I saw a man's yellow teeth under his mask. I heard the coins clink in their pants. It was them."

"Are you hurt inside?"

"They hurt me everywhere," she replied.

She refused to use the bed Abigail offered her and sat in the chair all night. Before dawn, without eating breakfast, she left the cottage and walked down Main and stood under the wood colonnade in front of McCain's Hardware. She wiped the film off the window with her hand in several places and tried to see inside. Then she walked out in the country to the laundry where she had worked. It and the cabins behind it were burned to the ground.

She walked back up the road to the back door of Carrie LaRose's bordello. She had to knock twice before Carrie came to the door.

"What you mean banging on my do' this early in the morning?" Carrie said.

"Need to earn some money," Flower said.

Carrie looked out at the fog on the fields and the blackened threads of sugarcane on her lawn, as though the morning itself might contain either an omen or threat. She wore glass rings on the fingers of both hands and a housecoat and a kerchief on her head and paper curlers in her hair that made Flower think of a badly plucked chicken inside a piece of cheesecloth.

"Doing what?" Carrie asked.

"Cleaning, washing, ironing, anything you want. I can sew, too. The Yankees are calling us contrabands. That means the Southerners cain't own us anymore."

"Already got somebody to do all them things."

"I can write letters for you. I know how to subtract and add sums."

"Want money? You know how to get it," Carrie said.

"Thank you for your time, Miss Carrie."

"Don't give me a look like I'm hard, no."

"You ain't hard. You just for sale."

"You like a pop in the face?" Carrie said.

Flower looked at the plank table under the live oak where Captain Rufus Atkins had counted out a short stack of heavy coins in the palms of the paddy rollers only yesterday afternoon.

"I axed for a job. You don't have one. I won't bother you anymore," Flower said.

"Wait up, you," Carrie said. She fitted the thickness of her hand under Flower's chin and turned it back and forth, exposing her throat to the light. "Who give you them marks?"

"I need a job, Miss Carrie."

"Abigail Dowling ain't gonna let you go hungry. You wanting money for somet'ing else, ain't you?"

Flower turned and walked down the steps and into the fog rolling out of the fields. It felt damp and invasive on her skin, like the moist touch of a soiled hand on her arm.

She wandered the town until noon, without direction or purpose. Many of the shops along Main Street had been broken open and looted, except the hardware store, which the owner, a man named Todd McCain, had emptied of its goods before the Yankees had come into town during the night. In fact, McCain had taken the extra measure of turning the cash register toward the glass window so passersby could see that the compartments in the drawer contained no money.

Yankee soldiers, some of them still drunk, slept under the trees on the bayou. She sat on a wood bench by the drawbridge and watched a steamboat loaded with blue-clad sharpshooters lounging behind cotton bales work its way upstream toward St. Martinville. The sharpshooters waved at her, and one pointed at his fly and held his hands apart as though showing her the size of an enormous fish.

The Episcopalian church, which had been a field hospital for Confederate wounded, had now been converted into a stable, the pews pushed together to form feed troughs. Flower watched the sun climb in the sky, then disappear among the tree branches over her head. She slept with her head on her chest and dreamed of a man holding a white snake in his hand. He grinned at her, then placed the head of the snake in his mouth and held it there while he unbuttoned and removed his shirt.

She woke abruptly and cleared her throat and spat into the dirt, widening her eyes until the images from the dream were gone from her mind. Then she rose from the bench and walked unsteadily through the shade, into the heat of the day, toward McCain's Hardware.

"You want to look at what?" the owner, Todd McCain, said.

"The pistol. You had it in the glass case before the Yankees came to town," she replied.

"I don't remember no pistol," McCain said. He had been a drummer from Atlanta who had come to New Iberia on the stage and married an overweight widow ten years his senior. His body was hard and egg-shaped, the shoulders narrow, his metallic hair greased and parted down the middle.

"I want to see the pistol. Or I'll come back with a Yankee soldier who'll help you find it," she said.

"That a fact?" he said.

He fixed his eyes on her face, a smile

breaking at the side of his mouth. She turned and started back out the door. "Hold on," he said.

He went into the back of the store and returned to the front and laid a heavy object wrapped in oily flannel on top of the glass case. He glanced at the street, then unwrapped a cap-and-ball revolver with dark brown grips. The blueing on the tip of the barrel and on the cylinder was worn a dull silver from holster friction.

"That's a Colt .36 caliber revolver. Best sidearm you can buy," he said.

"How much is it?"

"You people ain't suppose to have these."

"I'm a contraband now. I can have anything I want. No different than a free person of color."

"Twelve dollars. I ain't talking about Confederate paper, either."

"Maybe I don't have twelve right now. But maybe part of it."

"That a fact?" He looked into space, as though calculating figures in his head. "Under the right circumstances I can come down to ten, maybe eight."

"Right circumstances?"

"I could use a little hep in the storeroom. Won't take long. If you feel like walking on back there with me."

"I'll be back later."

"Tell you what, hep me out and I'll go

down to six. I cain't make it more right than that," he said. He wet his bottom lip, as though it were chapped, and looked away from her face.

"You all right, suh?" she asked.

He averted his eyes and didn't reply. After she was gone he threw the revolver angrily in a drawer.

She walked down the street toward Abigail Dowling's cottage and saw a carriage parked in front of the Shadows. Through the iron gate she caught sight of Ira Jamison, sitting at a table on a flagstone terrace under oak trees, with two Yankee officers and a cotton trader from Opelousas. The grass was sprinkled with azalea petals, the gazebo and trellises in the gardens humped with blue bunches of wisteria. The gate creaked on its hinges when she pulled it open.

She followed the brick walkway through the trees to the terrace. The four men at the table were drinking coffee from small cups and laughing at a joke. A walking cane rested against the arm of Ira Jamison's chair. His hair had grown to his shoulders and looked freshly shampooed and dried, and the weight he had lost gave his face a kind of fatal beauty, perhaps like a poisonous flower she had read of in a poem.

"I need you to lend me twelve dol'ars," she said.

He twisted around in his chair. "My heavens, Flower, you certainly know how to sneak up on a man," he said.

"The man at the store says that's the price for a Colt .36 revolver. I 'spect he's lying, but I still need the twelve dol'ars," she said.

The other three men had stopped talking. Ira Jamison pulled on his earlobe.

"What in heaven's name do you need a pistol for?" he said.

"Your overseer, Rufus Atkins, paid three men to rape Miss Abigail. She wasn't home, so they did it to me. I aim to kill all three of them and then find Rufus Atkins and kill him, too."

The other three men shifted in their chairs and glanced at Ira Jamison. He pinched a napkin on his mouth and dropped it into a plate.

"I think you'd better leave the premises, Flower," he said.

"You had that Yankee soldier killed at the hospital in New Orleans, just so you could escape and make everybody think you were a hero. Now I 'spect these Yankee officers are helping you sell cotton to the North. You something else, Colonel."

"I'll walk you to the gate," Ira Jamison said.

He rose from the chair and took her arm, his fingers biting with surprising strength into the muscle.

"Why's he letting a darky talk to him like that?" she heard one of the officers say behind her.

The cotton trader raised a finger in the air, indicating the officer should not pursue the subject further.

At the cottage she told Abigail Dowling what had happened.

"You should have come to me first," Abigail said.

"You would have bought me a gun?"

"We could have talked," Abigail said. Then she looked into space and bit her lip at the banality of her own words.

"You been good to me, but I'm going on down to the soldiers' camp," Flower said.

"To do what?"

"Someone said they're hiring washerwomen."

"Did you eat anything today?"

"Maybe. I don't remember."

Abigail pressed her hands down on Flower's shoulders until Flower was sitting in a chair at the kitchen table. She smoothed Flower's hair and caressed her cheek with her hand.

"Wish you wouldn't do that, Miss Abby."

Abigail's face flushed. "I'm sorry," she said.

Then she fried four eggs in the skillet and scraped the mold off a half loaf of bread and sliced it and browned the slices in ham fat.

She divided the food between them and sat across from Flower and ate without speaking.

"What are you studying on?" Flower asked.

"I was thinking of my father and what he would do in certain situations. You two would have liked each other," Abigail said.

Ten minutes later Abigail went out the back door and removed a spade from the shed and walked through the dappled shade along the rim of the coulee and began scraping away a layer of blackened leaves from under an oak tree. She dug down one foot to a tin box that was wrapped in a piece of old gum coat. Then she gathered her purse and a parasol from the house and walked down Main Street, past the Shadows, to the hardware store.

Todd McCain walked out from the back when he heard the bell tinkle above the front door. He and two black men had been re-stocking the front of the store with the inventory he had hidden from looters, and his shirt was damp at the armpits, his greased hair flecked with grit.

"Yes, ma'am?"

"You offered to sell a revolver to Flower Jamison for six dollars, provided she'd go in the back room with you," Abigail said.

"Sounds like somebody's daydream to me," he said.

She pulled open the drawstring on her purse. "Here are your six dollars. How much is it for the ammunition?"

He touched the inside of one nostril with a thumbnail, then huffed air out his nose.

"You got some nerve insulting me on the word of a nigger," he said.

He waited for a response, but there was only silence. When he tried to return her stare, he saw a repository of contempt and disgust in her eyes, aimed at him and no other, that made him clear his throat and look away.

"It's ten dollars for the pistol. I don't have any balls or powder for it," he said.

She continued to look into his face, as though his words had no application to the situation.

"Seven dollars, take it or leave it. I don't need any crazy people in my store," he said.

He waited while she found another dollar in her purse, then picked up the coins one at a time from the glass counter. "I'll wrap it up for you and throw in some gun oil so you don't have no reason to come back," he said.

"Don't presume," she said.

"Presume what?"

"That because I'm a woman your behavior and your remarks won't be dealt with."

He felt one eye twitch at the corner.

After she was gone he returned to the storeroom where he had been working and walked in a circle, his hands on his hips, searching in the gloom for all the words he should have spoken. She had made him play the fool, he told himself, and now his face felt as if it had been stung by bumblebees. Without his knowing why, his gaze rested on a saw, a short-handled sledgehammer, a can of kerosene, a barrel filled with serpentine coils of chain, a prizing bar with a forked claw on it.

One day, he told himself.

Down the street Abigail walked along the curtain of bamboo that bordered the front yard of the Shadows. The azaleas were a dusty purple in the shade, the air loud with the cawing of blue jays. The iron gate swung open in front of her, and Ira Jamison, the cotton trader, and two Union officers stepped directly in her path.

"Miss Abby, how are you?" Jamison said, touching his hat.

"Did you ask the same of your daughter?"

"My wife and I had no children, so I'm not sure whom you're referring to. But no matter. Have a fine day, Miss Abigail," he said.

"Your own daughter told you she was raped and you manhandled her. In front of these men. What kind of human being are you?" she said.

The street was deep in shadow, empty of sound and people. The oak limbs overhead creaked in the wind.

"I guess it's just not your day, Colonel

Jamison," the cotton trader said.

All four men laughed.

Abigail Dowling pulled the buggy whip from its socket on the side of Ira Jamison's carriage and slashed it across his face. He pressed his hand against his cheek and stared at the blood on his fingers in disbelief.

She flung the whip to the ground and walked to her cottage, then went through the yard and into the trees in back, trembling all over. She stood among the oaks and cypresses on the bayou, her arms clenched across her chest, her temples pulsing with nests of green veins.

A wave of revulsion swept through her. But at what? The owner of the hardware store? The rapists? Ira Jamison?

She knew better. Her violence, her social outrage, her histrionic public displays, all disguised a simple truth. Once again, an innocent person had paid for the deeds she had committed, in this case, Flower Jamison.

The wind swirled inside the trees and wrinkled the surface of the bayou, and in the rustling of the canebrake she thought she heard the word *Judas* hissed in her ear.

Chapter Nineteen

At Willie Burke's request, a Union chaplain secured for him three sheets of paper, three envelopes, a bottle of black ink, and a metal writing pen. He sat on straw against the wall of the storehouse, a candle guttering on the brick window ledge above his head, and wrote a letter to his mother and one to Abigail. There was a hollow feeling in his chest and a deadness in his limbs that he had never known before, even at Shiloh. The words he put in his letters contained no grand or spiritual sentiment. In fact, he considered it a victory simply to complete a sentence that did not reflect the fear and weakness eating through his body like weevils through pork.

His third letter was to Robert Perry, somewhere in the Shenandoah Valley of Virginia.

Dear Robert,
I was captured out of uniform and will be

shot in two hours. This night I have written Abby and told her I love her but I know her heart belongs to you. It could not go to a more fitting and fine man. I repent of any violation of our friendship, Robert, and want you to know I would never deliberately impair your relationship with another.

Jim Stubbefield and I will see you on the other side.

Your old pal and friend,
Willie Burke

He folded the three letters and placed them in their envelopes and sealed them with wax that had melted on top of the candle burning above his head. Then he gave them to the chaplain, who was consoling a man whose skin had turned as gray as a cadaver's.

Willie stood at the window and watched the stars fade and the light go out of the sky, and the scattered farmhouses and the trees along the bayou begin to sharpen inside the ground fog that rolled out of the fields. Roosters were crowing beyond his line of sight, and he smelled wood smoke and meat frying on a fire. Eight Union soldiers were camped in pup tents among the oaks on the bayou, their Springfield rifles stacked. The canvas sides of their tents were damp with dew, the flaps tied to the tents' poles. Willie's heart dropped when he saw an enlisted man emerge from his tent and stretch and look in the direction of the storehouse. He stepped back from the window and pressed his hand to his mouth, just as a half cup of bile surged out of his stomach.

Jim wasn't afraid when he went up the hill with the guidon at Shiloh, he thought. Don't you be, either, he told himself. A brief flash of light, perhaps a little pain, then it's over. There are worse ways to go. How about the poor devils carried into an aid station with their guts hanging out or their jaws shot away? Or the ones who begged for death while their limbs were sawed off?

But his dialogue with himself brought him no comfort and he wondered if his legs would fail when a Yankee provost walked him to the wall.

The soldiers camped on the bayou were gathered around their cookfire now, drinking coffee, glancing in the direction of the storehouse, as though preparing themselves for an uncomfortable piece of work that was not of their choosing.

A ninth man joined them, an erect fellow with a holstered sidearm and stripes on his sleeves. When the firelight struck his face Willie recognized the sergeant who had tried to prevail upon him to use his head and extricate himself from a capital sentence. What were his words, the only real pacifist was a dead Quaker?

Why had he not listened?

A man with a stench that made Willie think of cat spray elbowed him aside from the window.

"Sorry, I didn't know you had your name carved on the bricks," Willie said.

"Shut up," the man said.

His eyes, hair and beard looked as though he had been shot out of a cannon. He was barefoot and wore no shirt under a butternut jacket that was stitched with gold braid on the collar. His pants were cinched around his waist with a rope and stippled with blood.

"You ever kill somebody with your bare hands?" he asked. He pressed his face close to Willie's. The inside of his mouth was black with gunpowder, his fetid breath worse than an outhouse.

"Bare hands? Can't say I have," Willie replied.

"You up for it? Tell me now. Don't sass me, either."

"Could you be giving me a few more details?" Willie asked.

"Clean the ham hocks out of your mouth. Captain Jarrette is taking us out. Do you want to make a run for it or die like a carp flopping on the ground? Give me an answer," the man said.

"You were at the ambush on the St. Martinville Road."

"Of all the people I try to help, it turns

out to be another stump from Erin. Anyone ever tell you an Irishman is a nigger turned inside out?"

"I really don't care to die next to a smelly lunatic. Do you have a plan, sir?" Willie said.

"Go back to your letter writing, cabbage head," the man said.

The guerrilla turned away and stared at the locked door and front wall of the storehouse, his arms hanging like sticks from the ragged sleeves of his jacket, his pants reaching only to his ankles. Outside, the sun broke on the eastern horizon and a red glow filled the trees on the bayou and painted the tips of the sugarcane in the fields. Through the window Willie heard the sound of marching feet.

The sound grew louder and then stopped in front of the storehouse. Someone turned an iron key in the big padlock on the door and shot back the bolt through the rungs that held it in place. The light from outside seemed to burst into the room like a fistful of white needles. A captain and two parallel lines of enlisted men in blue, all wearing kepis, bayonets twist-grooved onto the muzzles of their rifles, waited to escort the prisoners to the barn and the firing squad of eight that had been camped in the pup tents by the bayou. In the distance Willie thought he heard the rumble of thunder or perhaps horses' hooves on a hard-packed road. Then he heard a solitary shout, like an angry man who had mashed his thumb with a hammer.

"Come out, lads. None of us enjoys this. We'll make it as easy and dignified as possible," the Yankee officer at the door said.

"Come in and get us, darlin'," a prisoner in the back of the room said.

Clouds moved across the sun and the countryside dropped into shadow again, the cane in the field bending in the breeze, the air sweet with the smell of morning. Willie heard horses coming hard across a wood bridge, then the shouts of men and the ragged popping of small-arms fire.

Suddenly there were horsemen everywhere, over a hundred of them, dressed like beggars, some firing a pistol with each hand, the reins in their teeth. The prisoners surged out of the storehouse, knocking the captain to the ground, attacking his men.

A wheeled cannon on one corner of the prisoner of war compound lurched into the air, blowing a huge plume of smoke across the grass. One second later a load of grapeshot slapped against the walls of the red barn used as the execution site, accidentally cutting down a squad of Yankee soldiers in its path.

Willie bolted from the door of the storehouse and ran with dozens of other men toward the bayou, while mounted guerrillas and what looked like regular Confederate infantry fired into the Yankees who were trying to form up in the middle of the compound. A shirtless man on horseback thundered past him, the guerrilla leader with the pinned-up hat riding on the rump, clinging to the cantle. The guerrilla leader looked back at him, his face like an outraged jack-o'-lantern under his hat.

Willie heard the whirring sound of minié balls toppling past his head, then a sound like a dry slap when they struck a tree. He plunged through a woman's front yard, tearing down her wash as he ran, scattering chickens onto the gallery. He crashed through her front door and out the back into a grove of pecan trees, then the lunatic from the storehouse was running in tandem with him, his vinegary stench like a living presence he carried with him.

They dove into the bayou together, swimming as far as they could underwater, brushing across the sculpted points of submerged tree branches, a stray minié ball breaking the surface and zigzagging through the depths in a chain of bubbles.

Their feet touched bottom on the far side, then Willie and what he had come to think of as his lunatic companion were up on the bank, running through a cane field, the blades of the cane whipping past their shoulders.

They fell out of the cane field into a dry

irrigation canal, breathless, collapsing on their knees in the shade of persimmon trees. Willie threw his arm around the shoulder of the lunatic.

"We made it, pard. God love you, even if you're a graduate of Bedlam and have nothing kind to say about His chosen people, that being the children of Erin," he said.

The lunatic sat back on his heels, his chest laboring, his blackened mouth hanging open. Willie fastened his hand on the man's collarbone, kneading it, grinning from ear to ear at his newfound brother-in-arms.

"Did you hear me? I bet you're a good soldier. You don't need to ride with brigands. Come with me and we'll find the 18th Louisiana and General Mouton," he said.

The lunatic's mouth formed into a cone and he pressed four stiffened fingers into his sternum as though he were silently asking Willie a burning question.

"You got the breath knocked out of you?" Willie said.

The lunatic shook his head. Willie cupped the lunatic's wrist and removed his fingers from his chest. A ragged exit wound the circumference of a thumb was drilled through his sternum. Willie caught him just as he fell on his side.

"The Yanks have fucked me with a garden rake, cabbage head. Watch out for yourself," the lunatic whispered.

"Hang on there, pard. Someone will be along for us directly. You'll see," Willie said.

The man did not speak again. His eyes stared hazily at the shadows the clouds made on the cane field and the mockingbirds swooping in and out of the shade. Then he coughed softly as though clearing his throat and died.

Willie rolled him onto his back, placed his ankles together, and covered his face with a palmetto fan. Then he buttoned the dead man's butternut coat over his wound and crossed his arms on his chest.

Other escaped prisoners ran past him, some of them armed now, all of them sweaty and hot, powdered with dust from the fields. He heard a rider behind him and turned just as the guerrilla leader reined his horse and glared down at him, his horse fighting the bit, spooking sideways.

The guerrilla hit the horse between the ears with his fist, then stood in the stirrups and adjusted his scrotum, making a face while he did it. The inside of his thighs were dark with sweat, as though he had fouled himself. "That's the body of my junior officer you're looting," he said.

Willie got to his feet.

"You're a damn liar," he said.

"I'll remember your face," the guerrilla said.

He galloped away, twisting his head to

look over his shoulder one more time.

Willie wandered the rest of the day. The sky was plumed with smoke from burning houses and barns, and by noon a haze of dust and lint from the cane fields turned the sun into a pink sliver. He saw a Confederate rear guard form up in a woods and fire a volley across a field at a distant group of men, then break and run through a gully and board a rope-drawn ferryboat and pull themselves across the Vermilion River, all before he could reach them.

He saw wild dogs attack and tear apart a rabbit in an empty pasture. He passed Confederate deserters who had hidden in coulees or who walked on back roads with their faces averted. He saw four wagons loaded with Negroes and their possessions stopped at a crossroads, wondering in which direction they should go, while their children cried and one man tried to jerk an exhausted horse up on its legs. At evening he saw the same people, this time on the riverbank, without the means to cross to the other side, frightened at the boom of distant artillery. He rooted for food in the charred ruins of a cabin and licked the fried remains of pickled tomatoes off scorched pieces of a preserve jar.

He climbed into a mulberry tree and watched a column of Union infantry, supply wagons, and wheeled field pieces that took a half hour to pass. When night came the sky was black with storm clouds, the countryside dark except for the flicker of cannon fire in the north. He lost the Vermilion River, which he had been following, and entered a high-canopied woods that swayed in the wind, that had no undergrowth and was thickly layered with old leaves and was good for either walking or finding a soft, cool place that smelled of moss and wildflowers where he could lie down and once more sleep the sleep of the dead.

He paused under a water oak, unbuttoned his fly, and urinated into the leaves. Out of the corner of his eye he saw movement back in the trees and heard the sound of field gear clanking on men's bodies. He mounted the trunk of a tree that had fallen across a coulee and ran along the crest of it to the other side, right into a Union sergeant who aimed the .50 caliber muzzle of a Sharp's carbine at his face.

Willie raised his hands and grinned as though a stick were turned sideways in his mouth.

"I'm unarmed and offer no threat to you," he said.

The sergeant's kepi was low on his brow, one eye squinted behind his rear sight. He lowered his carbine and looked hard into Willie's face. The sergeant had dark red hair and wore a mustache and goatee and a silver ring with a tiny gold cross affixed to it on his marriage finger. Willie could hear him breathing heatedly in the dark.

"No threat, are you? How about a fucking nuisance?" he said.

"The pacifist turned soldier?" Willie said.

"And you, a bloody hemorrhoid," the sergeant replied.

"Indignant, are we? I tell you what, Yank, within a span of five days you fellows have blown me up with an artillery shell, almost buried me alive, and tried to send me before a firing squad. Would you either be done with it and kindly put a ball between my eyes or go back home to your mother in the North and be the nice lad I'm sure you are."

"Don't tempt me."

"I'm neither a spy nor a guerrilla. Your general treated me unjustly back there. I reckon you know it, too."

Willie could hear the calluses on the sergeant's hands tightening on the stock of his carbine. Then the sergeant stepped back in the leaves, an air vine trailing across his kepi, and pointed the carbine's barrel away from Willie's chest.

"Pass by, Reb. When you say your prayers this night, ask that in the next life the Good Lord provide you with a brain rather than an elephant turd to think with," he said.

"Thank you for the suggestion, Yank. Now, would you be knowing where the 18th Louisiana Vols are?" Willie said.

"You ask the enemy the whereabouts of your own outfit?"

"No offense meant."

The sergeant looked at him incredulously. "My guess is somewhere north of Vermilionville," he said.

"Thank you."

"What's your name again?" the sergeant asked.

"Willie Burke."

"Get into another line of work, Willie Burke," he said.

Chapter Twenty

Flower Jamison had always thought the beginning and end of the war would be marked by definite dates and events, that great changes would be effected by the battles and the thousands of men she had seen march through New Iberia, and the historical period in which she was living would survive only as a compartmentalized and aberrant experience that fitted between bookends for people to study in a happier time.

But the changes she saw in 1864 and early 1865 were transitory in nature. The Yankee soldiers camped behind the Episcopalian church pursued the Confederates through Vermilionville and up into the Red River parishes, taking with them the money they spent in bordellos, saloons, and on the washerwomen by the bayou.

Many freed slaves returned to the plantations and owners they had fled and begged for food and shelter and considered themselves lucky if they were paid any wages at all. Others who preferred privation and even death from hunger over a return to the old ways were on occasion given a choice between the latter or execution.

Emancipation Day came to be known by people of color as June 'Teenth. Emancipated into what? Flower wondered.

She moved into an unpainted cypress cabin in the trees behind Abigail Dowling's house and did housework for wages. For a brief time she sorted mail for a nickel an hour at the post office, then was let go, with a sincere apology from the postmaster, Mr. LeBlanc, because he felt obligated to give the work to a woman whose husband had been killed at Petersburg.

Many of the Confederate soldiers from New Iberia returned home before the Surrender, either as paroled prisoners of war with chronic diseases or wounds that would not allow them to serve as noncombatants. Flower thought she would have little sympathy for them, regardless of the degree of their suffering. Why should she? she asked herself. The flag they had fought under should have been emblazoned with the overseer's lash rather than the Stars and Bars, she thought. But when she saw them on the street, or sitting on benches among the oaks in the small park across the bayou, the injuries done to some of them were so visibly grievous she had to force herself not to flinch or swallow in their presence and hence add to the burden they already carried.

Since the rape her anger had become her means of defense and survival. She fed it daily so that it lived inside her like a bright, clean flame that she would one day draw upon, like a blacksmith extracting a white-hot iron from a furnace. It was her anger and the possibilities of revenge that allowed her to avoid a life of victimhood. But an incident in the park almost robbed her of it.

An ex-soldier who had lost his eyes, his nose, and his chin to an exploding artillery shell was escorted each evening to the park by a child. A veil of black gauze hung from his brow, covering his destroyed face, but the wind blew it aside once and what Flower saw in a period of less than three seconds made her stomach constrict.

One week later, on a Sunday afternoon, when the park was almost deserted, the child wandered off. Rain began to patter on the trees, and the soldier rose to his feet and tried to tap his way with a cane to the draw-bridge. From across the bayou Flower saw him trip and fall, then gather himself up and walk in the wrong direction.

She crossed the bridge and took him by the arm. It felt as light as a stick in her hand.

"I can take you home if you tell me where you live," she said.

"That's very good of you, ma'am. I stay with my father and mother, just behind St. Peter's," he said.

The two of them walked the length of Main Street, then went through a brick alley toward the Catholic church.

"There's a café here on the corner. They have coffee. I'd love to treat you to a cup," the soldier said.

"I'm colored, suh."

The ex-soldier stopped, the gauze molded damply against the skeletal outline of his face. He seemed to be staring into the distance, although Flower knew he had no eyes.

"I see," he said. "Well, everyone looks the same to me these days, and you seem a very sweet person to whom I'm greatly indebted. I'm sure my mother has tea on the stove, if you would join me."

She refused his invitation and told herself she could not look any longer upon his suffering. But in the secret chambers of the heart she knew that the pity he inspired in her was her enemy and the day the clean and comforting flame of her anger died would be the day that every bruise and probing act of the hand and tongue and phallus visited upon her by the three rapists would take on a second life and not only occupy her dreams but come aborning in her waking day.

She and Abigail had driven out in the

country with the revolver Abigail had bought at the hardware store. An elderly Frenchman who lived in a houseboat on the bayou and spoke no English showed them how to remove the cylinder from the frame and pour powder and drop the conically shaped .36 caliber balls in each of the chambers and tamp down the wadding on top of the ball with the mechanical rod inset under the barrel and insert the percussion caps in the nipples of the chambers. Then he stepped back on the bank as though he were not sure in which direction they might shoot.

Abigail aimed at a dead cypress across the bayou and fired. The ball grazed an iron mooring plate nailed to a nearby oak and whined away in a field. She cocked the hammer with both thumbs, squinted one eye, and fired a second time. The ball popped a spout of water out of the middle of the bayou and clattered into a canebrake.

Abigail blinked her eyes and lowered the revolver, opening her mouth to clear her ears, then handed the revolver to Flower. "I think I'd have better luck throwing it at someone," she said.

Flower extended the revolver with both hands in front of her. The steel frame and wood grips felt cool and hard and solid in her palms as she forced back the hammer. But unlike Abigail, she didn't try to sight down the barrel at the cypress; she simply pointed, like a finger of accusation, and pulled the trigger.

The ball struck dead center.

She fired the remaining three rounds, each time notching wood out of the tree. Her palms stung and her ears were ringing when she lowered the revolver, but she felt a sense of power and control that was almost sexual.

"I'd like to keep the gun at my house, Miss Abby," she said on the way back to town.

"Maybe I should keep it for both of us," Abby said.

"Hitting a man with a buggy whip is a long way from being able to kill somebody."

"You're right, it is, and I think you're too willing to do that, Flower," Abby said. She turned and looked into Flower's face.

"You worry for my soul?" Flower asked.

"The commandment is that we don't kill one another," Abigail said.

"Rufus Atkins and those men who raped me already tried to take my soul. They wanted to take my soul, my heart, my self-respect, my mind, my private thoughts, everything that was me. If they could, they would have pulled off my skin. Pray to God men like that never get their hands on you, Miss Abby."

They rode in silence the rest of the way to the cottage. But that evening Abigail carried the pistol and the gunpowder, bullets, and caps for it to Flower's cabin.

"I was unctuous at your expense. There's no worse kind of fool," she said, and handed the gun and ammunition through the door.

In the evenings and at night Flower read. She now had sixteen books in what she called her "li'l library," the books propped up neatly on her writing table between two bricks she had wrapped and sewn with pieces cut out of a red velvet curtain a white woman down the street had thrown away. Some of the books were leather-bound, some had no covers at all; many of the pages in her dictionary were dog-eared and loose in the binding. Each day in her journal she recorded the number of pages she had read, the new words she had learned, and her observations about characters and events that struck her as singular.

Some of her entries:

"Mr. Melville must have known his Bible. Ishmael and Hagar were cast out and unwanted and I think that is why the story of Moby Dick is told by a sailor with the name of Ishmael. I think Mr. Melville must have been a lonely man."

"I like Mr. Poe. But nobody can tell a story like Mr. Hawthorne. He tells us about the Puritans but what he tells us most about is ourself."

"I saw ball lightning in the swamp last night. It looked like a mess of electric snakes rolling across the water, bouncing off the trees. I wish I could write about it in a way other people could see it but I cannot."

For the remainder of the war she did not see Rufus Atkins or Ira Jamison. As with the mutilated ex-soldier, she sometimes experienced feelings for Jamison that made her angry at herself and ashamed of her own capacity for self-delusion. When she had last seen him, on the lawn at the Shadows, he had walked her to the street, his hand biting into her arm, and had fastened the gate behind her, without speaking, as though he were locking an animal out of the yard. But she found excuses for him. Hadn't she deliberately embarrassed him in front of his friends, making him somehow the instrument of the assault on her person rather than his overseer, Rufus Atkins? In fact, for just a moment, she had enjoyed her role as victim. For once she had left him speechless and awkward and foolish in front of others.

But just when she had almost convinced herself that the problem was perhaps hers, not his, and hence her attachment to him was not a form of self-abasement, she remembered the hospital in New Orleans, Jamison's letter to General Forrest referring to the "unwashed niggers" who tended him, and the murder by his men of the young Union sentry. Then she burned with shame at her own vulnerability.

In moments like these she emptied her mind of thoughts about her father by concentrating her anger on the men who had raped her. Each day she hoped she would recognize one of them on the street. It should have been easy. Each was defective or impaired in some fashion. But the rapists seemed to have disappeared into the war, into the broad sweep of the countryside and the detritus of armies whose purposes made less and less sense. The injury done to her had become just another account among many told by the victims of Union soldiers, jayhawkers, Confederate guerrillas, stray minié balls and artillery rounds and naval mines, or wildfires that burned homes and cabins and barns to charcoal.

Most of the Yankee soldiers had gone somewhere up in the Red River parishes. The windows of their paddle-wheelers, headed up the Teche with supplies, were darkened at night because of sniper fire from guerrillas, but otherwise the war had simply gone away. Flower came to believe wars didn't end. People just got tired of them and didn't participate in them for a while.

On a Sunday in April 1865 she was sitting on a bench in the park when she picked up a discarded New Orleans newspaper and read an article that perhaps told more about the future of her race than she wanted to know. The article was about Ira Jamison and described his wounding at Shiloh and how his slaves had fled their master's protection and goodwill after his fields and storehouses had been burned by Yankees. But Flower sensed the article was more a promotion for a new enterprise than a laudatory account about her father. Ira Jamison was transforming Angola Plantation into a penal farm and would soon be in the business of leasing convict labor on a large scale.

The writer of the article said most of the convicts sentenced to Angola came from the enormous population of Negro criminals who had been empowered by the Freedmen's Bureau and turned loose upon the law-abiding whites of Louisiana. The writer also said the cost of convict labor would be far less than the cost of maintaining what he termed "servants in the old system."

A shadow fell across the page she was reading. She turned and looked up at the face of Todd McCain, the hardware store owner on Main Street. He had just come from church and was wearing a narrow-cut suit with a vest that made him sweat and a stiff white shirt with a high collar and one of the new bowler hats.

"I heard you could read," he said.

She folded the newspaper on her lap and looked through the oak trees at the sunlight on the bayou. His loins brushed the top of the backrest on the bench.

"I read that same article this morning. I don't agree with everything that's in it. But there's a mess of criminals out there belong on a chain gang, you ask me," he said.

"I'd like to read my paper, suh," she said.

"I got a lot of colored customers nowadays. I could use a clerk. I'll pay you fifty cents a day."

"Please leave me alone."

It was quiet a long time. "You're an uppity bitch, ain't you?" he said.

"Bother me again and find out," she replied.

"What did you say?"

She rose from the bench and walked out of the coolness of the trees into the sunlight, hating herself for her rashness. When she got to the drawbridge and looked over her shoulder, Todd McCain was still watching her.

Abigail did not believe in omens, but sometimes she wondered if human events and the ways of the season and four-footed animals and winged creatures did not conspire to weave patterns whose portent for good or evil was undeniable. If God revealed His will in Scripture, should He be proscribed from revealing it in His creations?

The azaleas and wisteria were in bloom, the destroyed countryside greening from the spring rains, and the telegraphic news bulletins from Virginia all indicated the same conclusion — that the surrender would come any day and all the soldiers who had survived the war, including Robert Perry, would soon be on their way home.

But instead of joy she felt a sense of quiet trepidation that seemed to have no origin. The night she heard that General Lee had given it up at Appomattox Courthouse she dreamed of carrion birds in a sulfurous sky and woke in the darkness, her heart beating, her ears filled with the sound of throbbing wings.

She went to the window and realized her dream of birds was not a dream at all. There were hundreds of them in the trees, cawing, defecating whitely on the ground, their feathers a purplish-black in the moonlight. They flew blindly about, without direction, thudding into the sides of her cottage, freckling the sky and settling into the trees again. One struck the window with such force she thought the glass would break.

In the morning she pulled on a pair of work gloves and went outside with a burlap sack and began picking dead birds off the ground. All of them were crows, their layered feathers traced with lines of tiny white parasites. They were as light as air in her hands, as though they had been hollowed out by disease, and she knew they had either starved to death or in their hunger broken their necks seeking food.

She dug a deep hole and buried the burlap sack and covered it with bricks so animals would not dig it up.

If birds could not find provender in a tropical environment like southern Louisiana, what must the rest of the South be like? she asked herself.

At noon she walked to the post office to get her mail, unable to rid herself of a sense of foreboding that made her wonder if she was coming down with a sickness. Mr. LeBlanc, the postmaster, stood up behind his desk at the rear of the building and put on his coat and came from behind the counter, an envelope in his hand. He had aged dramatically since the death of his son at Manassas Junction, but he never discussed his loss or showed any public sign of grief or indicated any bitterness toward those who had killed him. When Abigail looked at the deep lines in his face, she wanted to press his hands in hers and tell him it was all right to feel anger and rage against those who had caused the war, but she knew her statement would be met with silence.

Seated on a bench in the corner, hardly noticeable in the gloom, was a thin, solemn-faced boy in his early teens, wearing brown homespun, a Confederate-issue kepi, and oversized workshoes that had chafed his ankles. A choke sack containing his belongings

349

sat by his foot. Mr. LeBlanc studied him for a moment as though the boy were an on-going problem he had not found a solution for. Then his attention shifted back to Abigail.

"Do you know any way to contact Willie Burke?" he asked.

"No, I've heard nothing from him in months," she replied.

"I received a telegraph message for him this morning. I don't quite know what to do. His mother died in New Orleans."

"Sir?" Abby said.

"She went there to file a claim as a British subject. Something about getting paid for livestock the Yankees appropriated at her farm. She contracted pneumonia and died in the hospital. Do you want to sign for the telegram?"

"No."

He looked at her blankly. "I guess I can hold on to it," he said.

"I'm sorry, Mr. LeBlanc. I'm just not thinking very clearly right now."

"I have a letter for you from Johnson Island, Ohio. Maybe it's a little brighter in content," Mr. LeBlanc said.

"You do?" she said, her face lighting.

"Of course," he said, smiling.

Before he could speak further, she hurried out the door, tearing at the envelope's seal with her thumb.

"Miss Abigail, would you talk with me for a minute or two after you've read your mail?" he called after her.

She sat on a bench under a colonnade where the stage passengers waited and read the letter that had been written in a prisoner of war camp in Ohio.

Dear Abby,
Thank you for sending me the hat and suit of clothes. They are the exact size and right color (gray) and have been sorely needed, as my uniform had deteriorated into rags. As always, you have proved remarkable in all your endeavors.

But your letters continue to confuse me. You seem to be harboring a guilt of some kind, as though you've done me injury. Nothing could be farther from the truth. You are a true and compassionate and loyal friend. Who could have a better spiritual companion than one such as yourself?

Do you hear from Willie? Even though he has seen much of war, I think he has never gotten over the death of our friend Jim Stubbefield.

She folded the letter and replaced it in the envelope without finishing it. Robert Perry's words were like acid on her skin. Not only did they exacerbate her guilt over her self-perceived infidelity, the term "spiritual companion" reduced her to a presumption, an adjunct in Robert's life rather than a participant.

Why had she stayed in Louisiana? she asked herself. But she already knew the answer, and it had to do with her father and it made her wonder about her level of maturity. Sometimes she missed him in a way that was almost intolerable. In an unguarded moment, when the world surrounded her and her own resolve was not sufficient to deal with it, the image of his broad, jolly face and big shoulders and pipe-smelling clothes would invade her mind and her eyes would begin to film.

He was defrauded by his New York business partners and sued in Massachusetts by men who owed their very lives to him, but his spirits never dimmed and he never lost his faith in either God or humanity or the abolitionist movement, which he had championed all his life.

After his death she could not bear the New England winters in their family home up on the Merrimack, nor the unrelieved whiteness of the fields that seemed to flow into the horizon like the blue beginnings of eternity. The inside of the house had become a mausoleum, its hardwood surfaces enameled with cold, and by mid-January she had felt that her soul was sheathed in ice. In her mind she would re-create their clipper ship voyages to

Spain, Italy, and Greece, and she would see the two of them together in late summer, hiking with backpacks on a red dirt road in Andalusia, the olive trees a dark green against a hillside of yellow grass that was sear and rustling in the heat. She and her father would hike all the way to the top of the mountain and sit in the warm shade of a Moorish castle, then fix lunch and eat it, while in the distance the azure brilliance of the Mediterranean stretched away as far as the eye could see.

It was a place she went back to again and again in her memory. It was a special place where she lived when she felt threatened, if the world seemed too much for her late and soon, like a cathedral in which she and her father were the only visitors.

When she came to south Louisiana during the yellow fever epidemic and smelled the salt breeze blowing off Lake Pontchartrain and saw roses blooming in December and palm trees rising starkly against the coastline, like those around Cadiz, she felt that the best memories in her life had suddenly been externalized and made real again and perhaps down a cobbled street in the old part of New Orleans her father waited for her at an outdoor café table under a balcony that was hung with tropical flowers.

Perhaps it was a foolish way to be, but her father had always taught her the greatest evil

one person could do to another was to inter-
fere in his or her destiny, and to Abigail that
meant no one had a right to intrude upon either the province of her soul or her imagination or the ties that bound her to the past
and allowed her to function in the present.

But now, in the drowsy shade of a colonnade in April 1865, at the close of the
greatest epoch in American history, she
wished she was on board a sailing ship,
within sight of Malaga, the palm trees
banked thickly at the base of the Sierra Ne-
vada, like a displaced piece of Africa, the
troubles and conflicts of war-torn Louisiana
far behind her.

"You all right, Miss Dowling?"

She looked up, startled, at Mr. LeBlanc.
The boy in brown homespun and the Confederate-issue kepi stood behind him, his
choke sack tied with a string around his
wrist.

"This young fellow here says a preacher
bought him a stage ticket to find Willie
Burke," Mr. LeBlanc said.

The boy stared down the street, as though
unconcerned about the events taking place
around him.

"What's your name again?" Mr. LeBlanc
asked.

"Tige McGuffy."

"Where did you know Mr. Willie from?"
Mr. LeBlanc asked.

"Shiloh Church. I was with the 6th Mis'sippi. Me and him was both at the Peach Orchard."

"And you have no family?" Mr. LeBlanc said.

"I just ain't sure where they're at right now."

"Don't lie to people when they're trying to help you, son," Mr. LeBlanc said.

The boy's cheeks pooled with color.

"My daddy was with Gen'l Forrest. He never come back. The sheriff was gonna send me to the orphans' home. The preacher from our church give me the money for a stage ticket here," he said.

His skin was brown, filmed with dust, his throat beaded with dirt rings. He studied the far end of the street, his mousy hair blowing at the edges of his kepi.

"When did you eat last?" Abigail asked.

"A while back. At a stage stop," he replied.

"When?" Abigail asked.

"Yesterday. I don't eat much. It ain't a big deal with me."

"I see. Pick up your things and let's see what you and I can find for lunch," she said.

"I wasn't looking for no handouts," he said.

"I know you're not," she said, and winked at him. "Come on, walk me home. I never know when a carriage is going to run me down."

He thought about it, then crooked his arm and extended it for her to hold on to.

"It's a mighty nice town you got here," he said, admiring the buildings and the trees on the bayou. "Did Willie Burke make it through the war all right?"

"I think so. I'm not sure. The 18th Louisiana had a bad time of it, Tige," she said.

"Think so?" he said, looking up at her, his forehead wrinkling.

Ira Jamison sat astride a white gelding and watched his first shipment of convicts from the jails of New Orleans and Baton Rouge go to work along the river's edge, chopping down trees, burning underbrush and digging out the coffins in a slaves' cemetery that had filled with water seepage and formed a large depression in the woods.

Most of the convicts were Negroes. A few were white and a few were children, some as young as seven years old. All of them wore black-and-white-striped jumpers and pants, and hats that were woven together from palmetto leaves. They flung the chopped trees and underbrush onto bonfires that were burning by the river's edge and raked the rotted wood and bones from the slaves' coffins into the water. As Ira Jamison moved his horse out of the smoke blowing off the fires, he tried to form in his mind's eye a picture of the log skid and sawmill and loading docks that would replace the woods and the Negro cemetery.

He did not like the idea of the children working among the adults. They were not only in the way, they were not cost-effective. But his state contract required he take all the inmates, men, women, and children, from the parish jails throughout Louisiana; house, clothe and feed them; and put them to work in some form of rehabilitative activity and simultaneously contribute to the state's economy.

He watched a Negro boy, no more than twelve, clean a nest of bones and rags from a coffin and begin flinging them off the bank into the current. The boy picked up the skull by inserting his fingers in the eye sockets and pitched it in a high arc onto a pile of driftwood that was floating south toward Baton Rouge. The boy nudged a companion and pointed at his handiwork.

"Bring that one to me," Jamison said to Clay Hatcher, who was now back at his former job on the plantation, his blond hair the color of old wood, the skin under his right eye grained black from a musket that had blown up in his face at the battle of Mansfield.

"You got it, Kunnel," Hatcher said.

He walked into the trees and the trapped smoke from the bonfires and tapped the skull-thrower on top of his palmetto hat.

When the boy approached Jamison's horse he removed his hat and raised his face uncertainly. His striped jumper was grimed with red dirt, his hair sparkling with sweat.

"Yes, suh?" he said.

"It doesn't bother you to handle dead people's bones?" Jamison asked.

"No, suh."

"Why not?"

"'Cause they dead," the boy said, and grinned. Then his face seemed to brighten with curiosity as he gazed up at Jamison.

"You have a reason for looking at me like that?" Jamison asked.

"You gots one eye mo' little than the other, that's all," the boy replied.

Jamison felt the gelding shift its weight under him.

"Why were you sent to jail?" he asked.

"They ain't ever tole me."

"Don't be playing on the job anymore. Can you do that for me?" Jamison said.

"Yes, suh."

"Get on back to work now," Jamison said.

"Yes, suh."

By day's end the log skid was almost completed, the graves excavated and filled in, packed down with clay and smoothed over with iron rollers, the sides of the depression overlaid with cypress planks and stobs to prevent erosion. In fact, it was a masterpiece of engineering, Jamison thought, a huge sluice that could convert timber into money, seven days a week, as fast as the loggers could fell trees and slide them down the slope.

As he turned his horse toward the house he saw Clay Hatcher pick up an object from a mound of mud on the edge of the work area. Hatcher knocked the mud off it and held it up in the light to see the object more clearly. Then he stooped over and washed it in a bucket of water the convicts had used to clean their shovels in.

Jamison walked his horse toward Hatcher.

"What do you have there, Clay?" he asked.

"It looks to be an old merry-go-round. It's still got a windup key plugged in it. I wonder what it was doing in the graveyard," Hatcher replied.

Jamison reached down and took the merry-go-round from Hatcher's fingers and studied the hand-carved horses, the corroded brass cylinder inside the base, the key that was impacted with dirt and feeder roots. He had given it to Uncle Royal, who in turn had given it to his great-grandson, the one who died of a fever. Or was it an accident, something about an overturned wagon crushing him? Jamison couldn't remember.

He returned it to Hatcher.

"Wash it off and give it to the skull-thrower," he said.

"That little nigra boy?"

"Yes."

"Why would you be doing that, Kunnel?"

"He's intelligent and brave. You never make a future enemy of his kind if you can avoid it."

"I'll be switched if I'll ever understand you, Kunnel," Hatcher said.

Jamison flipped his reins idly across the back of his hand. The day you do is the day I and every other plantation owner in the South will have a problem, he thought, and was surprised at his own candor.

Willie Burke had long ago given up the notion of sleeping through the night from dark to dawn. His dreams woke him up with regularity, every one to two hours, and his sleep was filled with images and feelings that were less terrifying than simply disjointed and unrelieved, like the quiet throbbing of a headache or an impacted tooth. Tonight, as he slept under a wagon behind a farmhouse, he dreamed he was marching on a soft, powdery road through hills that were covered with thistle and dead grass. Up ahead, a brass cannon, its muzzle pointed back at him, flopped crazily on its carriage, and brown dust cascaded like water off the rims and spokes of the wheels.

His feet burned with blisters and his back ached from the weight of his rifle and pack. He wanted to escape from the dream and the heat of the march into the cool of morning and the early fog that had marked each dawn since he had begun walking back toward New Iberia from Natchitoches in north-western Louisiana. In his sleep he heard roosters crowing, a hog snuffing inside a railed lot, horses nickering and thudding their hooves impatiently in a woods. He sat up in the softness of the dawn and saw a pecan orchard that was still bare of leaves, the trunks and branches wet with dew, and the dream of the brass cannon barrel flopping crazily under a murderous sun gradually became unreal and unimportant, its meaning, if it had one, lost in the beginning of a new day.

He got to his feet and urinated behind a corncrib, then realized he was not alone. Between thirty and forty mounted men moved out of the fog in the pecan orchard and formed a half circle around the back of the farmhouse.

They wore ragged beards and bayonet-cut hair. Their elbows poked through their shirts; their pants were streaked with grease and road grime, their skin the color of saddle leather, as though it had been smoked over a fire.

The leader wore gray pants and a blue cotton shirt and a cavalry officer's hat that had wilted over his ears. A sword inside a leather scabbard and a belt strung with three holstered cap-and-ball pistols were looped over his saddle pommel. Even though the morning was peppered with mist, his face looked dilated, overheated, his eyes scalded.

"You Secesh?" he asked.

"I was," Willie replied.

"I've seen you. You was looting the body of one of my men at St. Martinville," the guerrilla said, his horse shifting under him.

"You're wrong, my friend. I won't be abiding the insult, either."

The guerrilla touched his horse's side with his boot heel and approached Willie, leaning down in the saddle to get a better look. His eyes were colorless, filled with energies that seemed to have no moral source. His coppery hair was pushed up under his hat, like a woman's.

"You know who I am?" he asked.

"I think your name is Jarrette. I think you rode with William Quantrill and Bloody Bill Anderson and helped burn Lawrence, Kansas, to the ground," Willie said.

"You got a mouth on you, do you?"

"I saw your handiwork on the St. Martinville Road. Your men give no quarter."

"That's life under a black flag. We recognize no authority except Jehovah and Jefferson Davis. What's inside that house?"

"A woman with a gun and a three- or four-day-old corpse."

The guerrilla leader stared at the house, then looked in both directions, as though he

362

heard bugles or gunfire, although there were no sounds except those of a rural morning and the buzzing of bottle flies inside the house.

One of the guerrilla leader's men leaned in the saddle and whispered in his ear.

"We was here?" the leader said.

The other guerrilla nodded. The leader, whose name was Jarrette, turned his attention back to Willie. "I don't want you walking behind me," he said.

"The war's over," Willie said.

"The hell it is."

Jarrette's face twitched under his hat. He glared into the distance, his back straightening, his thighs tightening on his horse. Willie looked in the direction of his interest but saw nothing but gray fields and a fog-shrouded pecan orchard.

"I gut blue-bellies and fill up their cavities with stones and sink them to the bottoms of rivers. Jayhawkers get the same. You saying I'm a liar?" Jarrette said.

Willie looked at his pie-plate face and the moral insanity in his eyes and the rubbery, unnatural configuration of his mouth. "I mean you no harm," he said.

"Stay out of my road," Jarrette said.

"My pleasure. Top of the morning to you," Willie said.

He watched Jarrette and his men ride out of the dirt yard toward the road, then scooped off his flop hat and began collecting chicken's eggs from under a manure wagon and in the depressions along the barn wall. He had put three brown eggs inside the crown of his hat and was walking toward a smokehouse that lay on its side, dripping grease and smoldering in its own ashes, when he heard the hooves of a solitary horse thundering across the earth behind him.

He turned just as the guerrilla leader bore down upon him, leaning from the saddle, the point of his hilted sword extended in front of him. The sword's sharpened edge knifed through the top of Willie's shirt, just above the collarbone, and sliced across the skin of his shoulder as coldly as an icicle.

Willie crumpled his hat against his wound and collapsed against a rick fence, the eggs breaking and running down his clothes. He stared stupidly at the guerrilla leader, who disappeared in the mist, an idiot's grin on his mouth.

Chapter Twenty-one

The two-story gabled house next to the Catholic cemetery had been built in the 1840s by an eccentric ornithologist and painter who had worked with James Audubon in Key West and the Florida Everglades. Unfortunately his insatiable love of painting tropical birds as well as Tahitian nudes seemed to be related to a libidinous passion for red wine, Parisian prostitutes, gambling, and trysts with the wives of the wealthiest and best duelists in southern Louisiana.

Residents of the town believed it was only a matter of time before a cuckold drove a pistol ball through his brain. They were wrong. Syphilis got to it first. Just before the first Federal troops reached New Iberia, he gave all his paintings to his slaves, put on a tailored gray officer's uniform he had worn as a member of the Home Guards, then mounted a horse and charged down the bayou road, waving a sword over his head, straight into an artillery barrage that blew him and his uniform into pieces that floated down as airily as flamingo feathers on the bayou's surface.

The first night Federals occupied the town they tore the doors off the house, broke out the windows and turned the downstairs rooms into horse stalls. After the Union cavalry moved on up the Teche into the Red River country, the house remained empty, the white paint darkening from stubble fires, the oak floors scoured by horseshoes, the eaves clustered with yellow-jacket and mud-dauber nests. The taxes on the house were not paid for two years, and on a hot afternoon in late May, the sheriff tacked an auction announcement on the trunk of the live oak that shaded the dirt yard in front of the gallery.

Abigail Dowling happened to be passing in her buggy when the sheriff tapped down the four corners of the auction notice on the tree and stood back to evaluate his handiwork. But Abigail's attention was focused on the gallery steps, where Flower Jamison was sitting with two black children, teaching them how to write the letters of the alphabet on a piece of slate. In fact, at that moment, the broad back of the sheriff, the auction notice puffing against the bark of the tree, Flower and the black children arranged like a triptych on the steps and the vandalized and neglected house of a sybaritic artist, all seemed to be related, like prophetic images caught inside a perfect historical photograph.

Abigail pulled the buggy into the shade and walked past Flower into the building, trailing her fingers across Flower's shoulders. She walked from room to room, computing the measurements in her mind, seeing furnishings and arrangements that were not there. Tramps or ex-soldiers passing through town had scattered trash through the rooms and built unconfined cook fires on the hearths, blackening the walls and scorching the ceilings. She could hear red squirrels and field mice clattering across the roof and the attic. The wind blew hot and dusty through the open windows and smelled of fish heads behind a market and horse manure in the streets. But when she looked out on the gallery and saw the two black children, both of them barefoot, bending down attentively on each side of Flower while she showed them how to print their names in chalk on the piece of slate, Abigail felt a prescience about the future that was more optimistic than any she had experienced in years.

Wasn't it time to put aside anger and loss and self-accusation and live in the sunlight for a while? she thought.

She went back out on the gallery and sat down on the top step next to Flower and placed her palm in the center of Flower's back. She could feel the heat and moisture in

Flower's skin through her dress, and she removed her hand and rested it in her lap. She looked at Flower's profile against the light breaking in the live oak, the clarity in her eyes, the resolute tilt of her chin, and experienced a strange tightening in her throat.

The two black children, a boy and a girl, both grinned at her. To call their clothes rags was a euphemism, she thought. Their poverty, the dried sweat lines on their faces, the untreated red cuts and abrasions on their black skin made her heart ache.

"You were born to teach," she said to Flower.

"That's what I'm doing. Every afternoon, right here on these steps," Flower replied.

Abigail touched Flower's hair. It felt as thick and warm as sun-heated cotton in a field. "Yes, you are. Like an African princess inside a painting. One of the loveliest, most beautiful creatures Our Lord ever made," she said.

She felt her face flush but knew it was only from the heat and the unnatural dryness of the season.

The next morning Abigail went to the brick jailhouse set between Main Street and Bayou Teche, where the sheriff kept his office in the front part of the building. When she opened the door, he glanced up from the paperwork on his desk, then rose heavily from his chair, hypertension glowing in his cheeks, his mustache hanging like pieces of hemp from each side of his mouth. The sheriff's name was Hipolyte Gautreau, and he wore a hat both indoors and outdoors, even in church, to hide a burn scar from Mobile Bay that looked like a large, hourglass-shaped piece of red rubber that had been inserted in his scalp. The cuspidor and plank floor by his desk were splattered with tobacco juice, and through an open wood door that gave on to the cells, Abigail could see several unshaved, long-haired white men standing at the bars or sitting against them.

"It's my favorite lady from Mass'chusetts," the sheriff said. He had such difficulty pronouncing the last word, even incorrectly, that he had to touch a drop of spittle off his lip.

"It looks like you're about to have a tax sale," she said.

He fixed his gaze out the window on a passing wagon, his eyes seemingly empty of thought.

"Tax sale? Oh, you seen me nailing up that notice on the tree yesterday."

"That's right. How much will I need to make a realistic bid?" she said.

"How much money? You want to have a seat?" he asked.

"No," she replied.

He remained standing and pushed some papers around on his desk with the tips of his fingers. The crown of his gray hat was crumpled and sweat-stained and worn through in the creases. He pulled his shirt off his skin with two fingers and shook the cloth, as though removing the heat trapped inside.

"You don't need no old building, Miss Abby. Why not leave t'ings be?" he said.

"What are you up to, Hipolyte?"

He raised his index finger at her. "Don't be saying that, no. I'm telling you somet'ing for your own good."

"Somebody else doesn't want a competitor at the auction?"

He pushed his hat back on his head. The skin below his hairline was white, prickled with rash.

"Tell her, you old fart. Yankee jellyroll like that don't come around every day," a voice shouted from one of the cells. The other men leaning or sitting against the bars laughed inside the gloom.

The sheriff got up from his chair and slammed the plank door that separated his office from the jail.

"Who are those men?" she asked.

"Guerrillas. White trash. They calling themselves the White League now. You heard about them?"

"No," she replied. "Who else wants to buy that house, Hipolyte?"

"Mr. Todd."

"Todd McCain? From the hardware store?"

"He's gonna make it into a saloon and dance pavilion. Them Yankees gonna be around a long time," the sheriff said.

"What an enterprising man."

"You a good lady. Don't mess wit' him, Miss Abby." The sheriff's voice was almost plaintive.

"I think Mr. McCain should have been run out of here a long time ago," she replied.

"I knowed you was gonna say that. Knowed it, knowed it, knowed it," he said. He picked up a ring of big iron keys from his desk, then dropped them heavily on the wood.

At dawn one week later and two days before the auction, Carrie LaRose drank coffee at the kitchen table in the back of her brothel and stared out the window at the red sun rising inside the mist on the cane fields. She stared at the plank table under the live oak where her customers drank and sometimes fought with fists or occasionally with knives, and at the two-hole privy that she herself would not use at gunpoint, and at the saddled black horse of a Yankee major who was still upstairs with her most expensive girl.

During the night she had felt chest pains that left her breathless, then a spasm had struck her right arm like a bone break. It was the second time in a month she had been genuinely terrified by premonitions of her own mortality. In each instance, after the pain had gone out of her chest, she had sat on the side of the bed and had heard heavy shoes walking in a corridor, then an iron door scraping across stone. She had pressed her hands over her ears, and her mouth had gone dry as paper with fear.

Now she sat in her kitchen and drank coffee laced with brandy and surveyed what she had spent a lifetime putting together: a termite-eaten house, a two-hole privy that her clientele shat and pissed upon, and a plank table under a tree where they got drunk and fought with fists and knives, then lumbered back into her house, stinking of blood and vomit.

The major, who was stationed in Abbeville, visited the brothel every Sunday night, mutton-chopped, bald, potbellied, effusive, his few strands of hair slicked down on his pate with toilet water. "Your randy fellow is back!" he would announce. Upon departure, he would wave in a jolly way and call out, "Just add it on my bill, Carrie!"

Last night he had sent an aide ahead of him to vacate an enlisted man from the only upstairs room with a tester bed, consumed two bottles of champagne, and started a fire by dropping a lit cigar in a clothes basket. But the major did not pay for services rendered, the liquor he drank, or the damages he did. One morning, when Carrie pressed him about his bill, he removed three pages of printed material from his coat pocket and unfolded and shuffled through them. At the bottom of the last page were a signature and official seal.

"Glance over this and tell me what you think," he said.

"T'ink about what?" she replied.

"Sporting places have been banned throughout the district. The proprietresses of such places can be sent to prison and their property seized. It's all written right there in the document," he said.

She stared at the page blankly.

"But you don't need to worry. This is a tavern and cotillion hall and nothing more. Don't you be long-faced now. I'm going to take care of you," he said, his eyes trailing after a girl whose breasts bounced inside her blouse like small watermelons.

Now Carrie sat alone in her kitchen, her body layered with fat, her nails bitten to the quick, her fate in the hands of a man who could threaten her with pieces of paper she could not read.

The day was already growing hot and humid, but she felt cold inside her robe and short of breath for no reason. She clutched the holy medal and cross that hung around her neck and tried to suck air down into her lungs, but her chest felt as though it were bound and crisscrossed with rope. Again, she thought she heard footsteps echoing down a long corridor and an iron door scraping across stone.

The major walked down the stairs, dabbing at the corner of his mouth with a folded handkerchief, the buttons on his blue coat tight across his paunch.

"Having a late breakfast?" he said.

"I don't eat breakfast, me," she replied.

He looked disappointed. Then his eyes lit on the coffeepot and a piece of carrot cake on a shelf.

"I thought I might join you," he said.

"Last night s'pposed to go on your bill, too?" she asked.

"Yes, that would be fine."

"I want my money," she said.

"Carrie, Carrie, Carrie," he said, patting her shoulder.

He leaned across her to pick up the piece of carrot cake from the shelf. She could feel the outline of his phallus press against her back.

Just before noon Carrie bathed and fixed her hair and dug in the back of her closet for a dress that had been made for her by a tailor in New Orleans. Then she powdered her face until it was almost white, rouged her cheeks, darkened her eyes with eyeliner and, with a silk parasol held aloft, sat regally in

374

the back of her carriage while a Negro driver delivered her to the front of Abigail Dowling's cottage on East Main.

"Could I help you?" Abigail said, opening the door, looking past Carrie, as though an emergency of some kind must have developed in the street.

"I want to talk bidness," Carrie said.

"I'm probably the wrong person for that," Abigail said.

"Not this time, you ain't," Carrie said.

They sat down in the living room. Carrie fixed her eyes out the window, her back not touching the chair. Her red-streaked black hair looked like a wig on a muskmelon. She took a deep breath and heard a rattling sound in her lungs.

"Are you feeling all right, Miss LaRose?" Abigail asked.

"I got chest pains at night," she said.

"You need to see a doctor."

"The only good one we had was killed at Malvern Hill. I want you to find out what's wrong wit' me."

"I'm not qualified," Abigail replied.

"I wouldn't take my horse to the doctor we got. What's wrong wit' me?"

"What else happened when you had the chest pains?"

"I couldn't breathe. It hurt real bad under my right arm, like somebody stuck me wit' a stick."

Abigail started to speak, but Carrie raised a hand for her to be silent.

"I hear a man walking in a long corridor. I hear an iron door scraping across a stone flo'," she said. "I t'ink maybe somebody's coming for me."

"Who?" Abigail said.

"I growed up in Barataria, right here in Lou'sana, but I run a house in Paris. A colonel in the French army kilt my husband over some money. When I got the chance I fixed him good. Wit' a poisoned razor in his boot."

Carrie paused, waiting to see the reaction in Abigail's face.

"I see," Abigail said.

"I was s'pposed to die on the guillotine. I done some t'ings for the jailer. Anyt'ing he wanted, it didn't matter. You know what I'm saying to you? I done them t'ings and I lived."

"Yes?" Abigail said.

"Anot'er woman went to the headsman 'stead of me. They put a gag in her mout' and tied her feet and hands. From my window I saw them lift her head out of the basket and hold it up by the hair for the crowd to see."

Abigail kept her eyes on the tops of her hands and cleared her throat.

"I think you've had a hard life, Miss Carrie," Abigail said.

"You been trying to borrow money around town. Ain't nobody gonna give you money to go up against Todd McCain. He's in the White League."

"How do you know?"

"He visits my house."

"You're offering to lend me money?"

"He's gonna set up a saloon, probably wit' girls out back. What's good for him is bad for me."

"And part of the deal is I help you with your health? I'd do that, anyway, Miss Carrie."

"There's somet'ing else." Carrie rotated a ring on her finger.

"What might that be?" Abigail asked.

"I cain't read and write, me. Neither can my brother, Jean-Jacques."

It was late evening when Willie Burke walked into town and stood in front of his mother's boardinghouse on the bayou. A rolled and doubled-over blanket, with his razor, a sliver of soap, a magazine and a change of clothes inside, was tied on the ends with a leather cord and looped across his back. A narrow-chested, shirtless boy, wearing a Confederate kepi, was sweeping the gallery, his face hot with his work, his back powdered with dust in the twilight.

The boy rested his broom and stared at the figure standing in the yard.

"Mr. Willie?" he said.

"Yes?"

"Miss Abigail and me thought maybe you was killed."

"I don't know who you are."

"It's me — Tige."

"The drummer boy at Shiloh?"

"Lessen hit's a catfish dressed up in a Tige McGuffy suit."

"What are you doing on my mother's gallery?"

"Cleaning up, taking care of things. I'm staying here. Miss Abby said it was all right."

"Where's my mother?"

A paddle-wheeler, its windows brightly lit, blew its whistle as it approached the drawbridge.

"She died, Mr. Willie."

"Died?"

"Last month, in New Orleans. Miss Abby says it was pneumonia," Tige said. He looked away, his hands clenched on the broom handle.

"I think you're confused, Tige. My mother never went to New Orleans. She thought it was crowded and dirty. Why would she go to New Orleans? Where'd you hear all this?" Willie said, his voice rising.

"Miss Abby said the Yanks took your mother's hogs and cows. She thought she could get paid for them 'cause she was from Ireland," Tige said.

"The Yanks don't pay for what they take. Where'd you get that nonsense?"

"I done told you."

"Yes, you did. You certainly did," Willie said.

He went inside the house and stamped around in all the rooms. The beds were made, the washboards and chopping block in the kitchen scrubbed spotless, the pots and pans hung on hooks above the hearth and woodstove, the walls and ceiling free of cobweb, the dust kittens swept out from under all the furnishings. He slammed out the back of the house and circled through the side yard to the front.

He squeezed his temples with his fingers.

"Where is she buried?" he said.

Tige shook his head.

"You don't know?" Willie said.

"No, suh."

Willie pulled his blanket roll off his shoulder and flung it at the gallery, then winced and clasped his hand on his left collarbone.

"There's blood on your shirt," Tige said.

"A guerrilla gave me a taste of his sword," Willie replied. He sat down on the steps and draped his hands between his legs. He was quiet a long time. "She went to the Yanks to get paid for her livestock?"

"I reckon. Miss Abby said 'cause your mother was from Ireland, the Yankees didn't have no right to take her property. How come they'd have the right if she was from here? That's what I cain't figure."

"This war never seems to get over, does it, Tige? How you been doin'?" Willie said.

"Real good." Tige studied the failing light in the trees and the birds descending into the chimney tops. "Most of the time, anyway."

"Will you forgive a fellow for speaking sharply?" Willie asked.

"Some folks say my daddy got killed at Brice's Crossroads. Others say he just run off 'cause he didn't have no use for his family. I busted a window in a church after somebody told me that. Knocked stained glass all over the pews," Tige said.

"I doubt Our Lord holds it against you," Willie said.

Tige sat down beside him. He aimed his broom into the dusk as though it were a musket and sighted down the handle, then rested it by his foot. "Miss Abby done bought a big building she's turning into a schoolhouse. Her and a high-yellow lady named Flower is gonna teach there. She talks about you all the time, what a good man you are and what kind ways you have. In fact, I ain't never heard a lady talk so much about a man."

"Miss Abigail does that?"

"I was talking about the colored lady — Miss Flower."

Chapter Twenty-two

Robert Perry was released from prison at Johnson's Island, Ohio, two months after the Surrender. The paddle-wheeler he boarded without a ticket was packed with Northern cotton traders, gamblers, real estate speculators, and political appointees seizing upon opportunities that seemed to be a gift from a divine hand. At night the saloons and dining and card rooms blazed with light and reverberated with orchestra music, while outside torrents of rain blistered the decks and the upside-down lifeboat Robert huddled under with a tiger-striped cat, a guilt-haunted, one-armed participant in the Fort Pillow Massacre, and an escaped Negro convict whose ankles were layered with leg-iron scars and who stole food for the four of them until they reached New Orleans.

Robert rode the spine of a freight car as far as the Atchafalaya River, then walked forty miles in a day and a half and went to sleep in a woods not more than two hours from the house where he had been born. When he woke in the morning he sat on a tree-shaded embankment on the side of the road and ate a withered apple and drank water from a wood canteen he had carried with him from Johnson's Island.

A squad of black soldiers passed him on the road, talking among themselves, their eyes never registering his presence, as though his gray clothes were less an indicator of an old enemy than a flag of defeat. Then a mounted Union sergeant, this one white, reined up his horse in front of Robert and looked down at him curiously. He wore a goatee and mustache and a kepi pulled down tightly on his brow and a silver ring with a gold cross on it.

"What happened to your shoes?" he asked.

"Lost them crossing the Atchafalaya," Robert replied.

"We've had trouble with guerrillas hereabouts. You wouldn't be one of those fellows, would you?"

Robert stared thoughtfully into space. "Simian creatures who hang in trees? No, I don't know much about those fellows," he said.

"Your feet look like spoiled bananas."

"Why, thank you," Robert said.

"Where'd you fight, Reb?"

"Virginia and Pennsylvania."

Cedar and mulberry and wild pecan trees grew along the edge of the road, and the canopy seemed to form a green tunnel of light for almost a half mile.

"I have a feeling you didn't sign an oath of allegiance in a prison camp and they decided to keep you around a while," the sergeant said.

"You never can tell," Robert said.

The sergeant removed his foot from the left stirrup. "Swing up behind me. I can take you into Abbeville," he said.

An hour later Robert slid off the horse's rump a half mile from his home and began walking again. He left the road and cut through a neighbor's property that was completely deserted, the main house doorless and empty of furniture, the fields spiked with dandelions and palmettos and the mud towers of crawfish. Then he climbed through a rick fence onto his father's plantation and crossed pastureland that was green and channeled with wildflowers. New cane waved in the fields, and in the distance he could see the swamp where he had fished as a boy, and snow egrets rising from the cypress canopy like white rose petals in the early sun.

The two-story house and the slave cabins seemed unharmed by the war but the barn had been burned to the ground and in the mounds of ashes and charcoal Robert could see the rib cages and long, hollow-eyed skulls of horses. He did not recognize any of the black people living in the cabins, nor could he explain the presence of the whites living among them. His mother's flowerpots and hanging baskets were gone from the gallery, and the live oak that had shaded one side of the house, its branches always raking across the slate roof, had been nubbed back so that the trunk looked like a celery stalk.

He lifted the brass knocker on the front door and tapped it three times. He heard a chair scrape inside the house, then heavy footsteps approaching the front, not like those of either his mother or his father.

The man who opened the door looked like an upended hogshead. He wore checkered pants and polished, high-top shoes, like a carnival barker might wear; his face was florid, whiskered like a walrus's. In his right hand he clutched a boned porkchop wrapped in a thick piece of bread.

"What do you want?" he asked.

"I'm Robert Perry. I live here."

"No, I don't hardly see how you could live here, since I've never seen you before. That would be pretty impossible, young fellow," the man said. His accent was from the East, the vowels as hard as rocks. His wife sat at the dining room table in a housecoat, her hair tied up on her head with a piece of gauze.

"Where are my parents? What are you doing in my house?" Robert said.

"You say Perry? Some people by that name moved into town. Ask around. You'll find them."

"He probably just wants something to eat. Offer him some work," the man's wife said from the table.

"You want to do some chores for a meal?" the man said.

Robert looked out at the fields and the pink sun over the cane. "That would be fine," he said.

"The privy's got to be cleaned out. Better eat before you do it, though," the man said. He laughed and slapped Robert hard on the upper arm. "Not much meat on your bones. Want a regular job? I run the Freedman's Bureau. You were a Johnny?"

"Yes."

"I'll see what I can do. We don't aim to rub your noses in it," the man said.

One week later, just before dawn, Tige McGuffy woke to a rolling sound on the roof of Willie Burke's house. Then he heard a soft thud against the side of the house and another on the roof. He looked out the window just as a man in the backyard flung a pinecone into the eaves.

Tige went to the dresser drawer, then walked down the stairs and opened the back door. Mist hung in layers on the bayou and in the trees and canebrakes. The man in the yard stood next to an unsaddled, emaciated horse, tossing a pinecone in the air and catching it in his palm.

"Why you chunking at Mr. Willie's house?" Tige asked.

"Thought it was time for y'all to get up. You always sleep in a nightshirt and a kepi?" the man in the yard said.

"If I feel like it," Tige replied.

"Where's Mr. Willie?"

"None of your dadburned business."

"I like your kepi. Would you tell Willie that if Robert Perry had two coins he could rub together he would treat him to breakfast. But unfortunately he doesn't have a sou."

Tige set a heavy object in his hand on the kitchen drainboard. "Why ain't you said who you was?" he asked.

Robert Perry walked out of the yard and onto the steps, his horse's reins dangling on the ground. His clothes and hair were damp with dew, his face unshaved, his belt notched tightly under his ribs. He came inside and glanced down at the drainboard.

"What are you doing with that pistol?" he said.

"Night riders got it in for Mr. Willie. I was pert' near ready to blow you into the bayou," Tige replied.

"Night riders?" Robert said.

Ten minutes later Willie left Robert and Tige at the house and went on a shopping trip down Main Street, then returned and fixed a breakfast of scrambled eggs and green onions, hash browns, real coffee, warm milk, bacon, chunks of ham, fresh bread, and blackberries and cream. He and Robert and Tige piled their plates and made smacking and grunting sounds while they ate, forking and spooning more food into their mouths than they could chew.

"I didn't know meals like this existed anymore. How'd you pay for this?" Robert said.

"Took advantage of the credit system . . . Then signed your name to the bill," Willie said.

"Tige was telling me about your local night riders," Robert said.

"Have you heard of the White League or the Knights of the White Camellia?"

"I heard Bedford Forrest is the head of a group of some kind. Ex-Masons, I think. They use a strange nomenclature," Robert replied.

"Some are just fellows who don't want to give it up. But some will put a bedsheet over their heads and park one in your brisket," Willie said.

"What have you gone and done, Willie?"

"Abigail and Flower Jamison started up a school for Negroes or anybody else who wants to learn. I helped them get started," Willie replied.

Robert was silent.

"You haven't seen her?" Willie asked.

"Not yet."

"You going to?" Willie asked.

Robert set down his knife and fork. He kept his eyes on his plate. "Her letters are confessional. But I'm not sure what it is that bothers her. Would you know, Willie?" Robert said.

"Would I be knowing? You're asking me?" Willie said.

Robert was silent again.

"Who knows the soul of another?" Willie said.

"You're a dreadful liar."

"Don't be talking about your old pals like that."

"I won't," Robert said.

The sun was in the yard and on the trees now, and mockingbirds and jays were flitting past the window. The horse Robert had ridden from Abbeville was drinking from the bayou, the reins trailing in the water.

"You were at Mansfield when General Mouton was killed?" Robert said.

"Yes," Willie replied.

"It's true that half the 18th was wiped out again?" Robert said.

Willie looked at him but didn't reply.

"You dream about it?" Robert asked.

"A little. Not every night. I've let the war go for the most part," Willie said. He twisted his head slightly and touched at a shaving nick on his jawbone, his eyelids blinking.

The wind blew the curtains, and out on the bayou a large fish flopped in the shade of a cypress. "Thank you for the fine breakfast," Robert said.

"I see grape blowing people all over the trees," Tige said.

Robert and Willie looked at his upturned face and at the darkness in his eyes and the grayness around his mouth.

"I drank water out of the Bloody Pond. I wake up with the taste in my throat. I dream about a fellow with railroad spikes in him," Tige said.

Robert lifted Tige's kepi off the back of his chair and set it on his head and grinned at him.

That evening Robert bathed in the clawfoot tub inside Willie's bathhouse and shaved in the oxidized mirror on the wall, then dressed in fresh clothes and went outside. A sunshower was falling on the edge of town and he could smell the heavy, cool odor of the bayou in the shadows. Willie was splitting firewood on a stump by the bayou and stacking it in a shed, his sleeves rolled, his cheeks bright with his work.

Robert suddenly felt an affection for his

friend that made him feel perhaps things were right with the world after all, regardless of the times in which they lived. There is a goodness in your face that the war, the likes of Billy Sherman, or the worst of our own kind will never rob you of, Willie, he thought.

"I received the letter you wrote me while you were waiting to be executed by the Federals," Robert said.

"You did?"

"A Yankee chaplain mailed it to me with an attached note. He thought there was a chance you had been killed while escaping and he should honor your last wish by mailing the letter you left behind," Robert said.

"Some of those Yanks weren't bad fellows," Willie said.

"You said you repented of any violation of our friendship and you never wanted to impair my relationship with another."

"A fellow's thoughts get a bit confused when he's about to have eight Yanks fire their rifles into his lights," Willie said.

"I see," Robert said. "Well, you're a mighty good friend, Willie Burke, and you never have to repent to me about anything. Are we clear on what we're talking about, old pal?"

"It's a tad murky to me. May I get back to my work now?"

Robert watched the wind blowing in the

Spanish moss and in the trees along the bayou and grinned at nothing. "Did you sign the oath of allegiance?" he asked.

"The oath? No, never got around to it, I'm afraid," Willie said.

"Thought not. My parents are living in a shack behind a Union officer's house."

"We had a good run at it. We lost. Accept it, Robert. When they give us a bad time, tell them to kiss our ruddy bums."

"A nation that fought honorably shouldn't be treated as less," Robert said. "There are men here who have a plan to take Louisiana back out of the Union. They fought shoulder to shoulder with us. They're fine men, Willie."

Willie set down his ax and wiped his hands on a rag and glanced furtively at his friend. Robert's face was wooden, his eyes troubled. Then he saw Willie watching him and he looked again at the wind in the trees and grinned at nothing.

At dusk the two of them walked through the streets to the house Abigail and Flower had converted into a school. Robert was not prepared for what he saw. Every room in the house, both upstairs and downstairs, was brightly lit and filled with people of color. They were of all ages and all of them were dressed in their best clothes. And those for whom there was no room sat on the gallery or milled about under the live oak in the front yard.

The desks were fashioned from church pews that had been sawed into segments and placed under plank tables that ran the width of the rooms. The walls were decorated with watercolor paintings and the numbers one to ninety-nine and the letters of the alphabet, which had been scissored from red, yellow, and purple pieces of cloth. Each student had a square of slate and a piece of chalk and a damp rag to write with, and each of them by the end of the evening had to spell ten words correctly that he could not spell the previous week.

Then Robert looked through a downstairs window and saw Abigail Dowling in front of a class that included a dozen blacks, Tige McGuffy, the bordello operator Carrie LaRose and her pirate of a brother, Scavenger Jack, who looked like a shaggy behemoth stuffed between the plank writing table and sawed-down pew.

Abigail wore a dress that had a silver-purplish sheen to it, and her chestnut hair was pulled back in a bun and fixed with a silver comb, so that the light caught on the broadness of her forehead and the resolute quality of her eyes.

Robert waved when she seemed to glance out the window, then he realized she could not see him in the darkness and she had been reacting to a sound in the street. He turned and watched a flatbed wagon loaded with revelers creak past the school. The revelers were drunk on busthead whiskey, yelling, sometimes jumping down to pick up a dirt clod, flinging it at a schoolroom window. A slope-shouldered man in a suit and a bowler hat followed them on horseback, a gold toothpick set in the corner of his mouth.

"Who's that fellow?" Robert asked.

"Todd McCain. Abby outbid him on the building," Willie said.

"Not a good loser, is he?" Robert said.

"Toddy is one of those whose depths will probably never be quite plumbed," Willie said.

The revelers got down from their wagon, uncorking bottles of corn liquor and drinking as they walked, watching the families of Negroes under the trees part in their path, like layers of soil cleaving off the point of a plowshare. One of them drained his bottle, carefully tamped the cork back down in the neck, then broke it on the roof of the school.

Robert walked through the revelers into the street, where Todd McCain sat on his horse under a street lantern that had been hoisted on a pulley to the top of a pole. McCain's face was shadowed by his bowler, his narrow shoulders pinched inside his coat. Robert stroked the white blaze on the nose of McCain's horse.

"A fine animal you have here," he said.

McCain removed the gold toothpick from his mouth, his teeth glistening briefly in the dark, as though he might be smiling. "You're Bob Perry," he said.

"My friends call me Robert. But you can call me Lieutenant Perry. Why is it I have the feeling this collection of drunkards and white trash is under your direction?"

"Search me," McCain said.

"Can I accept your word you're about to take them from our presence?"

"They're just boys having fun."

"I'll put it to you more simply. How would you like to catch a ball between your eyes?"

The wind had died and the air in the street had turned stale and close, stinking of horse and dog droppings, the lantern overhead iridescent with humidity. The joy in the revelers had died, too, as they watched their leader being systematically humiliated. McCain's horse shifted its weight and tossed its head against the reins. McCain brought his fist down between the animal's ears.

"Hold, you shithog!" he said.

"Give me your answer, sir," Robert said.

McCain cleared his throat and spit out into the street. He wiped his mouth.

"You've read for the law. I'm a merchant who doesn't have your verbal skills," he said.

He turned his horse in a circle, its hindquarters and swishing tail causing Robert to step backward. Then McCain straightened his shoulders and pulled the creases out of his coat and said something under his breath.

"What? Say that again!" Robert said, starting forward.

But McCain kicked his heels into his horse's ribs and set off in a full gallop down the street, his legs clenched as tightly in the stirrups as a wood clothespin, one hand dipping inside his coat. He jerked the bit back in his horse's mouth, whirled in a circle, and bore down on Robert Perry, his bowler flying from his head, a nickel-plated, double-barrel derringer pointed straight out in front of him.

He popped off only one round, nailing the lantern on the pole dead center, blowing glass in a shower above Robert's head. He held up the derringer in triumph, the unfired barrel a silent testimony to the mercy he was extending an adversary.

The revelers roared with glee and vindication and climbed aboard their flatbed wagon, then followed their leader back down the street to a saloon. Robert picked a sliver of glass off his shirt and pitched it into the darkness.

"The word is he's a White Leaguer," Willie said.

"I don't think they're all cut out of the

same cloth," Robert said.

Willie looked at Robert's profile, the uncut hair on the back of his neck, the clarity in his eyes. "How would you be knowing that?" he said.

"The carpetbaggers are pulling the nails out of our shoes. We don't always get to choose our bedfellows. Wake up, Willie," Robert replied.

"Oh, Robert, don't be taken in by these fellows. They do their deeds in darkness and dishonor our colors. Tell me you're not associating with that bunch."

But Robert did not reply. As Willie watched his friend walk inside the school to find Abigail Dowling, the sword wound in his shoulder seemed to flare as though someone had held a lighted match to his skin.

Chapter Twenty-three

Each morning Ira Jamison rose to greater prosperity and political expectations. Where others saw the collapse of a nation, he saw vast opportunity. He listened respectfully while his neighbors decried carpetbag venality and gave his money and support to the clandestine groups who spoke of retaking Louisiana from the Union, but in truth he viewed the carpetbaggers as cheaply dressed and poorly educated amateurs who could be bought for pocket change.

His summer days of 1865 began with a fine breakfast on his terrace, with an overview of the Mississippi and the trees and bluffs on the far side. He drank his coffee and read his newspapers and the mail that was delivered in a leather pouch from the plantation store. He subscribed to publications in New Orleans, Atlanta, New York, and Chicago, and read them all while a pink glow spread across the land and fresh convict labor throughout the state arrived by steamboat and jail wagon for processing in the camps and barracks they built themselves as the first down payment on their sentences.

Ira Jamison wondered if Abe Lincoln, moldering in the grave, had any idea what he had done for Ira Jamison when he emancipated the slaves.

Then he unwrapped the current issue of *Harper's Weekly*, read the lead stories, and turned to the second page. At the top of a four-column essay were the words:

The Resurrection of a Vanquished Enemy?
The Negro as Convict in the New South,
A View by Our Louisiana Correspondent

Jamison set down his coffee cup and began reading.

Even the apologists for Jefferson Davis would concede he spent a political lifetime attempting to spread slavery throughout the Western territories as well as the Caribbean. His close friend Confederate General Nathan Bedford Forrest has recently tried to influence congressional legislation that would bring about the importation of one million Cantonese coulees to the United States as a source of post-Emancipation labor.

However, an ex-Confederate colonel by

the name of Ira Jamison, who has converted his central Louisiana plantation
into an enormous prison, may have come
upon a profit-making scheme in the exploitation of African labor that outrivals
any precedent his peers may have set.

Mr. Jamison rents convicts to enterprises
and businessmen whose vested interest is
to keep costs low and productivity high.
The reports of beatings, malnutrition, and
deaths from exhaustion and exposure to
inclement weather are widespread.

Mr. Jamison, who prefers to be called
'Colonel,' is a wounded veteran of Shiloh.
But his name has also been associated
with the destruction of the 18th Louisiana
Infantry, who were sent uphill into Union
artillery and were unsupported on the
flank by the unit under Mr. Jamison's
command —

The name on the byline was Abigail
Dowling.

Ira Jamison rolled the journal into a tight
cylinder and walked into the house, tapping
it on his leg, puffing air in one cheek, then
the other, conscious each moment of the
anger she could stir in him, the control he
had to muster not to let it show in his face.
He stood by his fireplace, tapping the cusp of
the journal against the bricks, looking out the
window at the brilliance of the day. Then,

like a man who could not refrain from picking at a scab, his eye wandered to the fissure that cut across his hearth and climbed up one side of his chimney. Had it grown wider? Why was he looking at it now?

He took a lucifer match from a vase on the mantel and scratched it alight, then touched the flame to the rolled edges of the journal and watched the paper blacken along one side of the cylinder. He dropped the pages like burning leaves on top of the andirons.

He sent his body servant to find both Clay Hatcher and Rufus Atkins. A half hour later they tethered their horses in the backyard and walked into the shade of the porte cochere and knocked on the side door. He did not invite them in and instead stepped outside and motioned for them to follow him to the terrace, where his uneaten breakfast still sat, buzzing with flies.

"One of the niggers serve you spoiled food, Kunnel? Tell us which one," Hatcher said.

"Shut up, Clay," Rufus Atkins said.

Jamison stood on the flagstones of the terrace, his fists propped on his hips, his head lowered in thought. The green boughs and bright red bloom of a mimosa tree feathered in the wind above the three men.

"I understand Abigail Dowling has started up a school for freed slaves," Jamison said.

"She ain't the only one. Flower is teaching there, too," Hatcher said.

Atkins gave Hatcher a heated look.

"Flower?" Jamison said.

"Damn right. Teaching reading and writing and arithmetic. Can you believe hit?" Hatcher said.

"Who put up the money for the school?" Jamison said.

"I hear she got hit from the woman runs the whorehouse," Hatcher said.

"Who is *she?*" Jamison asked.

Hatcher started to speak, but Atkins cut him off.

"Abigail Dowling got the money from Carrie LaRose, Colonel," Atkins said. "Is there something you want done?"

"I've suspected for some time Miss Dowling is an immoralist. Do you know what I mean by that?" Jamison said.

"No, suh," Hatcher said.

"Listen to the colonel, Clay," Atkins said.

"She has unnatural inclinations toward her own gender. I think she has no business teaching anybody anything. She is also trying to embarrass us in the national press. Are you hearing me, Rufus?" Jamison said.

"Yes, sir. To borrow a phrase from my friend Clay here, maybe it's time that abolitionist bitch got her buckwheats," Atkins said.

"Yes, and leave footprints right back to my front door," Jamison said.

Atkins' gaze focused on the river bottoms

and a work gang hauling dirt up the side of a levee. The striped jumpers and pants of the convicts were stained red with sweat and clay. Atkins sucked in his cheeks, his eyes neutral, the colonel's insult leaving no trace in his face.

"I reckon we have a situation that requires a message without a signature," he said.

"Good. We're done here," Jamison said, and began to walk away. Then he turned, his hand cupped on his chin, his thoughts veiled.

"Rufus?" he said.

"Yes, sir?"

"No one is to harm Flower. Not under any circumstances. The man who does will have his genitalia taken out," Jamison said.

Jamison crossed the yard and walked under the porte cochere and into the house. Clay Hatcher stared after him, breathing through his mouth, his eyes dull.

"A little late, ain't hit? Don't he know Flower got raped by them lamebrains you hired?" he said.

Atkins used the flat of his fist to break Hatcher's bottom lip against his teeth.

Abigail Dowling had discovered she did not know how to talk with Robert Perry. The previous evening she had seen him for the first time in almost four years. When she had run out of the classroom into the hallway to greet him, he had placed his hands on her shoulders and touched the skin along her collar with one finger. Instead of happiness, she felt a rush of guilt in her chest and a sense of physical discomfort that bordered on resentment. Why? she asked herself. The more she tried to think her way out of her feelings, the more confused she became.

He had stood up to Todd McCain and the drunkards who were harassing the Negroes under the live oak; his manners and good looks and the brightness in his eyes and his obvious affection for her were undiminished by the war. He walked her and Flower home, dismissing the shot fired over his head by McCain, offering to sleep on her gallery in case the revelers on the flatbed wagon returned.

But she didn't even ask him in and was glad she could honestly tell him she was feeling ill. When he was gone she made tea for Flower and herself and experienced a sudden sense of quietude and release for which she could offer herself no explanation.

Who in reality was she? she asked herself. Now, more than ever, she believed she was an impostor, a sojourner not only in Louisiana and in the lives of others but in her own life as well.

The next morning she looked out the front window and saw Robert opening the gate to her yard. He wore a brushed brown suit, shined shoes, and a soft blue shirt with a black tie, and his hair was wet and combed back on his neck. In the daylight she realized he was even thinner than she had thought.

"I hope you don't mind my dropping by unannounced," he said.

"Of course not," she said, and unconsciously closed her left hand, which her father had told her was the way he could always tell when she fibbed to him as a girl. "Why don't we walk out here in the yard?"

They strolled through the trees toward the bayou. The camellias and four-o'clocks were blooming in the shade, and a family of black people were perched among the cypress knees on the bank, bobber-fishing in the shallows.

She heard Robert clear his throat and pull a deep breath into his lungs.

"Abby, what is it? Why is there this stone wall between us?" he said.

"I feel I've deceived you."

"In what way?"

Her heart raced and the trees and the air vines swaying in the breeze and the black family among the shadows seemed to go in and out of focus.

"You fought for a cause in which you believed. You spent almost two years in prison. I was a member of the Underground Railroad. I never told you that," she said.

"You're a woman of conscience. You don't have to explain yourself to me."

"Well," she said, her mouth dry, her blood hammering in her ears with a new deceit she had just perpetrated upon him.

"Is that the sum of your concerns?" he said.

She paused under an ancient live oak, one that was gnarled, hollowed by lightning, green with lichen and crusted with fern, the trunk wrapped with poisonous vines.

"No, I was romantically intimate with another," she said.

"I see," he replied.

His hair had dried in the heat and it had lights in it, like polished mahogany, and the wind blew it on his collar. His eyes were crystal blue and seemed to focus on a little Negro boy who was cane-lifting a hooked perch out of the water.

"With Willie?" he said.

"I can only speak to my own deeds," she said.

"Neither of you should feel guilt, at least not toward me. Nor does either of you owe me an apology."

"We're different, you and I," she said.

"And Willie is not?"

"You believed in the cause you served. Willie never did. He fought because he was afraid not to. Then his heart filled with hatred when he saw Jim Stubbefield killed," she said.

"I lost friends, too, Abby," Robert said.

But she was already walking back toward the house, her hands balled into fists, the leaves and persimmons and molded pecan husks snapping under her feet, the world swimming around her as though she were seeing it from the bottom of a deep, green pool.

"Did you hear me, Abby? I lost friends, too," Robert called behind her.

The following week, on a sun-spangled, rain-scented Saturday evening, Carrie LaRose entered St. Peter's Church and knelt down inside the confessional. The inside of the confessional was hot and dark and smelled of dust and oil and her own perfume and body powder and the musk in her clothes.

The priest who pulled back the wood slide in the partition was very old, with a nervous jitter in his eyes and hands which often shook uncontrollably, to such a degree he was no longer allowed to perform the consecration at Mass or to administer communion. Through a space between the black gauze that hung over the small window in the partition and the wood paneling, Carrie could see the hands and wrists of the priest framed inside a shaft of sunlight. His bones looked like sticks, the skin almost translucent, the veins little more than pieces of blue string.

The priest waited, then his head turned toward the window.

"What is it? Why is it you don't speak?" he said.

"You don't know me. I run the brot'el sout' of town," she replied.

"Could I help you with something?"

"You don't talk French?"

"No, not well."

"I done a lot of sins in my life. The Lord already knows what they are and I ain't gonna bore Him talking about them, no. But I done one t'ing that don't never let go of me. 'Cause for me to wish I ain't done what I did is the same t'ing as wishing I wasn't alive."

"You've lost me."

Carrie tried to start over but couldn't think.

"My knees is aching. Just a minute," she said.

She left the confessional and found a chair and dragged it back inside, then plunked down in it and closed the curtain again.

"Are we comfortable now?" the priest asked.

"Yes, t'ank you. I was in a prison cell in Paris. I could see the guillotine from the window. I kneeled down on the stone and practiced putting my head on the bench so I'd know how to do it when they took me in the cart to die. But I'd get sick all over myself. I knowed then I'd do anyt'ing to stay alive."

"I'm confused. You want absolution for a murder you committed?"

"You ain't listening. The other woman in my cell was a cutpurse. I done sexual t'ings for the jailer so he'd take her 'stead of me. I go over it in my head again and again, but each time it comes out the same way. In my t'oughts I still want to live and I want that woman to die so I ain't got to lay my head down under that blade way up at the top of the scaffold. So in troot I ain't really sorry for sending her to the headsman 'stead of me. That means I ain't never gonna have no peace."

The priest's silhouette was tilted forward on his thumb and forefinger. He seemed to rock back and forth, as though teetering on the edge of a thought or an angry moment. Then he closed the slide on the partition and rose from his seat and left the confessional.

She sat motionless in her chair, the walls around her like an upended coffin. Sweat ran down her sides and an odor like sour milk seemed to rise from her clothes. A hand that trembled so badly it could hardly find purchase gripped the edge of the curtain and jerked it back.

"Step out here with me," the priest said, and gestured for her to take a seat in a pew by a rack of burning candles.

He sat down next to her, his small hands knotted on his thighs. The rack of votive candles behind him glittered like a hundred points of blue light.

"You don't have to sort through these things with a garden rake. You just have to be sorry for having done them and change your way. God doesn't forgive incrementally. His forgiveness is absolute," the priest said.

He saw her forming the world "incrementally" with her lips.

"He doesn't forgive partway. You're forgiven, absolved, as of this moment," the priest said.

"What about the house I run?"

"You might consider a vocational adjustment."

"Ain't no one tole it to me this way befo'," she said.

"Come back and see me," he said.

The following night was Sunday, and the mutton-chopped, potbellied Union major was back at the bordello, charging his liquor and the use of Carrie's best girl to his bill.

"You're not still mad at me, are you, Carrie? Over my unpaid bill and that sort of thing?" he said. He held a dark green wine bottle in one hand and a glass filled with burgundy in the other. One button on his fly was undone and his underwear showed through the opening.

She was sitting in a rocker on the gallery, fanning herself, while heat lightning bloomed in the clouds. An oppressive weight seemed to be crushing down on her chest, causing her to constantly straighten her back in order to breathe.

"I'm glad you brought that up, you. Button up that li'l sawed-off penis of yours, the one all my girls laugh at, and get your ass outta my house," she said.

"*What* did you say?"

The coffee cup she threw at him broke on the wood post just behind his head.

There were lights in the sky that night, and wind that kicked dust out of the cane fields and dry thunder that sounded like horses' hooves thundering across the earth. She sat on the gallery until midnight, her breath wheezing as though her lungs were filled with burnt cork. In the distance she saw a ball of flaming swamp gas roll through a stand of flooded cypress, its incandescence so bright the details of the trees, the hanging moss, the lacy texture of the leaves, the flanged trunks at the waterline, became like an instant brown and green and gray photograph created in the middle of the darkness.

Some people believed the balls of light in the swamp were actually the spirits of the loups-garous — werewolves who could take on human, animal or inanimate forms — and secretly Carrie had always believed the same and had crossed herself or clutched her juju bag whenever she saw one. But tonight she simply watched the ball of lightning or burning swamp gas or whatever it was splinter apart in the saw grass as though she were looking back on a childhood fable whose long-ago ability to scare her now made her nostalgic.

In the morning she called her girls together, paid them their commissions for the previous week, gave each of them a twenty-five-dollar bonus, and fired them all. After they were gone she placed a black man in the front and back yards to tell all her customers the bordello was closed, then locked the doors, took a sponge bath in a bucket, dressed in her best nightgown, and lay down on top of her bedsheets.

She slept through the day and woke in the afternoon, thickheaded, unsure of where she was, the room creaking with heat from the late sun. She washed her face in a porcelain basin and shuffled into the kitchen and tried to eat, but the food was like dry paper in her mouth. It seemed the energies in her heart were barely enough to pump blood into her head.

The yard was empty, the servants gone. She soaked a towel in water and laudanum and placed it on her chest and went back to bed. The light faded outside and she drifted in and out of sleep and once again heard the rumble of horses through the earth. She heard rain sweep across the roof and shutters banging against the sides of the house, then she slipped away inside the dream where a man in heavy shoes walked down a long corridor and scraped an iron door across stone.

In her dream she saw herself rise from the bed and kneel on the floor and lift her hair off her neck and lay her head down on the mattress, for some reason no longer afraid. Then the year became 1845 and the place was not Louisiana but Paris, and a great crowd filled the plaza below the platform she knelt on, their faces dirty, their bodies and wine-soaked breaths emanating a collective stench that was like sewer gas in the bordello district in the early hours. The sun was bright above the buildings and the shadow of the guillotine spilled across the cobblestones and the rim of the crowd, who were throwing rotted produce at her. Out of the corner of her eye she saw a muscular, black-hooded man ease the top half of the wood stock down on her neck and lock it into place, then step back with a lanyard in his hand.

A man in a beaver hat and split-tail coat raised his hand and the crowd fell silent and Carrie could hear the wind blowing through the portals that led into the plaza and leaves scratching across stone. The light seemed to harden and grow cold, and she felt a sensation like a ribbon of ice water slice across the back of her neck. Then the headsman jerked the lanyard and she heard the trigger spring loose at the top of the scaffold and the sound of a great metal weight whistling down upon her.

The plaza and the upturned, dirt-smeared faces in it and the stone buildings framed against the sky toppled away from her like an oil painting tossed end-over-end into a wicker basket.

When a black man came to work at the bordello in the morning, he found the back door broken open and Carrie LaRose kneeling by the side of her bed, the pillow that had been used to suffocate her still covering her head. A white camellia lay on the floor.

Chapter Twenty-four

A week later the sheriff sent word to Flower that he wanted to see her in his office. She put on her best dress and opened a parasol over her head and walked down Main to the jail. She had never been to the jail before, and she paused in front of the door and looked automatically at the ground to see if there were paths that led to side entrances for colored. The sheriff, Hipolyte Gautreau, saw her through the window and waved her inside.

"How you do, Miss Flower? Come in and have a seat. I'll run you t'rew this fast as I can so you can get back to your school," he said.

She did not understand his solicitousness or the fact he had addressed her as Miss. She folded her parasol and sat down in a chair that was placed closely against the side of his desk.

He fitted on his spectacles and removed a

single sheet of paper from a brown envelope and unfolded it in both hands.

"You knew Carrie LaRose pretty good, huh?" he said.

"I did her laundry and cleaned house for her," Flower replied.

"A month befo' she died —"

"She didn't die. She was murdered."

The sheriff nodded. "Last month she had this will wrote up. She left you her house and one hundred dol'ars. The money is at the bank in your name. I'll walk you down to the courthouse to transfer the deed."

"Suh?" she said.

"There's fifty arpents that go wit' the house. A cane farmer works it on shares. It's all yours, Miss Flower."

She sat perfectly still, her face without expression, her hands resting on top of her folded parasol. She gazed through the doorway that gave on to the cells. They were empty, except for a town drunkard, who slept in a fetal position on the floor. The sheriff looked over his shoulder at the cells.

"Somet'ing wrong?" he said.

"Nobody is locked up for killing Miss Carrie."

"She knew a lot of bad t'ings about lots of people," he said. He seemed to study his own words, his expression growing solemn and profound with their implication.

"She gave Miss Abby the money to buy

our school. That's why she's dead," Flower said.

But the sheriff was shaking his head even before she had finished her statement.

"I wouldn't say that, Miss Flower. There's lots of people had it in for Carrie LaRose. Lots of —"

"There was a white camellia by her foot. Everybody knows what the white camellia means."

"Miss Carrie had camellias growing in her side yard. It don't mean a —"

"Shame on the people who claimed to be her friend. Shame on every one of them. You don't need to be helping me transfer the deed, either," Flower said. She looked the sheriff in the eyes, then rose from her chair and walked out the door.

She used the one hundred dollars to buy books for the school and to hire carpenters and painters to refurbish her new house. She and Abigail dug flower beds around the four sides of the house, spading the clay out of the subsoil so that each bed was like an elongated ceramic tray. They hauled black dirt from the cane fields and mixed it in the wagon with sheep manure and humus from the swamp, then filled the beds with it and planted roses, hibiscus, azalea bushes, windmill palms, hydrangeas and banana trees all around the house.

On the evening the painters finished the last of the trim, Flower and Abigail sat on a blanket under the live oak in back and drank lemonade and ate fried chicken from a basket and looked at the perfect glow and symmetry of the house in the sunset. Flower's belongings were piled in Abigail's buggy, waiting to be moved inside.

"I cain't believe all this is happening to me, Miss Abby," Flower said.

"You're a lady of property. One of these days you'll have to stop calling me 'Miss Abby,' " Abigail said.

"Not likely," Flower said.

"You're a dear soul. You deserve every good thing in the world. You don't know how much you mean to me."

"Miss Abby, sometime you make me a little uncomfortable, the way you talk to me."

"I wasn't aware of that," Abigail replied, her face coloring.

"I'm just fussy today," Flower said.

"I'll try to be a bit more sensitive," Abigail said.

"I didn't mean to hurt your feelings, Miss Abby. Come on now," she said, patting the top of Abigail's hand.

But Abigail removed her hand and began putting her food back in the picnic basket.

The next morning Flower woke in the feather-stuffed bed that had belonged to

Carrie LaRose. The wind was cool through the windows, the early sunlight flecked with rain. During the night she had heard horses on the road and loud voices from the saloon next door, perhaps those of night riders whose reputation was spreading through the countryside, but she kept the .36 caliber revolver from McCain's Hardware under her bed, five chambers loaded, with fresh percussion caps on each of the nipples. She did not believe the Knights of the White Camellia or the members of the White League were the ghosts of dead Confederate soldiers. In fact, she believed they were moral and physical cowards who hid their failure under bedsheets and she fantasized that one day the men who had attacked her would return, garbed in hoods and robes, and she would have the chance to do something unspeakable and painful to each of them.

Through her open window she could hear a piece of paper flapping. She got up from the bed and walked barefoot to the front door and opened it. Tied to the door handle with a piece of wire were a thin, rolled newspaper printed with garish headlines and a note written on a piece of hand-soiled butcher paper.

The note read:

Dear Nigger,
Glad you can read. See what you think

418

about the article on you and the Yankee bitch who thinks her shit don't stink.

We got nothing against you. Just don't mess with us.

It was unsigned.

The newspaper was printed on low-grade paper, of a dirty gray color, the printer's type undefined and fuzzy along the edges. The newspaper was titled *The Rebel Clarion* and had sprung to life in Baton Rouge immediately after the Surrender, featuring anonymously written articles and cartoons that depicted Africans with slat teeth, jug ears, lips that protruded like suction cups and bodies with the anatomical proportions of baboons, the knees and elbows punching through the clothes, as though poverty were in itself funny. In the cartoons the emancipated slave spit watermelon seeds, tap-danced while a carpetbagger tossed coins at him, sat with his bare feet on a desk in the state legislature or with a mob of his peers chased a terrified white woman in bonnet and hooped skirts inside the door of a ruined plantation house.

The article Flower was supposed to read was circled with black charcoal. In her mind's eye she saw herself tearing both the note and the newspaper in half and dropping them in the trash pit behind the house. But when she saw Abigail's name in the first paragraph of the article she sat down in Carrie LaRose's rocker on the gallery and, like a person deciding to glance at the lewd writing on a privy wall, she began to read.

While Southern soldiers died on the field at Shiloh, Miss Dowling showed her loyalties by joining ranks with the Beast of New Orleans, General Benjamin Butler, and caring for the enemy during the Yankee occupation of that city.

Later, using a pass from the Sanitary Commission, she smuggled escaped negroes through Confederate lines so they could join the Yankee army and sack the homes of their former owners and benefactors and, in some cases, rape the white women who had clothed and fed and nursed them when they were sick.

Miss Dowling has now seen fit to use her influence in the Northern press to attack one of Louisiana's greatest Confederate heroes, a patriot who was struck by enemy fire three times at Shiloh but who managed to escape from a prison hospital and once more join in the fight to support the Holy Cause.

Miss Dowling is well known in New Iberia, not only for her traitorous history during the war but also for propensities that appear directly related to her spinsterhood. Several credible sources have indicated that her close relationship with a freed negro woman is best described by a certain Latin term this newspaper does not make use of.

She set both the note and the newspaper under a flowerpot, although she could not explain why she didn't simply throw them away, and went inside her new house and fixed breakfast.

Several hours later a carriage with waxed black surfaces and white wheels and maroon cushions and a surrey on top pulled into the yard. A black man in a tattered, brushed coat and pants cut off at the knees sat in the driver's seat. A lean, slack-jawed outrider, wearing a flop hat, a gunbelt and holstered revolver hanging from his pommel, preceded the carriage into the yard and dismounted and looked back down the road and out into the fields, as though the great vacant spaces proffered a threat that no one else saw.

Flower stepped out on the gallery, into the hot wind blowing from the south. Ira Jamison got down from his carriage and removed his hat and wiped the inside of the band with a handkerchief as he nodded approvingly at the house and the mixture of flowers and banana trees and palms planted around it.

He wore a white shirt with puffed sleeves and a silver vest and dark pants, but because of the heat his coat was folded neatly on the cushions of the carriage. He carried an ebony-black cane with a gold head on it, but Flower noticed his limp was gone and his skin was pink and his eyes bright.

"This is extraordinary. You've done a wonderful job with the old place," he said. "My heavens, you never cease proving you're one of the most ingenious women I've ever known."

She looked at him mutely, her face tingling.

"Aren't you going to say hello?" he asked.

"How do you do, Colonel?" she said.

"Smashing, as my British friends in the cotton trade say. I'm in town to check on a few business matters. Looks like the Yanks burned down my laundry and the cabins out back with it."

"I'm glad you brought that up. My fifty arpents runs into seventy-five of yours. I'll take them off your hands," she said.

"You'll take them off —" he began, then burst out laughing. "Now, how would you do that?"

"Use my house and land to borrow the money. I already talked to the bank."

"Will you pay me for the buildings I lost?"

"No."

"By God, you amaze me, Flower. I'm proud of you," he said.

She felt her heart quicken, and was ashamed at how easily he could manipulate her emotions. She walked down the steps, then tilted up the flowerpot she had stuck the racist newspaper under.

"Read this and the note that came with it," she said.

Jamison set down his cane on the steps and unfolded the newspaper in the shade. Behind him, the outrider, whom Flower recognized as Clay Hatcher, stood in the sun, sweating under his hat. His bottom lip was swollen and crusted with black blood along a deep cut. He kept swiping horseflies out of his face.

Jamison tore the note in half and stuck it inside the newspaper and dropped the newspaper on the step.

"No one will dare harm you, Flower. I give you my word," he said.

"They already did. Three men raped me. They were paid by Rufus Atkins."

"I don't believe that. Rufus has worked for me thirty years. He does —"

"He does what you tell him?" she said.

His face seemed to dilate and redden with his frustration. "In a word, yes," he said.

"He made me go to bed with him, Colonel. Miss Abby told you about it. But you didn't raise a hand."

"I set the example. So you're correct, Flower. The guilt is mine."

He was speaking too fast now, his mercurial nature impossible to connect from one moment to the next.

"Suh, I don't understand," she said.

"Years ago I visited the quarters at night. I took all the privileges of a wealthy young plantation owner. People like Rufus and our man Clay over there are products of my own class."

"You helped them hurt me, suh."

"People can change. I'm sorry, Flower. My God, I'm your father. Can't you have some forgiveness?" he said.

After he was gone she sat on the top step of her gallery, her temples pounding, a solitary crow cawing against the yellow haze that filled the afternoon. She could not comprehend what had just happened. He had looked upon her work, her creations, her life, with admiration and pride, then had accepted paternity for her and in the same sentence had asked forgiveness.

Why now?

Because legally he can't own you anymore. This way he can, a voice answered.

She wanted to shove her fingers in her ears.

Willie saw reprinted copies of the article from the racist newspaper tacked on trees and storefronts all over town. One was even placed in his mailbox by a mounted man who leaned down briefly in the saddle, then rode away in the early morning mist. Willie had run after him, but the mounted man paid him no heed and did not look back at him.

Night riders had come into his yard twice

now, calling his name, tossing rocks at his windows. So far he had not taken their visits seriously. He had learned the White League and the Knights of the White Camellia, when in earnest, struck without warning and left no doubt about their intentions. A carpet-bagger was stripped naked and rope-drug through a woods, a black soldier garrotted on the St. Martinville Road, a political meeting in the tiny settlement of Loreauville literally shot to pieces.

But what do you do when the names of your friends are smeared by a collection of nameless cowards? he asked himself.

Make your own statement, he answered.

He saddled a horse in the livery he had inherited from his mother and rode out to the ends of both East and West Main, then divided the town into quadrants and traversed every street and alley in it, pulling down copies of the defamatory article and stuffing them in a choke sack tied to his pommel. By early afternoon, under a white sun, he was out in the parish, ripping the article from fence posts and the trunks of live oaks that bordered cane fields and dirt roads. His choke sack bulged as though it were stuffed with pinecones.

South of town, in an undrained area where a group of Ira Jamison's rental convicts were building a board road to a salt mine, Willie looked over his shoulder and saw a lone rider on a buckskin gelding behind him, a man with a poached, wind-burned face wearing a sweat-ringed hat and the flared boots of a cavalryman.

Willie passed a black man cooking food under a pavilion fashioned from tent poles and canvas. The black man was barefoot and had a shaved, peaked head, like the polished top of a cypress knee. He wore a white jumper and a pair of striped prison pants and rusted leg irons that caused him to take clinking, abbreviated steps from one pot to the next.

"You one of Colonel Jamison's convicts?" Willie asked.

"You got it, boss," the black man replied.

"What are you selling?"

"Greens, stew meat and tomatoes, red beans, rice and gravy, fresh bread. A plateful for fifteen cents. Or it's free if you wants to build the bo'rd road under the gun," the black man said. He roared at his own joke.

Willie turned his horse in a circle and waited in the shade of a live oak for the rider to approach him. The rider's eyes seemed lidless and reminded Willie of smoke on a wintry day or perhaps a gray sky flecked with scavenger birds. In spite of the heat, the rider's shirt was buttoned at the wrists and throat and he wore leather cuffs pulled up on his forearms.

"You wouldn't bird-dog a fellow, would you, Captain Jarrette?" Willie said.

"I make it my business to check out them that need watching," the rider replied.

"You put your sword to me when I was unarmed and had done you no injury. But you also saved me from going before a Yankee firing squad. So maybe we're even," Willie said.

"Meaning?"

"I'd like to buy you a lunch."

Jarrette removed his hat and surveyed the countryside, his hair falling over his ears. He leaned in the saddle and blew his nose with his fingers.

"I ain't got nothing against hit," he said.

Jarrette waited in the shade while Willie paid for their lunches. He watched the convicts lay split logs in the saw grass and humus and the black mud that oozed over their ankles. His nose was beaked, his chin cut with a cleft, his eyes connecting images with thoughts that probably no one would ever be privy to. Jarrette did not sit but squatted while he ate, shoveling food into his mouth as fast as possible with a wood spoon, scraping the tin in the plate, wiping it clean with bread, then eating the bread and licking his fingers, the muscles in his calves and thighs knotted into rocks.

"This grub tastes like dog turds," he said, tossing his bare plate on the grass.

Willie looked at the intensity in Jarrette's face, the heat that seemed to climb out of his buttoned collar, the twitch at the corner of one eye when he heard a convict's ax split a piece of green wood.

"Tell me, sir, is it possible you're insane?" Willie asked.

"Maybe. Anything wrong with that?" Jarrette replied.

"I was just curious."

Jarrette shifted his weight on his haunches and studied him warily. "Why you tearing down them newspaper stories? Don't lie about it, either," he said.

"They defame people I know."

Jarrette seemed to think about the statement.

"Cole Younger is my brother-in-law, you sonofabitch," he said.

Willie gathered up his plate and spoon from the grass, then reached down and picked up Jarrette's and returned them to the plank serving table under the canvas-topped pavilion. He walked back into the oak tree's shade. "As one Secesh to another, accept my word on this —" he began. Then he re-thought his words and looked out at the wind blowing across the saw grass. "May you have a fine day, Captain Jarrette, and may all your children and grandchildren be just like you and keep you company the rest of your life," he said.

When the sun was red over the cane fields

in the west, Willie pulled the last copy of *The Rebel Clarion* article he could find from the front porch of a houseboat far down Bayou Teche and turned his horse back toward town.

Now, all he needed to do was bury his choke sack in a hole or set fire to it on a mud bank and be done with it.

But a voice that he preferred not to hear told him that was not part of his plan.

Since his return from the war he had tried to accept the fact that the heart of Abigail Dowling belonged to another and it was fruitless for him to pursue what ultimately had been a boyhood fantasy. Had he not written Robert the same, in the moments before he thought he was going to be shot, at a time when a man knew the absolute truth about his life and himself, when every corner of the soul was laid bare?

But she wouldn't leave his thoughts. Nor would the memory of her thighs opening under him, the press of her hands in the small of his back, the heat of her breath on his cheek. Her sexual response wasn't entirely out of charity, was it? Women didn't operate in that fashion, he told himself. She obviously respected him, and sometimes at the school he saw a fondness in her eyes that made him want to reach out and touch her.

Maybe the war had embittered him and had driven her from him, and the fault was neither his nor Abby's but the war. After all, she was an abolitionist and sometimes his own rhetoric sounded little different from the recalcitrant Secessionists who would rather see the South layered with ash and bones than given over to the carpetbag government.

Why let the war continue to injure both of them?

If he could only take contention and vituperation from his speech and let go of the memories, no, that was not the word, the anger he still felt when he saw Jim Stubbefield freeze against a red-streaked sky, his jaw suddenly gone slack, a wound like a rose petal in the center of his brow —

What had he told Abby? "I'll never get over Jim. I hate the sonsofbitches who caused all this." What woman would not be frightened by the repository of vitriol that still burned inside him?

If he could only tell Abby the true feelings of his heart. Wouldn't all the other barriers disappear? Had she not come to him for help when she and Flower started up their school?

He tethered his horse to the ringed pole in front of Abby's cottage. The street was empty, the sky ribbed with strips of maroon cloud, the shutters on Abby's cottage vibrating in the wind. He walked into the backyard and set fire to the choke sack in Abby's trash pit, then tapped on her back door.

"Hello, Willie. What are you up to?" she said, looking over his shoulder at the column

430

of black smoke rising out of the ground.

"A lot of townspeople were incensed at your being slandered by this Kluxer paper in Baton Rouge. So they gathered up the articles and asked me to burn them," he said.

"What Kluxer paper?" she said.

He stared at her stupidly, then yawned slightly and looked innocuously out into the trees. "It's nothing of consequence. There's a collection of cretins in Baton Rouge who are always writing things no one takes seriously."

"Willie, for once would you try to make sense?" she said.

"It's not important. Believe me. I was just passing by."

"You look like a boiled crab. Have you been out in the sun?"

"Abby, love of my heart, I think long ago I was condemned to a life of ineptitude. It's time to say good-bye."

Before she could reply he walked quickly into the side yard and out into the street.

Right into a group of seven mounted men, all of whom had either black or white robes draped over the cantles of their saddles. Each of the robes was sewn with an ornate, pink-scrolled camellia. In the middle of the group, mounted on a buckskin gelding, was the man whose colorless eyes had witnessed the burning of Lawrence, Kansas.

"You was sassing me today, wasn't you?" he said.

"Wouldn't dream of it, Captain Jarrette," Willie said. He looked up and down the street. There was no one else on it, except an elderly Frenchman who sold taffy from a cart and a little black girl who was aimlessly following him on his route.

Another rider leaned down from his saddle and bounced a picked camellia off Willie's face.

"It's the wrong time to be a smart ass, cabbage head," he said.

"Get about your business and I won't tell your mother the best part of her sunny little chap dripped into her bloomers," Willie said to him.

The man who had thrown the flower laughed without making sound, then wiped his mouth. He had black hair the color and texture of pitch and was tall and raw-boned, unshaved, with skin that looked like it had been rubbed with black pepper, his neck too long for his torso, his shoulders sloping unnaturally under his shirt, as though they had been surgically pared away.

He lifted a coiled rope from a saddlebag and began feeding a wrapped end out on the ground.

"You were one of the convicts on the burial detail that almost put me in the ground," Willie said.

"I wasn't no convict, boy. I was a prisoner of war," the tall man said. "You sassed the captain?"

The summer light was high in the sky now, the street deep in shadow. Willie looked between the horses that were now circling him. The yards and galleries of the homes along the street were empty, the ventilated shutters closed, even though the evening was warm.

"Where's a Yank when you need one?" the convict said.

"Get on with it," Jarrette said.

The convict tied a small loop in the end of the rope, then doubled-over the shaft and worked it back through the loop.

"You listen —" Willie began.

The convict whirled the lariat over his head and slapped it around Willie's shoulders, hard, cinching the knot tight. Before Willie could pull the rope loose, the convict wrapped the other end around his pommel and kicked his horse in the ribs. Suddenly Willie was jerked through the air, his arms pinned at his sides, the ground rising into his face with the impact of a brick wall. Then he was skidding across the dirt, fighting to gain purchase on the rope, the trees and picket fences and flowers in the yards rushing past him.

He caromed off a lamppost and bounced across a brick walkway at the street corner. The rider turned his horse and headed back toward the cottage, jerking Willie off his feet when he tried to rise. Willie clenched both his hands on the rope, trying to lift his head above the level of the street, while dust from the horse's hooves clotted his nose and mouth and a purple haze filled his eyes.

Then the convict reined his horse and was suddenly motionless in the saddle.

A Union sergeant, with dark red hair, wearing a kepi, was walking down the middle of the street, toward the riders, a double-barrel shotgun held at port arms.

"The five-cent hand-jobs down in the bottoms must not be available this evening," he said.

"Don't mix in hit, blue-belly," Jarrette said.

"Oh, I don't plan to mix in it at all, Captain Jarrette. But my lovely ten-gauge will. By blowing your fucking head off," the sergeant said.

He lifted the shotgun to his shoulder and thumbed back the hammer on each barrel.

Jarrette stared into the shotgun, breathing through his mouth, snuffing down in his nose, as though he had a cold.

"How you know my name?" he asked.

"You were with Cole Younger at Centralia. When he lined up captured Union boys to see how many bodies a ball from his new Enfield could pass through. Haul your sorry ass out of here, you cowardly sack of shit," the sergeant said.

Jarrette flinched, the blood draining out of his cheeks. He rubbed his palms on his thighs as though he needed to relieve himself. Then his face locked into a disjointed expression, the eyes lidless, the jaw hooked open, like a barracuda thrown onto a beach.

"That was Bill Anderson's bunch. I wasn't there. I didn't have nothing to do with hit," he said.

"I can always tell when you're lying, Jarrette. Your lips are moving," the sergeant said.

"Hit's Cap'n Jarrette. Don't talk to me like that. I wasn't there."

"In three seconds you're going to be the deadest piece of white trash ever to suck on a load of double-ought buckshot," the sergeant said.

"Cap?" said a man in a butternut jacket cut off at the armpits. "Cap, it's all right. He don't know what he's talking about."

But there was no sound except the wind in the trees. The man in the butternut jacket looked at the others, then reached over and turned Jarrette's horse for him.

Willie watched the seven horsemen ride quietly down the street, the shadows and their wide-brim flop hats smudging their features, their voices lost in the wind. The sergeant released the tension in the shotgun's hammers. He wore a silver ring with a gold cross soldered to it.

"You again. Everywhere I go," Willie said, wiping the blood from his nose.

"Oh, had them surrounded, did you?" the sergeant said.

Willie touched a barked place on his forehead. "No, I allow you're obviously a much more resourceful and adept man than I. Truth is, Sergeant, I regularly make a mess of things," he said.

The sergeant's face softened. "Wasn't much to it. I know Jarrette's name and what he is. Hold up a mirror to a fellow like that and he's undone by what he sees."

"What's your name?"

"Quintinius Earp."

"It's what?"

"Ah, I should have known your true, lovable self was never far behind. The name is Quintinius Earp, lately of Ripton, Vermont, now obliged to baby-sit ex-Rebs who can't keep their tallywhackers out of the clothes roller."

"Earp? As in 'puke'?"

"Correct, as in 'puke.' Would you do me a favor?"

"I expect."

"Go home. Pretend you don't know me. Piss on my grave. Dig up my bones and feed them to your dog. Go back to Ireland and take a job in the peat bogs. But whatever it is, get out of my life!"

"Could I buy you a drink?" Willie asked.

Sergeant Earp shut his eyes and made a sound in his throat as though a nail had just been hammered into his head.

Abigail Dowling had been chopping wood for her stove and loading it into a box when she glanced through the side yard and saw a Yankee soldier armed with a shotgun disperse a group of men in front of her house. He had a red goatee and mustache and short muscular arms, and his dark blue jacket was pulled tightly down inside his belt so his shoulders and chest were molded as tautly as a statue's.

She set down the woodbox and walked through the side yard into the front. Down the street she saw a man walking away in the gloaming of the day, the back of his clothes gray with dust. The Union soldier had propped his shotgun against her fence and was buying a twist of taffy from a vendor. The soldier squatted down in front of a small Negro girl and untwisted the paper from the taffy and gave it to the girl.

"What happened out here?" Abigail said.

The sergeant stood up and touched the brim of his kepi. "Not much. Some miscreants giving a local fellow a bad time," he said.

"Was that Willie Burke?" she asked, looking down the street.

"Has a way of showing up all over the planet? Yes, I think that's his name."

"Is he all right?"

"Seems fine enough to me."

The black girl had finished her taffy and was now standing a few feet away, her eyes uplifted to the sergeant's. He removed a penny from his pocket and gave it to her. "Get yourself one more, then you'd better find your mommy," he said.

Abigail and the soldier looked at one another in the silence. "You sound as though you're from my neck of the woods," he said.

"On the Merrimack, in Massachusetts. My name is Abigail Dowling," she said.

"It's a pleasure to meet you, Miss Abigail," he said. He stepped forward awkwardly and removed his kepi and shook her hand. He continued to stare at her, his lips seeming to form words that were somehow not connected to his thoughts. He grinned sheepishly at his own emotional disorganization.

"Do you have a name?" she asked.

"Oh, excuse me. It's Sergeant Earp. Quintinius Earp."

She smiled, her head tilting slightly. A look of undisguised disappointment stole across his face.

"Quintinius? My, what a beautiful Roman name," she said.

When he grinned he looked like the happiest, most handsome and kindly man she had ever seen.

Chapter Twenty-five

Under a bright moon, deep inside the network of canals, bayous, oxbows, sand bogs, flooded woods, and open freshwater bays that comprised the Atchafalaya Basin, Robert Perry watched two dozen of his compatriots off-load crate after crate of Henry and Spencer repeaters from a steamboat that had worked its way up the Atchafalaya River from the Gulf of Mexico.

The wind was balmy and strong out of the south, capping the water in the bays, puffing leaves out of the trees, driving the mosquitoes back into the woods. Some of the men wore pieces of their old uniforms — a sun-faded kepi, perhaps, a butternut jacket, a pair of dress-gray pants, with a purple stripe down each leg. With just a little imagination Robert was back in Virginia, at the beginning of Jackson's Shenandoah Campaign, reunited with the bravest fellows he had ever known, all of them convinced that honor was its own reward and that politics was the stuff of bureaucrats and death was a subject unworthy of discussion.

In his mind's eye he could still see them, pausing among the hills in the early dawn to drink from a stream, to eat hardtack from their packs, or simply to remove their shoes and rub their feet. The fields and trees were strung with mist, the light in the valley a greenish yellow, as though it had been trapped inside an uncured whiskey barrel. Propped among the thousands of resting men were their regimental colors, the Cross of Saint Andrew, and the Bonnie Blue flag sewn with eleven white stars.

The denigrators and revisionists would eventually have their way with history, as they always did, Robert thought, but for those who participated in the war, it would remain the most important, grand and transforming experience in their lives. And if a war could make a gift to its participants, this one's gift came in the form of a new faith: No one who was at Marye's Heights, Cemetery Ridge, or the Bloody Lane at Sharpsburg would ever doubt the courage and stoicism and spiritual resolve of which their fellow human beings were capable.

Robert did not know all of the men who came into the Atchafalaya Basin either by boat or mule-drawn wagon that evening. Some were White Leaguers, others Kluxers;

some probably belonged to both groups or to neither. How had he put it to Willie? You don't always choose your bedfellows in a war? But none of these looked like bad men; certainly they were no worse than the carpet-baggers appointed to office by the provisional governor.

They had shot and butchered a feral hog and great chunks of meat were now broiling on iron stakes driven into the ground by a roaring fire under a cypress tree. The crates of Henry and Spencer lever-action repeaters and ammunition were stacked in the wagons now and within a week they would be distributed all over southern Louisiana. If events turned out badly, the Yankees had cast the die, not these fellows in the swamp, he told himself.

But his thoughts were troubled. A guerrilla leader in a flop hat, a man named Jarrette, was squatting on his haunches by the fire, sawing at a shank of broiled meat, sticking it into his mouth with the point of his bowie knife. Some said he had ridden with Quantrill, a psychopath and arsonist whom Robert E. Lee had officially read out of the Confederate army. Jarrette spoke little, but the moral vacuity in his eyes was of a kind Robert Perry had seen in others, usually men for whom war became a sanctuary.

The other men were eating now from tin plates, passing around three bottles of clear whiskey someone had produced from under a wagon seat. Their faces were happy in the firelight, the whiskey glittering inside the bottles they tilted to their mouths. In this moment, in their mismatched pieces of uniform, they looked as though they had stepped out of a photograph taken on the banks of the Rappahannock River.

Then a man he recognized all too well walked out of the darkness and joined the others. His hair was greased and parted down the middle, his body egg-shaped and compact, his brow furrowed, the corners of his mouth downturned, as though he did not quite approve of whatever his eyes fell upon.

The egg-shaped, narrow-shouldered man sat down on a log and unfolded a sheet of paper and began reading off the names of people in the community whose activities were, in his words, "questionable or meriting further investigation on our part."

A two-shot nickel-plated derringer was stuck down tightly in the side of his belt.

"It looks like you've got the dirt on some right suspicious folk, Mr. McCain," Robert said.

" 'Dirt' is a word of your choosing, not mine," McCain replied.

Robert sat down on the log next to him. "Do you mind?" he asked, lifting the sheet of paper from McCain's hands. "Which outfit did you serve in?"

"I was exempted from service, although that was not my preference," McCain replied.

"How is it you were exempted, sir?" Robert asked.

"Provider of war materials and sole support of a family."

"Some used to call those fellows 'the Druthers.' They'd druther not fight," Robert said. Then he popped the sheet of paper between his hands and studied the list before McCain could reply. "Well, I see you have the name of Willie Burke down here. That disturbs me."

"It should. He's a nigger lover and he regularly insults the leadership of the Knights of the White Camellia," McCain said

"That sounds like Willie, all right. There's a little boy in town, a veteran of the 6th Mississippi, who says Willie told off Bedford Forrest. Can you believe that? May I see your gun?" Robert said.

Without waiting for an answer he lifted the derringer from McCain's belt. The nickel plate on it was new, unscratched, the pearl handles rippling with color in the firelight. Robert broke open the breech and looked at the two brass cartridges inserted in the chambers. He snicked the breech shut.

"Fine hideaway," he said, and tossed the derringer into the fire.

"What are you doing?" McCain said.

"No, no, don't get up," Robert said, resting

his arm across McCain's shoulders. "Those are peashooter rounds in there. I doubt they could do any serious harm. Let's see what happens."

The derringer rested between two red-hot logs, which were crumbling into ash. One cartridge detonated and a bullet clattered through the top of a tree. The recoil flipped the derringer backward, burying it in a pile of soft ash.

"Don't know where it's aimed now, do we? I guess it's a bit like attacking across an open field against a rifle company that's set up inside a woods. You feel a terrible sort of nakedness, not knowing which fellow is about to park one in your liver," Robert said.

McCain pushed himself to his feet and jumped back into the darkness. The pistol popped again, this time driving the bullet into a log.

Robert stared silently into the flames, the list of names pinned between his arm and thigh. The other men formed a semicircle behind him, looking at one another, kicking at the ground, their food forgotten.

"How about a drink of liquid mule shoe, Robert?" one man said.

"I think I'll be having no more of this, but thanks just the same," he said.

He picked up the list of names and held it loosely in his fingers. The breeze puffed the fire alight so that he only had to lean forward slightly to drop the list onto the flames.

"You're our friend, but don't challenge us, Robert," another man said.

Robert flattened the sheet of paper on his thigh and removed a pencil stub from his pocket and blackened out one name on the list. Then he folded the paper and stuck it under the log.

"Good night and God bless you all," he said, rising to his feet. "But the man who brings injury to my pal Willie Burke will wish Billy Sherman had heated a train rail and wrapped it around his throat."

Perhaps obsession had sawed loose his fastenings to a reasonable view of the world, Willie thought. Or maybe he was diseased and pathologically flawed, to the extent he was no longer repelled by death and mortality and defeat and was instead drawn to the grave, to leaf-strewn arbors and green-stained markers fashioned from fieldstones, where the air was vaporous and tannic and the light always amber and the voices of friends rose from the ground, whispering lessons he wanted to reach out and cup in his hand.

And what a companion he had chosen for his return to Shiloh — a one-eyed, barefoot, British-born minstrel named Elias Rachet who constantly plucked at a banjo and twanged on a Jew's harp and wore his shoes

445

tied around his neck, in case, as he said, "we have to walk in nasty water and through cow turds and such."

The two of them stood in the early morning haze at the bottom of an incline that was dotted with wildflowers. At the top of the rise was a clump of hardwoods, dark with shadow, the canopy denting in the breeze. Willie thought he heard the iron-rimmed wheels of caissons knocking across rocks and the popping of flags in the wind, the jingle of a bridle and the nicker of a frightened horse in the trees. He yawned to clear his ears and turned in a circle and saw only the vastness of the forests and the dark, metallic-blue dome of sky overhead.

"Jim Stubbefield died right where the gray stones are at. See, there's five of them, just like big Indian arrow points that's been pressed down in the ground," Elias said, pointing. He leaned over and spit tobacco in the grass, then plucked at his banjo. The tremolo from his strings seemed to climb into his voice. "Lordy, I can still hear all our boys yelling. Would you go through it again, knowing what you know now?"

"Maybe."

"I tell myself the same thing. I always reckon God forgives liars and fools, being as He made so many of us," Elias said.

Elias was slat-toothed when he grinned, his face crinkling with hundreds of tiny lines. He looked away at a tea-colored creek that coursed through the edge of a woods. The wrinkles in his face flattened and his solitary eye became a blue pool of sadness. "I kilt a boy out there in them trees maybe wasn't over fifteen. He came busting down the hill and I whipped around and shot him right through the chest. A little bitty Yankee drummer boy, much like your friend Tige."

Elias sat down on a large rock, his legs splayed, and picked at his banjo. His callused feet were rimmed with mud, his mouth downturned, his jug head silhouetted against the pinkness on the bottom of the horizon.

"You're not going to cut bait on me, are you?" Willie asked.

"Both Jim's folks is passed?"

Willie nodded.

"Then I don't reckon they'll mind. I wish I was a darky," Elias said.

"Why's that?"

" 'Cause I'd have an excuse for taking other people's orders all my life." Then he slapped the tops of his thighs and laughed and stomped his feet up and down in the grass. He laughed until a tear ran down from his empty eye socket. "Ain't this world a barrel of monkeys?"

"Take me to the grave," Willie said.

"Jim don't hold it against you 'cause you lived and he died."

Elias started to smile, then looked at

Willie's expression and got up from the rock and arched a crick out of his back, his face deliberately empty.

The water in the creek was spring-fed and cold inside Willie's shoes as he and Elias waded across, a freshly carpentered, rope-handled box strung between them. The trees were widely spaced on the far side of the creek, the canopy thick, the ground gullied, crisp with leaves that had settled into the depressions scattered through the woods. Up the incline Elias studied an outcropping of rock that was cracked through the center by the trunk of a white oak tree.

He set down his end of the box. "We didn't have time to dig deep. Don't be surprised if animals has had their way with things," he said.

Willie opened the box and removed a shovel and a large square of sail canvas. He spread the canvas on the ground and began to dig at the base of the outcropping. The ground was carpeted with toadstools and mushrooms with purple skirts and moist from a spring farther up the incline. Overhead, squirrels clattered in the white oak and he felt himself begin to sweat inside his clothes. The soil he spaded to the side of the depression was dark and loose, like coffee grinds, and was churning with night-crawlers and smelled of decay and severed tree roots. The tip of Willie's shovel scraped across metal.

He got to his knees and began brushing the dirt from a copper-colored belt buckle embossed with the letters CSA, then his fingers touched cloth and wood buttons and the skeletal outline of a rib cage, wrist bones, and fingers that were like polished white twigs.

"His shoes are gone. When we put him in the ground I was sure his shoes was on. I didn't let nobody take Jim's shoes, Willie," Elias said.

"I know you didn't," Willie said.

"Maybe it ain't Jim. There was shooting going on in the trees and people running everywhere."

Willie hollowed the dirt away from the corpse's shoulders and arms and sides, then brushed at the face, touching a piece of cloth that had moldered into the features. He picked up the bottom of the fabric and peeled it back from the chin and nose and forehead and looked down into a face whose skin had turned gray and had shrunken tautly against the skull. The mouth was open and a tin identification tag, still attached to a leather cord, was wedged perpendicularly between the front teeth. Willie clasped the tag between his thumb and index finger and lifted it from the dead man's mouth.

Willie spit on the tag and rubbed it clean on his pants, then read the name on it and wrapped it carefully with the frayed leather cord that had held it around Jim's neck and placed it in his shirt pocket and buttoned his shirt flap on top of it.

Then he took Jim out of the grave and laid him on the piece of canvas. He could not believe how light Jim was, how reduced in density and size he had become. There was no smell of corruption in Jim's body, no odor at all, in fact. The spring water had washed the blood from the wounds in his head, and the wind touched his hair and his mouth seemed to form a word.

Where have you been, you Irish groghead?

Had to take care of a few Yanks, run them out of New Iberia, set General Banks straight about a few things. Ready to go home, you ole beanpole?

"You're giving me the crawlies," Elias said.

Willie folded the corners of the canvas across Jim's body and face and lifted him in both arms, then laid him down in the wood box, with the knees propped against one wall, the head bent against another.

Then, on his hands and knees, he shoved the dirt back into the hole at the foot of the outcropping, packing it down, smoothing it, raking leaves across the topsoil. When he had finished, he glanced up at Elias and saw a mixture of pity and sadness in his face.

"He carried the guidon. He was braver than me. I loved Jim and care not if anyone calls me a ghoul. To hell with them," Willie said.

"Oh, Willie, would that I could change your soul as easy as I can rub the burnt cork on my skin," Elias replied.

Ira Jamison never got over being surprised by the way white trash thought. He assumed their basic problem was genetic. They were born in ignorance and poverty, with no more chance of success than a snowball in a skillet, but as long as they were allowed to feel they were superior to Africans, they remained happy and stupid and believed anything they were told.

They worked from dawn to dusk on other people's farms, bought at the company store, lived in cabins a self-respecting owl wouldn't inhabit, saw their children grow up with rickets and rotted teeth, and with great pride became cannon fodder in wars whose causes had nothing to do with their lives.

Then a day came when, through chance or accident, the great scheme of things crashed on their heads like an asteroid.

What better example than Clay Hatcher, Ira Jamison thought. A man who had lived most of his life with expectations of a reward that most people would consider a punishment. More specifically, a lifetime spent coveting a desiccated, worm-eaten house that had so little structural value a man with heavy boots could kick it into kindling.

But Clay Hatcher was not most people and Angola Plantation was not the rest of the world. The house had four rooms, a cistern and a chicken run, and was built on a bluff overlooking the river. Its geographic prominence meant it went to only one person, the chief overseer. The homes of the other whites who worked on the plantation, now becoming known in the prison nomenclature as "free people," were situated down the back slope, at best on dry ground that didn't breed mosquitoes. Farther on, in acreage that never quite drained or was full of clay, were the old slave cabins, now used by convicts.

The house on the bluff was sunny in winter and cooled by a breeze off the river in summer. Mimosa trees bloomed in the front yard and peach trees in back. The soil was black and loamy, too, wheelbarrowed up from the compost heaps behind the barns, and the vegetable garden produced tomatoes as big as grapefruit.

Hatcher had knocked on the side door under the porte cochere, his battered excuse for a hat in his hand, his bottom lip crusted with a scab that looked like a black centipede.

"I hear Rufus is buying the property where the laundry was at in New Iberia," he said.

"That's right, Clay. Looks like Roof is about to become a gentleman planter," Jamison said.

"Then he'll be moving out directly?"

"Yes, directly it is."

Hatcher cut his head and grinned and fiddled with his hat, his gaze never quite meeting Jamison's.

"Reckon me and my old woman should get our things together, huh?" he said.

"I'm not following you."

"Seeing as how I'm second overseer, I figured you'd want me moving on into Rufus's place. It goes with the job, don't it?"

Jamison heard a boat on the river and looked in its direction. "You're a good man, Clay. But we're in the penal business now. An oldtime jail warden from New Orleans will be replacing Rufus. I'll be relying on you to get him oriented."

Hatcher turned his hat in his hands, his face reddening, his jawbones knotting, a band of sunlight slicing across his eyes.

"Oldtime jail warden, you say?" he said.

But Jamison did not reply, his eyes taking on a glint that Hatcher failed to read.

Hatcher licked the broken place on his lip. "I seen a heap of shit happen on this place. But this takes all," he said.

"I advise you not to create a problem for yourself, my friend."

"Twenty-five years of herding niggers and living one cut above them? Listening to my old woman bitch about it from morning to night? Four goddamn more years of ducking

Yankee bullets? Me create a problem? Kunnel, when it comes to putting a freight train up a man's ass, you know how to do it proper," Hatcher said.

"Go down to the store and get you a bottle of whiskey and charge it to me. Then come back and talk to me in two days."

"You'll see the devil go to church first," Hatcher said.

He started down the drive, then stopped and turned, glaring at Jamison, all his servile pretense gone now, his hands opening and closing at his sides.

That had been three hours ago. Now Ira Jamison stood on the upstairs veranda, surveying all that he owned, the breeze cool on his skin, the air aromatic with the smell of flowers hanging in baskets from the eaves. But neither his prosperity nor the loveliness and unseasonable coolness of the day brought him comfort. Why had he not acted more diplomatically with Hatcher? Had his father not taught him never to provoke white trash, to treat them as one would coal oil around an open flame?

He had placed a ball of opium the size of a child's marble in his jaw, more than he usually ingested, but it did not seem to be taking effect. The wind gusted against the house and for a moment he thought he felt a vibration through the beams and studs, a tremolo that seemed to reach down into the foundation. But that was foolish, he told himself. His house was solid. An engineer had told him the fissure in his hearth and chimney was cosmetic. Why did Ira worry so much about his house? the engineer had asked.

Because not one person in the world cares whether you live or die. Because you are the sum total of your possessions and the loss of any one of them makes you the less, a voice said to him.

"That's not true. One person does care," he said to the wind.

Then he wondered at his own sanity.

That night Clay Hatcher left the plantation. But not before tying both of his bird dogs to a catalpa tree and shooting each of them with a revolver, then setting fire to his shack with his dead wife inside it.

Chapter Twenty-six

It had rained all afternoon and Flower Jamison's yard was flooded. Through her front window she saw mule-drawn wagons carrying green lumber down to the site of the old laundry, where Rufus Atkins was building a home for himself and pretending to be a member of the local aristocracy. Sometimes the wagons sunk almost to the hubs in the mud and the convict teamsters would have to unload them, free the wheels, then restack the pile before they could continue on in the rain.

While he oversaw the building of his home Rufus Atkins lived in a huge canvas tent, one with crossbeams and big flaps and individual rooms inside. Oil lanterns hung from the tent poles, and when they were lit the tent looked like a warm, yellow smudge inside the mist. He had laid out plank walkways to the entrances and in the morning he walked to the privy in an elegant bathrobe to empty his chamber pot, like a scatological parody of a Victorian gentleman.

He asked others to call him "Captain," reminding them of his service to the Confederacy but never mentioning that his rank was given to him only because he was the employee of Ira Jamison and that during four years of war he was never promoted.

In public places he talked loudly of what he called his "land transactions." Ex–paddy rollers cadged drinks from him in the saloons around town and White Leaguers like Todd McCain visited him in his tent late at night, but the invitations that went to Ira Jamison as a matter of course did not go to Rufus Atkins.

So he abused Negroes to show his power over others, flew a Confederate battle flag over his tent in defiance of the Occupation, and kept late hours in the saloon down the road. Twice Flower saw him stop his horse, a black mare, in front of her house and stare at her gallery for a long time, his stiffened arms forming a column on the saddle pommel. But when she went outside to confront him, he was gone.

It was still raining when she started supper, which meant Abigail Dowling would probably show up soon in her buggy and take the two of them to the school for night classes. She poured a cup of coffee and added sugar to it and drank it at the stove, her thoughts on the school, the field hands who worked ten-hour days and tried to learn reading and writing and arithmetic at night, and the meager donations on which she and Abigail operated.

She heard a horse in the yard and foot-steps on the gallery. She pulled open the front door and looked into the face of Clay Hatcher, his clothes drenched, the brim of his hat wilted over his ears and brow. A knife was belted on one hip, a pistol on the other. He looked up and down the road, then back at her, the skin of his face stretched against his skull. His breath smelled of funk and boiled shrimp.

"Got something to tell you," he said.

"Not interested," she answered.

"It's about your mother. Her name was Sarie. Her teeth was filed into points 'cause there was an African king back there in her bloodline or something."

She wanted to tell him to get off her gallery, to take his repository of pain and grief and hatred off her land and out of her life. But she knew the umbilical cord that held her to Angola Plantation was one she would never be able to sever, that its legacy in one way or another would poison the rest of her days. So she fixed her eyes on his and waited, her heart pounding.

"Rufus tole Kunnel Jamison your mama killed one of the overseers and that's how come he hit her so hard with his quirt," Hatcher said. "That was the lie he covered his ass with. He beat Sarie's brains out 'cause she sunk her teeth in his hand, and I mean plumb down to the bone. I don't know about no African king in her background, but she was one ferocious nigger when she got a board up her cheeks."

Flower felt the gallery tilt under her, as though she were on board a ship. The wind gusted and a tree slapped the side of the house and rain swept under the eaves.

"They said she was kicked by a horse. She shot the overseer and tried to run away and a horse trampled her," she said.

"That's the story the kunnel wanted us to tell folks. He didn't want other white people knowing his slaves got beat to death. You don't believe me, look at that half-moon scar on Rufus's left hand."

"Leave my property," she said.

"I'm hell-bound, Flower. I kilt my old woman. Look at my face. Devil's done got my soul already. Ain't got no reason to deceive you," he said.

Then he plunged into the rain and mounted his horse, jerking its head about with the reins and slashing it viciously with his boot heels at the same time.

But he had set the hook and set it deep.

She went to the school that evening and

taught her classes but said nothing to Abigail about Clay Hatcher's visit. That night she dreamed of a man's callused, sun-browned hand, the heel half-mooned with a string of tiny gray pearls. She woke in the morning to the sound of more thunder. She started a fire in her woodstove and fixed coffee and drank it while she watched the wind flatten the cane in the fields and wrinkle the water in her yard. Then she put on a gum coat and wrapped a bandanna on her head, and with her parasol popped open in front of her face she began the long walk down to Rufus Atkins' tent.

The convicts building his house were working under tarps. An empty jail wagon sat forlornly under the live oak in front. Bearded, filthy, lesioned with scabs, the convicts stared at her from the scaffolding as she passed on the plank walkway. Then a guard yelled at them in French and their hammers recommenced a rhythmic smacking against nails and wood.

She pulled open the flap on Atkins' tent and stepped inside. He was standing at a table, studying the design of his house, his white shirt and dark pants unspotted by the rain. An oil lamp burned above his head, lighting the grainy texture of his face and the flat, hazel eyes that never allowed people to read his thoughts.

He placed one hand on his hip, his booted

feet forming a right angle, like a fencer's.

"I don't know what it is, but it's trouble of one kind or another. So get to it and be on your way," he said.

"Clay Hatcher came to my house last night," she said.

"You should have gone for the sheriff. He went crazy and killed his wife. You didn't hear about it?"

His left hand rested on the table, behind him, in a pool of shadow.

"How did my mother die?" she asked.

"Sarie? A horse ran her down," he replied. His face seemed to show puzzlement.

But Rufus Atkins had made a lifetime study of not revealing his emotions about anything, she thought. Not even puzzlement. So why now?

"She shot a man, Flower. Right in the head. Then took off running," he said, although she had not challenged his statement.

"She'd just given birth."

He shook his head. "I'm telling you how it happened, girl." He raised his left hand and touched at his nose with his wrist. Then she saw it, a barely noticeable half-circle of tiny scars on the rim of his hand.

Her gum coat felt like an oven on her body. She could smell all of his odors in the tent's stale air — testosterone, unwashed hair, shaving water that hadn't been thrown out, a thunder mug in a corner. She unbuttoned her coat and pulled her bandanna off her head and pushed her hair out of her eyes, as though she were rising out of dark water that was crushing the air from her lungs.

"She bit you and you beat her to death," Flower said.

"Now, hold on there." He looked at her open coat and at her hands and involuntarily backed away from her, knocking into the tent pole. The oil lamp clattered above his head.

She stepped toward him and saw his mouth open, his hand clench on the edge of the table.

"I can hurt you, Flower. Don't make me do it," he said.

She gathered all the spittle in her mouth and spat it full in his face.

Rain swept in sheets across the wetlands throughout the day, then the storm intensified and bolts of lightning trembled like white-hot wires in the heart of the swamp, igniting fires among the cypress trees. Long columns of smoke flattened across the canopy and hung on the fields and roads in a dirty gray vapor.

Flower told no one of her encounter with Rufus Atkins nor of the knowledge that had come to her about the nature of her mother's death in 1837. Who besides herself would care? she asked herself. What legal authority would concern itself with the murder of a slave woman twenty-eight years in the past?

But she knew the real reason for her silence and it was not one she would share, not even with herself, at least not until she had to.

The cap-and-ball revolver Abigail had bought from McCain's Hardware was wrapped in a piece of flannel under Flower's bed. She removed it and set it on the kitchen table and peeled back the cloth from the frame. The metal and brown grips glistened with oil; the caps were snug in the nipples of each loaded chamber. She touched the cylinder and the barrel with the balls of her fingers, then curved her hand around the grips. The cylindrical hardness that she cupped in her palm caused an image to flit across her mind that both embarrassed and excited her.

That evening the rain stopped, but fires still burned in the swamp and the air was wet and heavy with the smell of woodsmoke. She drove with Abigail in the buggy to the school, passing the saloon often frequented by Rufus Atkins. His black mare was tethered outside, and through the doorway she caught a glimpse of him standing at the bar, by himself, tilting a glass to his mouth.

That night she taught her classes, then extinguished all the lamps in the rooms and locked the doors to the building and climbed up on the buggy for the trip home.

"You're sure quiet these days," Abigail said.

"Weather's enough to get a person down," Flower said.

"Sure you haven't met a fellow?"

"I could go the rest of my life without seeing a man. No, I take that back. I could go two lifetimes without seeing one."

Both of them laughed.

By the drawbridge over the Teche they saw a crowd of workingmen from the Main Street saloon, Union soldiers, the sheriff, their faces lit like tallow under the street lamps. Two Negroes had tied a rope around a body that was caught in a pile of trash under the bridge. They pulled the body free, but the wrists were bound with wire and the wire snagged on the rootball of a submerged cypress tree. A barrel-chested, red-faced white man, with a constable's star pinned to his vest, rode his horse into the shallows and grabbed the end of the rope from the Negroes, twisted it around his pommel, and dragged the body, skittering like a log, up on dry ground.

The dead man was white, without shoes, his eyes sealed shut, the belt gone from his pants, the pockets turned inside out. His head rolled on his neck like a poppy gourd on a broken stem. The sheriff leaned over him with a lantern in his hand.

"They mark him?" someone in the crowd called out.

"On the forehead. 'K.W.C.,' " the sheriff

said. Then the disgust grew in his face and he waved his arms angrily. "Y'all get out of here! This ain't your bidness! What kind of town we becoming here? If the Knights can do that to him, they can do it to us. Y'all t'ought of that?"

Abigail slapped the reins on her horse's rump and headed down the road toward Flower's house. She glanced back over her shoulder at the crowd by the bridge.

"Wasn't that the man who worked for Ira Jamison, what was his name, a posse was looking for him yesterday? He murdered his wife up at Angola Plantation," she said.

"Cain't really say. I've shut out a lot of bad things from Angola, Miss Abby," Flower replied.

Abigail looked at her curiously. "What are you hiding from me?" she asked.

Flower read in the front room of her house until late, getting up to fix tea, silhouetting against the lamp, twice stepping out on the gallery to look at the weather, the light from the doorway leaping into the yard. At midnight she heard the sounds of the saloon closing, the oak door being secured, shutters being latched, horses clopping on the road, men's voices calling out a final "good night" in the darkness.

But she saw no sign of Rufus Atkins.

She stood at the front window, the lamp

burning behind her, until the road was empty, then blew out the lamp and sat in a chair with the cap-and-ball revolver in her lap and watched the sky clear and the moon rise above the fields.

The revolver rested across the tops of her thighs, and her fingers rested on the grips and coolness of the barrel. She felt no fear, only a strange sense of anticipation, as though she were discovering an aspect of herself she didn't know existed. She heard a wagon pass on the road, then the sounds of owls and tree frogs. The curtains fluttered on the windows and she smelled the odor of gardenias on the wind. In a secure part of her mind she knew she was falling asleep, but her physical state didn't seem important anymore. Her hand was cupped over the cylinder of the pistol, the back of the house locked up, the front door deliberately unbolted, cooking pots stacked against the jamb.

She awoke at two in the morning, her bladder full. She locked the front door and went out the back into the yard, locking the door behind her. Then she sat down on the smooth wood seat inside the heated cypress enclosure that had served the patrons of Carrie LaRose's brothel for over twenty years, the revolver next to her. Through the ventilation gap at the top of the door, she could see the sky and stars and smell the faint tracings of smoke from the fires burning in the swamp. The only sounds outside were those of nightbirds calling to one another and water dripping from the yard's solitary live oak, under which Rufus Atkins had paid the men who raped her.

She had overestimated him, she thought. Perhaps a lifetime of being abused by his kind had made her believe men like Atkins possessed powers which they did not, not even the self-engendered power or resolve to seek revenge after they were spat upon.

She wiped herself and rose from the seat, straightening her dress, and crossed the yard with the pistol hanging from her right hand. She turned in a half circle and looked about the yard one more time, then unlocked the door and went inside.

She rechecked all the doors and sashes to see that they were locked, then ate a piece of bread and ham and drank a glass of buttermilk and went into her bedroom. She put the revolver under the bed and left two of the windows open to cool the room and balanced a stack of cook pots on each of the sills in case an intruder tried to climb in. Then she lay down on top of the covers and went to sleep.

When she woke later it was not because she heard glass breaking or a door hasp tearing loose from wood or pans clattering to the floor. It was a collective odor, a smell of whiskey and horses and crushed gardenias and night damp trapped inside cloth.

And of leather. The braided end of a quirt that a man in a black robe and a peaked black hood teased across her face.

She sat straight up in bed, at first believing she was having a dream. Then the man in the peaked hood sat next to her on the mattress and fitted the quirt across her throat and pressed her back down on the pillow. Behind him was a second man, this one in white, her cap-and-ball revolver clutched in his hand.

"How did you get in?" Flower said.

The man in the black robe and hood leaned close to her, as though he wanted his breath as well as his words to injure her skin. The image of a camellia was stitched with pink and white thread on the breast of his robe. "A hideaway door with a spring catch on the side of the house. Lots of things I know you don't, Flower," the voice of Rufus Atkins said. "I know the places you go, the names of the niggers you teach, the time of day you eat your food, the exact time you piss and shit and empty your thunder mug in the privy. Have you figured out what I'm telling you?"

"Explain it to her," the other visitor said.

Flower recognized the voice of Todd McCain, the owner of the hardware store.

"You think you're free," Rufus Atkins' voice

said, the mouth hole in his hood puffing with his breath. "But you spit in the wrong man's face. That means no matter where you go, what you do, who you see, either me or my friend here or a hundred like us will be watching you. You won't be able to take a squat over your two-holer back there without wondering if we're listening outside. Starting to get the picture? We own you, girl. Throw all the temper tantrums you want. That sweet little brown ass is ours."

When she didn't answer, he moved the quirt over her breasts, pressing it against her nipples, flattening it against her stomach.

"Damned if you're not prime cut," he said. He blew his breath along the down on her skin and she felt her loins constrict and a wave of nausea course through her body.

The two hooded figures left the front door open behind them. She sat numbly on the side of her bed and watched them ride away, their robes riffling over their horses' rumps, the cap-and-ball revolver on which she had relied thrown into the mud.

Chapter Twenty-seven

Early the next morning she took the sheets off her bed, not touching the area where the man in the black hood had sat. She put them in a washtub, then bathed and dressed to go to school. When she tried to eat, her food tasted like paper in her mouth. The sky had cleared, the sun was shining, and birds sang in the trees, but the brilliance and color of the world outside seemed to have nothing to do with her life now.

She drank a cup of hot tea and scraped her uneaten food into a garbage bucket and washed her dishes, then prepared to leave for school. But when she closed and opened her eyes, her head spun and bile rose in her throat and her skin felt dead to the touch, as though she had been systemically poisoned.

You've gone through worse, she told herself. They raped you, but they didn't make you afraid. They murdered your mother but they couldn't steal her soul. Why do you keep your wounds green and allow men as base as Atkins and McCain to control your thoughts? she asked herself.

But she knew the answer. The house, the land, the school, the flower beds she and Abigail had planted, her collection of books, her new life as a teacher, everything she was and had become and would eventually be was about to be taken from her. All because of a choice, a deed, she knew she would eventually commit herself to, because if she did not, she would never have peace.

She went outside and picked up the cap-and-ball revolver from the edge of a rain puddle. She carried it into the kitchen and wiped the mud off the frame and the cylinder and caps with a dry rag and rewrapped it in the flannel cloth and replaced it under her bed.

In the corner of her eye she saw a black carriage with a surrey and white wheels pull to a stop in front of the gallery. Ira Jamison walked up the steps, his hair cut short, his jaws freshly shaved, looking at least twenty years younger than his actual age.

"I hope I haven't dropped by too early," he said, removing his hat. "I was in the neighborhood and felt an uncommonly strong desire to see you."

"I'm on my way to work," she said.

"At your school?"

"Yes. Where else?"

"I'll take you. Just let me talk with you a minute," he said.

She stepped back from the doorway to let him enter. She reached to take his hat but he took no heed of her gesture and placed it himself on a large, hand-carved knob at the foot of the staircase banister. He smiled.

"Flower, I'm probably a fond and foolish man, but I wanted to tell you how much you mean to me, how much you remind me of —" He stopped in mid-sentence and studied her face. "Have I said the wrong thing here?"

"No, Colonel, you haven't."

"You don't look well."

"Two men got in my house last night. They had on the robes of the White Camellia. One was Rufus Atkins. The other man owns the hardware store on Main Street."

"Atkins came here? He touched you?"

"Not with his hand. With his whip. He told me he'd be with me everywhere I went. He'd see everything I did."

She saw the bone flex along his jaw, the crow's feet deepen at the corner of one eye.

"He whipped you?"

"I don't have any more to say about it, Colonel."

"You must believe what I tell you, Flower. This man and the others who ride with him, I'm talking about these fellows who pretend to be ghosts of Confederate soldiers, this man knew he'd better not hurt you in any way. Do you understand that?"

"He beat my mother to death."

The colonel's face blanched. "You don't know that," he said.

"Clay Hatcher was here. He told me how you made him and Rufus Atkins lie about how my mother died."

"Listen, Flower, that was a long time ago. I made mistakes as a young man."

"You lied to me. You lied to the world. You going to lie to God now?"

Jamison took a breath. "I'm going to get to the bottom of this. You have my word on it," he said.

She rested her hand on the banister, just above where his hat rested on the mahogany knob. Her eyes were downcast and he could not read her expression.

"Colonel?" she said.

"Yes?"

"You started to say I reminded you of someone."

"Oh yes. My mother. I never realized how much you look like my mother. That's why you'll always have a special place in my heart."

Flower stared at him, then picked up his hat and placed it in his hand. "Good-bye, Colonel. I won't be seeing you again," she said.

"Pardon?" he said.

"Good-bye, suh. You're a sad man," she said.

"What? What did you say?"

But she stood silently by the open door and refused to speak again, until he finally gave it up and walked out on the gallery, confused and for once in his life at a loss for words. When he glanced back at her, his forehead was knitted with lines, like those in the skin of an old man.

When he got into his carriage she saw him produce a small whiskey-colored ball that looked like dried honey from a tobacco pouch and place it inside his jaw, then bark at his driver.

Willie Burke's return journey from Shiloh had been one he did not measure in days but in images that he seemed to perceive through a glass darkly — the emptiness of the Mississippi countryside that he and Elias traversed in a rented wagon, a region of dust devils, weed-spiked fields, Doric columns blackened by fire and deserted cabins scrolled with the scales of dead morning glory vines; the box that held Jim's bones vibrating on the deck of a steamboat and a gaggle of little girls in pinafores playing atop the box; a train ride on a flatcar through plains of saw grass and tunnels of trees and sunlight that spoked through rain clouds like grace from a divine hand that he seemed unable to clasp.

Willie's clothes were rent, vinegary with his own smell, his hair peppered with grit. He drank huge amounts of pond water to deaden his hunger. When the train stopped to take on wood he and Elias got into a line of French-speaking Negro trackworkers and were given plates piled with rice and fried fish that they ate with the trackworkers without ever being asked their origins. At a predawn hour on a day that had no date attached to it they dragged the box off a wagon in front of Willie's house and set it down in the grass. The sky was the color of gunmetal, bursting with stars, the surface of the bayou blanketed with ground fog.

"Come in," Willie said.

"I think I'll go out to my mother's place and crawl in a hammock for six weeks," Elias replied. His face became introspective. "Willie, the next time I say I'll help you out with a little favor?"

"Yes?"

"Lend me a dollar so I can rent a gun and stick it in my mouth," Elias said.

Willie walked into the house, not pausing in the kitchen to either eat or drink, and on out the back door to use the privy. He dragged Jim's box onto a wagon at the barn, shoved it forward until it was snug against the headboard, then began stacking bricks in the wagon bed. The stars were fading from the sky now, the oaks along the bayou becoming darker, more sharply edged, against the fog. He heard footsteps behind him.

Tige McGuffy heaved a wooden bucket filled with cistern water across Willie's head and face and shoulders.

"Good God, Tige, what was that for?" Willie asked, spitting water out of his mouth.

"You trailed a smell through the house I could have beat down on the floor with a broom."

"Would you be going out to the cemetery with me this fine morning?"

"Cemetery? What you got in that box?" Tige replied. But before Willie could speak Tige waved his hand, indicating he wasn't interested in Willie's response. "The Knights or them White Leaguers lynched a fellow last night. A bunch of them rode through our yard. Where you been, Willie? Don't you care about nobody except a dead man or a lady ain't got no interest in you? Why don't you wake up?"

At the school that same morning Abigail Dowling noticed the circles under Flower's eyes, her inability to concentrate on the content of a conversation. During recess Flower shook a ten-year-old boy in the yard for throwing rocks at a squirrel. She shook him hard, jarring his chin on his chest, squatting down to yell in his face. The boy lived in a dirt-floor shack with his grandmother and often came to school without breakfast. Until today he had been one of her best students. The boy began to cry and ran into the street.

Flower caught him and led him by the hand into the shade.

"I'm sorry, Isaac. I was sick last night and I'm not feeling good today. Just don't be chunkin' at the squirrels. You forgive me?" she said.

"Yessum," he said.

He rubbed the back of his neck when he spoke and she could see that neither the pain nor the shock had left his eyes. She got to her knees and held him against her breast. Then she walked to the gallery, where Abigail had been watching her.

"I'm going home, Miss Abby," she said.

"Tell me what it is," Abigail said.

"I don't think I'll be back."

"That's nonsense."

"No, it's a heap of trouble," Flower said.

"I'm going to dismiss the children and take you home," Abigail said.

"I don't need any help, Miss Abby."

"We'll see about that," Abigail said.

It was almost noon, and Abigail told the children they could leave the school early and not return until the next day. While they poured out the front door into the yard and street, she brought her buggy around from the back and went after Flower.

"Get in," she said in front of the hardware store.

"Miss Abby, you mean well, but don't mix in this," Flower said.

"Stop calling me 'Miss Abby.' I'm your friend. I admire you more than any person I've ever known."

Flower paused, then stepped up into the buggy and sat down, her face straight ahead.

"There's a door with a secret catch on it in the side of my house. Last night I woke up with Rufus Atkins and Todd McCain standing by my bed," she said. She glanced back at the hardware store. "They were wearing Kluxer robes and hoods, but it was them."

Abigail reined up the horse and started to speak, but Flower grasped the reins and popped them down on the horse's rump.

"Atkins touched me with his whip, like I was a piece of livestock. He wanted me to know I'd never be free, that he or a hundred like him could come for me anytime they wanted," Flower said. "I'll never get them out of my life."

"Oh yes, we will," Abigail said.

"It's a nigger girl's word against a captain in the Confederate army, Miss Abby. Plus I didn't see his face."

"Don't you dare call yourself that. Don't you dare."

But Flower refused to speak the rest of the way home.

The house and yard and flower beds were marbled with shadows, the wind touched with rain, the cane rustling in the fields. Down the road Abigail could see convict carpenters in striped pants and jumpers framing Rufus Atkins' new house, hammering boards into place, sitting on the crossbeams like clothespins. Farther down the road, past the burned remnants of the laundry, she thought she saw the polished, black carriage of Ira Jamison disappearing around a bend.

Flower got down from the buggy and went inside the house, leaving the door open behind her. Abigail followed her.

"What are you planning to do?" Abigail asked.

"Go to the privy and make water."

"You answer my question, Flower."

"I aim to put Rufus Atkins in hell for what he did to my mother and me. And before he dies I aim to make him hurt."

"It doesn't have to be like this."

"Yes, it does. You know it does. Don't lie. You don't realize how much some folks can hate a lie," Flower said, and went out the back door.

Abigail stood for a long time by the entrance. She felt the wind blowing through the house, twisting the curtains, flipping the pages of a book in Flower's bedroom. She could smell rain outside and see the sunlight disappearing from the yard. She stared through the open door of the bedroom and at the bedroom floor and the pool of shadow under the bed.

When Flower returned from the privy, the house was empty.

"Abigail?" she said into the silence.

She looked outside. The buggy was gone. She glanced through the doorway into her bedroom. The piece of oily flannel in which she had wrapped her revolver lay discarded on the floor.

For Ira Jamison anger had never been a character defect to which he attached any degree of seriousness. If your business or personal adversaries tried to injure you, you did not brood over biblical admonitions about an eye for an eye. You buried your enemies alive. Anger wasn't a problem.

If someone challenged your authority, as the dandruff-flecked minister had when he allowed Ira's wife to confide her husband's sexual habits to him, you publicly humiliated the person in such a way he would dread sleep because he might see you in his dreams.

In fact, when anger was controlled and carefully nursed, then sated at the expense of your enemies, the experience could be almost sexual.

But disobedience on the part of people whose wages he paid was another matter.

These were usually white trash whom a Bedouin would not allow to clean his chamber pot, self-hating and genetically defective creatures whom he had housed, fed, and provided medical care for, given their children presents at Christmas and on birthdays, and sometimes seen commissioned in the army. Disobedience from them amounted not only to ingratitude and betrayal but contempt and arrogance, because they were indicating they had read his soul and had concluded he could be deceived and used.

Clay Hatcher was a perfect example, a self-pitying imbecile who blamed his stupidity on his wife and killed her with an ax while she was fixing his supper, then burned down his own house with all his possessions in it to hide his crime.

Ira had to laugh thinking about it. He wondered what Hatcher had to say when the Knights of the White Camellia told him the law was the law and they hoped he wouldn't hold it against them when they broke his neck. After all, they were just poor whites like himself, trying to do the right thing.

But Ira had to take himself to task for not anticipating Rufus Atkins' treachery. Atkins was a cynic and pragmatist and knew how to eat his pride when a greater self-interest was involved. But under those flat, hazel eyes and skin that was like seared alligator hide lay a mean-spirited, sexually driven, and resentful man who, like all white trash, believed the only difference between himself and the rich was the social station arbitrarily handed them at birth.

Ira Jamison had left Flower's house that morning and had gone immediately to Rufus Atkins' newly acquired property, but he was nowhere in sight. The prison guards overseeing the convict workmen were no help, either, shaking their heads, speaking in demotic French that Ira could barely understand.

So he tried to put himself in the mind of Rufus Atkins, hung over, probably filled with rut, growing more depleted as the sun climbed in the sky, realizing he had fouled his own nest and made an enemy of the only man in Louisiana who could give him access to the social respectability he had always coveted.

He had his driver take him to the saloon on Main Street, to the jail, to a row of cribs on a muddy road out by the Yankee camp, and finally to McCain's Hardware Store.

McCain's eyes were scorched, his face discolored, as though it had been parboiled, his breath like fly ointment. Ira saw him swallow with fear.

"How do you do, sir?" Ira said.

"Mighty fine, Colonel. It's an honor to have you in my store."

"Do you know Captain Atkins?" Ira asked.

"Yes, suh, I do. Not real well, but I do know him."

"If you see him, would you tell him I wanted to pay my respects, but regrettably I have to return to Angola this afternoon," Ira said.

"Yes, suh, I'll get the message to him. He's building himself a fine house. He comes in here reg'lar for nails and such."

"That's what I thought. Thank you for your goodwill, sir," Ira said.

Ira had his driver take him back to Rufus Atkins' tent, where, as he expected, Atkins was not to be found. He instructed the driver to take the carriage down the road, out of sight, and not return until Ira sent for him.

A light rain began to fall and Ira sat on a cane chair by Rufus Atkins' worktable and looked out the tent flap at the convicts perched on top of the framing for Atkins' house. He wondered what kind of thoughts, if any, they had during their day. Did they ever have an inkling of the game that had been run on them and their kind? Did they ever think of possessing more than a woman's thighs and enough liquor to drink? The best any of them could hope for was to become a trusty guard and perhaps survive their sentences. If their fate was his, Ira believed he would either take out a judge's throat or open his own veins.

But ultimately most of them deserved whatever happened to them, he thought. They were uneducable, conceived and born in squalor and hardly able to concentrate on three sentences in a row that didn't deal with their viscera. Even Flower, who was the most intelligent Negro he had ever known, was somehow offended because he had told her she reminded him of his mother. His father had said there was no difference between the races. That morning Flower had certainly proved she was half-darky, acting rudely after he had journeyed all the way from Angola to see her. What a waste of his time and affections, he thought.

Ira heard a sound like a music box playing in the rain, rising and falling as the wind popped the tent flaps and the canvas over his head. Perched up high on the framing of Rufus Atkins' house he saw an elderly Negro man fitting a board into place, his face as creased as an old leather glove, his purple pants shiny with wear above his bare ankles.

Why was this man wearing purple pants instead of the black-and-white stripes that were standard convict issue? The convict's hair was grizzled, his cheeks covered with white whiskers. What was a man that age, probably with cataracts, doing on top of a second-story crossbeam? Again Ira heard the tinkling of music in the rain, a tune that was vaguely familiar and disturbing, like someone rattling a piece of crystal inside his memory. He rose from his chair and looked out the flap at the Negro carpenter, who had paused in his work and was looking back at him now.

Uncle Royal? Ira thought. He pinched his eyes. My God, what was happening to him? Uncle Royal had been dead for years. What was it his father had once said, Niggers would be the damnation of them all? Well, so be it, Ira thought. He didn't create them nor did he invent the rules that governed the affairs of men and principalities.

He walked out into the rain, splattering his white pants with mud. "Get that old man off there!" he yelled at the foreman.

"Off what?" the foreman asked.

"Off the house. Right there. Why is he wearing purple pants?" Ira replied.

"That ain't no old man up there, Kunnel," the foreman said, half grinning. Then he looked at the expression on Ira's face. "I'll get him down, suh. Ain't nothing here to worry about."

"Good," Ira said, and went back inside the tent and closed the flap.

The rain was clicking hard on the canvas now. It had been a mistake to come here, one born purely out of pride, he thought. What was to be gained by confronting Rufus Atkins personally? He was going to pull his convict labor off Atkins' property and ruin his credit by running a newspaper notice to the effect he would not co-sign any of Atkins' loan applications or be responsible for his debts. Ira computed it would take about six weeks for Atkins' paltry business operations to collapse.

When you could do that much damage to a man with a three-dollar newspaper advertisement, why waste time dealing with him on a personal basis?

It was time for a fine lunch and a bottle of good wine and the company of people who weren't idiots. Maybe he should think about a trip to Nashville to see his old friend General Forrest.

He smiled at a story that was beginning to circulate about the regard in which Forrest had been held by General Sherman. After Forrest had driven every Yankee soldier from the state of Mississippi, Sherman supposedly assembled his staff and said, "I don't care what it takes. Lose ten thousand men if you have to. But kill that goddamn sonofabitch Bedford Forrest."

Nathan should have that put on his tombstone, Ira thought.

But where was that tune coming from? In his mind's eye he saw hand-carved wooden horses turning on a miniature merry-go-round, the delicately brushed paint worn by time, the windup key rotating as the music played inside the base.

For just a moment he felt a sense of theft about his life that was indescribable. He tore through the other rooms in the tent, searching for the origin of the sound, kicking over a chair with a black Kluxer robe hung on the back. Then, through a crack in the rear flap, he saw it, a wind chime tinkling on a wood post. He ripped it from the nail that held it and stalked back through Atkins' sleeping area, then ducked through the mosquito netting and curtain that separated it from the front room.

He smelled an odor like camphor and perfume, like flowers pressed between the pages of an old book or blood that had dried inside a balled handkerchief. He straightened his back, the chime clenched in his hand, and thought he saw his mother's silhouette beckoning for him to approach her, the wide folds of her dark blue dress like a portal into memories that he did not want to relive.

Willie tethered his team under a huge mimosa tree on the edge of St. Peter's Cemetery, mixed mortar in a wheelbarrow, and bricked together a foundation for Jim's crypt. Then he dragged Jim's box on top of the foundation and began bricking and mortaring four walls around the box. Clouds tumbled across the sky and he could smell wildflowers and salt inside the wind off the Gulf. As he tapped each brick level with the handle of the trowel, the sun warm on his shoulders, he tried to forget the insult that Tige had flung in his face.

If it had come from anyone else, he

thought. But Tige was uncanny in his intuition about the truth.

Was it indeed Willie's fate to forever mourn the past, to dwell upon the war and the loss of a love that was probably not meant to be? Had he made his journey to Shiloh less out of devotion to a friend than as a histrionic and grandiose attempt at public penance? Was he simply a self-deluded fool?

There are days when I wish I had fallen at your side, Jim.

You were always my steadfast pal, Willie. Don't talk like that. You have to carry the guidon for both of us.

I'll never get over the war. I'll never forget Shiloh.

You don't need to, you ole groghead. You were brave. Why should we have to forget? That's for cowards. One day you'll tell your grandchildren you scouted for Bedford Forrest.

And a truly odious experience it was, Willie said.

He thought he heard Jim laugh inside the bricks.

He saw a shadow break across his own. He turned on his knee, splattering himself with mortar from the trowel.

"Sorry I said them words," Tige said. He took off his kepi and twirled it on the tip of his finger.

"Which words would those be?" Willie said, grinning at the edge of his mouth, one eye squinted against the sunlight.

"Saying Miss Abigail didn't have no interest in you. Saying you didn't care about nobody except dead people."

"I must have been half-asleep, because I have no memory of it," Willie said.

"You sure can tell a mess of fibs, Willie Burke."

"You didn't happen to bring some lunch with you, did you?"

"No, but Robert Perry was looking for you."

"Now, why would noble Robert be looking for the likes of me?"

"Ask him, 'cause there he comes yonder. Y'all are a mysterious kind," Tige said.

"How's that?"

"You lose a war, then spend every day of your life losing it again in your head. Never seen a bunch so keen on beating theirself up all the time."

"I think you're a man of great wisdom, young Tige," Willie said.

Robert Perry walked through the rows of crypts and slung a canvas choke sack on the bed of Willie's wagon. It made a hard, knocking sound when it struck the wood. His skin was deeply tanned, freckled with sunlight under the mimosa, his uncut hair bleached on the tips. The wind gusted behind him, ruffling the leaves in the tree, and the countryside suddenly fell into shadow.

"It's going to rain again," Robert said.

"Looks like it," Willie replied.

"Why don't you tell people where you're going once in a while?" he asked.

"Out of sorts today?" Willie said.

"That worthless fellow Rufus Atkins was drunk down in the bottoms this morning. The word is he and this McCain character, the one who runs the hardware store, put on their sheets last night and paid Flower Jamison a call," Robert said.

"Say that again?" Willie said, rising to his feet.

"Ah, I figured right," Robert said.

"Figured what?"

"You couldn't wait to put your hand in it as soon as you heard," Robert said.

"What's in that bag?" Willie asked.

"My law books."

"What else?"

"My sidearm," Robert said.

Chapter Twenty-eight

Abigail Dowling whipped her buggy horse down the road and into the entrance of Rufus Atkins' property. She felt a sickness in her chest and a dryness in her throat that she could compare only to a recurrent dream in which she was peering over the rim of a canyon into the upended points of rocks far below. She waited for the voices to begin, the ones that had called her a traitor and poseur who fed off the sorrow and the inadequacies of others, the voices that had always drained her energies and robbed her of self-worth and denied her a place in the world that she could claim as her own. But this time she would fight to keep them in abeyance; she would rid herself of self-excoriation and for once in her life surrender herself to a defining, irrevocable act that would not only set her free but save an innocent like Flower Jamison from bearing a cross that an unjust world had placed on her shoulders.

What would her father say to her now? God, she missed him. He was the only human being whose word and wisdom she never doubted. Would he puff on his pipe silently, his eyes smiling with admiration and approval? But she already knew the answer to her question. That jolly, loving, Quaker physician who could walk with beggars and princes would have only one form of advice for her in this situation, and it would not be what she wanted to hear.

She cracked the whip on her horse's back and tried to empty her mind of thoughts about her father. She would think about the pistol that rested on the seat beside her, substituting one worry for another, and concentrate on questions about the residue of dried mud she had seen wedged between the cylinder and the frame and inside the trigger guard, about the possibility the caps were damp or that mud was impacted inside the barrel.

The rain was as hard and cold as hail on her skin. The convicts were climbing down from the house frame, raking water out of their hair and beards, grinning at the prospect of getting off work early. She reined up her horse and stepped down into the mud.

"Hold up there, missy," the foreman said.

His stomach was the size of a washtub and he wore an enormous vest buttoned across it and a silver watch on a chain. A black trusty guard in prison stripe pants and a red shirt and a palmetto hat stood behind him, the stock of a shotgun propped casually against his hip, his ebony skin slick with rain, his eyes fastened on the outdoor kitchen under the live oak where the cooks were preparing the midday meal.

"My business is with Mr. Atkins," she said.

"Hit ain't none of mine, then. But, tell me, missy, what's that you got hid behind your leg?" the foreman said.

"Are you a Christian man?"

"I try to be."

"If you'd like to see Jesus today, just get in my way and see what happens," she said.

The foreman snapped open the cover on his watch and looked at the time, then snapped the cover closed again and replaced the watch in his vest pocket. "I reckon I've had enough folks fussing at me in one day. How about we eat us some of them beans?" he said to the trusty guard.

Abigail stepped up on the plank walkway that led to Rufus Atkins' tent. The rain was slackening now, the sun breaking from behind a cloud, and the sky seemed filled with slivers of glass. She paused in front of the tent flap and cocked back the hammer on the revolver with both thumbs.

Then her hands began to shake and she lowered the pistol, her resolve draining from her like water through the bottom of a cloth sack. Why was she so weak? Why could she not do this one violent act in defense of a totally innocent creature whom the world had abused for a lifetime? In this moment, caught between the brilliance of the rain slanting across the sun and the grayness of the cane fields behind her, she finally knew who she was, not only a poseur but an empty vessel for whom stridence had always been a surrogate for courage.

She heard a rumbling sound on the road and turned and saw Willie Burke and Robert Perry crouched forward in a wagon, the boy named Tige clinging to the sides in back. Willie had doubled over the reins in his hands and was laying the leather across his horses' flanks.

So once more she would become the burden of others, to be consoled and protected and mollified, a well-intended, neurotic Yankee who was her own worst enemy.

But if she couldn't kill, at least she could put the fear of God in a rotten piece of human flotsam like Rufus Atkins.

She raised the pistol and threw back the tent flap and stepped inside just as a man emerged from a curtain and a tangle of mosquito netting in back, his posture stooped in order to get through the netting, a metal object in his right hand. His eyes lifted to hers, just before she pointed the revolver with both hands and squeezed the trigger and a dirty cloud of smoke erupted into his face.

Her ears rang from the pistol's report. Then she heard his weight collapse as he sank to one knee, a bright ruby in the center of his forehead, the muscle tone in his face melting, his arm fighting for purchase on top of a worktable, like an unpracticed elderly man whose belated attempt at genuflection had proved inadequate.

Outside the tent, she dropped the revolver from her hand and walked toward the stunned faces of Willie Burke, Robert Perry, and Tige McGuffy.

"I killed Ira Jamison by mistake. But I'm glad he's dead just the same. God forgive me," she said.

"You shot Ira Jamison?" Willie said.

"He had a wind chime in his hand. A silly little wind chime," she said.

She buried her face in Willie's chest. He could feel the muscles in her back heaving under the flats of his hands and could not tell if she was laughing or sobbing.

The rain stopped and the air filled with a greenish-yellow cast that was like the tarnish on brass. The wind came up hard out of the south, flattening the cane in the fields, whipping the tent in which Ira Jamison died, riffling water in the irrigation ditches, scattering snow egrets that lifted like white rose petals above the canopy in the swamp. Out over the

Gulf a tree of lightning pulsed without sound inside a giant stormhead.

As an old man Willie Burke would wonder what the eyes of God saw from above on that cool, windswept, salt-flecked August day of 1865. Did His eyes see the chime pried from Ira Jamison's dead hand and Robert Perry's revolver substituted for it?

Or did His eyes choose not to focus on an individual act but instead on the great panorama taking place below Him, one that involved all His children — leased convicts perched like carrion birds on a house frame in the middle of a wetlands, abolitionists and schoolteachers whose altruism was such they flayed themselves for their inability to change the world's nature, slavers whose ships groaned with sounds that would follow them to the grave, mothers and fathers and children who had no last names and would labor their lives away for the profit of others without ever receiving an explanation?

Did God's eyes see the past, present and future taking place simultaneously, perhaps on a mist-shrouded, alluvial landscape threaded by Indians and Spanish and French explorers and Jesuit missionaries, its hummocks surrounded with either saw grass or endless rows of cotton and cane, its earth pounded with the hooves of mounted jayhawkers and Confederate guerrillas or covered with flocks of birds and roving herds of wild animals, its mists flaring with either the spatter of musket fire and the red glow of burning crosses or lanterns lighting quiet residential streets and children at play in the yards?

Sometimes in the clarity of his sleep Willie Burke saw the same protean landscape he believed God saw, and a long column of soldiers wending their way toward the horizon, their butternut uniforms crusted with salt, their bullet-rent flags aflame in the sunset, a sergeant-major in a skull-tight kepi counting cadence, "Reep, reep, reep," while a brass band thundered out a joyful song like the one that had made Jim Stubbefield wonder if there wasn't something glorious about war after all. For reasons Willie did not understand, he wanted to join their ranks and disappear with them over the rim of the earth.

But in the mornings the dream escaped his grasp and his days were often filled with memories he shared with no one.

Then, five years after that late August afternoon when Abigail Dowling shot down Ira Jamison, Willie woke to an early frost, to the smell of wood smoke and the sound of trees stiff with ice and breakfast wagons creaking across stone. He walked out into the freshness of the dawn and, in a place inside his mind that had nothing to do with reason, he once again remembered his speculation about how the eyes of God viewed creation. He stood on the gallery in his nightshirt, the sunlight breaking on his bare feet, and imagined himself caught between the Alpha and the Omega, in the hush of God's breath upon the world, and for just a second believed he actually heard the words *I am the beginning and the end. I am He who makes all things new.*

In that moment he let go of his contention with both the quick and the dead and experienced an unbridled gladness of heart. He was a participant in the great adventure, on the right side of things, a celebrant at the big party, a role that until the day of his death no one would ever be able to deny him.

Epilogue

In the year 1868, one year after her release from the women's prison at Baton Rouge, Tige McGuffy, Flower Jamison, Robert Perry, and Willie Burke stood on the gallery of the school and watched Abigail Dowling become Mrs. Quintinius Earp.

Later the same year Lieutenant and Mrs. Earp would find themselves stationed on the Bozeman Trail, in southern Montana, in the middle of Chief Red Cloud's War. After the discovery of gold in the Black Hills, she testified before the U.S. Congress in hopes of gaining support for the protection of Indian lands, but to no avail. Until her husband's retirement from the army, she worked as a volunteer nurse and teacher among the Oglala Sioux and the Northern Cheyenne. Later, she moved with him to a small town outside Boston, where she became active in the Populist and early feminist movements of the 1890s. In 1905 she became a founding member of the

Industrial Workers of the World, was the friend of Molly Brown and Elizabeth Flynn, and before her death in 1918 marched with the striking miners at Ludlow, Colorado.

Willie Burke became a teacher and later the superintendent of schools in New Iberia. For the remainder of his life he was known for his bravery as a soldier, his refusal to discuss the war, his prescience about human events and his irreverence toward all those who seek authority and power over others.

Flower Jamison married a black veteran of the Louisiana Corps d'Afrique and taught at the school she and Abigail Dowling founded until her seventy-ninth year. The school remained open well into the twentieth century and changed the lives of hundreds, if not thousands, of black children. Among the many distinguished educators who visited it were George Washington Carver and Booker T. Washington.

Robert S. Perry read for the law and practiced in St. Martin Parish, served in the state senate, and was appointed an appeals judge in 1888. He died in the year 1900 and is buried in New Iberia, in St. Peter's Cemetery, not far from his friend Willie Burke.

Jean-Jacques LaRose moved to Cuba and became a planter and shipbuilder and supposedly increased his fortune during the Spanish-American War by scuttling a ship loaded with gold coin off the Dry Tortugas and salvaging the wreck after the owner, who had made his money in the illegal arms and slave trade, committed suicide.

Captain Rufus Atkins continued to prosper immediately after the war, buying up tax-sale cotton acreage in the Red River parishes and supplying convict labor in the salt and sulfur mines along the coast. Then he began to drink more heavily and wear soft leather gloves wherever he went. After a while his business associates were bothered by an odor the nostrums and perfumes he poured inside his gloves could not disguise. The lesions on his hands spread to his neck and face, until all his skin from his shirt collar to his hairline was covered with bulbous nodules.

His disfigurement was such that he had to wear a hood over his head in public. His businesses failed and his lands were seized for payment of his debts. When ordered confined to a leper colony by the court, he fled the state to Florida, where he died in an insane asylum.

A guerrilla leader by the name of Jarrette, who was brought to Louisiana from Missouri by the Confederate general Kirby Smith and who claimed to be the brother-in-law of Cole Younger, left the state after the war and lived out his days as a sheep rancher in Arizona Territory.

The White League and the Knights of the White Camellia continued to terrorize black voters throughout the Reconstruction era and were instrumental in the bloody 1874 take-over of New Orleans, which they occupied for three days, before they were driven out of the city by Union forces partially under the command of the ex–Confederate general, James Longstreet.

The convict lease system at Angola Plantation, which became the prototype for the exploitation of cheap labor throughout the postbellum South, lasted until the beginning of the twentieth century. The starvation and beating and murder by prison personnel of both black and white convicts at Angola Farm was legendary well into modern times. The bodies that are buried in the levee rimming the prison farm remain unmarked and unacknowledged to this day.

Tige McGuffy, at age twenty-two, became one of the first cadets admitted to Louisiana State University, which was created out of the old United States Army barracks at Baton Rouge, largely through the efforts of General William T. Sherman, the same Union general who burned Atlanta and whose sixty-mile scorched-earth sweep into northern Mississippi became the raison d'être for the retaliatory massacre of black troops at Front Pillow by Confederate soldiers under the command of Nathan Bedford Forrest.

Tige McGuffy received the Medal of Honor for his heroism at the battle of Kettle Hill during the Spanish-American War of 1898.